SILENCE

Unbound Book Two

NICOLI GONNELLA

Copyright © 2022 by Nicoli Gonnella

All rights reserved.

No part of this book may be reproduced in any form or by any electronic or mechanical means, including information storage and retrieval systems, without written permission from the publisher, except for the use of brief quotations in a book review.

This is a work of fiction. Names, characters, places, and incidents either are the products of the author's imagination or are used fictitiously. Any resemblance to actual persons, living or dead, businesses, companies, events, or locales is entirely coincidental.

*To my daughter and son.
You kids are everything.*

PROLOGUE

PRESENT DAY

In the Eyrie of the Protector's Guild, a manic intensity reigned.

Men and women—most of them Human—ran down corridors with freshly inked missives and requests, many of them on their way to Eliza DuFont's desk. As the Elder of Acquisition, she was responsible for the harvesting and distribution of all resources gained by Guild employees and affiliates. Typically, this meant she dealt with the back-end of board requests and Guild hunts, taking in whatever skins, meat, and the odd cracked artifact her people brought home. In turn, her office would dole out a reasonable payment.

But now, the dreaded and mysterious fog of the eponymous Foglands had faded entirely. All of the riches within those wild forests, untamed mountains, and deadly hills were now within reach. In a single instant, DuFont had been catapulted to the upper echelons of the Elder Council as her domain would now affect the fortunes of all those within the Eyrie.

She thumbed through page after page detailing Tier I herbs and Tier II lumber already hastily harvested, each entry growing the power of their Guild branch. They may even overtake Setoria as the most prosperous in the west. Already DuFont envisioned the new assets the main branch would afford them if that happened. The Eyrie was a strong, powerful construction, but the city of Haarwatch was a backward hovel that almost didn't deserve the services the Guild provided. She almost laughed when she found the letter from the Governor's office requesting a tithe of rare materials to be provided to the city's Craft Quarter.

"When did this arrive, Vera?" she asked, holding up the letter for her secretary to see. It was just the one today, as her twin sister was off on other important duties.

"Just this morning, ma'am," her secretary said, pausing the scratching of her quill. "And it's Tera, ma'am."

"Of course," DuFont said offhandedly before snorting in amusement. "The fog has been gone less than a week, and already we have demands of 'recompense' and 'taxes on behalf of the people of Haarwatch.'" The Elder let the heat within her core spin off, spraying from her hand in a wash of bright yellow vapor. The paper blackened before turning entirely to ash. "Pathetic. They wouldn't know what to do with the materials we've collected already, let alone those deeper within."

The city of Haarwatch was and always had been little more than a jagged stone planted at the end of a mountain pass, designed as a bulwark against the dangerous Foglands. It was built upon ruins older than itself, older than the Hierocracy if legends were true, but it was a backwater. Luxury crept into Haarwatch slowly as the mines were found to be ample, and the steady attacks of monsters provided a tithe of monster cores to fuel enchantment arrays or to sell for profit. Mining and hunting flourished, and all of it was under the Guild's charter and Provisional System Authority. They had made changes to improve the city, but they would never match the splendor of the continental interior. A few taxes to the governor were tossing a flagon of water on a house fire.

"Pen a response to the governor, Vera," she commanded,

and her secretary took out a new scroll of parchment. "I'll nip this line of thinking in the bud—"

The doors were kicked in.

Tera screamed, and the slamming wooden doors were accompanied by the tinkling of glass. DuFont came to her feet, her senses stretched taut as her heat Mana cycled through her channels. Framed in the door was a slight figure wearing matte black armor and a half mask that left only her mouth exposed. Eyes the color of cataracts stared at her, sharp as the daggers lining her hips and chest.

DuFont's stance slackened and she gave a wide smile. "Ilia. You have returned, and none too soon."

"I'm just a simple courier, ma'am. Here to drop off my package and be on my way," Ilia said through her perfect smile. "After I've collected my payment, of course."

DuFont looked around the Sworn agent and took in the ragged appearance of a young woman slumped in one of the plush chairs in reception. Dark of skin and darker of hair, the girl was beautiful in a way that had nothing to do with Tempering, even unwashed and bruised as she appeared. Vessilia Dayne, heiress of Pax'Vrell and future duchess. DuFont Analyzed her, noting that her Health was untouched but that her Stamina was lingering near the bottom. She switched Skills, checking on the girl's Status Condition.

"Poisoned?" she asked.

"A baby poison. Barely hurts." Ilia shrugged as her secretary shouldered the girl out of the armchair. "She was a scrappy one, and I had to transport her somehow."

DuFont regarded the Sworn with her steady eyes. "Vera," she called out.

"It's Tera, ma'am," her secretary said quietly.

"Vera, arrange for Lady Dayne to be taken to the Healer's Ward on the lower levels. Tell them she was found in the Foglands, injured."

"...Yes ma'am," she replied, before carrying the unconscious heiress out of the reception chamber and into the hall.

When DuFont returned her attention to the Sworn, Ilia was reclining in a settee along the wall.

"There you have it. Girl delivered, plan foiled, Shieldwitch destroyed," she said, extending her hand. "Payment, if you will."

"You brought her into my offices like this? Did anyone see you?"

"Please. Your Eyrie is protected by Iron and Bronze Rank fools, none of whom have a Perception Skill higher than Uncommon," Ilia scoffed so hard she came to her feet. "They weren't able to even spot my shadow."

"And Aren died? You are sure of that?" DuFont pressed. It was a stroke of luck she hadn't quite expected, for all that she factored it into her plans.

"She was thrown into a nest of vipers so nasty I'd doubt you'd survive," Ilia said with a disbelieving headshake. "If she's still alive, I'll eat my own poison."

DuFont closed her eyes, letting a rare feeling wash over her. It was so infrequent in this wretched place that truly it was a moment to be savored. Money and power were flowing into her hands, while those that had opposed and threatened her had perished.

"There are survivors, though. People who know exactly why they had gone out there in the first place," Ilia said with a sly smile. That smile transformed into pleased surprise as a heavy pouch twice the size as what she was promised fell into her arms.

"Take it all for services rendered and discretion kept," DuFont said with a toothy smile. "I would not concern yourself with the others. They will be taken care of in due time."

Eliza DuFont turned to her large window, peering at the smudge that was the Foglands, now bathed in cleansing daylight. So great was her mood that she barely cared when the Sworn left without any parting words, or when her secretary returned with a new stack of sealed letters.

All was finally right with the world.

SILENCE

Far away, and far too close, an ancient mountain range rumbled. Beneath its deadly slopes, filled with dire creatures and ancient magics, down deep under the darkened earth was a skein of darkness. Beyond that skein, past where the Realms dragged against one another, beneath the bones of that aged mountain, cacophony reigned.

Within a chamber large enough to swallow a city, a legion of misshapen figures worked over forges designed out of molten lava. The air was filled with the stench of charred minerals, the ozone of discharged force, and the noisome clatter of hundreds of hammers. Said hammers struck and refined the metal pulled from these forges, shaping the dark materials into barbed, ominous forms.

Eddies of Mana vapor flowed through the chamber, orange and dusty brown mingling freely with the dark gray of shadow. The smiths, inelegant and malformed, grasped at the vapor, drawing it into themselves before working the confluence of energies into their craft. What power remained was funneled out of the forge room, down passageways so twisted and bent no right angles survived. Shimmering, mangled sigils inscribed in the walls pulled at the vapor, guiding the power with their invisible influence. Openings in the top of the passageways let in more vapor, pulled from other sources within the dark demesne. Emerald-gold and deep crimson streamers joined the rest.

The jagged sigils pulsed with every new wave of Mana, growing imperceptibly larger each time.

Spreading.

The corridors wound downward, delving deeper into the earth as the ambient Mana began to riot. As dozens of twisted passageways terminated at another massive chamber, the air itself seemed to thicken and congeal with near-physical power. Blood-red crystals rose from every surface in the spherical chamber, glinting with a dark, pulsating potency. At the center of the spherical room's base, an oubliette shot straight down, into a deeper dark.

But from this shaft arose a sense of plenitude and surcease. Faint, emerald-gold Mana began to outweigh the crimson waves as a garden thrived within.

The garden was fecund and beautiful, filled with colorful blooms and tall, impossible growths. Artificial lights shone from above, closely mimicking the absent sun, and a gentle, warm breeze rustled leaves and branches. Were it not for the terrible sense of crimson death that hung like a gallows' ax in the air, the garden would have been a place of true serenity.

This effect was particularly spoiled by an immense iron desk.

Situated within the center of the garden, it was huge. Built on the scale of giants and their ilk, it was accompanied by an equally massive chair. Said chair was occupied by a huge figure, composed of an elaborate golden armor and full helm. Eyes like burning brands flared and narrowed as he considered the desktop before him. A dagger-sized stylus laid in the creature's metallic hand, small in comparison to his huge frame, and he was carefully etching something onto a thick ream of hide.

Profane Sigaldry is level 120!

"Almost. Almost ready to Tier," the golden figure sighed before sitting back with an exaggerated groan. The Archon no longer felt fatigue or needed to sleep, but he found some satisfaction in mimicking the feeling. He always hoped it might remind him what it was like to be alive.

It had not proven successful yet.

The Archon stared at his handiwork, admiring the steady hand and fine edge to his work. The sigils almost crawled across the page, power baked into their forms, his dire Intent harnessed by their unsettled lines. They were a cage for his dire Will, and the Archon had more than enough of that to go around. Intent and Might and Alacrity. Strength of Body, of

Mind, but focus above all else. They were Harmonic Stats not typically used together, not anymore. The fools of the world had forgotten the truth that underpinned their flimsy reality. For that reason alone, he would be more than justified in wiping them all out.

Clear the board. Start anew.

The Archon was ancient, this much he knew. How ancient precisely was a mystery even to him. Long enough that his makers were but dust.

Save for that fool boy.

A rage stoked inside of him, one that had been tended to for an Age or more. The reemergence of the Nym, here, in his Domain was untenable. Only his Wurms' insistence that he perished along with the Mother had the Archon advancing his plans. But a voice, a familiar one, whispered in the back of his mind.

The Nym are devious and powerful. They cannot be trusted.

He trusted the voice. It had been his sole companion for an Age, the only thing he could cling to in the endless dark. His earliest memories were bits of a blank, ceaseless void, and the voice was there. Speaking such things that made his infant Mind tremble. Over the centuries, it dwindled, speaking up less and less. Once the Archon had awakened from his slumber, the voice had become a rare whisper. That it chose now of all times to return meant the Archon was right.

"Something turns Desolation's Wheel," the Archon boomed to himself, his Spirit flaring.

There was the sound of a startled gasp and the clatter of metal. The Archon looked up to see one of his Arcids collapsed upon the verdant ground. It trembled beneath the golden giant's glare, the silver wisps of its eyes gone wide.

"Number 54773. Report."

As if invisible strings pulled it up, the Arcid snapped to attention. It was more patchwork than some of his better creations, but the Archon had only been able to salvage most of its predecessor, Number 54768. The *boy* had damaged too much of its false Body when he had assaulted the Archon's Domain. As recompense, the Archon had been able to put more resources in its Mind, and that had proven remarkably effective.

"Master, we have found evidence of one of the Mother's brood," it rasped in a metallic tone, like a file scraped along a tin cylinder.

"Alive?" the Archon sat forward, the fires of his eyes burning brighter. The Mother was one of many names for the dreaded Maw, a Primordial of exceptional power long held captive in a nearby ruin. It had been one of the few creatures that could contest him without issue…but that had been changed. The *boy* had seen to that, ironically enough.

"N-no, Master. Dead for weeks. Killed by the Nymean child, we think."

"Tsk."

"But its Mana signature is unmistakable. There was a…stench in the air, despite its sublimated Body." Number 54773 trembled slightly under the weight of his regard. "It was large, and clearly a Blood Beast of the Mother's making. Perhaps derived from the Geist Race?"

"Yes. The Maw had several of its twisted children around my Domain. You found it close?" The Archon had bare control of only a few dozen square miles of the surface, thanks to his minions. He could not leave his Domain, but a few of them at a time could manage it. As such, that area was growing, but not nearly fast enough. "Can I reach it?"

"I-It lies beyond your Domain, closer to the Bitter Sea. We are bringing samples back, but—"

A Harmonic trace of a Primordial. So close, yet so far. "No matter. I'd have thought to use the Primordial's power for my own ends, but its potency has been all but wiped from these lands. Just as the Labyrinth is empty now. Impossible, but then, so is defeating one." The Archon shook his head. That Nym had done so much in his short time in the Archon's lands, and thankfully he could take advantage of the chaos he left behind. "What of the Nymean ruins? Where that child found his Crescian blade."

"Near the corpse, we believe," 54773 replied, puffing out its meager chest. "The trace leads westward. The Wretches and Reforged are searching as we speak."

The Archon fingered his sharp chin, the tarnished Nymean Bronze scraping against his articulated fingers. "Good. And the envoy was dispatched to Haarwatch, yes?"

"Yes, Master. Integrated with the survivors. They'll never sort them out, not until it's too late." 54773's rusted voice bloomed with unmistakable pride.

"Plan for it to happen, anyway," the Archon waved the Arcid away. "Humans are wily, despite their weaknesses. Or perhaps because of them." He snorted. "Still, they shall fall."

"Y-yes, Master. Of course."

The Archon turned away, regarding the twisted sigils he had written out. They had already blackened the durable hide upon which they were penned, breaking the powerful skin down under their power.

"Midsummer," he said to himself. The Arcid looked up at him, a question in its gaze. "We have five months until all my plans come to fruition."

Then his great work would truly begin.

CHAPTER ONE

"The Continent dwells within the Corporeal Realm. This is known. The Realms number three, as do our Aspects. Body, Mind, and Spirit. But whose Body? Whose Mind? Do we toil upon the literal shoulders of giants? If one were cast into the Void, what would they find?"

-Vilas Tern, Pagewright of the Violet Tower

Pit squawked in alarm, and Felix stumbled back, putting as much distance as he could between himself and the Maw. That was easy, as the Void stretched between them, infinite darkness without a speck of light or life.

It appeared before him as a statuesque woman with long black hair and vivid blue-green eyes—the form of Lhel, a Nymean woman from thousands of years ago. Its face was cadaverous and gaunt, as if it hadn't eaten in weeks. The Maw snarled at him, and Felix noticed that its teeth were blunt and flat. Not a fang in sight.

"Why are you here?" Felix asked, trying to keep his Perception spread out as wide as possible. Who knew what sort of tricks it would pull? "You're supposed to be dead!"

I am Unending, fool! I cannot die. The Maw looked around at the featureless darkness all around them in disgust. *Though I may wish for it before long. The Void is not a realm I ever wanted to visit, let alone be trapped within. Why are you not dead?*

Pit growled and shrieked angrily at the creature, while Felix frowned, having thought the same thing. More worryingly, he wasn't sure why both he and his Companion survived. He checked his neck, and a pulse still beat strong and quick beneath his fingers.

Does your heart still pump? The Maw snarled. *Let me fix that for you!*

With a furious yell, the Maw crossed the intervening distance, a blur of emaciated rage. Felix barely got his guard up, and the Maw's chipped nails pierced right through his throat… and out the other side. In fact, its entire body sailed through Felix's like a ghost.

WHAT!

Felix spun around, facing the creature while running his hands across his body and throat. He was completely unharmed, his Health unmoved aside from his busted nose. The Maw laid upon the ground, staring at its hands in shock. It was wearing the same pale dress it had worn in its prison, and in fact looked exactly as it did right before it attempted to hijack his body. Right after—

"You gave up your power," Felix muttered. That had to be it: the majority of the Maw's Mana had been torn away and siphoned off into the Essence Anchor, as what little there was left was more than enough to deal with him. Or should have been.

YOU! You did this to me! You used that stolen Skill to…to…You consumed my power. The Maw paused, her luminous eyes wide. *Blasted Affinity. We are…connected.*

Felix couldn't argue. He felt it too, disgusted as he was. What's more, his new quest confirmed it.

Escape the Void!
You have saved the Continent from the Maw, but all choices have consequences. As a result of becoming the Maw's Vessel, however briefly, you have been banished to the Void!
Find a way out, if you can!
Rewards: Freedom, Title, Varies

He had become her Vessel, at least for a little while, and he had... eaten her essence while she attempted to devour him in return. Almost in response to that thought, a new notification flashed across his vision.

Hidden Quest Complete!
Defeat the Unending Maw!
Stop the Unending Maw's escape, by any means necessary!
Due to foiling its escape as well as banishing it into the Void, you have gained increased rewards!
Due to killing the majority of the Risi and their Chieftain, you have gained increased rewards!
Due to killing 3 of 6 Blood Beasts hidden in the Foglands, you have gained increased rewards!

You Gain:
+3 Levels
+3 Titles
+1 Bronze Chest
Be Aware! A Bronze Chest cannot be rewarded at this time. Please return to the Corporeal Realm to receive your prize.

You Have Gained 3 Levels!
You Are Now Level 25!
+9 to WIL! +6 to INT! +12 to DEX! +3 to END! +6 to PER! +6 to VIT! +12 to AGL!

You Have 20 Unused Stat Points!

Your Companion Pit Has Gained 3 Levels!
+6 VIT! +6 PER! +12 AGL! +12 DEX! +9 WIL! +3 END! +6 INT!

New Title!
Titan Slayer (Epic) - You have triumphed over a foe that is double your level and advancement. +10% STR, VIT

New Title!
Indomitable (Epic) - Against all odds you rise, again and again. +10% WIL, END

New Title!
Primordial Slayer (Transcendent) - +50% All Stats - You have killed a Primordial, an ancient enemy of—

ERROR!
Primordial still living—
ERROR!
Primordial not alive—
ERROR!
Correcting Reward...

New Title: Cage the Beast (Epic) - You have survived the Maw's plan, becoming both more and less than a Vessel, connected by tethers of Affinity. A piece of the Maw now lives within you, forevermore. Be wary. +10% ALA, REI, INE

Felix's eyes bulged as another storm of power thundered through him, though this time it felt muted somehow. A flaring ring of luminous vapor poured off of him, spreading outward in a rapid pulse that vibrated the nothingness beneath his feet.

The sensation vanished quickly, swallowed by the Void fast enough that Felix noticed Pit had briefly glowed with System energy as well, his wingspan growing another few inches. The Titles he'd received were...well, honestly appropriate for what he'd done. Far more strange, however, was the last two lines of his rewards.

+1 Bronze Chest
Be Aware! A Bronze Chest cannot be rewarded at this time. Please return to the Corporeal Realm to receive your prize.

Return to the Corporeal—the Continent? Felix grunted. *Of course. Why make it easy?*

He turned back to the Maw, who had watched the two of them spasm with power with a sour look on its face.

There, you see? Connected forevermore. Whether we like it or not.

Felix curled his lip in disgust, pushing aside the heady joy of his level gains. He looked over the Titles he'd earned, especially the last one, and started piecing it all together. When he had dropped onto the Essence Anchor, instead of killing him, it had transported both of them into the Void. The sigils written on the artifact said as much when he'd translated them: *Anchor The Beast and Draw Its Power Into The Infinite Void*. The Maw was part of Felix now; the System itself confirmed it, so he was shunted off with it. And since Pit was connected via the Convergence ability, he came along for the ride.

"Damn," he muttered. He was glad not to be dead, but this was a wrinkle he hadn't expected. He looked at the Maw. "Why can I see you?"

The Maw looked at its own hands, Lhel's hands. *I am a...projection of your Mind and Spirit, apparently. Fah! This is untenable!*

"And you can't hurt me, or even touch me or Pit." Felix nodded. "Good."

Felix immediately ignored her and inspected himself, noticing he was still shirtless and wearing the same ragged boots and tattered pants. His belt was gone, as was his journal and sword. They had been left behind, he assumed, somewhere in the Maw's prison. He cursed inwardly and ran his hands through his hair. It was messy and too long, dangling about his ears.

"I need to find out what our new baseline is," he mused, bringing up his Status with a thought.

Name: Felix Nevarre
Level: 25
Race: Nym*
Omen: Magician
Born Trait: Keen Mind

Health: 852/864
Stamina: 861/861
Mana: 1458/1458

STR: 156
PER: 154
VIT: 172
END: 156
INT: 188
WIL: 272
AGL: 129
DEX: 123

BODY
Resistances: Acid Resistance (C), Level 24; Fire Resistance (C) Level 19*; Cold Resistance (U), Level 20; Heat Resistance (U), Level 21*; Pain Resistance (U), Level 42; Poison Resistance (U), Level 28; Lightning Resistance (R), Level 1*

Combat Skills: Axe Mastery (C), Level 5*; Blunt

Weapon Mastery (C), Level 10*; Dodge (C), Level 25; Long Blade Mastery (C), Level 15*; Parry (C), Level 4*; Small Blade Mastery (C), Level 10; Staff Mastery (C), Level 7*; Thrown Weapons Mastery (C), Level 11; Unarmed Mastery (C), Level 25; Blind Fighting (R), Level 21; Corrosive Strike (R), Level 25

Physical Enhancements: Running (C), Level 21; Stealth (C), Level 25; Swimming (C), Level 6; Acrobatics (U), Level 25*; Breath Control (U), Level 22*; Free Climbing (U), Level 15; Relentless Charge (U), Level 9; Armored Skin (R), Level 38; Physical Conditioning (R), Level 23

MIND
Mental Enhancements: Intimidation (C), Level 8*; Make An Entrance (U), Level 10; Meditation (U), Level 33; Bastion of Will (E), Level 42; Deep Mind (E), Level 30; Ravenous Tithe (E), Level 1

Information Skills: Analyze (C), Level 25; Tracking (C), Level 13; Exploration (U), Level 25; Herbalism (U), Level 17

SPIRIT
Spiritual Enhancements: Dual Casting (U), Level 21; Mana Manipulation (U), Level 6; Manasight (U), Level 40; Etheric Concordance (L), Level 26

Spells: Cloudstep (R), Level 8; Fire Within (R) Level 33; Influence of the Wisp (R), Level 26; Invocation (R), Level 1; Mantle of the Long Night (R), Level 13; Shadow Whip (R), Level 26; Stone Shaping (R), Level 25; Reign of Vellus (E), Level 28; Sigils of the Primordial Dawn (E), Level 13; Wrack And Ruin (E), Level 26

Unused Stat Points: 20

Harmonic Stats
RES: 103
INE: 88
AFI: 57
REI: 60
ALA: 136

Felix's stats had jumped significantly, owing to the large stat bonuses gained per level. Unlike a vanilla Human, he gained quite a few, not to mention the extras earned from his bond with his Companion. The Harmonic Stats were also increased, though they were harder to get a read on. He still wasn't entirely sure what most of them did, though he was fairly certain Resonance (RES) and Resilience (REI) had to do with Mana and Health regeneration in some capacity.

Name: Pit (Companion)
Level: 16
Race: Chimera - Tenku

Health: 388/388
Stamina: 347/347
Mana: 462/462

STR: 52
PER: 69
VIT: 77
END: 64
INT: 50
WIL: 87
AGL: 110
DEX: 87

Bite (C), Level 24

Rake (C), Level 23
Cry (R), Level 24
Skulk (C), Level 25
Etheric Concordance (L), Level 26
Wingblade (U), Level 19
Frost Spear (C), Level 17
Cold Resistance (C), Level 16
Poisonfire (R), Level 13

Active Titles:
Survivor III
Butcher III
Unconquered
Face the Charge
Bulwark of the Innocent
Pactmaker
Work Horse
Blind Pugilist
Hero
Iron Will
Apprentice Magus
The Broken Path

Even omitting all his Titles and Apprentice Tier notations, his Status page was impressive and Pit's wasn't far behind. He felt strong and capable… and being alive was a heady rush far different than a System stat bump.

He'd survived. He hadn't expected that. Everything after this was gravy.

Though even gravy goes bad.

Felix noted that a number of his Skills had asterisks next to them. When he focused on them, he swallowed. Bad news.

Be Aware! The following Skills are damaged!

Acrobatics

Axe Mastery
Blunt Weapon Mastery
Breath Control
Fire Resistance
Heat Resistance
Intimidation
Lightning Resistance
Long Blade Mastery
Parry
Staff Mastery

Be Aware! Damaged Skills will not function optimally!

Ho ha! The Maw clapped its hands, a spiteful glee on its face. *Just noticing that, hmm? So tasty, your Skills! A choice spread, haha!*

Felix stared at the list, aghast. None were his foundational Skills, those with which he'd Tempered his Body, Mind, and Spirit, but they were all useful, Acrobatics especially. Felix looked up at the Maw, jaw clenched.

"Fix it!"

More laughter, cackling and mad. *I can't! Haha! What's done is done! You'll just have to sunder them and start over!*

The Maw couldn't touch him, but unfortunately that meant Felix couldn't touch the Maw either. Pit screamed at her, his ears laid back on his skull, no more than feathery tufts. Felix wanted nothing more than to punch its smug face in and... he took a breath. Then another. He could manage. He checked the list again, and only Acrobatics had made it to Apprentice Tier. That meant it wasn't too terrible, though he'd lost about half the bonuses for Tiering up. He'd survive. He had to.

Felix looked at Pit, who tilted his head, then nodded. The two of them started walking.

Hey! Where are you going? The Maw shouted after them.

"Away." Felix replied without turning. Sound didn't work the same way here as it did back on the Continent. Everything felt immediate, like it was ringing in his own head. "From you, if I can manage it."

Felix shouted in alarm when the Maw materialized before him. One moment it was twenty feet away, the next...

You cannot be rid of me, Felix Nevarre. We are one.

Felix pushed past it, not wanting to even touch their ghostly form. "Then leave us alone. We won. You lost. Go die in a hole or something."

The Maw kept pace with him, not even walking, but floating beside him. *Can't die. I'm dead already. But not... truly strange. I've met my share of Unbound in the past, and few managed to twist the System into such knots. I almost admire you, Felix.* Her voice had gone soft again, a faint echo of the false persona of Lhel she had used on him. *But aren't you curious?*

Felix tried not to respond. Truly he did. But after twenty minutes of apparently pointless walking through the featureless Void, he turned in annoyance. The Maw still floated apace, smiling serenely at him.

"What?"

The Maw shrugged. *Nothing important, I suppose. Just your Race.*

"My Race? Why--?" He stopped mid-sentence as a blue screen was shoved in his face... by the Maw.

Race: Nym*

"How did you--? Why's there an asterisk?" Felix focused on it as before, and a new notice came up.

Further Bloodlines Have Been Found. Processing 1%

"What?" Felix looked at the Maw, who was smiling innocently. "What does this mean?"

The Maw's grin widened, sharpening at the corners as it floated away. Felix's expression soured. He was about to say something when a sudden bellow shook the Void.

Above, a massive whale-like creature rolled across the sky, if the Void had such a thing. Distances were strange there, but it felt both impossibly far away and entirely too close. It was like a mountain, swimming across the black like a ponderous fish, its body more like craggy stone than blubber or flesh. It had huge paddles in place of flippers and a tail that fanned out in a spray of vibrant, multi-colored Mana streams. Felix gasped and flared his Manasight. The creature blazed like a sun in the darkness, a riot of color that exploded with power with each lumbering flex of its tail. It was too far to Analyze, but he tried anyway.

Analyze...

Target Out Of Range.

Tch. That was pathetic. The Maw whispered over his shoulder, and before he could flinch away, it shoved its hand into Felix's head.

Synergy Detected Between Nascent Bloodline, Born Trait, and Tempered Skill!
Primordial Essence Introduced To System!
ERROR!

Felix fell to the ground as his eyes *burned*. Literal smoke poured from his sockets, turning his vision into crackling static. Distantly, he heard Pit shrieking at the Maw, while the latter laughed insanely. A notification popped up, visible despite his lack of vision.

Analyze has become Voracious Eye (Epic), Level 25!

Voracious Eye (Epic), Level 25!
Your avaricious quest for knowledge knows no bounds! You devour everything you see, committing it all to your hungry Mind. Can be used as long as the object or creature is within line of sight. Detail

increases with Skill level, sensory input increases with Skill level.

Further Bloodlines Have Been Found. Processing 2%

Slowly, the burning faded, and the pops of static turned into washes of blue and gold that quickly faded into the darkness of the Void. Felix pressed gingerly at his face, but everything was pain-free again, though his hands came back wet with blood. He whipped toward the Maw.

"What the hell was that! What's Primordial Essence!?"

The Maw floated upside down, chortling. *I guess I can touch you, in some ways...*It leered at him, turning right side up again. Felix bared his teeth, ready to fight the thing to the death (*again*) if he had to, when a screaming cry sounded above them.

The massive creature was still close by, but in the light of its strange tail there cavorted thousands upon thousands of mottled...*things*. Without conscious thought, his eyes flared with a sudden heat.

Voracious Eye...

Name: Tenebril
Type: Voidborn
Level: 33
HP: 545/545
SP: 434/588
MP: 184/0
Lore: As all Voidborn, the tenebril love the light and power of Mana. They feed upon it and nothing else. Tenebril flock together by the thousands, usually following a Narhollow as it traverses the black.
Strength: More Data Required
Weakness: More Data Required

Felix blinked in surprise, the information flowing into his brain the instant he activated the Skill. He looked to Pit, who seemed to be enraptured by the swirling chaos of tentacular horrors. Their movements were truly mesmerizing, flowing and swimming among each other, their long, tangled bodies mottled gray and black. They appeared to be lumpy masses of tentacles, and Felix couldn't spot a body among the appendages, only the occasional flash of rainbow light within them. Felix could practically smell the things just by looking at them, his new eyes somehow doing things his Perception never had.

Remarkable...and delicious. I've never tried Tenebril, they so rarely leave the Void! You absolutely must *eat one.* The Maw turned to Felix with bright eyes, spittle flecking its lips. Felix furrowed his brow and curled his lip again.

"The last thing I'm doing is taking dietary advice from you. What did you do to my Analyze Skill? Why is it...Maw-flavored now?" Felix demanded.

The Maw drifted higher, as if it were going to inspect the flock of tenebril. It turned back at him, head tilted at an unpleasant angle. *You are what you eat, hmm?*

Felix was viscerally reminded that this was a Primordial terror that had tried to kill him. To *wear* him, like a suit. Something about it kept easing his mind into complacency, something insidious. He checked his HUD, but other than his slowly healing broken nose, there were no blinking icons indicating an ongoing Condition. Just like in the prison, when the Maw kept toying with his mind. Except now...

How do I protect myself from... myself?

The Maw began humming to itself from slightly above Felix, contemplating the dark not-sky. *Hmm. You should run.*

"What?" Felix stopped and looked up. He saw nothing. "What are you talking about?"

The Maw just smiled at him.

Then the darkness attacked.

It was fast and silent and utterly invisible. Felix felt a flash of awful heat as something tore at his unprotected chest. Blood sprayed outward as he fell back, which was the only thing that saved him from a follow up strike from another set of ebon claws.

Armored Skin is level 39!

Disoriented and in pain, Felix reeled, his head almost muddied after the attack. The darkness loomed, textureless and infinite, and he was blind to it all.

Pit leaped atop the shadow, wings wide in challenge and beak open for a trumpeting cry. Spears of ice and visible blades of wind crashed into a wide shape, delineating its form and allowing Felix to fire off his Skill.

Voracious Eye...

Name: Harrowing
Type: Voidborn
Level: 41
HP: 832/944
SP: 344/687
MP: 1384/0
Lore: Feeding off Mana, the Harrowings gather in small flocks to trace the path of the Narhollow, picking off any Tenebril that get separated. They are opportunistic and will attack anything they consider weak. Their attacks drain Mana and Health.
Strength: More Data Required
Weakness: More Data Required

Even with his evolved Skill, the creature practically vanished before his eyes. Still, he rolled to his feet, feeling his wound pull with every movement, and waited for an opening. Pit had crawled atop the thing, which flapped its angular wings in furious agitation and tried to buck the tenku. But his Companion had grown hefty, easily the size of a full-grown Rottweiler now, and it buried its beak into the Harrowing's nape.

Now, Pit!

Pit leaped aside, some sort of pale, viscous fluid pouring out as he disengaged, and Felix flared his Skills.

Relentless Charge!
Influence of the Wisp!
Corrosive Strike!
Corrosive Strike!
Corrosive Strike!
Corrosive Strike!

Felix flashed through the intervening distance, which was no more than ten or fifteen feet, appearing instantly by the creature's side. A bloom of blue-white fire limned both of them as his wisp magic activated, Enthralling the Harrowing for 5 seconds. More than enough time for his fists to go to work. Felix unleashed Corrosive Strike after Corrosive Strike, acid splashing around the beast as parts of it were torn off and dissolved. It still got some hits in, as its talons were impossible to track, each one leaving a jagged gash in his body.

Then Felix noticed that, while his Health took a hit with each slash, his Mana drained even more.

"Shit!" He sped up the pace, but so did the Harrowing.

At one point, it broke free and immediately flew away. Wheeling through the darkness, leaking a bright fluid from its wounds, it was far easier to track than before… until it disappeared completely. Felix held still, extending his senses outward and feeling Pit do the same. The Maw floated nearby, watching with a sort of gleeful disdain.

It's invisible, you know.

I'm aware! Felix spun, checking behind him and activating Voracious Eye as often as possible. His eyes felt warm each time it discharged, like staring into a desert wind. Then he heard it, a faint, fleshy creak, and Felix pivoted. He leaped into a sideways spin as the Harrowing swooped toward him, but his body spasmed mid-turn. Daggers of molten pain stabbed into his side and back, and Felix fell directly on top of the Harrowing.

It screeched in dismay and anger, and Felix tried to shake

off the sudden agonizing spasms. By the time he did, the creature had brought its talons down on his exposed back, slashing him deeply. His Health dropped by 20% and his Mana dropped by 30%; he was below half in both, which set his heart frantically pumping. Pushing with pure Strength, Felix threw himself up and out of the Voidborn's reach. Then he unleashed a kinetic blast directly into its center mass.

Reign of Vellus!

Lightning arced across the beast, tearing open its dark body and releasing a flood of shimmering fluid that boiled into the air. Abruptly, a wave of light burst from it, discharging into the not-sky like a lightning bolt.

You Have Killed A Harrowing!
XP Earned!

Panting, Felix stepped back from the pile of glowing mush and watched as remnant streamers of multi-colored Mana poured into the air. It was almost beautiful. Pit's anxious squawk drew him away from the sight, and when Felix looked over, his Companion pointed with an outstretched wing.

Voracious Eye...

Six more were on the way. The Maw flashed him a smile.

I would suggest running, Unbound.

CHAPTER TWO

He was wrong.

It was way more than six.

They were impossible to count as they flew toward him deceptively fast. Not only were they practically invisible, they didn't move like natural creatures at all. Their wings flapped rarely, but they sped up and slowed down abruptly, as if inertia didn't apply to them. But it certainly applied to Felix and Pit, as the two of them weren't able to outrun the Harrowings for more than a few seconds.

Talons flashed and Voidborn beasts shrieked while Felix and Pit unloaded their arsenal of Skills. Wrack and Ruin tore through two of them, boring sizzling holes through their wings, which unfortunately had zero effect on their ability to fly. Pit flared with green Poisonfire, blindingly bright in their black surroundings, and got up close and personal with Rake and Bite. For a few blessed seconds, the two of them fought the Harrowings back.

Then three others attacked. From *below*.

Flying just as if the ground were air, the Harrowings burst from below them, and both Felix and Pit took raking talons to their backs and sides. The Reign of Vellus that Felix was holding stuttered and went out, the Mana flow somehow interrupted by the Voidborn's attack, and Felix's sharp eyes caught a trailing tendril of crackling azure light fading behind the beast.

His Mana was low, lower than it had been in a long while, and even though it regenerated at a ridiculous pace, it wasn't quite enough. These monsters tore it from him faster than he could use it, dropping his Health by significant numbers as well. Ten seconds into the fight, Felix was torn and bloody, with Pit not far behind. The tenku, while not as magically potent as Felix himself, was still a tasty morsel to creatures that fed on Mana.

And feed they did. The Harrowings grew bloated and fat on their meal, though they flew no less gracefully.

They're so fast! How? His new and "improved" Analyze no longer told him their highest stats, so he could only guess. *Their Agility has to be through the roof!*

The Maw floated off to the side, watching with rapt eyes as Felix and Pit were sliced and diced. Fury rose inside Felix at the sight, a real and physical hate for the creature that had messed with his life so thoroughly. It had denied bringing him to the Continent, but he couldn't trust anything it said. Felix channeled his rage into his fists, lashing out with standard unarmed strikes that didn't cost Mana. They were agile but so was he, and—damn it—he was strong.

He hit one of them with a straight jab, and its Health dipped fast, and before it died completely Felix grabbed it. He felt something grip him in turn, and a stinging heat flashed in his chest.

Ravenous Tithe!

Ravenous Tithe (Epic), Level 1!
Consume completely an object or creature which you have claimed and can physically touch. Uses Mana to power conversion. Chance of gaining Skills and/or Memories from target if applicable.

His Mana sank, dropping nearly three hundred points, and the Harrowing was suddenly torn asunder. Its strange, rubbery body shredded into strips that faded into motes of white light and were sucked immediately into Felix's mouth. It all happened in a millisecond, less than a blink, and Felix felt a burning heaviness settle in the pit of his stomach. No, his core.

Harrowing Consumed!

But not all of it: the creature had a bellyful of stolen Mana, and Felix screamed as much of it crawled out of his throat and exploded in a massive shockwave. A ripple tore through the Void, an expanding circle of Mana vapor that shot off into the black. The remaining Harrowings darted off after it, wheeling their unnatural bodies with reckless speed.

Felix's scream cut off abruptly, and he fell to his knees. His body blazed with energy, his core packed to bursting.

Ravenous Tithe is level 2!

His hands shook as he pushed back into a standing position. Felix was a mess of blood, and Pit was little better. Both of them were dangerously low on Health, Stamina, and Mana.

"I'm...sure...that's gonna be fine," Felix huffed with all of the sarcasm in his bones as he nodded at the receding wave of power. He was a torch made of Mana out here. No wonder they were getting mobbed.

Pity. The Maw pouted, floating in lazy circles around him. *You survived.*

Felix snapped. "You realize that if I die, you'll die too, right?"

The Maw waved a pale hand. *Impossible. I am Unending. I believe I've said that already.* It looked up, as if noting something in the distance. *I also said running is the better option. I suggest you listen this time.*

Felix ground his teeth, almost tempted to stay still out of sheer spite. Instead, he ran.

While the act of running was not difficult, the lack of anything in the Void meant it felt a little like spinning in a hamster wheel. There was no wind against his skin, no objects moving in the distance, only the faint resistance of the "ground" beneath him giving any sense of motion. Pit had trouble as well, loping alongside him. Felix frowned, then looked at the Maw. It was easily keeping pace, floating after them like the ghost it was.

Felix growled, low and in the back of his throat. He pushed himself, all while constantly scanning in all directions. Voracious Eye couldn't find anything, but he didn't trust it. Too new, too...tainted.

Felix had to slow down slightly, however, as Pit couldn't move as fast as he could. As Felix adjusted his speed, he caught a glance of the Maw who was flying slightly behind him. It looked...pensive.

"What?" he snapped.

The Maw didn't answer, only frowned and looked away. As far as Felix was concerned though, that was nothing but a gift.

They sped through the Void. For all that he felt he'd achieved no distance, Felix's Stamina ticked steadily downward, and his muscles had begun to burn. His Born Trait gave him perfect recall, so keeping track of time wasn't hard, just tedious. He did the math: they had been running for six entire hours.

Running is level 22!

Holy shit. Felix couldn't believe it. It had felt like, at most, an hour. The unique combination of featureless landscape mixed with a Body that had reached the First Threshold seemingly meant fewer mile markers, either geographical or physiological. They hadn't been going full tilt at all times, however. Pit was straining to keep up, and Felix had adjusted to keep his friend nearby. Last thing he was gonna do was leave his Companion behind.

"Hey, you," Felix grunted at the Maw. It still floated, seemingly unaffected by their travel. Only the rippling flow of its tattered dress and hair indicated any movement at all. "Be useful: what does First Threshold mean?"

The Maw smirked, lines gathering on its gaunt face like a traffic jam. *First Threshold is when your Primary Stats reach a point of conflux. It is rare to reach it so early, but less rare for the Unbound. And one of the many reasons I wished you as my Vessel. Your kind has a certain knack for the unexpected.*

Felix frowned, but ignored the jab about Vessels. "You're not answering the question, Maw. What does that mean? I get the impression that my stats work... better than before. Is that what you mean by 'conflux?'"

Yes. And no. The Maw grinned, and though its teeth were flat and Lhel-shaped, its mouth looked entirely too wide.

"And that's all you're going to tell me?" Felix panted. His lungs were beginning to burn.

You haven't earned more, yet.

Pit screeched, his voice entirely too loud in the dead air, and Felix felt a surge of hate-rage through their bond.

"Yeah, what he said."

Only a few minutes later, Felix found out that the Harrowings had never stopped pursuing them. As his muscles flagged, they came like invisible assassins. Influence of the Wisp caught many, rendering them immobile while he pummeled them with his acidic fists. But his Mana was slower than usual at recharging in the Void, and Felix only had so many castings available to him.

They all were hurt, again and again, while the Maw watched on in silence. Its blue-green eyes were riveted to Felix at all times, measuring and weighing him on scales he neither understood or appreciated. It was his rage against the Primordial's continued existence as much as survival instinct that guided Felix to victory. After a vicious battle lasting all of fifteen minutes, he and Pit had killed seventeen more Harrowings.

In the distance, another cry.

Better keep running, Unbound.

Felix bit off his curses and did just that.

The Harrowings dogged them through the next few hours. Furious battles interrupted by long, boring stretches of featureless running. Eventually, the Voidbeasts gave up. "Why" was a question Felix didn't care to discover, instead hoping it was a lucky break that would continue.

Then it was just running.

Running is level 23!

Moving through the Void felt like falling, no matter the direction he turned. Stuffed as he was by the Harrowing he ate, it only added to Felix's growing discomfort. He felt like he'd eaten a double helping of Thanksgiving dinner, and unfortunately, he was not wearing stretchy pants.

Yet, far more than the physical exertion, the silence gnawed at Felix. Never before had he been somewhere so still. No grass to rustle, no crickets to chirp, not even any wind. It was a silence that was almost like those nights as a kid, when he'd stay up far past his bedtime then wander out of his room. The house became a strange, alien place. Unknown.

The memory of it hit Felix hard, more clear than it had been in years as his Mind and Perfect Recall activated. He had been four, nearly five, and it was the night before Labor Day. He'd stayed up late because he was a big kid, about to go to school for the first time. To prove to himself that he was brave, he had wandered out into the dark living room, passing by the night-stranged knick-knacks and tchotchkes. The room had felt cold and weird, and noises had crept out at him, things that he'd never heard in the day. Car alarms, shifting floors, the pitter-patter of geckos on the lattice.

Something moved in the dark, and the memory was so vivid Felix felt the remembered terror as if it were real. His little self didn't run away or run toward it or even boldly challenge it. He had cried. Oh lord, he had cried a *lot*, until his mom had bustled out of her room.

"Shh shh shh, what's wrong, Bumble? Why're you out of bed?" she'd said. Her voice, even in memory, was a soft, soothing melody. She sounded so *young*.

He hadn't been able to make much sense of it all, merely blubbering about monsters and the dark. His mom had whispered comforting words like, "you're safe now" and "don't worry." Mom things. And he had promptly fallen asleep.

His thoughts turned inevitably toward the dream that wasn't... the memory he walked into just before he "died." His mom, his sister Gabby. Felix hoped they were okay, that his trusting sister had made it off the boat in that storm. And... and he hoped they didn't miss him.

He really didn't think he'd ever make it back to them. Felix was surprised at how much that hurt to admit. He'd thought he'd come to grips with it when he'd fallen on the Essence Anchor, but it was still just as raw.

What is wrong, Felix Nevarre?

When the memories released him, Felix felt like he had been transported all over again. It hadn't been like when he'd stolen a Memory in the past, but his perfect recall had made it so damn realistic. Smells, sounds, even emotions felt viscerally true. He brushed a hand across his cheeks and found them wet. Pit bumped at his leg, hard enough to nearly knock him over, and a fuzzy warmth spread through their bond. Comfort.

Felix Nevarre?

He ignored the Maw and started running again. He might share a body with the damn thing, but his memories were his own.

A few minutes later, they came across a few rocks floating in the Void. No bigger than his torso, Felix almost missed it as they whizzed by the formation. A strange quirk of perception meant it looked like the rocks were the ones moving. When they slowed and backtracked, Felix found the rocks to be hovering in place; just a touch was enough to send it moving away. After a moment, it was pulled back by some unseen tether. They were bare of anything but stone, yet excitement coursed through him.

"If there are rocks, that means the Void isn't completely empty," Felix said to Pit. The tenku joined him in his excitement. "There are monsters, there are floaty rocks. There's gotta be a way out."

Optimism, rasped the Maw. *The smiling Fool's lie he tells himself. I thought you drew the Magician, Felix Nevarre?*

Felix ignored it as best he could, but the Maw was insidious. It crept into sight over and over, floating into his peripherals or in front of him as he ran. By the end of another two hours, Felix and Pit had crossed the path of numerous floating stones. Some were lone formations, while others were conglomerated into tiny floating archipelagos.

Felix knelt atop a particularly large formation, perhaps as large as a basketball court. He swept his Perception and, with some reluctance, his Voracious Eye around the area.

What are you doing?

Felix didn't bother to answer it, merely grunting in annoyance. He sought some sign of life and hoped the larger islands would have *something*. But there was nothing growing on them, just rock and rock dust. Still, hope buoyed his heart. He knew they could find a way out. Why else would the System assign a quest?

You're an idiot, Felix Nevarre.

Felix rolled his eyes. "What is it this time?"

There is no escaping this. The Void is... You cannot escape it. Your Grand Harmony lies to you. You cannot even hear it in this wretched place!

"I recall someone telling me I couldn't fight you off, yet here we are." Felix spread his arms wide. The Maw only bared its flat, human teeth at him. Felix scoffed and dropped his arms to slap at his sides. "If you—"

A foghorn-like bugle rocked the Void, a description that was both apt and totally misleading. It was deep, sure, but strange and multitudinous undertones laced the bugle, the cry of a creature that was far larger than even the whale-thing he had seen earlier. Felix's vision blurred with the strength of the cry, the rock beneath him vibrating like an earthquake. Then suddenly and without warning, a massive creature flew above them.

It looked like one of those rocky whale beasts, except far bigger and more gruesome. Where the former had skin of craggy stone, this… *thing* had reddened, blubbery flesh that visibly pulsed even from a distance of what had to be miles. All over its long, bulky form, rows and rows of serrated teeth formed strange mouths surrounded by patches of rust-colored scales.

Name: Corrupted Narhallow
Type: Voidborn*
Level: 73
HP: 3944/3944
SP: 2489/4375
MP: 862145769/0
Lore: Normal Narhollow siphon Mana from the Void with their specialized mouth filters, releasing excess through their tails to move their impossible bulk. This Narhollow has been corrupted by foreign power, its very nature altered by its ingestion.
Strength: Unknown
Weakness: Unknown

Voracious Eye is level 26!

As they watched, it tore into a flock of Harrowings that Felix hadn't spotted, eating a huge mouthful of them. Silhouetted against the Narhollow, hundreds of the things appeared to be after them now. The Corrupted Narhallow snapped up several more with one of its side mouths, the teeth working like a horrific venus fly trap. Just looking at it, Felix could sense a dire sort of connection to the creature. A visceral reverberation shot through his guts before coiling and leaping back out toward the creature.

Oh Ruin, whispered the Maw.

"What?" Felix couldn't tear his eyes away from the corpulent monstrosity, but he felt the Maw float next to him, could feel the tension pouring from it. He turned and saw a flurry of emotions moving across the Maw's face, some far too fleeting to identify.

My power. My beautiful strength! It TOOK IT! The Maw raised a pale hand in a snatching motion. *GIVE IT BACK!*

A dissonant note cracked across the silent expanse, a burr in the fabric of reality that shook from Felix's own core at the Maw's gesture. In the distance, the Corrupted Narhallow's massive eye rolled toward them with distinct clarity. Another foghorn shook the Void.

And the creature began heading in their direction.

"What've you done?" Felix glanced at the Maw only a moment before calling out for his friend. "Pit! Run!"

CHAPTER THREE

Felix took off like a shot, sending the floating island bobbing in place.

Racing among the hovering stones, Felix could finally appreciate the speed at which they were moving. Small, hanging rocks whizzed by at incredible velocity, more blurs than solid shapes. Pit zipped ahead for only a moment, wings tucked back and legs pumping furiously, but unable to keep up his pace for long. Felix panted, straining himself, heaving his Strength against the soft not-ground of the Void to propel himself faster.

Faster! Faster, you fools!

The Maw zipped alongside them both, hair and dress streaming in a phantom wind. Its cadaverous face looked back in a confused mixture of fear and bright, naked lust.

Felix didn't have time to break down the thing's strange, unsettling emotions. His muscles burned, and his joints ached. They had been on the move for so long, and there was only so much his Body could take. Tempered or not.

Silence filled the Void. The lack of wind in his ears was an eerie sensation as they dodged and dove over the few rocky obstacles they encountered. The silence was misleading, however, as the gargantuan Corrupted Narhollow was still in pursuit. It had simply not yet reached their cluster of rock motes. The sharp cries of Harrowings flared louder for only a moment before the Void was filled with the cacophonous sound of the Narhollow crashing through. Felix risked a glance backward, and his eyes grew wide.

The Corrupted Narhollow simply obliterated the islands it came across, the massive bulk proving too much. Distances were so hard to judge, but Felix guessed it was maybe a mile away and gaining fast. The monster fixed him with a beady-eyed stare before manifesting several dozen other eyes along the front of its wide, blunt head. Each one spun a moment before fixing on Felix and Pit.

Holy fucking shit! There wasn't a chance in hell he wanted to be anywhere near that thing.

Relentless Charge!

Relentless Charge is level 10!

Felix physically grabbed his Companion and chained together as many Relentless Charges as his Mana and Stamina allowed, each one sending them further and further from the abomination's massive gullet. All the while, the Maw kept pace, passing right through the scattered floating stones like a ghost as Felix navigated through the treacherous terrain. Through clenched teeth, he gasped a question.

"What do you mean, it took your power?"

The Maw's glance at him was filled with such hatred that Felix felt his heart skip a beat. But then it answered. *Because I gave it up.*

"The Anchor," Felix realized. It had soaked up the huge majority of the Maw's power, siphoning it off to who knows where. To *here*, he realized. "So then that… thing has your power?"

Obviously. It fed on it, grew stronger, and its flesh form couldn't handle my majesty. Now it's transforming from the inside out. The Maw spun until it was floating backward, contemplating the raging beast. *It is surviving far longer than Grimmar did.*

Larger stone islands loomed ahead, some of the largest he'd seen yet. They blocked the path enough to either side that going around was just as arduous as going over. Felix flared his Perception, searching for a path, a crevice, *something.*

"There! Pit!" Felix shouted, flexing a strange new feature he could feel coiling within his Skills. Etheric Concordance flared.

Convergence!

Felix leaped into the not-air, accompanied by a flash of vivid white light. Pit disappeared, only to manifest as a strange, heavy weight in his chest. He couldn't hold his Companion like this long, only for as many minutes as the Etheric Concordance had levels, but it helped. Landing atop the side of the monolithic crag, Felix stabbed his hands into it. His Body was strong and tough, he'd learned that much, but it didn't stop him from wincing at each impact. He made his own handholds and scrambled up the side of the fifty-foot stone to the booming sound of cracking rock.

Climb, Felix Nevarre! Climb as if your life depended on it, the Maw hissed from beside him. *I do believe it does!*

A wide crevasse loomed in the stone, and Felix reached for the easy handhold. The moment he did, however, a swarm of mottled gray Tenebrils flooded out, chittering wildly. Rubbery, barbed tentacles lashed all around and struck Felix across the head and shoulders. They didn't get past his Armored Skin, but it was painful regardless.

"Ah, fuck!"

Stop fooling around and continue! Or else ready yourself for a brief and humiliating fight. The Maw wasn't quite screaming, but her—*its!*—face looked far more gaunt than usual. For a lightning-quick second, Felix felt a thrill of fear that wasn't him or Pit. It came from the Primordial.

Felix spared a look backward and immediately wished he hadn't. The Corrupted Narhollow was shattering all of the stone motes it encountered, and its hundreds of blue-green eyes were fixed upon Felix. It was close, maybe a half mile away, but its bulk made distances misleading.

With a writhing flap, the last of the Tenebrils rushed out, but Felix could sense more within. His Perception twinged on the rustle-scrape of thousands of limbs dwelling deeper within. Those that emerged fell quickly before the host of nigh-invisible Harrowings that crowded the almost featureless Void. Even the Narhollow's attention was briefly diverted as its massive, fanged mouths snapped at the flood of prey.

Felix got an idea, and from within him came a series of fluting calls. *Shush, you. It's a great idea. We can't run forever.*

Relentless Charge!

Relentless Charge is level 11!

The Skill threw his body past the crevasse and onto the very top of the huge stones. Sounding the pattern, Felix manifested twin whips of shadow in each of his palms; thick, four-inch diameter cables of vaguely tacky shadow Mana that extended nearly fifteen feet each. With every ounce of his Strength, he lifted them up and brought them slamming down.

KRAK!

The stone islands, each of them as big as buildings, shuddered.

What are you doing!? the Maw screamed. *Flee! It smells your Mana with each spell you cast!*

Felix ignored her and lifted his whips up and down again.

KA-KRAK!

In the distance, closing ever faster, the horrifying whale let out a bellow that Felix could only describe as *eager*. And *hungry*.

KRAK!

KRAK!

KRAK!

"C'mon, you stupid whale!" Felix growled. He was sweating with panic. This had to work. They couldn't outrun the creature, and they couldn't fight it. He'd barely won against a weakened Maw. "What more could you want—?"

It smells my Mana. So did the voidbeasts!

Cloudstep!

With a series of uncertain hops, Felix coalesced what remained of his Mana into tiny, crackling platforms. He stood on them only moments before leaping to the next, their thin solidity holding just enough.

Cloudstep is level 9!
Cloudstep is level 10!
Mana Manipulation is level 7!
Mana Manipulation is level 8!

The steps firmed under him, just a touch more as the Skill reached that first threshold of understanding. Felix shifted how he was exuding his Mana vapor, and the crackling clouds almost made sense, somehow. Regardless, once he was far enough out, he spun and glanced down at the rock faces.

"Come on out!" Felix shouted, his voice echoless in the Void. He pumped more Mana vapor from his hands until his Manasight detailed a waterfall of crackling blue-white vapor cascading down the surface of the stone. "Time to eat!"

This time, it was like an avalanche of mottled gray flesh that came pouring out of the stones. A twisting, conglomerate ribbon, the Tenebrils swarmed his Mana with all the savagery of starving vultures. Soon it was gone, but Felix wasn't done.

Wrack and Ruin!

An orb of acid hit them with a splash of viscous green, but he ignored the kill notifications that flickered across his vision. He had their attention now. Felix poured all the Mana he could manage into a single, wobbling orb of acidic Mana. The Tenebrils' inscrutable forms stared at him, writhing across their unfortunate broodmates. With a scream of effort, Felix sent this one streaming into the black.

Wrack and Ruin!

Wrack and Ruin is level 27!

The Tenebrils pivoted and immediately chased after the massive, clearly unstable spell. They thundered past him, battering his Body with their lashing limbs, but wholly focused on their meal. It arced through the darkness, going farther than even Felix had anticipated.

Directly toward the Corrupted Narhollow.

A tidal wave of Tenebrils crashed into the disgusting whale's strange, scaled flesh. Harrowings dove, consumed by a hunger Felix could almost *feel*, and their ebon claws tore into the endless wave of mottled tentacles. A terrifying bellow shook the Void, scattering some of the voidbeasts, but not nearly fast enough. The Corrupted Narhollow banked, ponderously slow but inevitable, and opened its million-fanged maw. A net of crimson tendrils snapped outward, so many that it looked like an expanding gas cloud. Thousands of voidbeasts were snagged and pulled into its cavernous insides.

The abomination fed.

"Run," he whispered to himself. Felix's insides shook with each crunch and despairing shriek, Pit equally awed. "Now!"

Relentless Charge!

They fled into the black.

CHAPTER FOUR

Relentless Charge is level 12!
Running is level 24!

Felix fell atop a craggy stone, one of many that had begun to litter the Void. He panted harshly, cramps seizing along his gut as he did. The voidbeast he'd eaten sat in him like a rock. But Pit was exhausted too; the tenku's thin chest heaved, both of them taking huge, gasping gulps of air. They'd run as fast and as far as they could, and it wasn't until Felix could no longer see the hulking, crimson mass of the Corrupted Narhollow that he dared rest.

That had proven to be farther than he had imagined. There was air in the Void—he was breathing *something* after all—but it was something *else* that slowly occluded objects in the distance. A darkness that slowly engulfed things too far to sense, and Felix feared it was tied directly to his Perception. It had made him run farther and farther, even going so far as to dump 10 of his free points into Agility and boosting his speed. His Stamina had almost bottomed out six or seven times, but eventually the panic that seized him had settled.

Felix leaned his head back against a rocky outcropping and clutched his Companion to his side.

"Where the hell did we end up, Pit?"

Pit cooed in tired sympathy.

"Yeah. I'm pretty sure we don't deserve this, either," Felix said, rolling his eyes toward the specter of the Maw. She hovered high above them, apparently no longer concerned with the mountain-sized whale. Felix squeezed his tired eyes shut. "It does, though."

The Maw had done terrible things in just the half-hour he'd known it, let alone the breadth and scope of its massive life. From all the things it had confessed to, the Primordial had deserved eternal banishment to the Void. Felix looked back up, but the Maw had vanished.

We have lost it.

"Jesus!" Felix nearly shouted. The Maw fixed him with its intense eyes, a swirl of green and blue that still unsettled Felix.

Feeding those voidbeasts your Mana was an... acceptable tactic, Felix Nevarre.

Felix blinked in surprise. He hadn't been expecting praise from the world-eating abomination.

But, it continued. *You still leak that Mana like a sieve. Your Mana system is patchwork, and your core is pitifully crude. You will kill us, given half the chance, with nothing more than your ineptitude.*

"Oh," Felix let out a pent up breath. He was almost relieved. "For a minute, I thought you were being helpful." He settled back against the stone and fixed the apparition with a glare. "You were afraid of it."

What? I was not, mortal. I was enraged. The Maw's gaunt face took on shadows that were impossible in the strange, even lighting. It looked feral. *That thing has taken hold of my power. You would have no idea how that burns.*

"Does it feel like someone stole your body? That they planned to walk around in it like a meat puppet?" Felix asked in mounting frustration. "You're no different from that thing."

The Maw did not respond. It merely regarded Felix with those blue-green eyes, so similar to the... the *Whalemaw.*

"What?" Felix snapped.

You must fix your Mana.

Felix ran his hands over his face, close to ripping his hair out. "What are you talking about!?"

You are Unbound, so I shall forgive your lack of knowledge, but if we're to remain hidden from that beast, *then you need to fix yourself.* The Maw floated closer until it was only feet away.

"That's close enough," Felix warned. He didn't have a clue what he could do to her—it!—but he was willing to try anything he could. "You've already altered one of my Skills, and don't think I didn't notice my Bloodline progress increasing after you did it! I don't need you touching me again."

...Very well. Then at least listen, you quibbling wretch. The Maw put its spindly arms on its stolen hips. *Your Mana system is paltry, but you've begun to enter the Visualization Stage. So, you should be at least capable enough to manage this.*

"Visualization Stage?" Felix asked, interested despite himself. Cautiously interested. "What are you talking about?"

Your core, fool. Can you not feel it? Feel the power surge through your veins?

"You're talking about my channels? Where my Mana moves?" Felix asked. He knew relatively little about the channels in his body, except that they were extant. He recalled the mural in the Waterfall Temple, a cross-section of a humanoid body that depicted a circular orb above the navel and looping veins throughout the torso, head, and limbs. If he concentrated, he could envision a blue-white vapor pulsing through him, traveling along those veins before returning to his core. "What about them?"

Not just your channels, your core itself. You leak your Mana out of your Gates like a chimera taking a piss. The Maw sneered at him. *The voidbeasts are tracking your scent.*

Felix sat up, his attention well and truly grabbed.

I thought that might stir you. The Maw smirked. It looked more like a sneer, though. *You've not progressed far into the Visualization stage, I felt that much when I was... making myself at home. There's still time to fix you.*

Felix was positive he didn't want the Maw doing any "fixing." But he also didn't want to lead the Whalemaw back toward them, or any of the voidbeasts for that matter.

"Talk."

You have seen your core, the blue-white flame within, yes? Felix nodded, and the Maw pointed at her own navel. *All have such cores, though they are not the same. Your... disposition will shape it, your unique vision reflected in its composition.*

"Okay," Felix said slowly. "So, mine is a ball of blue-white fire, and it has little lightning bolts around it. You're saying it looks like that because I *want* it to?"

The Maw made an exasperated noise. *It is as it appears, but it only appears as it is due to your perception of it.*

"That's... okay." His core was what he wanted it to be, but it was colored by his preconceptions. He first unlocked a smattering of it when he gained the Fire Within Skill. He had thought the warmth inside him was a flame, and so it was. "So when I envisioned my center as fire that spread outward to warm myself—"

You created a connection between your Mind and Spirit, beginning the process of Visualization. The Maw rolled her eyes. *I'd be disappointed if you were not completely foreign to these concepts. Your world is practically barren in comparison to mine.*

"Does that extend to Skills, as well?" Felix asked.

The Maw raised a thin eyebrow. *Quicker than expected. That boost to Intelligence seems to be kicking in, finally.* Felix frowned, but the Maw kept talking. *Your core is the amalgam of all three of your Aspects. Body, Mind, and Spirit. Of course your Skills are intrinsic to that amalgamation. Each one you learn is stamped into the fabric of your core space, however you visualize it, and only grow more entrenched as they level.* It waved a clawed hand in a careless fashion. *None of that is important in the now, Felix Nevarre. What is of gravest concern are your Gates.*

"My... Gates," Felix said. "Part of my channels, the pathways through my Body?"

Indeed. They are apertures through which your Mana escapes to affect the world around you, as well as where ambient Mana is pulled back in, *to regenerate your core.* The Maw pointed to several spots on her—its—own body. *Your palms, the base of your skull, elbows, knees, and feet. Nine Gates, corresponding to the nine major channels that move through you. Each one acts as a reservoir meant to purify the ambient Mana around you, but yours are... sloppy. They simply pull in Mana constantly, no matter the type, and release it just as readily.* The Maw gave him a grin dominated by its overly large, Human teeth. *You're ravenous.*

Felix felt a quiver of unease, but tried to keep it off his face. "So you're saying I'm... releasing a trail of my Mana through the Void?"

The Maw nodded. *And in this dead place, it burns like fire.*

Felix looked down at his hands and flared his Manasight. He'd never noticed anything odd about himself, but then, he hadn't really spent much time looking at his hands and whatever. Mana in the Void was... thin was the best word. There wasn't even much shadow Mana either, as there wasn't exactly any light. It was all a sourceless illumination that hit everything equally.

So, it was far too easy to spot tiny puffs of multicolored light coming from his palms.

Fire Within is level 34!
Mana Manipulation is level 9!

"Shit," Felix said, clenching his fists. It was like trying to catch smoke. Pit quirked his head and nipped at the floating vapor. "I'm losing Mana? How long has this been happening?"

Since you arrived. Those not as blessed as you would feel their reserves drop continually until they were barely functional. It's why most learn early to develop better internal Mana control. Your Mana regeneration though is...abnormal. You suffer no ill effects from losing a bit of your Mana like this—not yet, at least.

At later Stages, you'll find the world far less agreeable to such weaknesses. As it is, every voidbeast close enough to sense you will come swarming. We must fix this now, or else you'll die. Something in the Maw's tone pulled Felix's eye from his fists. It was looking into the darkness of the Void and touching its own throat.

"Or else *we* die," Felix corrected. "We're tied together, Maw."

Unfortunately, you are correct. The creature gathered itself and floated closer. *So I shall deign to fix your deficiencies. It will take but a second to—*

"No," Felix said, and put every ounce of his Willpower into his voice. "I don't need you to fix this for me. Explain what has to be done, and I'll do it."

The Maw regarded him with a sour expression, but its clawed hand dropped back. *Fine. Choose the Fool's path, despite your Omen.* It floated backward, putting a few more feet of distance between them again. *Listen closely then, Felix Nevarre. I'll not be repeating myself.*

Pit nudged against Felix's elbow, and he absently scratched his Companion. He listened.

He wouldn't forget a word.

CHAPTER FIVE

Felix clenched the Mana Gate located in his right palm. It wasn't visible on the surface of his skin. In fact, it didn't even seem to be there except to his more arcane senses. The Gate sent out a quiver of searing pain that felt like holding a bolt of lightning in his hand.

"MMMPH!" Felix grunted, but kept applying pressure. According to the Maw, the process for strengthening one's Mana Gates was relatively easy. His problem, however, lay in another issue.

Ah yes, the other reason you mortals choose to train your Mana Gates so early is to prevent them from locking open. Quite painful to rectify, I've been told. The Maw's false concern would have been better sold without the contemptuous sneer on its face.

Painful was an understatement. It was like forcing closed an iron door that had fused its hinges into a solid whole. His nerves screamed in agony, despite his Pain Resistance, and he could only imagine how much worse it would have felt at full blast. The searing agony meant he could only focus on one Gate at a time, but it was a grueling experience just the same.

Pit tried to help, attempting to send Felix's sensations of

warmth and comfort through their bond, but they all came out a bit sour. The tenku kept pacing around Felix's supine form, his body language betraying the unease that boiled within his Rottweiler-sized physique. Felix felt for the poor guy, but he didn't have the attention to spare. Already, one small slip had resulted in the loss of all his efforts up to that point, and Felix wasn't willing to do that again.

Focus!

Felix marshaled his Willpower, easily his greatest stat, and pushed through the pain. He felt *something* tear in a blinding burst of anguish before something slammed shut. It felt like a tiny jolt in his right palm, vibration more than anything else, but… he'd done it.

Fire Within is level 35!
Mana Manipulation is level 10!

Excellent. You've done that faster than I had hoped. The Maw glanced around at the darkness again. *We don't want to remain here much longer.*

But Felix wasn't listening to the Primordial; instead he was focused on his palm and the deep, uncomfortable pressure that had immediately started to build. It felt like… like sticking his face out of the window of a moving car. He felt clogged. He couldn't take a breath. He—

He released his Gate. Mana belched from his palm, vibrant and blazing bright in the Void, before his Gate began to draw in more from the ambient levels around them. What little there was.

Tch. The Maw had its arms akimbo as it regarded Felix. It watched his puff of Mana vapor as it spiraled off into the Void. *Now we run. Before the beasts arrive. Fool boy.*

Felix learned two things during their renewed flight.

One, the Maw hadn't been lying when it had said the Void was a desert in terms of Mana. His regeneration, so impressive on the Continent, wasn't even keeping up with his expenditures of Relentless Charge. According to the Maw, he'd been venting Mana ever since he'd started developing his core, only the abundance of Mana had hidden it from him.

The second thing he discovered was, while his Endurance was more than impressive for his level, the constant, low-level drain on his Mana and Stamina burrowed into his bones. Felix had been running for… a day? Time was uncertain in the unchanging Void, and the nigh-featureless terrain was impossible to measure distances. He was *tired*, and Pit was no better.

Eventually, what felt like hours later, he was able to close his first Mana Gate at will.

Acceptable. Now you must learn to fluctuate the opening to let Mana in and out, the Maw instructed. It had been floating beside him, tireless as ever.

"Let it out? I thought the purpose was to keep us from being tracked?" Felix asked.

For now, yes. But you'll need an influx of Mana, just as you'll need to release it to activate your Skills. If your core starves of Mana, it will be snuffed out. That is not a fate you wish to put upon yourself, Felix Nevarre.

The tone of its voice was stern, and Felix couldn't help but envision a possible result of his core winking out. He doubted it would be pleasant.

"How will I avoid the voidbeasts? Or the Whalemaw?" Felix asked, blowing his breath as he walked to recoup his energy.

Whale—? The Maw fixed Felix with a gimlet eye. *The Whalemaw is sensing me, my influence on your Mana. You've been Marked boy, Body, Mind, and Spirit. Every part of you has been touched by my power. That you walk free is a testament to your idiocy. What fool would kill themselves rather than attain apotheosis?*

Felix could tell the Primordial didn't like what he'd done, but he was rather proud of the achievement. Existential terror notwithstanding. "So it will find us again? No matter what I do?"

SILENCE

Most likely, yes. What I teach is to avoid the voidbeasts we pass more than preventing the thief from tracking us down. The Maw floated onward. *The Void is… annoyingly vast. Control your Gates, reduce your vented Mana, and it will buy us time.*

"Time enough to kill the Whalemaw?" Felix asked, disbelieving. The Maw didn't bother to answer him.

Time kept trudging forward, as did Felix and Pit. They snatched bits of sleep when they could, but fear and the knowledge that any of the floating rocks could house hordes of voidbeasts did not let him rest. His Endurance and Vitality meant sleep wasn't as necessary as it once was; his Aspects had also undergone the First Threshold—having all risen above 100 points before level 50—and worked as a more unified whole than before. It did not stop exhaustion from stripping away at his concentration, blurring the hours even more than the repetitive terrain.

He refused to stop and had taken to carrying Pit in his arms to let the tenku rest. All the while, Felix fought with his "rusted" Mana Gates. He managed his left palm perhaps a half day after his right palm, but had barely scraped the edges of his right elbow when the Maw stopped them.

Something is wrong, it muttered.

Felix focused ahead, looking beyond his flesh for the first time in hours, and his eyes spasmed in pain. Light bloomed just beyond a series of large stone islands, each one double the size of where he'd lost the Whalemaw. As he watched, the light filled with the flicker of green flame, and he could hear a faint booming. It was muted, like all sound in the Void, but the fact that he could hear it from such a distance meant it must have been *loud*.

"What is that?" Felix swallowed. He set Pit down next to him, waking the dozing chimera, and readied himself to fight. "Is it more voidbeasts?"

No, it's—the Maw hesitated, before baring her flat, yellowed teeth—*Mortals.*

People, Felix translated, and a desperate sort of joy rose up in him. *There are people beyond that ridge.*

Yet before he could make a move toward it, a small shape crested the floating rocks and slalomed down it's craggy side. It was long and thin, and a single triangular sail was mounted atop it.

A... boat?

A Manaship, the Maw hissed. There was joy in its voice. *We have but to steal it, and our pace will be greatly enhanced.*

The boat—Manaship—seemed to use the floating ridge as a speed ramp, increasing its velocity with every passing second before pulling up sharply and rocketing outward. Toward them.

Hide, but ready yourself, Felix Nevarre. You must take them out as they draw near, but do not *damage the ship!*

"I'm-I'm not attacking some random person," Felix protested. "They can help us!"

They are likely fleeing a heinous deed. Or do you think explosions of fire are commonplace in the Void? The Maw sneered at him and flexed her skeletal thin hands. *And do innocent mortals typically emblazon a grinning skull upon their standards?*

Felix focused on the speeding ship, and just as the Maw indicated, the triangular sail was inked with a dark skull. His Perception was enough to pick out that a single Human was piloting the ship, and was frantically looking behind them far more than ahead. The reason why was soon clear.

"Holy shit," Felix breathed as a far larger ship crested the ridge. It had two masts, each festooned with multiple sails and a prow designed to mimic some sort of undulating monstrosity. A massive sea monster was detailed on its main sail, one eating smaller ships.

"More pirates."

Bolts of green flame launched through the air as the bigger ship coursed after the smaller. Despite his dislike of the new Skill, Felix flared his Voracious Eye at them both.

Name: Death's Companion
Type: Manaship (Damaged)
Lore: Manaships are vehicles designed from rare

materials and powered by Mana to propel them through the skies. Or, in this case, the Void. This Manaship is classified as a Sloop and takes a crew of at least one to sail.

Name: Night's Wake
Type: Manaship (Damaged)
Lore: Manaships are vehicles designed from rare materials and powered by Mana to propel them through the skies. Or, in this case, the Void. This Manaship is classified as a Schooner and takes a crew of at least six to sail.

"Those are cheery names," he muttered, hunkering lower behind a floating rock. He wasn't planning on stealing either ship, but hiding was at least a good idea. "What is going on?"

Death's Companion was the smaller vessel, and it raced ahead, weaving a serpentine trail as it attempted to dodge the flood of green fire bolts from the *Night's Wake*. But it was doomed to fail. The *Night's Wake* suddenly glowed a brilliant, multicolored hue, the light shining from the planks of its sides, and put on an immense burst of speed. Within seconds, the larger vessel had overtaken the smaller, and hooked ropes had latched onto it like a spider catching a fly.

"Wind 'er in, boys! We're havin' meat tonight!"

Catcalls and jeers met the boisterous cry, and the man on *Death's Companion* blanched in fear. He was a stocky Human, with an ill-kept beard, dozens of scars, and a number of cruel weapons strapped to his person.

Name: Keggus Pike
Race: Human
Level: 37
HP: 427/613
SP: 164/483
MP: 15/54

Strength: More Data Required
Weakness: More Data Required

Felix had started to mentally edit out the Lore on Humans; he'd read it enough at this point. To his surprise, the Skill complied, and it vanished. He didn't have time to investigate that more, because the two ships collided relatively violently only feet from his location.

"You'll never take me alive! The Keelhaul Krew will never work under the likes o' Captain Nokk!" Keggus declared, drawing two cutlasses from his belt. He charged across his ship's deck and leaped into the air, as if the mad man intended to board the *Night's Wake* and fight.

A bolt of green fire tore through the man, killing him instantly.

*Holy—that—*Felix flinched and hid again, but he was unable to suppress his curiosity. He peeked back over the edge of the rocky island, just in time to see a collection of strangely dressed men and women lean over the railing. A Dwarven woman with her face covered in geometric line tattoos stood with one foot on the prow of the ship, grinning down at her prize. Unfortunately for Felix, she was sharp as well as bloodthirsty.

"Oi! Who do we have 'ere?" The Dwarven captain met Felix's eyes and grinned. Her teeth had been filed down to points. "Another of the Keelhaul Krew, eh?"

The entire motley crew turned their venomous stares on Felix, and he ducked back below. He heard the Dwarf laugh.

"Get 'im."

CHAPTER SIX

The pirates screamed as they charged him, and both Felix and Pit ran.

Pit! Circle wide! They split as they ran, each of them running in a different direction around the floating rock motes. *We're fast, we can outrun—*

One of the pirates, a burly bastard with tusks, landed in front of him.

Did he jump over me?

Corrosive Strike!

Felix didn't have time to worry about it, so he lashed out with a straight jab. His fist zipped forward, wreathed in Mana vapor that bubbled out of his Mana Gate. The Orc pirate blocked with his left forearm and was promptly knocked flat on his ass. He wailed, but Felix kept running, only managing to glance at the bloody hole being eaten into the pirate's flesh.

A squawk came from the other side of a rock mote, and a bolt of terror coursed through their bond. A wave of jagged icicles shot up into the air.

Shadow Whip!

Using the shadowy tether, he grasped the top of the intervening rock and pulled. Felix rocketed up and over in an arc, rising above the stone impediment in time to see an absolute beast attacking his Companion. Pit dodged aside, fast enough to evade, but the pirate was huge.

Voracious Eye...

There was a brief moment of resistance, as if something blocked him, but Felix *focused*.

Name: Stiilgar "The Ram" Raamstell (Hidden)
Race: Ogre
Level: 28 (Hidden)
HP: 1242/1242 (Hidden)
SP: 644/851 (Hidden)
MP: 75/118 (Hidden)
Lore: Ogres are generally known for their large reserves of Endurance and Strength, as well as their prodigious appetites. They are often predisposed for melee combat and are considered half-feral by many Races.
Strength: More Data Required
Weakness: More Data Required

Voracious Eye is level 27!

Wrack and Ruin!

Felix got off the shot just as he landed, but his aim was fouled by a second pirate coming from nowhere. It was a Dwarf, covered in faded tattoos and hair. Felix danced backward, just out of range of a horizontal swipe from a cutlass.

You're too scattered! the Maw said, floating somewhere below their fight. *I did you a favor by breaking your Skills. If you—we—are to survive, then you must be more than this. You must let me refine you. Turn you into something greater.*

Screw off! Felix fumed. *Wrack and Ruin!*

This time, the dark orb of acid took the Dwarf right in the

chest, melting through his thin armor and putting him down, hard.

**You Have Killed An Unknown Dwarf!
XP Earned!**

Wrack and Ruin is level 28!

Felix turned back to the Ogre, finding Pit circling him cautiously. He was seven feet tall with pale green skin and yellow eyes. His head was big, but his shoulders and paunch dwarfed it considerably, leaving his thick, muscle-bound arms to hang low like a gorilla's. He wore a pair of leather trousers and a linen vest that strained to contain his bulk. Blunt, yellowed tusks extended from his lower jaw, and he thrust his chin out at them both in challenge.

"You gonna fight the Ram?" he raised his huge fists, miming fisticuffs. "Or you gonna run, Keelhaul?"

"I'm not a pirate!" Felix shouted and activated Relentless Charge.

"Hurk!" the Ram choked. Felix all but vanished and reappeared inches from the Ogre, close enough that his two-fisted Corrosive Strike was impossible to dodge.

Corrosive Strike is level 26!

The Ram stumbled backward, but recovered enough to take a downward swipe at Felix. He dove out of the way, but the Ogre's reach was greater than Felix anticipated. The blow clipped his shoulder—it didn't hurt, but it threw Felix off-balance—making him a prime target for the Ram's follow-up haymaker.

"Hah!" the Ram crowed.

Tsk tsk, I thought you were faster than that, the Maw chided.

Felix bounced off the not-ground of the Void, which was still disconcerting. Again, his Pain Resistance kept the blow from hurting, but his Health took a ten percent dip. Stiilgar bleated out a laugh that was echoed back by a number of rogues around him. Felix's face heated up and his heart raced; he hadn't noticed the rest of the crew catch up.

Armored Skin is level 39!

Damn it.
Felix rolled clear and stood back up, wiping the blood that dribbled from his nose. A slender female, a Goblin, came at him screaming. Felix threw himself aside, easily dodging the slash of her crooked blades. Less than easy was avoiding the discharge of some sort of Skill, one that sent a wash of pale blue up and over his arms. Something latched onto his arms and yanked them aside, opening his chest for a second Goblin's flaming cutlass.

Mantle of the Long Night!
Purple-white ice Mana surged out of his Gates, snuffing the dim orange flames on the cutlass and pushing back at the slighter Goblin. He kicked out, hitting his attacker's hand, before snapping his head backward. His skull hit the first pirate in the face, spraying his hair with warm liquid. The binding Skill failed.

However, over a dozen more pirates closed in, weapons leveled, and a few with the Mana-filled hands of mages. Pit squawked in fear, unleashing a blast of Wingblades that brought several to the ground, but the rest charged forward with reckless abandon.

Reign of Vellus!
A storm of electricity burst outward in all directions, an orb of lightning and kinetic force that threw every single pirate back at least fifteen feet. Even the Ram foundered, screaming against the crackling blast of blue-white lightning.

KRAKOOM!
Without warning, the rock island Felix had leaped on exploded in a shower of dust and brilliant emerald flames. Felix

threw his arms up against the blooming heat, and spun toward the source. The ship, the *Night's Wake*, had crept up on them while they fought, and at the prow was their Dwarven leader. She smiled at him over the edge of a massive ballista, lit up with green Mana vapor that matched the detonated island.

"You're not a Keelhauler," she said, her tattoos wrinkling with her raised brow. "Why're you in our territory, mage?"

Territory? Felix shared a glance with Pit. "I'm sorry. I've only just got here, and I don't really know where I am."

The Dwarven woman—the captain, he assumed—looked him over. It was just a look at first, but then it got weird. Felix felt something scrape along his senses, though he was hard pressed to tell if it was touch or sight or taste. It felt as if someone had just seen him naked. He felt exposed and in danger.

Now that *is interesting,* the Maw said. To Felix's surprise her tone was a mix of caution and curiosity. *Very interesting, indeed.*

Felix abruptly realized the Dwarf had Analyzed him. *That* was what he had felt.

The captain grunted in surprise before letting out a wry chuckle. "A new arrival? And an interesting one to boot. The Captain will certainly want to meet you." She gestured, and a gangplank extended from the side of the ship. "Get aboard. You're comin' with us, pretty boy."

Pretty boy? That was new. This time, he didn't need to look at Pit to sense the wary confusion they both shared. "Coming with you where?"

"To the Keep of the Ten Hands. Greatest pirates in all the Void!" she shouted the last to a cheer from her crew. Felix's hesitation must have been obvious, or the Dwarf was used to coercion because her light tone dropped immediately. "Or ye can refuse. My crew could eat your little dog there. Good meat's scarce in the Void. I never seen what my girl would do to a body this close."

The Dwarf lifted her ballista to her shoulder, and light bloomed along the shaft of a massive arrow.

Felix licked his lips and offered a half-hearted smile. "Always wanted to see a castle."

The Dwarf grinned. "Wise decision, pretty boy."

Soon after, Felix was shuffled aboard the *Night's Wake* at swordpoint. But after a vague warning not to touch anything or get in their way, the captain—named Veris Shirtwaist—had left him to his own devices. He was allowed to roam about the deck completely free from manacles or chains. Pit was free as well, thankfully, and the two of them were huddled along the prow of the ship while pirates bustled all around them.

Felix could somehow sense the murderous gazes directed his way, though he never actually saw them. Whenever he panned around, all the crew were busy hauling on lines and sails—or whatever sailors did. Their apparent lack of concern for him was not a balm. He was a prisoner, and a knot of tension settled between his shoulders and refused to ease.

They're afraid of you, the Maw said. It floated above him, hanging onto a braided line and staring into the dark distance. He noticed that none of the pirates seemed to take notice of the Maw, and had even seen one of the crew climb *through* it. Neither of them acknowledged the other. The ship rose into the Void and slowly banked, turning back the way they had come.

Felix snorted and scratched Pit's silky head, careful to keep his mouth as still as possible and his voice low. He had enough trouble without the pirates labeling him insane. "Why? They captured me."

Because you killed two of them, and you fought off the rest. The Maw looked down at him and her blue-green eyes were intense. *You've the scent of a predator, Felix Nevarre, and you've shown them your teeth. They will not trust you, for they, too, are predators. Behold.*

The ship moved surprisingly quickly, and it had crossed over the rocky ridge. Below, Felix could spy a burning island. It was far larger than most, and a sort of structure was built on top of it, maybe a house or fort. Now it resembled nothing so much as a bundle of burnt matchsticks, while the rock around it crackled with emerald flame.

Prey, it said with a flash of teeth.

Felix's Perception was far better than it had ever been at home, but even pre-System, he would have recognized the shape of corpses. His gut dropped and his throat tightened. There were ten, twenty—Felix counted thirty-two bodies before the *Night's Wake* was too far away to make them out. *Thirty-two victims.* Felix looked at the pirates, and this time caught a few grinning at him before they returned to their work.

"Bastards," Felix muttered. From what he'd gathered, this was the base of the Keelhaul Krew, and they sounded like pirates themselves. But to kill everyone? And some of those shapes were awfully small. Were they Goblins or children? Would it have mattered to them?

A pain lanced through his gut—his core, he supposed. Felix gasped and leaned on the railing while Pit cooed in concern. It felt like a cramp, or like when you ate too much.

I still haven't digested that Harrowing, he realized. Typically, his old Title had let him drink down blood or Mana and gain a memory and/or Skill in quick succession. This had been the first time he'd used Ravenous Tithe, and he'd eaten the whole damn voidbeast. "That's probably not good."

You'll be fine, the Maw assured him. It had changed to hovering upside down, inspecting the sailcloth. *The first meal is always the roughest. Though, I'd prefer if you hurried up your digestion. You'll need the room.*

Felix frowned at the Primordial. "What are you talking about?"

It smiled at him, a cadaverous grin on its wasted face. *You're headed to their lair, no? First rule of all predators: never show weakness. But, if you do, then you eat them before they can eat you.*

Felix blanched, and the Maw's cackle faded as she—*it!*—swept away along the deck.

CHAPTER SEVEN

In the lower chambers of the second floor of the Eyrie, Vessilia Dayne, daughter and heir-apparent to the duchy of Prax'Vrell sat with her hands folded neatly in her lap. The second floor—typically called the Tribunal by the local Guilders—housed the judiciary arm of the Protector's Guild, itself ensconced in the soaring tower at the very center of Haarwatch. The heiress sat upon a blocky stone bench, carved of a uniformly gray granite and enchanted with a subtle durability array. She wasn't bound in any manner, but it felt that way.

Vess sighed and rubbed her right index finger along the web of her left thumb. The room itself—a holding area outside the Tribunal—was warded against sound and other eavesdropping Skills. She even had trouble pushing Mana through her channels, so great was the pressure put out by the numerous hidden arrays. It was uncomfortable, to say the least, and the pressure made it hard to even practice her simpler Skills. There was little for her to do but worry, but at least she was alone.

Ever since she had woken up in the Eyrie's infirmary with six Bronze Rank healers fussing around her, Vess had been lavished with attention. The Silver Rank First Alchemist, Aenea

Ty'nel, had ground poultices and brewed potions for Vess' recovery herself. It was both expected for the ducal heir and utterly stifling. She had been lambasted with questions by an endless parade of Guilder officials the moment she had been deemed recovered enough to answer them, but hadn't been afforded any satisfaction herself.

Then she heard about the Foglands.

"Vessilia," a voice called out. The smooth sides of her chamber opened, a door appearing from the seamless stone. In walked a tall man with dark hair, dark eyes, and a glower enough to grind a mountain to dust. "I had requested you wait for me, my lady."

"I could not wait on you all morning, Darius," Vess responded, glancing at him with a glare. "This is important."

And I might actually hear something of use! Vess fumed silently. Darius Reed had ample sway within the Guild. He was her Father's Chosen Hand—his military aide for tasks beyond the duke—and the highest-ranking member of the peerage in Haarwatch (excluding herself). Yet, he denied her answers to any of her many questions, instead insisting that she remained within the Guild tower—the Eyrie—and convalesce.

"You cannot expect—"

"Why are you here, Darius? In Haarwatch. Who sent for you?" Vess demanded. "Answer me true, and I'll let you remain."

Darius, true to form, let his mouth close into a grim line. The man was an Adept Tier combatant, with more Skill levels in Deception than an entire squad of Tin Ranks. She knew, because he had shown her, once upon a time. She had no hope of reading his expression, and he knew it.

"Fine," Vess said with a cold finality. "Then leave."

"Vessilia—" he started.

"Leave."

Vess did not raise her voice or even look at him, but she was not proficient at Deception and never had been. Her emotions were plain as day. She didn't hear him move, but she heard the seamless door close with the whisper of grinding stone.

She was alone, again. Vess sighed, part frustration and part confusion.

Darius Reed had traveled, post-haste, the moment she had been suspected missing in the Foglands. He had to have done so, or else he wouldn't have reached the city so fast. The distance between Haarwatch and Pax'Vrell was immense. Clearly, her father himself had ordered Darius to move with all speed, and perhaps even granted him leave to use his personal Manaship, though she hadn't seen it. How her father had learned of the issues in the Foglands at all was frustratingly unknown.

It had to have been someone of rank, she surmised. *An Elder. One who had been against Magda's plan, perhaps even the same one who had organized the failed operation in the first place.*

They had traversed the treacherous wilds to—unknowingly, at first—rescue the survivors from a failed Guild operation to occupy and lay claim to the Foglands. Magda's former teammate and longtime lover had been among the missing. She had gathered a team to penetrate the Foglands and recover them or their bodies. And, it had been a success! Vess knew it had, deep in her bones, though Darius refused to shed any light on that, either.

The Tribunal she awaited involved that failed operation; that much she did know. She had been asked to offer testimony on Magda's activities within the Foglands, and the heiress had jumped at the chance. Not only to get more information or to share her side of the situation, but because she knew her friends would have to be in attendance.

On the other side of the room, a more ornate door slid open with a muffled boom. A voice spoke, its words dripping with a regal tone and gravitas.

"Lady Vessilia Dayne, Heiress of the duchy of Pax'Vrell, Tin Rank of the Protector's Guild. Please step forward."

She exhaled, stood, and exited the chamber.

They were situated among a large crowd in a chamber as big as any Evie had seen before. Seating was tiered, with one's Rank determining their positions. Silver were at the first, lowest row, with Bronze, Iron, and Tin Ranks above that. The floor of the Tribunal was for the defenders and the Council itself, all of whom were Gold Ranked by Guild law. That didn't mean they actually were strong enough for that Rank, but the medallion hung heavy and shiny from their chests regardless.

From left to right were the Elder of Spirit, the Elder of Mind, the Elder of Body, the Elder of Acquisitions, the Elder of Craft, and the Elder of the Barricade. Each was sat upon a high dias, a bench that let them loom over the defenders. Callie, Harn, and Evie were seated at the bottom level, each on an uncomfortable wooden bench and dressed in itchy, stiff clothing. The Inquiry had started half a glass ago, but the elders hadn't said a word. They were just… whispering to each other.

Evie alternated between drumming her hands on her lap and tugging at her collar.

"Stop fidgeting," Harn grunted. "You look guilty."

"Why do I have to wear a burnin' dress? It's uncomfortable," Evie said. "And aren't we, though? We didn't exactly just *happen* to wander into a restricted area."

"Quiet. Ya didn't do anythin' wrong," he corrected her. He frowned at the dark wooden bench ahead of them, twice as tall as their own seats and emblazoned with a sword and spear crossed over a shield. The Protector's Guild crest. "Remember that."

After slogging through the bright, fog-free, and unexpectedly beautiful Foglands, their group, along with over thirty survivors, had come knocking on the Haar Gate. It had taken them two weeks, but they had finally reached Haarwatch. Soon after, however, Silver Ranks had appeared to take them all into custody. The why hadn't been fully explained, not to her at least, but everything happened so fast. She didn't even know where they'd taken Atar or the survivors of the Frost Giant's prison.

Truth was, Evie felt numb. She hadn't been solid since Cal had come back without—Someone sneezed in the peanut gallery, and she flicked her eyes in their direction. It was well-lit in the center, but that left the tiered seating in more of a murky shadow.

Night Eye.

Her natural green eyes glowed a brighter shade, vivid were she in the dark herself. The shadows were peeled back, but all that greeted her were the stoic faces of people she barely knew. Evie had spent the last five years in Haarwatch, but her familiarity was with Cal and her crew. Magda—

Breathe.

She took a breath.

It was damn hard to do. But she did it, and it wasn't a gasp, either. *Keep it together, dummy.*

She would—she would be fine. She just had to control her thoughts. But that was easier said than done.

Maggie would be so mad at me for being in a Tribunal. Disappointed. Evie blinked rapidly. *Joke's on her, I guess. Can't tell me what to do anymore.*

She grimaced at her own Mind. Rude, even to herself. Either that or accept that—

Breathe.

For a moment, she thought of her Born Trait, the random gift the System bestowed upon every newborn. Evie's was called Mass Shift, and it allowed her to transfer up to a third of the mass of any object to any other object she could touch. It was a powerful Trait, more suited to a brawler than a Guilder, and one she had spent years learning to grasp. She gave away her mass to the bench beneath her. The bench creaked as it strained, but it held, and Evie felt light.

Fall down or float away. I know what I prefer. Evie swallowed. *Wish I had my chain.*

She wanted to fight something. Anything.

Another breath, and Evie settled back into that comfortable numbness, even if her dress still itched. She had to be here, and not just because they dragged her in. She needed to find her friends. Vess was taken by the Sworn, and Felix had disappeared in the Labyrinth. But no one would tell them anything. Were they already here, in town? In the Eyrie itself?

Were they even alive?

That was when the door behind the Council bench opened up. It creaked and groaned, as if the weight of it was too much for it to function. Evie frowned because it had to be for effect—everything within the Eyrie was kept in pristine condition. Striding out of the door and up to the central seat, was a tall man with a graying beard and sharp eyes.

High Elder Fairbanks, Evie sneered internally. *Spirelord himself.* She had heard he didn't often attend hearings like this one, leaving it to the lower-ranked elders. Evie supposed she should be flattered, but bile rose in her gorge instead. He was cold and emotionless, a statue of a man come to serve out judgment. Fairbanks stood a moment, surveying the audience around them.

"We are here today to find out the truth," he said with a deep, baritone voice. Numb and floaty, she still gritted her teeth at how *pleasant* he sounded. "We are here to right grievous wrongs committed under the Protector's Guild's name and charter. We are here," he said, and this time his voice shook the air. Evie could feel it in her bones, almost. "We are here for *justice.*"

Murmuring broke out among the crowd, and the High Elder let it linger. Evie couldn't help it. She scoffed. The High Elder's eyes pivoted to hers, and she felt the man's Spirit press against hers, ever so slightly. Her mass squirreled away as it was, Evie was still pressed *hard* into the bench below. She broke out into a sweat.

Burnin' ash, he's strong, she thought.

The all-too-physical sensation lingered for only an instant

before the chimera-stain looked away. His Spirit retracted, and Evie took in a sharp gasp.

"Let us begin with our first witness." The old bastard sat down in the central chair—more a throne, really—and gestured to Evie's right. "Lady Vessilia Dayne, Heiress of the duchy of Pax'Vrell, Tin Rank of the Protector's Guild. Please step forward."

Evie's scowl turned to surprise, and she shared a look with Harn and Callie. Neither of them looked particularly stunned, so maybe they'd expected this. Evie sure hadn't.

It's good though, right? She was there, she's on our side.

Evie hadn't had many friends growing up, for whatever reason. Mags had called her "sour, abrasive, and a jerk" but Evie was pretty sure that was unrelated. With the time they spent together in the mists, Vess had swiftly taken the top spot in a pretty spare list. So her heart had soared at hearing Vess' name.

The far stone wall split open like a door, and Vess walked out, dark head held high like the duchess she would one day become. The low murmuring in the audience stopped immediately, and a hush fell over the Tribunal. Evie half-suspected that it was because of how beautiful Vess was; the woman was tall, shapely, had flawless dusky skin and hair that was annoyingly glossy. And that was *without* Tempering.

All things considered, it was downright unfair.

She sat down at a bench on the far end, squinting into the inscribed light that focused directly on her. Evie doubted she could even see them, and Callie's warning grip told her that shouting across the dais wasn't a good idea.

"Lady Dayne, thank you for agreeing to speak," Fairbanks began.

"My pleasure, High Elder. I am willing to be of service to the truth." Vess' voice was firm and stately.

"Very good," Elder Fairbanks said. "Elder Teine, you have the floor."

A man with silver hair and a matching silver goatee leaned

forward. His robes, too, were silver—or at least close enough not to matter. He looked down at Vess from atop his narrow nose, and Evie immediately didn't like him. "You were lured into the Foglands under false pretenses, yes?"

"Yes," Vess admitted slowly. "But that mission was predicated upon—"

"Were you used as a tool, a way for Magda Aren to further her own personal agenda?" Elder Teine continued, flicking through a sheaf of papers. Evie's heart hammered in her chest, and Callie's grip on her arm became a painful shackle. She looked at Callie, and the woman's eyes were practically burning.

"To an extent, I suppose. Magda did not tell us all that she planned when we set out. But we were told once we were within the Foglands—"

"—When you had no means of escape. She told you when there was nothing for you to do but rely upon her and her accomplice, Harn Kastos," Teine stated. His voice betrayed no emotion, whether anger or snide amusement, just irrevocable facts. "Is this not correct?"

Vess paused, and Evie thought her face was... considering. "It is... factually accurate, yes."

"Did Magda flout Guild protocol in any way?" asked another Elder, this one a woman who absently plucked imaginary dirt from her elaborate metal gauntlets. Elder DuFont, Acquisitions. She felt Harn stiffen in his chair beside her. "Did she not attempt to slay an incursion from the Hoarfrost? Alone?"

"To save the prisoners, yes she—" Vess began, but loud, scandalized murmurs from the crowd cut through her words.

"Silence," Elder Fairbanks said, slamming a small cylinder on the bench. Evie almost thought he used his Spirit to quell them, so fast did the audience shut their traps. "I will have silence in this Tribunal." He turned back to Vess. "My lady, please continue."

"Um," Vess ventured. Evie could see sweat beading on her brow. She raised a hand, blocking the light from her eyes. "My thanks, High Elder. Magda Aren did attempt to fight off an incursion of Risi from the Hoarfrost. However, this was in service of saving the lives of many Guild members who had been imprisoned by the Frost Giants."

The murmuring picked up again, but this time it was quieter. Fairbanks let it continue, unabated.

"Ahem, yes. We have read the reports from you and your associates, that the Frost Giants had captured a contingent of lost Guilders in the Foglands. We thank you for their rescue. You are a hero for the risks you took on our Guild's behalf." Elder Teine's words were smooth and sweet, but they felt oily to Evie. "But the fact is, Magda Aren lied to the Guild when she applied to bring you and two other Tin Ranks into a restricted zone. And those false pretenses led to her death."

"Yes, she lied to the Guild," Vess admitted. "She as much as admitted to it. But it was to save people that your Guild seemed to have conveniently disregarded!" The heiress' voice shook and she stood from her seat. Like the High Elder, her voice resonated slightly, filling up more space than the slender woman embodied. "Why were these Guilders never rescued before Magda's interference? Why were *they* within the restricted zone of the Foglands?"

The terraced seating around them burst into furious conversation, and Evie grinned wide. "Got 'em. Now they gotta admit to their illegal operation." She glanced at Callie, but the woman wasn't smiling. "They gotta? Right?"

"Silence!" Fairbanks barked again, but this time, the crowd quieted only after several minutes. "As I was not involved with the original operation, I ask that Elder DuFont answer the Lady Dayne's question. Elder DuFont, you have the floor."

Everyone's attention shifted to the Elder of Acquisitions. The woman was slight, with the face of an aristocrat—all fine lines and rounded edges. She inclined her head to the High Elder. "As you wish. The original operation was a fact-finding mission designed to find and—on the off chance they could—secure a way to stop the chimeric hordes from attacking our city.

Unfortunately, before it could prove fruitful, we lost contact. The last communication we had with the mission was six months ago, when we had word of a dangerous monster attack. Frost Giants, we now know."

DuFont took a sip of water at her side. It was purely for show, to prove how unconcerned she felt. Evie wasn't fully Tempered yet, but there was little chance a Gold Rank Elder couldn't ignore their Bodily needs for a few minutes. DuFont continued, "After that, we heard nothing more. It was assumed the operation was a failure and, as the Foglands began to fill with an influx of monstrosities once again, it was ruled too dangerous to attempt a rescue." DuFont leaned back and spread her hands helplessly. "All of this would have been provided to Miss Aren, had she simply asked through the proper channels. Had she done so, we could have lent support and prevented her death, as well as the risk of three of our most promising recruits."

The woman's words were so earnest that even Evie was taken in for a moment. A traitorous thought drifted through her Mind, and Evie wondered what might have been had Magda trusted the Guild Elders. *Would they have never gone, and would Maggie still be alive?* Her common sense caught up with her though. *No. They simply would have let Cal and everyone else die. I'm no genius, but I don't gotta be to know the math doesn't add up. They were assumed dead. Why save the dead?*

Discussion among several Elders had begun the moment DuFont stopped speaking, and the crowd grew more and more rowdy. Evie looked around, Night Eye activated. There were far too many heads nodding and pointing than she liked.

"Avet's teeth," Callie swore. Her Tempered fingers had pressed furrows into the bench beside her. "We won't win this."

Harn grunted, but it wasn't in disagreement.

"That is not how—" Vess began.

"I have the floor, Lady Dayne," DuFont insisted in a clear but calm voice. "Had Miss Aren chosen to go into the Foglands alone, that is one thing, but she decided to endanger the life of her charges. *That* is unacceptable."

"The way Magda took action might have been in error, but her choice to save the lives of this Guild were not," Vess said, incensed. Her voice cut through the hubbub and returned silence to the Tribunal. Her brows were furrowed, and she looked out at the Elders and crowd with a storm in her features. "Thirty innocent lives were saved by Lady Aren's and Lord Kastos' choices. I ask that this Council truly consider the weight and significance of what they accomplished, when all of you refused to lift a finger. You condemned those people to die. Magda saved their lives."

"Lady Dayne, you would be wise to watch your tone," growled another Elder, a hamfisted man that filled his robes to bursting. "I don't care if your father is the Duke of Pax'Vrell. Here, you're a Tin Rank and nothing more."

"And you would do well in remembering the men and women you sent into the Foglands to die!" Vess shouted, and Evie's heart soared. The crowd burst into excited whispers.

"Silence," Fairbanks ordered, banging his little cylinder again. "We will have silence!"

Before the Elder stopped speaking, a tall figure in dark, lacquered armor appeared at Vess' side. The man had moved so fast that, seconds after his arrival, the air he displaced boomed. Errant breezes whipped across the chamber. He was handsome in the way folks beyond Journeyman were: perfect skin, perfect teeth, and a sort of symmetry to his features that was both pleasing and cold.

"Darius..." Vess whispered.

"We're done here," he said with a glare at the Council. With a gentle touch, he led Vess from the witness stand. For a moment, the heiress tossed a glance backward, and the two of them locked eyes. Evie tried to smile, and Vess tried right back. The man and heiress were gone a moment later with another swirl of violent wind.

"We shall have a brief recess before proceeding," Elder Fairbanks announced after a moment. He looked... ruffled. His hair had been blown out of order by the wind, and papers had scattered from the bench. "We have heard from the Lady Dayne, and even more testimonials have been rendered unto the council in anonymity. The truth has been laid bare, and we will have our decision shortly."

The Elders stood as one, and all of them filed out of the chamber. Evie stared them down, hard enough to spot the considering gaze of Elder DuFont. The woman raised an eyebrow before gathering her robes and exiting.

Evie suppressed a groan. Callie was right. There was no way they'd win against the Guild in its own Tribunal. The fix was in.

Maggie, she thought, turning her eyes skyward. Her gut sank low, sour and upset. *This is a ripe mess you left us.*

"Let it be known: Magda Aren, the woman once known as the Shieldwitch and Silver Rank of the Protector's Guild, is hereby stripped of her rank posthumously and all benefits therein."

Atar stared at the little green stone set into the wall amid an elaborate array. It flashed with every syllable of the recorded message.

"Likewise, her accomplice, Harn Kastos, the Silver Rank known as Onslaught, will also be stripped of his rank. However, in respect of services rendered and a bright future, Harn Kastos will be merely demoted to Bronze Rank and be forbidden to train new recruits ever again."

"Burning ash," he said. "No word on Vessilia? Or even that layabout chain wielder?"

The green stone quit blinking, its message delivered. To his understanding, similar stones were placed around the Eyrie so that warnings and important messages could be spread quickly and easily. That the Council had decided to announce the results of the Tribunal in this way said a lot about their stance.

Frankly, Atar was on the fence about how he felt. Magda

and Harn had lied to him and nearly gotten them all killed. Sure, they'd saved people from a nasty fate, and yes, the Foglands were now fog-free for the first time in Ages, but at what cost? Magda had died and Felix... they had never found a body. That's what Cal had said. Just when he was starting to like the backwater idiot.

After they had returned to Haarwatch, Atar and the survivors had been separated from Cal, Harn, and Evie. They'd been taken to the Healing Ward up on the fifth floor, while Atar had been brought to the Archives, where he'd been told to stay put. No guards or anything to keep watch on him, at least none that he could see, magically or otherwise. Not that he had anywhere to go, or any wish to flee the Guild. His Master had paid a fortune to get him there; the last thing Atar was going to do was jeopardize that.

Not any more than I already have, he thought with a frown.

"You are not allowed in this section, Tin Rank," a voice said from behind him. Atar turned to find a woman with ochre skin and bright, sky-blue eyes staring at him over the rims of spectacles. Her seagreen hair was done up in a messy bun, and her formal robes were buttoned all the way up her neck, but she was quite beautiful, until she smiled. She had shark teeth. "I'll be happy to escort you to the tomes you are allowed to visit."

Naiad, he thought. A Race born of the rivers, same as Nixies, and entirely alien to Atar's desert upbringing. "If, ah, if you don't mind. I seem to have gotten turned around."

He hadn't; he had just gotten bored and wanted to explore. But the last thing he wanted to do was piss off a librarian of the Archive, no matter how unsettling he found her. The Naiad led him down a maze of stacks and shelves, somehow bringing the fire mage back to his starting spot in a fraction of the time it took him to wander about.

"Here you are, Atar V'as," she said.

Atar started. "How do you know my name?"

"We keep an eye on the most promising recruits," the

librarian said with another unnerving smile before turning and walking away.

Atar gathered his nerve and Analyzed the woman.

Analyze.

ERROR.
Analyze Failed.

The pasty fire mage paled even further. Aside from special places like the Foglands, Analyze always worked on those of roughly equal power and advancement. Even for those farther above you, say at Journeyman or Adept Tier, Analyze should have brought up *something*.

"Ah, you're still here. Very good."

Atar turned, once again surprised by a voice at his back. Standing near the desk he'd been left at was a man in silver-gray robes embroidered with swooping shapes in emerald green. He was older, though his face was unlined and ageless—evidence of significant advancement—and his hair and goatee were as silver as his robes. Atar immediately knew who it was—his Master had sent him to Haarwatch with the express purpose of studying with this man.

"Elder Teine," Atar gushed, stepping forward and bowing. "It is an honor to finally meet you, sir."

"I have heard much of you, Atar V'as. Not just from your Master, either," the man said with a smile. "Your exploits in the Foglands have reached us, too. The capability you have shown with your chosen element is remarkable for one so young. Have you considered expanding your studies?"

"Expanding them, sir? How do you mean?" Atar asked. The flame of hope ignited in his chest. His Master had paid to have Atar sent north, but getting into Elder Teine's good graces was based entirely off personal effort. "I am willing to learn. Sigaldry is my craft of choice, of course."

"Ah! Excellent! Mine as well," Teine beamed at him. "If you are willing to join me in my private classes, then I can help you finish your advancement into Apprentice. You are just the kind of forward-thinking mage this Guild needs, and a worthy inheritor of the magic I have in store." He looked at Atar and extended his hand. "Are you willing to become one of my Apprentices, Atar V'as?"

Atar took his hand, overjoyed.

This was a *great* day.

CHAPTER EIGHT

The monotonous terrain whipped past them at incredible speeds. Sitting on the prow of the Manaship, the only place he felt somewhat safe, Felix marveled at their pace. Some sort of magic propelled the ship forward, and he could see it looping around the innards of the ship in bright, green-gold lines. Life Mana, he was certain, pulsing excitedly despite the lusterless gray of the strange deck. It wasn't made of wood, that was clear—where would someone find wood in the Void? But he couldn't place its construction, and it rebuffed his attempts with Voracious Eye.

So instead, Felix spent his time watching the crew. He marveled at the speed and grace with which the crew operated the Manaship. Orcs, Goblins, Humans, Dwarves, even a few birdlike creatures called Korvaa flitted up and down the ropes and decks. They moved nearly as fast as he did, and Felix couldn't figure out why. Each pirate had been analyzed and cataloged in his perfect memory, and he'd soon discovered his Voracious Eye had the ability to sense a target's Tier in a vague way. The crew—with the exception of Captain Shirtwaist—were on the higher end of Apprentice Tier. Felix had only just entered Apprentice Tier, but his Primary Stats had reached the First Threshold. He imagined that some would be stronger or faster than him, but all of them?

He was missing something.

Felix tried to investigate further, but every single one of them had that same resistance to being analyzed. His Voracious Eye had pushed through it, but it was odd. The Maw, feeling particularly helpful, had said it was the nature of their core. The Void had infected them, she said, influencing the composition of their Mana systems. That concerned him, yet when he'd asked for clarification, the Primordial had simply drifted away.

The knowledge that the Void itself was invading the pirates made him want to shut all of his Gates. Ye,t he had made little progress on that front. Felix had only successfully freed up both palms and elbows while traveling; he still had five more Gates to go, and his everything was sore. It hurt even thinking about freeing any more. Mana Manipulation had boosted, at any rate.

Moreover, the few times he'd seen the pirates activate an external Skill, the Mana vapor that had poured from their Gates was dim and washed out. He recalled seeing a similar phenomena during his fight; the flaming cutlass had seemed awfully feeble. He had chalked it up to weaker Skills, but that didn't feel right. In comparison, Felix's own released Mana vapor was vivid and rich.

The only exception among the pirates was Captain Shirtwaist and the ballista she kept slung on her back. She all but glowed with a green radiance, similar in effect to the Manaship itself.

It replaces them with itself.

Felix started, nearly falling over the prow of the Manaship. A few pirates nearby pivoted to watch him, their hands on their weapons, but Felix made a show of inspecting some coiled rope. When they were sure he wasn't trying to escape, they went back to "ignoring" him. Felix hissed under his breath. "What are you talking about?"

Pit swiped at the Maw's location, but his claws passed right through the spectral Primordial.

Get away, beast. The Maw hovered a bit higher, out of the Rottweiler-sized tenku's reach. *The Void is replacing their cores with itself. You asked for elucidation, so there you are.*

"What? That's not clarification, that's a bomb. What—how does it do that? Is it dangerous?" Felix's breath came a little quicker, and he felt a fissure of pain as he tried to calm it down. *Damn broken Breath Control.*

Dangerous? The Maw let out a bitter laugh, like a buzzsaw cutting steel. *Only in the sense that it gradually weakens your Skills—a decay that happens faster the more you use them—while they advance at a progressively slower pace. Once your Skills break apart, your core soon follows. And after that?*

The Primordial spread its skeletal hands, palms up.

Felix licked his lips and regarded the crew around him. A few on the lines were using some sort of utility Skill, letting their knife float alongside them. The Mana that surrounded it was fitful and pale, barely visible were it not for the ceaseless black around them. "So the System just… falls apart out here?"

Again, that same buzzsaw laugh. *You think the Grand Harmony reaches us here? In this dark silence? You've banished us to the end of all things, Felix Nevarre.*

"Grand Harmony. You mentioned that before, and I've got things called Harmonic Stats. What is it?" Felix had some ideas, but they were guesses at best. In spite of the Maw's antagonistic attitude, he hoped it was feeling generous again.

The Maw was silent a moment, as if contemplating something. Its stolen face looked almost sad, but Felix knew better than to believe it. It was a creature of madness as much as hunger. When the silence stretched on for several minutes, he chastised himself for even expecting some sort of answer.

The Grand Harmony is the music of the spheres, it said without preamble. Felix looked back up at the Maw. *The great vibrations that are and always have been. The foundations of creation.* It met his gaze, and its eyes glowed with a bloody crimson light. *It is your System you so foolishly clutch to.*

"The System doesn't reach out here? That's why Skills grow weaker and people don't level up and advance properly?" Felix asked.

An apt summary, if limited. The resonance of the Void is all but nonexistent. The music is thin here, enough that even I am beginning to feel some light strain.

"Music," Felix snapped his fingers and frowned. "You used music before, in the Labyrinth. But it wasn't a harmony."

The Maw smiled, showing too many teeth. *No. No it was not. But the Void is something else. It is an absence, a Realm of silence. It is slow, but that silence will weaken a mortal's foundation until it simply crumbles apart. The Void is averse to life. It does not want us here.*

"How long, exactly?" Felix asked, poking at his core. Everything felt normal, but who was he to say? "How long before it starts affecting me?"

If I were to guess, I would say the youngest of these pirates is two centuries old, the Maw said with a careless shrug. *It's likely the Void has deeply affected them for the last century.*

"Two hundred years? There's a few that are human. How's that possible?" Felix asked.

Advancing increases your lifespan by a significant amount, though...most of these creatures should have withered to dust long ago. The Maw ran its fingers through the air, as if playing an invisible harp. *Time... time is strained here in the black. It does not flow as it does upon the Continent, nor does it touch the denizens of the Void more than it has to. Tempered as you are, without a single ounce of further growth, I expect you would live for several centuries here in the Void, Felix Nevarre. Plenty of time for your core to wither and die.*

The Maw let loose a louder, even more atonal guffaw. *Congratulations, Unbound.*

Their journey was perhaps half a day, if Felix's internal clock was any measure. He snatched some desperate bits of sleep while Pit watched his back, and vice versa, but the two or so hours he'd managed only left him grumpier.

The Maw's words of warning were still on his mind, writ large across his thoughts like a countdown clock. How long before the Void broke him down? Years, surely, but what if it was happening as he sat there?

He poked at his core space, watching as his Skills slowly rotated around a blue-white ball of fire and lightning at the center. It resembled a solar system, with his highest-level Skills closer to the blue-white sun and revolving quickly around it, while his lower-leveled Skills lingered in the back. The Skills were three-dimensional etchings of light, drawn on the darkness of his core space and filled with humming noises. Each one looked and sounded different, unique patterns for each Skill.

A few of those Skills were darkened, even sparking in places where the patterns were severed and dangling. These were the broken Skills the Maw had savaged during their fight. They did not revolve as the rest, or glow. In fact, each tiny pulse of light through them sent a stabbing pain into Felix's Aspects that was hard to ignore when he was within his core space.

Is the Void affecting me now? Nothing really looked different. He looked up, above the spread of his personal solar system, to a cluster of roiling clouds. The clouds were dim and barely perceptible, but Felix had grown, and he could sense a vague shape and pale colors slowly manifesting. A part of him knew it was a representation of the Harrowing he had eaten, just as he sensed a sort of... connection between it and his Ravenous Tithe Skill.

I've eaten a voidbeast. What'll happen when it's finished digesting?

Fire Within is level 35!
Mana Manipulation is level 17!
Mana Manipulation is level 18!

Felix worried at his core and Mana Gates all the while, slowly chipping away at the metaphysical rust that had accumulated on them. He had sequestered himself at the prow of the ship, just before the bowsprit and an elaborate carving of a man and woman in agony. It was remarkably well-done, but it skeeved him out a bit, and he'd tucked down below the railing to better focus on his Gates.

Shouts in the rigging soon stopped him though; they were approaching a massive stone island. It was far away, but the details were picked out in his Tempered vision as if they were an arms-length away. A collection of eclectic and ramshackle structures sat on the island, all of which were combined into something approaching a castle. There were parapets and even a few towers.

That impression was further cemented as they drew closer. Felix could see at least two dozen ballista that were pointed in the ship's direction, mounted atop crenelated walls and easily twice the size of the one Captain Shirtwaist wielded. Two or three figures were manning each huge weapon, though they looked more bored than hostile. A dim Sparkbolt shot into the sky—a signal, no doubt—and the *Night's Wake* dropped elevation until it came down under the makeshift castle.

At that moment, a massive flock of invisible Harrowings made themselves known. Screeching out of the dark, the triangular monstrosities attacked the *Night's Wake*, only to be met by the quick fire of green Mana cannons. The bulk of them fled, angling instead for the defenders on the castle walls. Though they had ballista lined up, not a single one fired.

What? Why aren't they doing anything? Felix stared as the pirates began to get out... ropes?

Just as the Harrowings reached the walls, a shimmering plane of white force suddenly snapped up around their impacts. With a pang, it reminded Felix of Magda's Force Wall, but the power felt different, more primal. Terrifyingly so.

The Harrowings crashed into it, and those in the lead immediately began to dissolve, flesh and bone and tooth and a thousand eyes all turned to blackened mush. The rest banked hard, their inertia still seeding destruction among the flock. Bone and cartilage and gooey red muscle turned to carbonized nothing as the white shield atomized their bodies.

Blighted Night, the Maw muttered. Felix glanced at it in surprise. There was fear in its voice.

They tried to fly away only to fall into the sparkling nets of the pirates. In short order, the majority of the flock had been captured and was hauled into a side hatch. The Harrowings' screeches turned quickly from rage to dismay and fear.

"What the hell was that?" Felix muttered to his friend, but Pit wasn't paying attention.

The tenku chirruped in clear awe as the shadow of the massive stone island drifted over them, bigger than any they had seen yet. There were holes cut into it above them, and Felix spotted some movement among the openings. He shivered. *Murder holes*, he realized, where people could dump boiling oil down on them. Yet they were unaccosted as the *Night's Wake* slipped into a large, open-air dock.

The shouting only increased as the pirates boiled across the deck like ants on an anthill. Curses and washed-out Skills bloomed with light around him, and the Manaship was guided into a set of blocks along the stone dock. The entire area was wide open and featured at least six other ships, of varying sizes, including an absolutely massive ship. It was easily twice the size of the *Night's Wake* with masts as large as redwoods.

Voracious Eye!

Name: Hippocamp's Fury
Type: Manaship
Lore: Manaships are vehicles designed from rare materials and powered by Mana to propel them through the skies. Or, in this case, the Void. This one has been modified with extra weaponry and is larger in all dimensions than those you have seen. This Manaship is classified as a Frigate.

Interesting. Analyze is comparing things now. That's... useful.

"All right, boy. Time to disembark," Captain Shirtwaist said behind him.

Felix spun, his hands already out, before he realized she was standing at least ten feet away. He felt his face flush but refused to be embarrassed. These people had kidnapped him, after all.

"My, you're jumpy."

"I wonder why," Felix muttered.

She heard him, though, and gave him a sharp smile. "You're a funny one, eh? Here." She threw him a black cloth. It was threaded with golden stitching along the edges, small shapes embroidered in a complex sequence. Felix's Manasight flared, and he saw remnant Mana flowing through them, like a thick grease.

Voracious Eye!

Name: Deadman's Blindfold
Type: Cloth (Enchanted)
Lore: Stitched with sigaldry to dampen the senses and dizzy the Mind. Effect only active when worn.

What an excellent item name, murmured the Maw. She floated around him in a small circle. *Doesn't seem ominous at all!*

"We don't got any elision collars, so this'll have to do. Put it on. If you don't, well..." She smiled wider than before. The two Orcs beside her fondled the swords at their sides. Felix knew they were only ten or so levels higher than him, but their position at the upper end of Apprentice Tier had him nervous. Plus, their Strengths and Weaknesses were still a mystery. Only the "Ram" had given him more information, likely because they had actually fought.

Felix put the blindfold on, which was large enough that it covered his entire face. It smelled like an armpit.

"Good boy," Shirtwaist whispered in his ear, and Felix jumped. He hadn't heard her move at all. In fact, he found he couldn't hear much at all, not to mention see, and the armpit smell was invading his sinuses as if it meant to take up residence. He could, however, sense the Mana that began to circulate around the cloth. It tasted like the color puce and glooped through the sigils like mud. "Put one on the mutt, too."

It took some coaxing, but Pit let them blindfold him as well. Simmering with anger, Felix silently coaxed the tenku down from attacking the pirates outright. *We might defeat some now, but not all of them. Not here.*

They were led down the gangplank, one of the burly Orcs having grabbed the back of his tattered collar and led him downward, across a deceptively wide expanse of relatively flat ground, then up a series of stairs. The path wound left and right, up and down; Felix was certain they were intentionally misleading him, in spite of the blindfolds.

**Blind Fighting is level 22!
PER +1!**

The joke was on them, however, as his passive Blind Fighting Skill helped boost his Perception enough to make things out. Added to that was his perfect recall, thanks to his Born Trait, and Felix could repeat the same pathway as many times as they asked. He had even gained a point of Perception, which would have been amusing were Felix not scared for his life.

Eventually, they came to a halt in a room that felt large, but not excessively. Without warning, the blindfold was ripped off Felix's face, and he was greeted by a blazing fire and several figures. Blinded by the fire's relative intensity, it took him a heartbeat or two to focus enough and see a trio of men sitting at a wide table spread with maps. The two on the sides were Half-Orcs, each glowering and betusked, while the central figure was quite a bit shorter.

"Captain, I'd like to introduce ya to our new find," Shirtwaist said, gesturing to Felix. "The one I sent word about. He's freshly arrived to the Void, he says."

"Oh, really?" asked a voice, and the shorter figure stepped closer. It was a small gray-skinned man, shorter than Felix by a head, wearing a tricorn hat and long, dark coat that swirled behind him. It was made of a thick, rough leather dyed a dark, dark purple and beneath it, he wore a white shirt with a puffy collar. Suddenly smiling, the man tipped his hat back with a finger and huffed a breath. His teeth were sharp, like a shark.

Voracious Eye!

Name: Captain Ruan Nokk
Race: Nixie
Level: (Hidden)
HP: (Hidden)
SP: (Hidden)
MP: (Hidden)
Lore: Nixies have a deep connection to the waters of the Continent. Though related closely to the Naiads, they are distinct Races. Most notably is their gray-green skin and gills that allow them to breathe both water and air.
Strength: More Data Required
Weakness: More Data Required

Voracious Eye is level 28!

"So you're the one that fought my whole crew. You're a tough sonuvabitch, ain't ya? Not many folk get slammed by the Ram and get back to their feet!" Captain Nokk laughed, showing off two rows of those sharp fangs.

Felix smiled as well, showing his own teeth. Something inside of him bristled at the man, and it wasn't his gray skin or strange, colorless eyes. "I'm full of surprises, Mister...?"

"Captain, actually. Which you know, seeing how you already Analyzed me." Nokk smirked. "Captain Nokk, infamous leader of the Ten Hands, the rough company you've had the pleasure of meetin' and the bloodiest killers in all the Bitter Sea."

The others in the room shifted slightly, and Felix felt the vaguest sense of threat from all of them. Like he was smelling violence.

Captain Nokk grinned again, shrugging a single shoulder. "Back when we sailed it, that is. Now it's the Void for us."

"Sounds like quite the story, Captain," Felix said cautiously, Perception spreading out farther and farther, watching for any sudden movements. "I'd love to hear it."

Nokk laughed, a hissing thing that slithered across the dark air. "And I'd love to tell it, me boy! Come! You and your friend look ravenous. We've lived another day in this benighted pit!" He turned to his crew and threw out his arms. "So what happens next?"

The men and women around him smiled with rotten teeth. Those that came in with Shirtwaist cheered. "We drink!"

Everyone began filing out of the chamber, through a wide doorway and down a set of uneven stairs. The two Half-Orcs—J'thok and P'then according to his Skill—stared at Felix a while longer, baring their teeth at him and caressing their sheathed blades before following the rest down the stairs. Captain Nokk turned back to Felix and extended a hand. "I promise my men will not attack again. Will you join us, Mister...?"

"Felix. Felix Nevarre." Felix realized he *was* hungry. It had been... several days since he last ate? Was that right? Pit trilled across their bond, agreeing. "We'd be happy to join you."

Felix was led down, into the darkness.

CHAPTER NINE

The pirates of the Ten Hands knew how to throw a party. After a cramped and rickety stairway down, the entire fortress below seemed to be one huge chamber. It was at least three thousand square feet, filled to the brim with tables and bars, but still had several open spaces where various forms of betting occurred simultaneously.

Shimmering multicolored lights hovered at ceiling level, sometimes zipping across the room at the gesture of someone wearing a fancy hat, reorienting around some new game or diversion, be it a dice game or knife fighting. A band had struck up a lively tune, a sea shanty that was all sorts of dirty. The overall ambiance was ribald decadence and violent debauchery.

Felix was on edge, and Pit was not much better. The tenku pressed tight against his legs, unwilling to be parted from Felix... until he caught the tantalizing scent of food.

Captain Nokk seemed right at home, of course. A king in his castle, the master of all he surveyed. As Felix and Pit followed the shark-toothed man, folk of all stripes bowed and stepped out of his way quickly. Felix's sharpened eyes recognized the looks on their faces: fear and hunger.

From the whale to the shark. Why can't we have a nice, quiet life, Pit?

The tenku ignored him though, more intent on stalking a table full of steaming meat that had been slathered with a sweet-smelling sauce. Felix didn't know what it was, but the combination of Pit's hunger and his own made his mouth water. A hissing laugh came from behind him, and Nokk had turned back toward him and beckoned.

"Come, lad! I have food aplenty at my table." Felix cast a glance back at Pit, who had jumped atop a table and started eating, to the annoyance of a Gnome and Goblin. He followed the captain, sending a quick word back to his Companion.

Be careful.

Nokk led them up a set of stairs and onto a wide open dais at the far end of the hall. A large, rectangular table sat here, made of some sort of dark material polished so brightly it gleamed, and was surmounted by an elaborate throne made of the same stuff, except built far more angular. The back of the throne extended high up, at least twice the captain's height and ending in a series of spiked protrusions that looked like a rising sun… or a crown. Nokk settled into the throne, then gestured to the set to his right.

"Take a rest, friend Felix. Food is on its way." He smiled his sharp teeth and handed him a large mug that looked fashioned from a horn. "Drink! I have a story to tell you."

The captain knocked back his own drink, and Felix eyed the liquid before him.

Name: Twice-Boiled Swill
Type: Poison
Lore: Alcohol made from the twice-boiled gastric juices of a Harrowing. Very strong.
Effect: Chance of alcohol poisoning increased by 95% for all those below Apprentice Body Formation. 65% chance for those below Journeyman.

Nokk was eyeballing him, having finished his own drink,

and though suspicious, Felix quaffed his. He didn't want to stand out, not yet. Besides, he had Poison Resistance, right?

You Have Poisoned Yourself!
-50% Dexterity and Agility for 1 Hour
-60% Intelligence and Willpower for 1 Hour

Poison Resistance is level 29!
Poison Resistance is level 30!
...
Poison Resistance is level 35!

Felix's eyes widened a moment when he saw the instant effect.

You fool, hissed the Maw. *Never drink what an enemy offers you! This Nixie is dangerous.*

Shut up, Felix thought at her. It was harder to do than ever before, though. *I know what I'm doing.* His Resistance began to rise, he let his eyes drift closed, looking at Nokk with a faked, half-lidded gaze.

Stop, Felix Nevarre. You threaten us all, even your precious mutt!

SHUT UP!

Felix flared his Bastion of Will, one of his Epic Skills, imaging the dark stone walls that guarded his innermost thoughts and slamming them down. To his surprise, the Maw flickered and vanished, like a cell phone with a bad connection, though it returned within seconds. The Primordial was visibly alarmed, staring at Felix with something he didn't recognize at first. But then he understood.

It was fear.

You Have Poisoned Yourself!
-40% Dexterity and Agility for 45 Minutes
-50% Intelligence and Willpower for 45 Minutes

The Maw fled, flitting into the crowd like the ghost it was.

Felix put it out of his mind entirely and focused on his situation. His Resistance had already cut the penalty and timer down on the drink, so in Felix's mind there was only one thing to do: Resistance training.

"Oh this is delicious," he drawled. "Can I have some more?"

"More?" laughed Nokk. "As much as you like! Barkeep! Another for our honored guest!"

His horn was refilled by an attentive Korvaa, their dark feathers reminding him of a raven or crow. *Like Pit!* Felix crushed that stray thought before it burst from his mouth. The Intelligence penalty was doing strange things to him. Plastering a not-entirely-faked grin on his face, Felix tossed that one back too.

Poison Resistance is level 36!
Poison Resistance is level 37!
Poison Resistance is level 38!

You Have Poisoned Yourself!
-37% Dexterity and Agility for 40 Minutes
-46% Intelligence and Willpower for 40 Minutes

Captain Nokk had started talking at some point, and Felix had to struggle to follow for a moment. Once his Resistance hit level 38, the fog lifted slightly more.

"—yes, privateers we were. Sailing high on the riches of the Bitter Sea! I still miss that acrid spume, the smell of vinegar on the fresh mornin' breeze." Nokk sighed wistfully, then clacked his teeth together. "But it were not to be. Swallowed up we were, ship an all me crew. A leviathan as big as a city, and in its belly we floundered into the Void. The how, I can't be tellin', as I don't understand it much myself. Old Mungle had a theory once, though the damn fool has forgotten much else besides."

Poison Resistance is level 39!

A pain started up in his core, faint but noticeable. Felix blinked actual haze from his eyes as the swill began affecting him more and more. He gathered his thoughts. "How long have you been here, then?"

Nokk leaned back and looked out at his people, many of which had started singing along to the newest song, one about a long lost love. "Two hundred and thirty seven years, three months, and twelve days. Entirely too long, stuck in this endless nothin'. You? Veris says you only just arrived, but time be a bit fluid in the black."

"My condolences, Captain. I've just found myself here two or three days ago, actually."

This time Nokk looked sympathetic, quirking his sharp mouth. "Ach, so recent. A pity. You must have been near the Bitter Sea as well, yes?" Felix nodded. "Live here long enough, and you see patterns, lad. Folk appear in the Void round about where they got swallowed up, or fell; it's different for most. This section is roughly the same as the Bitter Sea back home, give or take a dozen miles. I've seen travelers pop into the Void many a time, but rarely out here. It's why I picked this place. Nice and private, away from… distraction."

Distraction from what? Other pirates? Authorities? Were there cops in the Void? He took another small sip of swill. "You being out here saved me, Captain. So I have to thank you… but, what was that white barrier I saw earlier? Your men used it to ward off a flock of Harrowings."

Nokk looked inordinately pleased, as if someone had just complimented him. He smiled smugly and waved a hand. "Oh that? Desolation magic. Powerful stuff, indeed. Thirty six years ago, we found a sigil stone grown into this island that can make a smallish dome of it for a little while. Our trump card against the big nasties out here, and one o' the reasons we're still alive. It's also good for fishin', so anytime we get a ship coming back, we make sure to vent our Mana and lure in a good haul."

A plate of steaming… something was placed in front of both of them. It was gray and puckered, marinated in some sort of oil and garnished with long, hooked… talons. Felix looked up to see Nokk happily slurping down pieces of the meat before him.

"Only real pity is that we can't move the damn thing. Ah, to have such a dome around our ships!"

"Desolation? What's that?" Felix asked. He identified the meat as from the Harrowings, and that it was safe enough to eat. He muscled past his distaste and dug in.

"Ach, of course. So new and shiny." The captain held out his hands, both dripping grease. In his right hand flared a smoky ball of darkness. "There is the Void, endless span of rocks and not much else, flotsam and jetsam mostly. Castoffs. Then," here he summoned a bright ball of white light in his left hand. "Then ya got the Desolation itself. A sorta flipside to the Void. A light to the dark. Except anything that falls into the Desolation ain't just castoff, it's gone. Forever. Like these Harrowings that was chasin' ya. We had to catch these. The ones that hit the shield? Barrier ate 'em up. Desolation rips apart anything ya throw at it."

Felix eyed the light show. Illusion magic, his Manasight told him. How much of what he was seeing was real here? Felix pushed that thought aside. "So, it's an energy?"

Nokk half shrugged, the lights in his hands going out. He returned to shoveling more pieces of grub into his mouth. "More like a place, but ya can find holes to Desolation all over the Void. Sometimes they even move." He took a drink from a small horn, something bright orange and bubbling. "There's even one nearby. Suckin' in all the rocks and debris around it; it'll collapse soon enough and reappear elsewhere."

The sharp-toothed man shifted in his throne and threw a leg over the armrest. "Now onto the important stuff! Who are you, and what, by all the broken gods, is a Nym?"

CHAPTER TEN

Pit was full.

So full.

The big folk had brought so much meat and he had eaten it all. Pit had not had such abundance in what felt like many many days.

'Weeks.' The word is 'weeks.'

Thoughts had been coming easier to Pit ever since Felix had saved him under the mountain. It was like a whole new world opened up, one where Pit could explore and fight and eat side-by-side with his Companion. It was a good feeling.

But then the giants. And the Maw. Pit's hackles rose unconsciously, and the greasy-looking Gnome nearby scooted a few inches away from the table.

And now the Void, this terrible dark place where there wasn't much more than rocks and dust to smell, and not a single tree to scratch against! And still, he could not fly. His wings were all but useless. His mother could fly, and some of Pit's earliest memories were of sitting in her forelimbs as she would glide above the fog-shrouded trees.

Pit whimpered slightly, partly because of his pained tummy,

and partly because those memories made him feel... sad. Yes. Sad was the word, like when Felix would sit against a rock or tree and sigh into the night.

Sad. His stomach grumbled again, rebelling against all of that delicious food. He was lying upon one of the stout tables, panting. *Sad and painful. Felix feels that one a lot, too.*

A brief flare of woozy panic came across their pact, though it mellowed out into a wary resignation and... determination. Felix was fighting again, though not with his strong fists like usual. With... words?

How strange. Pit tilted his head, the triangular tufts of his ears twitching. He remembered Felix's parting words, before he followed Bad Teeth. *Be careful,* he had said. *This place is dangerous, like the bad mountain. But different. Odd smells. What are they?*

Pit turned an eye to the stinky Gnome and Goblin that were watching over him, much as they tried to hide the fact. He waited until they distracted each other with another fight.

"No! Dice roll six! Six win!"

"Yer a shifty little cheat, Garlak! I saw you touch that die!"

"I no touch! Gnome is stupid! Eat my butt!"

"*Raaagh!*"

Pit rolled off the table as a fight broke out. He landed lightly on his feet, wings tucked close to his body and ducked beneath. The two small folk were busy with one another, if the grunts and screams were any indication. He shook his head and Skulked away.

Follow the odd smells. He thought, then brightened. *Maybe it's more food!*

Felix froze with a piece of charred meat halfway to his mouth. Mouth suddenly dry, he gave a hesitant shrug.

"Mostly just Human, really. I don't really like to talk about it, but we're an offshoot. Some encounters with Elves a few generations ago, and bam, here I am." Felix forced a laugh, trying to keep his cool. "Aside from some talent with Mana Skills, we're no better than the standard Human."

For some reason, Felix's vision flashed red, sparks of blue and gold flaring at the edges. He forced himself to ignore it. He'd seen sparks like this before, back in the Foglands...

"Fascinating." Nokk drew out the word, staring at Felix like he was an animal at a zoo... or a pet. "An offshoot of Humans, hah! Those bastards'll bed anything that moves, right enough! Then again, who am I ta judge!" He laughed and Felix joined him.

The sparks intensified, fireworks exploding just out of sight. Pressure built in his head and chest, like something was trying to push through.

Felix took a swig of Swill again.

You Have Poisoned Yourself!
-35% Dexterity and Agility for 37 Minutes
-44% Intelligence and Willpower for 37 Minutes

Poison Resistance is level 40!

Gasping for breath as the rotgut burned down his throat, Felix felt excruciating pain as something burst inside of him. The world lit up in a blue-gold radiance, covered in a sheen of crimson. A surge of music blared in his mind before fading away quickly... the sound unraveling as if it weren't allowed there.

New Skill!
Deception (Uncommon), Level 1!
Once you knew the Acting Skill, but it was sundered. Now you've distilled the essence of it and emerged from the other side with Deception, the art of managing perceptions. Chance of misleading someone increases moderately by Skill level.

Captain Nokk didn't notice a thing, and had in fact turned to speak to a passing server.

"...and more Swill for our guest! Of course! He's a thirsty lad!" Nokk turned back to Felix, who was blinking the stars out of his eyes. "Talented with Mana Skills, though? Must be from the Elf side. Not a path many of your kind take. Too few stats, generally speaking. You must have quite the Omen, hmm?"

"Um, yes. It's quite helpful." Felix said through the pain, though it was nothing new. Pain was an old friend at this point.

"I can imagine. Veris tells me that lightning storm you summoned was impressive. The power needed to throw so many of my men with their Will and Strength engaged. Remarkable!" Nokk laughed, his sharp teeth flashing in the conjured lights above. Felix smiled along with him, but this all felt...off.

When Nokk had stopped laughing, a new round of drinks were delivered to the table. Nokk took one and handed Felix the other.

"Drink up! This be your welcome party, friend Felix!" He took a swig at that, and Felix mimed the same. His head was already feeling woozy and his hands didn't quite want to move the way he wished. The Swill was affecting him more than he realized.

Deception is level 2!

"Ahh," Nokk sighed then smacked his lips appreciably. "I miss the vintages of home, but the local stuff hits the spot. Don't ya think?"

Felix grunted, not trusting himself to answer. The pain in his chest had dimmed to a dull roar.

"Not many Humans wind up in the Void, or Human-adjacent in your case. At least, none that live for long." Nokk said after a moment.

Felix looked up, eyebrow quirking. "Why? There's plenty of

Humans on the Continent." As far as Felix understood, they were one of the most populous Races.

"Too weak. Won't survive a few hours in the Void, let alone the time it'd take to make it to one of the safe havens. But you," he snapped his fingers and pointed at Felix. "You've got that lightning. Big and bad and you can cast it, what? Two times a day? Three?"

"Something like that," Felix replied cautiously. He wasn't sure what the Nixie was getting at, but it put his back up.

Nokk clapped his hands. "Haha! Yes! You're a strong one. Which makes sense why we found those Harrowings so close to you. You practically smell like magic, lad." He held out his gray hands in placation. "Take no offense! My kind's got magic in our very bones, as do most of my crew. Makes us all tempting meals for the Voidborn."

He leaned out toward the crowd below, and shouted. "That's why I say: not if we eat 'em first!"

A ragged cheer went up all around them.

"Do you know what the Void is?" Felix asked.

"Nah. Don't care neither. Fer me and my crew, it was a second chance at life. We all thought we was dead, staring down that leviathan's teeth." Nokk shrugged, his clear eyes shining in the low light. "Now we sail on, raidin' and pillagin' and takin' whatever we want!"

Another cheer, this one much more deafening.

"Ahh, but Old Mungle calls the Void a 'place between minds,' whatever that means. Man's gone a bit daft in his dotage. All I need to know is where to find the treasure, the women, and to keep two steps ahead of my enemies. What more could ya want?"

Felix didn't have an answer for that. Not one that would satisfy the strange man.

Pit ended up somewhere brighter than the big room, but just as hot and loud. The sound of sizzling and popping filled the air, followed by the most delectable scents he'd ever smelled. This was where the food lived, he realized.

The sound of clacking drew him forward, past dark tables and toward the legs of another big folk, though she was different from anyone Pit had ever seen. She had pale ochre skin and dark green hair that was bound into a loose coil behind her neck, and wore a once-white apron that was smudged with all sorts of vile fluids. She was busy, moving across the room with purpose and several huge knives. Those blades flashed, chopping mottled tentacles into tiny pieces, and ripping strange Void bugs and frying their Mana-rich innards. Pit could smell the power in the air, a vapor that drove him wild despite his full belly.

Four other folks were in the kitchen—*yes, right, that's the word*—and Pit hid under one of the many tables as their booted feet scrambled around the room. The woman in the apron was shouting at them, and everyone was stumbling and trying to follow her orders. She seemed quite annoyed, and Pit was happy to avoid her, as tempting as those wonderful smells were...

"And who is this? A stowaway?"

Pit's golden eyes widened as he saw the woman had bent down and was regarding him. She smiled, kindly Pit thought, despite her jagged teeth. One of the small folk cooking with her, one with pimply green skin and claws squealed.

"Dahlia, that's the mutt! The one what come with the fresh meat--huak!"

Pit tilted his head, ears pricking as the green-haired woman shoved a hot metal pan into the gut of the Goblin. The small pointy eared creature took the red hot pan and whimpered. Pit turned back to the woman, who was saying something to the others. Pit raised his beak inquisitively.

This is interesting. I smell... bones.

It was a familiar scent, one of many that had been plaguing

him since they had arrived. It wasn't exactly the odd smell he'd caught earlier, but it was similar. Pit wandered closer, snuffling at the woman's dark, angular leg. It appeared to be made of the same material as the floor and tables, attached to her at mid-thigh with various leather straps. There was a deep scent of blood to it. It made him hungry. Hungrier, at least.

"Oh ye like my leg?" The woman smiled again. "Made it from a critter no bigger'n you, though it wasn't so skinny. Here." She tossed a gooey globule of mottled grey flesh onto the ground, where it immediately began leaking a rainbow-hued vapor. "A Mana-bladder from a Tenebril. Go ahead. It honors me to have a tenku in my kitchen."

Pit didn't waste time. He gobbled it up. A flaring explosion went off in his head, as if his Companion's lightning sizzled across his mind.

+1 PER
+1 INT

"It's a good rush, innit? Chimera's need plenty of Mana to grow up big and strong." She threw down another Mana-bladder, rainbow light escaping in wisps. "Eat up."

Felix felt a jolt of energy through the pact bond, a rush of energy not unlike a System stat bump. Small, far-off flutes trilled in his mind. Pit had just done something.

But what?

Nokk was still talking. They'd been chatting at length about, yikes, everything it felt like. The Captain had quite a lot to say on just about any subject, and Felix had taken his complacency as a great opportunity to gather information on him and everyone within eyesight.

The Captain was a Nixie, and his stats were hidden behind a similar sort of veil he'd encountered before, though stronger.

Felix figured he could break through it eventually, but was positive the pirate would notice. So instead, he focused on his crew as the garrulous captain continued.

The crew all around them were a wide variety of Races, even more so down below. There were perhaps two hundred folk moving in and out of the massive chamber, and a great deal of them had only just reached their Apprentice Formation. Like on the ship, his Voracious Eye could spot their advancement like a vague brand hovering around them. A goodly number were on the higher end of Apprentice Tier, like the entire crew that had brought him there, and a few stood out even among them.

That Captain Shirtwaist was managing the bartenders around the area—sometimes cracking the literal whip she carried for emphasis. Celat, an aloof Elven person Nokk had mentioned earlier, prowled the edges of the party, not partaking in anything and always moving. Their easy grace made Felix feel ungainly, but it was the series of long knives the Elf carried that made him truly wary. At the opposite end of the room was a raised stage, upon which a band bellowed out various shanties and ballads to the roaring approval of the crowd.

The lead singer was Bridgven Parsdattir, a Half-Orc with white hair, dark green skin, and bright, attentive eyes, ones that moved around the room almost as fast as her fingers on her mandolin. Nearby, against the opposite wall as the Half-Orc was Korm Rocksplitter, a huge Ogre wearing a mishmash of half-plate and leather armor. He slowly polished and sharpened an increasing variety of martial weaponry.

He filed away every detail he could, carefully putting together an escape plan for when the time came. The debuff from the alcohol was close to wearing off, and he'd been miming any further drinks at this point. He wanted a clear head and all of his stats in order. The Nym wasn't sure whether he'd have to fight his way out of here yet, but he'd rather plan for the worst and survive. The Risi had taught him how quickly plans could go awry.

Classic adventuring party if I've even seen one, though, he thought. These four, plus any hidden members were the backbone of the crew. They were all at their Journeyman Formation, perhaps beyond it. Voracious Eye only gave him a feeling on this count, but it was strong. The Captain himself had completed his Journeyman Formation, he was sure, though the Nixie was far better at concealing it than the others.

What have I gotten myself into? The thought was loud, but he kept it off his face with some effort. No need to tip his hand yet.

The drinks kept flowing, and Felix tried to keep Nokk talking as long as possible. Occasionally, he'd feel a thrill of System power, as if Pit were eating elemental cores again. He glanced around the room, unable to find the tenku.

"Lookin' fer yer friend?" At Felix's nod, Nokk belched and smiled. "I'm sure he's fine. I had a Companion once, ya know? A hippocamp I'd saved from a fisherman's net. A great beastie, one I sorely miss. Lost her when the leviathan attacked." He sighed, a touch bitterly. He seemed more than a little drunk. "I miss the sea."

"Thirty seven years is a long time," Felix agreed.

"Aye, and that's thirty seven years in here. Blind gods suspect how long it's been back on the Continent." Nokk spat something thick onto the ground. "Either way, been long enough for most of the boys to get comfortable, settle in. We're losing our edge. Goin' soft, I fear."

"You all seem pretty tough," Felix said.

"Not tough enough to hurt you too badly!" Nokk laughed, and Felix faked a smile.

Deception is level 4!

"Ah but there's plenty to see here in the black. When we aren't holed up here, we ply the skies with our ships, searching for treasure and plunderin' what grabs our fancy."

Treasure sounded nice, but Felix didn't like the sound of the last bit. The captain had gone off on the subject a couple times, but hadn't hit on the part in which Felix was most interested.

"So there's other folks out here?" Felix tried to keep the question casual and off-hand, hoping his Deception was enough.

"Oh aye, plenty of islands like ours, some even bigger. Spread out, o'course, like everything in the Void. Takes weeks to reach most places, even at full speed." Nokk burped.

"Ships? You've mentioned them a few times. How do you have ships in the Void?"

"By bein' awful clever, that's how." Nokk spread his hands and grinned. "You see this place? The walls, the floors, the table in front o'you? Ya think it's wood? Have ya seen a tree, Felix?"

Felix ran his hand over the table before activating Voracious Eye.

Name: Narhollow Bone Table
Type: Furniture
Lore: Known for its strength and Mana-conductivity, Voidborn bone is often used by locals for many items of convenience.

"It's bone?" Felix exclaimed. The table was an odd color, sure, but it's dark surface was heavily grained and seemed more like stone. He knocked on it, and it sounded hollow.

"Aye, bone. We make everythin' out of it. The ships are made of it, and given the Mana to fuel it, we can sail straight across the Void."

"Must take quite a bit of Mana to get a ship of this moving." Felix ran his hands over the table again, marveling at its smoothness. It felt polished.

"Ye can't imagine how much," Nokk muttered.

Pit was full again. Fit to burst, he thought.

He had gained another 6 points in STR and 4 points in VIT from the feast. The Mana-sacs were only the start, though they were the most delicious and beneficial. The rest were choice cuts of a marbled white meat, covered in sweet juices that Pit hadn't the words for yet. Dahlia said something about "honoring the chimera," and "harmony," but Pit hadn't really paid attention.

Eventually they stopped feeding him and left him alone. The woman was busy rushing more food out the doors as music swelled in the main chamber. Alone again, Pit huffed a contented sigh.

Then the smell came back.

Boots clomped through the kitchen, big ones covered in some sort of muck. They were on the feet of one of the big folks, something he'd heard Felix call a Half-Orc with dark green skin and small tusks in her mouth. She passed through the area without a single glance at him, tracking that dark gunk all through the kitchen and out into the main chamber.

It smelled odd. Like the smell Pit had chased into the kitchen originally.

Heaving his meat-stuffed bulk off the floor, Pit waddled down the hall, tracing back the footsteps of the Half-Orc. He followed the path back along several darkened hallways and down a rickety flight of stairs. Pit had to extend his wings to balance on the poorly made steps, but he made it down with only a little sound. Below it was darker, the magical lights few and far between.

The smell was stronger.

Skulk is level 26!

The area opened up quickly as Pit slunk through the shadows, his golden eyes wide to catch any stray movements. The roof above disappeared, replaced instead by a huge cavern that was probably three times as high as the previous ceiling. It was where they had first arrived. The stinky cloth he had to wear had muddled the scent, but he recognized it now. Great stone blocks were all over, and it looked like massive black wedges were nestled on top of them.

Ships. Manaships. Pit recalled the word from Felix. In fact, a large board dropped from the side of one of the ships—the one they arrived on—and a couple of figures started struggling down it. Though it was dark, Pit had excellent sight, and he easily identified three big folk: two Orcs and a thin Elf.

They carried something wrapped up in a thick cloth.

Pit sniffed. The smell was strongest with these people. It clung to them. Hiding behind a stack of barrels, Pit watched as the big folk spoke.

"Another one down, eh?" an Orc said.

"Can't keep em long enough! These weaklings ain't enough to power a skiff, let alone the Captain's flagship." Cruel laughter followed the second Orc's words. The Elf's sharp voice cut through it, however.

"Ya know the rules. Swap it out. Get a spare from down below."

The Orcs headed into a darkened doorway with the shrouded thing, and as they moved a hand fell free of the cloth, one covered in scars and dripping blood. The Elf, apparently in charge, marked something off on a board.

Terror welled up inside him. He'd seen plenty of dead bodies, had even made quite a few of them. This was different. The figure wasn't dead.

It was hollowed out.

CHAPTER ELEVEN

The night wore on.

Felix wasn't sure if it was even nighttime, but even his high Endurance was reaching its end. The party kept going, drinks served, shouts sounding, and music blaring. The various tables for dice and other gambling expanded as more pirates sought out its pleasures, while other members disappeared into back rooms. Presumably for other delights.

He continued miming his sips at his drink; however, the captain's eyes weren't easy to fool. He'd had to take a few real gulps to sell it. His Poison Resistance had even leveled up to 42, which was remarkable. He checked the Status Condition.

Status Condition: Poisoned
-25% Dexterity and Agility for 10 Minutes
-35% Intelligence and Willpower for 10 Minutes

As female servers squealed nearby and grizzled crew (male and female) guffawed at a lucky dice throw or play, Felix found the atmosphere of the Ten Hand's Fist was very… comfortable. It was a sentiment that popped into his head several times that night during his winding conversations with the captain, the mischievous Nixie continually plying him with drinks.

The clock was winding down on his poisoned condition, but Felix was certainly feeling the effects of the Swill. His eyesight was blurry, and the urge to wallow in the casual hedonism of Captain Nokk's generosity was strong. Luckily, Willpower was Felix's highest stat, and he shook off the sensation whenever he felt it creep upon him.

Felix shook himself, focusing on burning away the last vestiges of the poison from his system. Its effects swirled in his channels, not his blood or guts, but as a vapor similar to his Mana. Felix still recalled the sensation of burning away poison that had earned him his first Tempered Skill, though before he had done it blindly. Now he could see the looping veins and the pulses of blue-white light that surged through them. As his core pulsed and the blue-white vapor shifted, Felix gripped at the green and dragged it along. Each throb sent more of the poison into the crackling flame of his core, where it burnt away.

It was a slow task made all the harder due to his core being absolutely *stuffed*. The remnants of the Harrowing were still in there, slowly being broken down by his Ravenous Tithe. Felix wondered how much longer it might be. It had been days since that fight.

"Yes! Come here!" Nokk was calling out to someone in the crowd, pulling them up onto the dais with Felix. The Nym looked up from his drink and saw three scantily clad figures fawning over the captain. "Felix, my boy, yer too stressed! Time to relax! Take one of my luscious foundlings and retire for the night. You won't regret it, believe you me!"

Felix blinked and regarded the three who leaned against Nokk. They were all Elves, two women and one man, and all dressed equally provocatively. However, Felix's sharp eyes caught the presence of concealed weapons in their hair, hips, and even the sheer-seeming bodices on the women. Felix had no interest in bringing anyone into his bed who could stab him in the back.

"That is very... generous, Captain Nokk. But I'll have to decline." Felix gestured helplessly. "It's getting late, and it's been a long and stressful day. So I will take you up on that offer of a room to rest, if you don't mind."

Nokk frowned, his fangs disappearing in a wrinkled grimace. "Very well. Rooms're up one floor. You get yer rest, and we can talk in the mornin'. I'd like to see you bright and early. I have a request for you that is quite urgent." He smiled, shark teeth gleaming in the magelights. "Life or death, you might say."

Felix made his exit, slipping from the table and down into the crowd with a final farewell. His last sight of the captain was of his wandering hands gripping all three Elves possessively. Shaking his head, he dove into the shifting crowd.

A frantic looking Goblin in a stained white apron stood atop a nearby table, scanning the massive chamber. His eyes alighted on Felix, and the little guy jolted, as if surprised. Felix's Eye identified him as Snurl the Whelp.

"Hey there, Snurl," Felix waved at the Goblin and got closer. "Do you know where the private rooms are? I'm looking to bed down for the night."

Snurl gave him a strange look then pointed to his left, where a darkened alcove extended back into a hallway.

Felix smiled."Thanks! You looking for something?"

Snurl hopped again and shook his head emphatically. "No no no. Not nothing! Go 'way!"

Nonplussed, Felix held up his hands and backed away. Soon, the strange Goblin was lost in the press of bodies, and Felix found his way into the side hall. It was immediately quieter and cooler, the cloying meat-heat of bodies only a vague emanation there. The flooring was covered in a threadbare rug that extended for several dozen feet before terminating at a blank wall. A few doors stood along either side, and to his right was a set of stairs leading up and down. The darkened hallway was empty of anyone else, and Felix cast his eyes and senses out over the crowd, still looking for Pit.

"Where are you, buddy?"

Movement to his side caused Felix to flinch, his hands going up to guard his head. But all he saw was the Maw, standing inches away and regarding one of the walls.

"Where have you been?" Felix hadn't realized it until then, but the Maw had been curiously silent since landing on the wall. She (*it*, he reminded himself) hadn't spoken to him in hours.

It didn't reply, only glancing over at Felix with hate-filled eyes as it ran a hand over the smooth, dark gray walls. They were made of bone too, just as Nokk had said. The Maw suddenly scoffed at him. *Tried their noxious brew, did you? Foolish boy.*

Felix frowned and wanted to say something scathing back, but it had the right of it. He'd been too confident in his Poison Resistance—he shouldn't have drank anything these pirates put in front of him. Luckily, they hadn't done anything to the meat, disgusting as it was, but the Swill would make fighting a nightmare if it came down to it. And other than being pirates, these people seemed off; Felix was missing something that hid beneath their pleasant veneer.

As if waiting for that admission, the poison debuff deactivated. Felix's cognition rose to full instantly, and it was like a muffling shroud had been pulled from his thoughts. His mind was clear, and his body so much more responsive. Not willing to acknowledge the Maw's point, he looked at her hand, still being run along the wall.

"What're you doing?" Felix asked.

Do you know what these walls are made of, child? Felix shrugged and nodded. *Then don't ask stupid questions. There is something baked into these walls that I've not seen before. It*—She (*it, damnit!*) trailed off, blue-green eyes going distant.

"What's wrong with you? Still afraid of that shield?"

The Maw gave him an affronted look. *I fear nothing, Unbound. It is you that should fear. Something is happening here. Something I—*

The Maw cut itself off, suddenly looking down sharply. Without another word, it disappeared.

Felix grunted and shook his head. He wasn't sure that he'd ever understand the Maw, and the sooner he could get to civilization and have it removed, the better. Magic being real, there must be *someone* on the Continent who could do it.

Maybe Vessilia's dad could do it? A duke has to have a lot of pull. If I can convince her to ask… and if I can ever get out of here. Felix sighed and trudged up the stairs. It was definitely time to rest and get his shit together. In the morning they'd leave, whether Nokk liked it or not.

But *where* was Pit?

Pit panted as quietly as he could. His little bird beak hung open and tongue lolled to the side as he hid beneath another overhang. Booted feet ran by, and voices shouted over one another frantically. Pit wasn't sure, but he worried the big folk were looking for him. He slunk low to the ground and kept to the shadows the entire way from the big dock (that's what they called it), and was just outside the kitchens again.

Skulk is level 28!

The door into the kitchen opened and closed several times as big folk and small folk alike rushed in and out. They all smelled frantic, some with food on trays, others with that foul stench clinging to their bodies. From *below*. However, the route ended here, so if Pit wanted to get back to Felix he'd have to get through the kitchens again.

He waited for some time, straining his senses for any hint of another. Eventually he was able to dart into the kitchen and under a nearby countertop.

Skulk is level 29!

Good. Unseen.

Pit stepped lightly, keeping his wings tight to his body and his tail tucked. He keenly missed when he was smaller—the entire endeavor would have been far easier a few levels ago. He could see legs from the knee down move to and fro, hustling around the kitchen doing something that resulted in a bounty of delicious smells. He was full, yet it took all his Willpower to keep from trying to steal more food. Then, as he drew near the end of the first counter, someone stomped into the room.

"Dahlia!" It was the shrill voice of someone who loved to yell. "Dahlia dammit! Where's the mutt?"

"What?" There was a clatter of metal as someone threw down a pan or pot. Then the *thump-tik* of the ochre woman's steps. Pit tilted his head as she walked by. "What do you want?"

"I want that winged thing the newcomer brought with him. The Captain is looking for it." The shrill voice wore soft leather shoes that curled slightly at the tip. They stomped in impatience. "I know it was here."

"Oh aye, it were here. Some time ago. Ain't seen it since." Dahlia turned and started walking away.

"Don't—you—!" The shrill one stomped their feet again and stormed out. Dahlia simply strolled back to her stove and scooped up her implements. The sound of sizzling filled the air.

Pit cooed internally, pleased. *A nice one.*

There had been so few of those.

Sneaking again, Pit exited the kitchens and started making his long trek across the main chamber. He stuck to the shadows, keeping out of sight. He was careful.

―――

The second floor hall was longer than the first floor, and seemed to extend parallel to the main chamber. A number of mage lights were stuck to the walls, one every ten feet or so, leaving gloomy patches of shadow down the corridor.

Do I just… pick a room? There were many, one every twenty

feet or so, built sturdy and not-quite square. The first few were locked, and the next one was occupied. He could tell because of how... boisterous they sounded. He walked past that one as quickly as possible.

Further down the hall, he picked out a pile of rags that had been deposited by a doorway. They looked dirty and dingy, the kind of things you'd use to clean the floor and then throw away. Made sense that they'd launder that kind of stuff; not a lot of fresh cloth in the Void, he imagined. Felix walked right on by, intent on finding an unlocked room. So it was downright terrifying when the rag mound grabbed him by the wrist.

"*Ghost!*"

Felix twisted his arm, grabbed the rags, and threw the entire pile across the hallway. They fluttered wildly through the air, thumping against the far wall and sliding down to their feet.

Feet?

The pile of rags had booted feet, though they were boots in name only. Far more beaten up than his own, these were cracked and split, barely held together with spit and wishes. More importantly, they were surmounted by a cloak of tattered rags, soiled and torn and faded until they resembled no one particular color. A mélange of dirty beige. A ratty beard cascaded from an equally shabby hood, made up of the same rags as the rest of the cloak, and watery gray eyes popped at him from above a huge hooked nose.

It was...a Human.

Voracious Eye...

Name: Daedalus Mungle IV, Sage of Vellus (former)
Race: Human
Level: 64
HP: 254/254 (3446)
SP: 94/132 (2243)
MP: 189/189 (5784)
Strength: More Data Required
Weakness: More Data Required

Felix regarded the strange man before him, who even now was holding out a shaking hand, as if warding the Nym away. *What the hell is a Sage of... does that say Vellus? Like my Skill?*

"Stay back, ghost! I deny you! You have no cause to be here!"

"Mungle... Old Mungle?" Felix thought the name was familiar. The captain had regarded him as someone who had theories about the nature of the Void. "Is that your name?"

"I deny you!" The man was howling and pressing himself so hard against the wall Felix felt either the man or the wall would break. "I deny your presence, specter!"

"Hey, hey, easy. I'm not a ghost. I'm flesh and blood, see?" Felix slowly raised a hand and poked his face, squishing in his cheek. "What's a Sage?"

The man blinked owlishly, his watery eyes wide but uncomprehending. Felix took a slow step away, further down the hall. It was a shame, but he wasn't gonna get anywhere with this guy. "I'm just gonna go, then. Okay?"

Felix turned to try one of the door latches, but felt a hand land on his shoulder. He spun to find Mungle inches away from him, invading the entirety of his personal space. Pock marks riddled his grizzled and wrinkled face, and his ratty beard brushed against Felix's chin as he spoke.

"You've questions of the Void?"

His voice had deepened into something approaching a genteel accent. British-sounding, almost. Felix blinked and tried to step back, away from the door and wall. Old Mungle stepped forward at the same time, keeping them within inches of each other.

"Uh, yeah. What is it?"

"It is the place between Minds." Came the reply, the same as what Nokk had quoted at him.

"What does that mean? Whose Minds? Mine and yours?"

"No, no ghost. Not even your Mind, great as it may be, can hold the infinite Void." His laugh was soft and gentle, and his breath smelled of mint. "Think bigger. Greater. Divine."

"Divine? The Void is the space between the gods' Minds?" Felix couldn't help his skeptical tone. He'd seen some weird stuff so far, but real, actual gods were a bit much.

"The whispers between departed divinities! Echoes unfurling into eternity, null of all things intrinsic to life, save for those shadows it twisted for purposes unknown." Old Mungle's voice rang out down the hallway, so loud that the rhythmic banging of a headboard ceased for a few seconds... before resuming.

"Departed divinities—What does that mean? You mean the 'blind gods' people talk about? Like Vellus?" Felix asked. He was groping for sense in the madman's ramblings, but the moment he said the last, it was like he'd splashed water in his dirty face.

"*Lost!* Lost to blood and sea and storm!" Mungle howled into the corridor, and his voice was filled with so much grief he fell to the floor.

"Um, yes. Sorry to hear that. I guess I'll be headed to sleep. Sorry to bother you." Felix attempted to disengage from the old man, but Mungle leaped to his feet and grabbed him by the shoulders. His fingers dug *hard* into Felix's skin.

Armored Skin is level 40!

"Ask yer question! The true one, the one I see shifting about in your Mind. A question with Teeth." He pushed his face into Felix's. "*Ask!*"

Felix winced at the old man's volume and squirmed from his grip. "Whoa, okay! Do you know how to get out of the Void?"

Mungle's eyes went strangely blank, as if he stared into the middle distance yet deeply into Felix's soul. His voice returned to that deeper, more polished tone. "Seek the tumbled rock, the Temple at the Edge. Hanging at the precipice of Desolation. My once-home away from home, now lost to the between."

"A Temple? Like a Nymean Temple?" He asked. When Mungle didn't answer, he tried another tack. "Temple of what?"

"Of who, you mean. Of who, you daft, dead bastard. And

you know who. You have to!" The mad gleam was back in the man's eye, and he smiled. His teeth were blackened and cracked. "I recognized you, ghost. The holy Reign of your Spirit is damning. To me and you. She works her wiles still, though she be Lost and gone. Lost for so long."

He fell to his knees again, reaching out to grab Felix's tattered pant legs. "Please ghost, take me from this place. Take me home, beyond the Lady's gate!"

"Gate?"

But Old Mungle had broken down into mad, gurgling sobs. With some effort, he pushed himself into a corner of the hallway and moaned to himself.

"Mungle! What gate? Who's the Lady? Is that Vellus?" It was no use. The old man had checked out, leaving Felix to stare sadly at him. For all Felix's newfound power, he had no ability to heal the body or mind, and wouldn't even know where to start if he did.

A short *chirp* followed by a knee-buckling headbutt nearly sent Felix sprawling, but he pushed out a leg and turned to see Pit nuzzling against him.

"Pit! You're back! Where've you been?" Felix said in relief. "No, wait. Get in the room. We've gotta talk."

He chose a room at random and threw the latch and lock behind him. The lock was a simple bolt-style one, something that wouldn't keep out a determined person. Especially not if they were strong enough to break rocks barehanded, and that was most people in that pirate castle. The room was small, only ten-by-ten square and containing a twin-sized bed, a footlocker-style chest, and a small desk and chair. Modest accommodations, but better than he'd hoped for; Felix grabbed the chair and wedged it under the latch, just in case.

Turning back, Felix flared his Manasight to see in the dark room. While the Void seemed to offer an omnipresent ambient light, it did not affect the interior of objects somehow. The physics of it made no sense, but all it meant was that he had to work a bit harder to see. Thankfully, the ambient Mana from the bone walls and floors was more than enough to see by—Pit, meanwhile, just had great vision and could pick out most details by the faintest of lights. In this case, that meant the strip of light under the doorway from the hall.

"Ok, buddy. Time for a recap. I—" Pit held up a paw, almost as if... "You got something to share?"

Pit nodded, and his little ears perked up. Felix marveled at the level of intelligence his Companion was showing. It had been rising recently but this was—where would it go from here?

While he mused, Pit seemed to be concentrating. A vague warmth built in Felix's chest, slightly alarming until he realized it was just their bond, their Etheric Concordance. It was the only Legendary-ranked Skill he had, and it was capable of some strange things. Like Convergence, which allowed the two of them to share a body, among other effects. The heat built in Felix's chest for nearly thirty seconds, growing warm enough that he started to sweat. Without warning, Felix's mind went blank—

—and he was flooded with sensory impressions from smell, touch, taste, hearing, and sight. It lasted only a few seconds, but it burned into his indelible memory. His strong, Apprentice Tier Mind took only seconds to parse it all, replaying it back at speed.

"Holy shit," Felix gasped, then looked down at the tenku. "I'm glad you're ok, buddy. That is some messed up shit. You're sure they didn't catch sight of you?"

Pit nodded. A sense of utter certainty washed across their bond. Felix ran a hand through his hair and let out a weary breath. "Man, this is heavy. They're... draining people? For the ships? Nokk said their ships require Mana, but I never would've imagined..."

He went over their conversations, replaying them at triple speed. He easily remembered Nokk's words:

"But you," he snapped his fingers and pointed at Felix. *"You've got that*

lightning. Big and bad and you can cast it, what? Two times a day? Three?"

"Something like that," Felix replied.

"Shit. Shit. He knows my regen is higher than normal. He's gonna drain me dry and use me as a Mana battery or something." Felix sat down next to Pit, idly scratching his friend's neck. One of the tenku's wings half-extended and shook involuntarily. "So what do we do? Escape?" He was dead-tired and needed sleep, but the idea of being literally dead was far less appealing. He stood again and clapped his hands.

"Alright Pit. We gotta move, then. First, down to the kitch—the kitchen—"

You Have Finished Digesting Your Target's Mana!
You Have Gained A Memory From A Harrowing!
Would You Like To Review It Now?
Yes/Yes

The last thing he saw before he blacked out was Pit's dark pinions, rushing toward him.

———

Darkness.
All the world stretched before him, and before his family. Endless, eternal. A comforting shroud that he wore like a second skin, a flickering illusion that covered his flesh. All of their flesh.
Safe in the dark.
Something bright and Mana-rich was spotted down below, and with a near-silent cry, his family wheeled themselves in pursuit.
Dinner would be fresh tonight.

———

Felix jerked to consciousness, his eyes snapping open to the full dark of the room. His Manasight had deactivated. He couldn't see. He couldn't see!

New Skill!
Dark Mimic (Uncommon), Level 1!
Mimic your surroundings for concealment. Duration increases with Skill Level, detail increases with Skill level.

Be Aware!
Synergy Detected between Stealth (level 25), Breath Control (level 22), and Dark Mimic!
Do you wish to create a new Skill?

Be Aware!
Stealth (Apprentice Tier) Level 25 will be lost.
Breath Control Level 22 will be lost.

Continue?
Yes / No

    Relieved that he hadn't gone blind, Felix didn't even think about it; he chose yes.
    From far away, the sounds of a string quartet plucked across his senses. The volume swelled rapidly, pushing against an invisible barrier. There was a great tearing sound, and a tidal wave of chords and notes bore down on his Mind, Body, and Spirit like the end of all things. It fell, a mountain of sound, and Felix's body spasmed violently. Distantly, he was aware that his arm broke the leg of the desk and his leg shattered the foot of the twin bed, but it was happening to another him, one divorced from the sonic cavalcade that thrummed across his being.
    At some point, a notification popped up, but it was a while before he read it.

New Skill!
Abyssal Skein (Rare), Level 1!
Draw the Void within yourself as you become one with your surroundings. Costs Mana. Duration lasts as long as breath is held. Duration increases with Skill Level, detail increases with Skill level. Due to combination with Stealth, each increase in level also slightly decreases all sensory cues given to opponents.

Felix blinked at the bright notification in the dark room, not quite believing his eyes.

Huh. Magic stealth? Hell yes.

CHAPTER TWELVE

Felix was still lying on the floor when the Maw appeared in the room.

"Ugh. What do *you* want?" Felix still hadn't bothered to reactivate his Manasight, but the Maw was clearly visible even in the darkened room, untouched by the shadows. The creature looked at him like he was a bug beneath its feet.

The world moves in cycles, Felix Nevarre. The sun rises, the moons turn, the seasons dance endlessly. The look of condescension shifted subtly to one of derisive amusement. *You were groomed to be devoured, used as a Vessel to fuel my emancipation. It was foiled by my own hubris and your desperate idiocy. So we are here again.*

"Yeah, we already figured that part out," he said as he stood. "Bit late on the uptake, O Great and Powerful Maw."

The Maw sneered and pointed at the door. *They're coming, you fool!*

Then she was gone.

"What? Who?" Then Felix heard the faint creaks outside his door, and he put it together. The pirates.

Glancing about, Felix summoned a Shadow Whip to either of his hands. Whipping them into the support beams above, he hauled himself up off the ground with a flare of his Strength and Agility. It was only ten feet up, but it was only his excessive Dexterity that let him flip and orient himself up between the shallow beams. He tucked himself into a corner and sent thoughts along his bond to Pit. *Get up here!*

Pit leaped upward, wings outspread. He only managed to scrabble a bit before falling again.

The latch jiggled.

Shadow Whip!

Shadow Whip is level 27!

One of his tendrils dissipated, and Felix hurled another around Pit's middle. The shadowy Mana secured itself and he hauled back, lifting the tenku with a muffled squawk. The door creaked. Felix sucked in a breath and activated his new Skill.

Abyssal Skein!

Felix's view of the world altered, the colors inverting disconcertingly as the symbol in his core began to shimmer in his mind's eye. He couldn't do anything to hide Pit, but hopefully he could end this before the tenku was discovered. He could hear two people shifting their weight just outside his door. They were whispering.

"This ain't gonna work! You heard the Ram same as me! He's a mage or somefin', fer sure!"

"Shut up! It *will* work. An' sides, we ain't got no choice. The Swill'll have knocked him out by now. He's easy pickins."

The latch jiggled again, and this time, the door started to open. Then it caught on the chair Felix had braced against it. A slender hand slipped through the narrow opening and touched the back of the chair, and the thing simply disintegrated. The door swung open.

Felix widened his eyes, refusing to squint against the relatively brighter light outside in the hallway. There were two figures, backlit by the dim magelights, the one in the lead barely cresting three feet in height and the other towering closer to six and a half. Felix's eyes adjusted quickly, and as the two of them crept into the room, he could make out their features and identify them.

They were a male Gnome named Orfin and a male Hobgoblin named Pasquale, both of them level 29 and neither with a single complete Apprentice Tier Formation. They were dressed in patchwork leather armor, and each had a dark green sash across their waist alongside simple cutlasses. But neither of them had those blades in hand. If they weren't here to attack him, then why—?

"I can't see nuffin, Orf. Is he on tha bed?"

The Gnome gestured at the Hobgoblin. "I'll get 'im. Stay back, idiot. Ya don't want this on ya."

As the Hobgoblin backed up, Orfin the Gnome started reaching for a sack tied to his hip. Felix didn't let him get whatever it was. He kicked hard off the ceiling.

Corrosive Strike!

Corrosive Strike!

Two simultaneous chops struck the Hobgoblin and Gnome. It was over, instantly; the flat of his hand shattered their vertebrae and severed them completely, shoulders to hips. Blood arced across the room, splattering against the floor and walls like a gruesome Jackson Pollock painting as their bodies collapsed into a limp pile.

Felix regarded his hands, which still dripped sizzling acid, but were otherwise clean of blood. More importantly, they were colored a matte black, dark as the Void itself. Lungs beginning to burn, he released his breath and both his skin and vision returned to normal. Felix took a few gulps of fresh air.

Instant regret. Freshness was not on the menu today. The bodies and their resultant mess stank to high heaven, so bad it almost felt like an attack.

You Have Killed Orfin And Pasquale!
XP Earned!

SILENCE

Abyssal Skein is level 2!

Oh god, this is awful. The two men were all over the place, with pieces of their chests and arms fallen down beneath the bed. Felix winced and turned from the awful sight, but then movement caught his eye. Something wriggled within the spilled offal. He inched forward, hand out in preparation for a spell, and saw an open burlap sack with a glistening slime trail coming from its wide mouth. A short distance away, Felix saw a writhing, gooey creature attached to the gruesome end of the Hobgoblin.

Eugh. It was a creature that resembled a leech the size of Felix's hand, except with ten spindly legs and a face full of wriggling appendages that pulsed rhythmically on the Gnome's decapitated head. It's body was a dark, dark gray, but it was swelling as it writhed, pouches along its back filling with light.

Name: Gnarlock
Type: Voidborn
Level: 10
HP: 86/86
SP: 25/52
MP: 61/0
Lore: An ambush creature born of the Void, a gnarlock will wait patiently for long periods of time for a sentient being to come across its path, at which point it leaps onto them and injects them with a paralytic poison, feeding on their Mana until sated. Victims are usually left alive, only drained and easy prey for other creatures.
Strength: More Data Required
Weakness: More Data Required

They were gonna use this on me? Felix shuddered and discharged a kinetic blast from Reign of Vellus. The Gnarlock exploded into a bloody smear while faint wisps of rainbow light escaped its burst sacs. Felix stepped back and, with a jolt of realization, reached to close the door. Before it closed Felix realized that Old Mungle was still there, across the hall, rocking in the corner of a doorjamb. Had he seen anything? Did it matter?

"We gotta move, Pit. No time to sleep." He looked to his friend, who had fallen to the floor when Felix had attacked. Pit let out a disgusted chirp but moved to the door, nimbly avoiding the mess.

At least I have a new sneak Skill to work with... but is it better than my Apprentice Tier Stealth? Felix had no numbers to compare the two Skills, but he was sure he'd soon find out how easy it was to sneak with the new ability. However, he quickly realized he had lost his Apprentice Tier gains from Stealth. That was -3 to PER, AGL, and WIL, which wasn't crippling at this point, but he couldn't deny that it sucked.

The main effect of the Skill seemed to make him blend into his environment, like a chameleon or something, and lasted as long as he could hold his breath. Unfortunately, it seemed his Breath Control had also been reverted to level 1 when it was combined into Abyssal Skein. His chest felt tight and constricted.

So Abyssal Skein at level 2 can last, what? Half a minute? Maybe longer? Does my Endurance mitigate my ability to hold my breath? Only one way to find out—trial by fire was his only real mode of learning, at this point.

He didn't really have time to practice and theorycraft anything; the two of them had to get moving. Yet something else was troubling him, and he didn't know when else he'd be able to address it in the near future. He looked around in annoyance before sending out a mental call.

Maw! *Where are you?*

Without a sound, it reappeared, hovering over the bed. It looked down distastefully and sniffed. *So you survived. Bravo.*

Felix narrowed his eyes. "Bravo. That's an Italian word. How do you know it?" He shook his head. "Nevermind. That doesn't matter right now. I just learned a Skill from Ravenous

Tithe, but it took hours to digest the Mana. And before, at the party, I learned Deception, and it was also a literal pain to do. Why?"

The Maw rolled her blue-green eyes, vivid despite the dark. *This is the Void, you imbecile. That you can learn new Skills at all is a testament to your Unbound nature. Truly, the laws of Creation hold you but lightly.*

Felix frowned. His ability to learn new Skills had come in handy in the past, and likely would again. Knowing that he could was a relief, but the restriction of it was not. His mind drifted again to the fact that the Void was infiltrating his core even now, and he shuddered. *All the more reason to get outta here.*

Felix turned back to the bodies and checked their pockets, pointedly ignoring the look of smug superiority on the Primordial's face. Looting corpses wasn't as fun and exciting as video games made it out to be, but perhaps these pirates had something that'd help them escape. On the Gnome, aside from his cutlass, he found a few silver coins of strange mint, emblazoned with a seven-pronged crown on one side and a single eye on the other. On the Hobgoblin, he found another cutlass and a similar purse of coins, these a dark red coloration and pressed with a woman's face on both sides. There was no way for him to hold two swords, but one might come in handy at some point. He was increasingly competent with unarmed strikes, but a sword could scare people, even if he couldn't use one anymore without pain.

Strapping the Hobgoblin's belt, sheath, and purse around his waist, Felix sidled back up to his door. Carefully, he opened it a touch and peered out, pushing his senses into the space beyond. It was hard to filter out the scent of blood and worse in his room, but the hallways sounded empty and smelled only faintly of smoke and whatever it was Old Mungle had going on. He opened it fully. The hallway was empty.

Mungle must have left. Felix gestured for Pit to follow before padding down the hall. A brief spasm of pity roused in him at the thought of the addled old man, but he quashed it. The pirates wished him harm and worse than death, according to Pit. He couldn't afford to feel bad for any of them.

Nearly at the end of the hall at this point, Felix could hear the banging of drums and piping of flutes down below, echoing up the staircase. It was just loud enough to distract him from the sound of an Orc stumbling out of one of the rooms.

"Heeeey! Who're you?" The Orc squinted and slurred his words. Felix didn't reply, he simply unsheathed his new cutlass and swiped it across the Orc's face, all in one motion. The Orc coughed once, then fell to his knees as his head detached at the neck.

A terrible shooting pain blazed across Felix's arms and torso, as if red hot needles were being stabbed into his veins. His lungs seized. He tried to scream in pain, but couldn't suck in a breath to manage it. Felix fell to his knees while the body of the orc fell forward, pumping out gouts of dark blood.

You Have Killed An Unknown Orc!
XP Earned!

The Maw floated above him, its lank hair dangling in his face. *You might not want to try that again, boy.*

Perhaps thirty seconds later, Felix gasped as his breath returned to him, Pit nudging him urgently in the shoulder all the while. With the tenku's help, he regained his feet.

"That was way worse than before, with Acrobatics." He sheathed the cutlass. "No using this again until I can get that resolved."

A wise decision from the Earth child, the Maw said with a sarcastic gasp. *I've been blessed with eternal surprises.*

Ignoring it, Felix stepped around the widening pool of blood and made to walk past. Then stopped. He glanced down at the Orc, who was a bit bigger across the shoulders than Felix, but maybe...yeah.

He was sick of being shirtless.

SILENCE

Five minutes later, Felix was at the edge of the main chamber, now wearing a slightly stained faded blue tunic and a short brown canvas jacket. The jacket only went down to his hips, but it flared in the back, allowing for excellent movement. Which made sense for a pirate. He figured he cut a pretty dashing figure, though he still hadn't located a mirror. His pants were still tattered and his boots nearly worn out; the Orc's were not the right fit, having had stocky legs and oddly big feet for his height.

Now at the edge of the party, Felix peered carefully around the archway. The blocky sides of the arches and general shadowy nature of the hallways kept him from sight, but Felix couldn't rely on that forever. Especially in the main chamber, the magelights seemed to move around without pattern, and eyes were everywhere. The kitchens were just near the stage, on the far side from the dais where Captain Nokk sat. Dozens of men and women of all sorts of Races milled about, most of them drinking from bone mugs and drunkenly singing along to the band's song. It was a sad one, something about a lost love and a crab, as far as Felix could tell.

Here goes nothing.

He took a breath.

Abyssal Skein!

Felix's vision inverted and he stepped out into the chamber, making sure to stick to the wall.

No one so much as glanced at him.

It's working! Maybe!

When he glanced down at himself, he had a dizzying sense of dislocation, as he couldn't quite see his body. His skin had changed to match what was behind him; not perfect invisibility but better than just running in a crouch. Still, moving slowly and carefully was the best way forward, except within seconds his lungs began to burn. The loss of Breath Control had hurt him more than he realized, and Felix figured he had been right before: he had about a minute before he'd *have* to breathe again. He moved quicker.

He dodged between chairs and pillars, sticking to the darker edges and having to time his movements with the erratic magelights. He was doing fairly well, as long as he didn't think about breathing. Three quarters of the way across the room however, Felix hit an impasse. A clutch of unkempt men and women leaned together, blocking the path forward as they discussed something in a low whisper. He ducked behind a nearby empty table, and listened. Felix's Perception carried their voices to him easily.

"Have you seen 'em?" A lantern-jawed Half-Orc asked.

"Nah. Not since he went upstairs. Orfin and Pasquale took a leech and followed." A dusky-skinned Elf replied, scratching at her neck. It was covered in tattoos that resembled cursive writing. "That was, say, ten minutes ago?"

"Long time to deal with a drunk wanderer." Grunted the Half-Orc.

"Cap'n talked with 'em a long time. Maybe he's tough?" Suggested a short and stocky Hobgoblin. His big nose was as red as his eyes, and he kept wiping at it with a handkerchief. "Snnf. Why else would Cap'n care about some new meat?"

Felix's lungs were burning fiercely. He was low and hidden by nearly everyone by the table, so he took a chance. He released his breath and let Abyssal Skein drop at the same time as attempting to quietly suck in a few more lungfuls of air.

"*What's goin' on here?*"

The booming voice shocked the gathered pirates, and Felix could hear them shift and turn toward the clomping steps of what felt like a huge creature. Checking his Mana, Felix saw he was down about 30% from the last thirty seconds; the Skill was pretty Mana-intensive. He had plenty to spare, thankfully, so Felix took a deep breath and reactivated it. The colors around him inverted again, and Felix crept slowly out from under the table to get a peak at what was happening.

Abyssal Skein is level 3!

Shit. Sauntering up to the group of pirates was the Ogre Korm Rocksplitter in his mismatched armor. Twice as tall as the others, he absolutely *bristled* with weapons.

"Lollygaggin' when we 'ave business? I'll lay out the lot a ya!" Korm's neck bulged with veins and spittle dropped from his tusks. He was much bigger than Stiilgar.

"No, no Korm! We're just waitin' fer Orfin!" The Half-Orc had begun sweating and waving his hands. "They left to get the new meat."

The Ogre grunted and eyed the darkened hallway toward the rooms. Felix tried to keep perfectly still, terrified that he'd be spotted, but Korm only snorted and shook his head.

"I hate waitin'. We need that new ship for raidin'! Veris!" He turned toward the bar and the tattooed Dwarf running it. "Your newbie is makin' me thirsty! Gimme a barrel a the hard stuff!"

"Ain't my newbie! And get it yerself, ya lazy ponce!" she shouted back.

"Woman! Ye ain't half the size a' me usual, but I'll end ya!" Korm growled back.

"Prove it, Rocksplitter!"

Felix's breath was starting to run out again, and he hadn't moved. He couldn't wait here any longer; sooner or later they were gonna figure out what happened to their friends, and then they'd find him. He needed a distraction.

Pit trilled in his head, a series of flashing images shared between them. Felix grinned in response, and mentally thanked the tenku.

Reign of Vellus!

The Skill was showy, but it always produced lightning on the target of the kinetic force. A series of arcing blue lightning skittered across a chair and table next to the darkened hallway, before the entire set lifted and was flung outward. The racket was enormous, but not as much as Korm's shout.

"A *fight! Yes!* The new meat is feisty!" The huge Ogre thundered past, followed closely by the rest of the pirates. Felix ducked beneath the table again, releasing and taking another quick breath to refresh his Abyssal Skein before crawling out. "Come! Lock down this bastard before he flees!"

The crew distracted, he slunk his way toward his destination. The kitchens.

The room was bright, the magelights unwavering along the ceiling. Felix had to squint. Aside from the counters, floors, and walls being made of the gray-black Void bone, it seemed utterly normal. There was a huge stove along the far wall where a few pots and pans steamed and boiled, and various items hung from the ceiling on hooks. Meat, mostly, but also wrinkled and dried roots and weedy looking plants. Felix kept his Abyssal Skein going, but had to drop it about halfway through the room.

Abyssal Skein is level 4!

Luckily, no one was there.

They almost made it to the far door, the one Pit's memories confirmed was the way to the docks below. Then Felix heard a *clomp-tak* from behind him and he spun in place, a dark green orb already formed in his left hand.

A woman, with ochre skin and dark green hair stood before him. She wore a stained once-white apron and held out a *very* large butcher knife. She snarled at him, her teeth as sharp as the Captain's own.

"You're the newcomer." She looked to his side, eyes briefly darting about at waist level. "Where's yer friend?"

Pit chirruped happily at her presence, and before Felix could stop him, disengaged their Convergence. With a flash of light, Pit reformed next to Felix. The Naiad stepped back in surprise.

"What in Avet's name—?"

"Pit is my Companion, and we have certain... abilities." Felix smiled and spread his hands, not dismissing the acid orb from his grip. "Far easier to escape a trap when you're one person instead of two, right?"

The woman, Dahlia Sa'thys by his Eye, blinked and nodded slowly. Pit let out a low warble and the Naiad's mouth quirked in a smile. She lowered her knife.

"I'll not be raisin' weapons against a Tenku." She directed a nod at Felix that was begrudgingly respectful. "That you earned its trust speaks highly of ya. Here."

She tossed a burlap sack the size of Felix's torso at him. He caught it easily, but it was surprisingly heavy. Not taking his eyes off the woman, Felix opened it and let his Perception flow into it. It was full of food and flasks of water. Felix blinked.

"What's this for?" he asked.

Dahlia ignored Felix and turned to Pit. She bowed at the waist. "Thank you fer blessing my kitchens, Honored Chimera. This is all I can manage, but take it with my heartfelt gratitude. I'd thought I'd die before I'd see another Guardian Beast." She flicked her finger across her left eye, and Felix thought he spotted a tear. "Now go. I'll distract the crew if they come looking. Go!"

Felix didn't need to be told twice. He beckoned Pit and pushed open the door. His friend lingered, letting out a mournful note. The Naiad only smiled at Pit with sad eyes and shooed them away. They left.

"Honored Chimera, huh?"

Pit only chirruped brightly. Images of meat and the words *"nice lady"* came through the bond. Felix just smiled. Unwilling to waste any more time, Felix unleashed the full power of his Agility, and urged Pit to do the same. They fairly flew down the corridors and staircases, following Pit's remembered path back down to the dock.

The dock was just as dark as Pit recalled, but Felix flared his Manasight and the place lit up to him like it was midday. There was a significant amount of ambient Mana in the air, much of it generated by a gargantuan warship. It was three or four stories tall and had to have been half the length of the island itself. Four masts stretched up into the cavernous ceiling, and some sort of dark cloth was bunched there: sails waiting to be unfurled. Most amazing of all was the deep, multicolored glow of the ship's heart. Felix thought heart because the flow of Mana seemed to *pulse* through the ship, as if the craft was living.

"Just like the *Night's Wake*," Felix said as he looked up at the Ten Hands' flagship. "But way bigger. You weren't kidding about the size. This is the same place we docked, right? So that means, aha!" It only took a few seconds to find the wide open hatch leading out into the darker Void. Yet, before they could contemplate escape, the grisly phantom of the Maw appeared before them.

Idiot child. You can't outrun these craft. It threw a hand toward the flagship. *Look at them! Primitive or not, these are Manaships.*

"Your point? I don't exactly know how to pilot a ship, Mana or otherwise," Felix growled back.

Just find the smallest one! Or do you want to be slaved to their ship for the rest of your pitiful life?

Grumbling to himself, Felix turned back. They had to travel to the other side of the huge flagship, but Felix and Pit were able to find a sloop. Like the rest of the crafts, the sloop was made of voidbeast bone and had sails of some dark, leathery material. Being small, it only had a single mast and a minimal amount of ropes and pulleys. Felix and Pit alighted on its deck and he stared around fairly helplessly.

"I don't know… how do I do this?" he asked the air.

The Maw sucked at its teeth in annoyance, which set Felix's own nerves on edge. *See the plinth there? Where the rudder should be?*

Felix turned and spotted a blocky construction at the far rear of the boat. He nodded.

Good, there should be an interface node there. Grab it and feed it your Mana through one of your Gates. We have to be quick. The Maw pivoted her attention to their right and up. *They're coming.*

Felix swallowed and hovered over to the rudder. The Maw was right, there was a polished gray orb in place of the rudder handle, and it was surrounded by small inscriptions. The inscriptions were similar to the Primordial Dawn sigils he knew, but only barely. He squinted at it, but it didn't really make much sense.

Hurry!

Groaning, Felix placed his hand on the orb and felt it grow warm slightly. "That's not too bad." Then he made use of his Mana Manipulation Skill and sent out a larger stream of Mana vapor.

Mana Manipulation is level 19!

The orb came to flickering life, sucking in the vapor and pulling insistently at Felix's Mana channels. With a grimace, he relaxed against it. A full third of his remaining Mana disappeared into the hungry guts of the ship, and abruptly, the entire thing thrummed with vibrant energy. The sails lowered and affixed themselves, and the entire craft lifted off the ground.

"Whoa." Felix could feel his regeneration battling with the pull of the orb, but it wasn't too hard to maintain...

Go, you fool! They're here!

Acting on instinct, Felix willed the sloop forward, and they shot off into the Void.

CHAPTER THIRTEEN

Piloting the sloop was a lot like riding atop the *Night's Wake*, only faster. The leather sails cracked and the braided ropes snapped tight as veins of Mana spread from the Control Node down into the bone of the craft, each pulse somehow propelling them through the dark nothingness all around them. There was no wind in the Void, which was a very strange sensation to Felix, but the sails billowed and shifted regardless.

They moved fast. The small craft didn't have weapons or enough room for more than Pit and himself, but it was apparently built for speed. The Maw had been right: there was no way they could have outrun even their smallest ships on foot. Now, however, rock formations whizzed past them as Felix guided the ship into the black.

Well, "guided" was a strong word.

The speed the sloop traveled combined with the asteroid field nature of the area meant Felix spent most of his time dodging up and down or side to side. After some experimentation, Felix found that, as long as he fed it Mana, the ship responded to his Willpower, moving how he directed it. His Willpower was easily his highest stat, which presumably meant that the boat responded better than if he had less points, but it was still enormously taxing. He felt his mental strength draining almost as fast as his Stamina. A nameless feeling in his bones told him that moving so fast strained his Perception as well as his Dexterity and Agility, and that he couldn't keep it up for too long. After an hour of full speed flight and two near-crashes, Felix reigned it back in and began to cruise at half-speed.

Mana Manipulation is level 20!
Mana Manipulation is level 21!

What are you doing? The Maw spun toward him, its pale dress floating ephemerally behind it as if in a breeze. Even as a construct of his own mind, the Maw kept up its tricks. *They are surely chasing you!*

Felix frowned and steered the sloop up and over another rocky island half the size of their craft. "Maybe. But I sure as hell can't keep that speed up all the time. I'll end up crashing." He looked over at the Maw and raised an eyebrow. "And what do you care?"

I told you. Your life is my own for now.

"No, my life is *my* own. You're just a temporary passenger," Felix said, jerking the ship up and over another house-sized rock. "A parasite."

The creature didn't respond to that, which surprised him. Felix was coming to realize the Maw was a study in contradictions. He'd noted before, when he still thought it was a Nymean woman named Lhel, that the Maw was insane. Felix didn't know what new twist the Primordial's mind would take, but it was capricious at best. He was only glad that it couldn't physically harm him or Pit.

It can affect my Skills and core though, he recalled. *That's more than enough damage to stay wary.*

Pit warbled in agreement, though it sounded muted. Felix heard snuffling and rustling somewhere forward of the cabin, where the deck dropped a foot or so. Pit's butt was in the air, and his wings were askew as the snuffling sounds continued. Piloting the ship around another obstacle, Felix stood slightly and saw the tenku's head was in the burlap bag they'd been given.

"Hey! Cut it out, little pig!" Felix felt a smile curl his lips involuntarily as Pit lifted his head and looked back. A string of what Felix assumed was sausages hung from Pit's neck, and a faintly glowing piece of meat was clenched in his beak. The chimera slurped up the meat and a radiant glow flickered around him for an instant.

+1 to END

"What are you eating?" The only thing Felix knew that gave Pit bonuses like that were elemental cores. He recalled the distant swells of System energy he'd sensed throughout his evening with Captain Nokk. "Have you been eating those things all night?"

Pit's only reply was a small burp. However, it was followed up by a curious trilling. Pit emerged from the sack with a thick, rolled up piece of paper in his beak.

What is that? Bring it here. Pit trotted over to him and dropped the thick paper into his lap. It was grayish-pink, and when he unrolled it, Felix found it was a map, easily two-by-three feet in size.

A map! He immediately attempted to find their location. The map was littered with lines of different varieties, some solid, some dashed or dotted, each one denoting a path or heading. Felix wasn't really sure. Navigation and sailing had never been a thing he'd gotten into back on Earth. His family was entirely too poor to own a boat, and his recent history with yachts wasn't something he liked remembering.

The lines were all over the map, but many of them intersected in an oversized drawing of a castle: the Ten Hands' secluded home, Felix guessed. There were a number of places marked out on the map with curious symbols, a language he didn't understand. He figured they were things like outposts and towns floating off out there in the Void. Felix's eyes focused on one particular spot that was marked with a series of skulls and crossbones. That, at least, he could recognize. A dangerous place.

A groaning call echoed all around them, startling Felix up onto his feet. Suddenly, a pod of Narhollows—normal ones, his Eye assured him—rose up from below, not a hundred yards from the port side. *Starboard?* he briefly wondered. *No, port is left. I remember that at least.*

The creatures were majestic, craggy forms somehow sinuous from a distance. There were three of them, one larger than the others, and they each paddled their massive tails and left brilliant streamers of Mana behind them. Huge and slow, they spun and undulated like an earthquake given form, their flippers nudging rock formations out of their path. Felix smiled as he saw them, then frowned. In their wake traveled hundreds of Tenebrils, and he didn't doubt a flock of invisible Harrowings were lurking behind them.

"More monsters. We should put some distance between us and them." Last thing Felix wanted was the voidbeasts catching scent of his Mana. He shifted the sloop into a faster speed, angling it to the right and upward. Starboard and… was there a nautical term for up?

KATHOOOM!

The small rocky island next to them exploded in a shower of gray shrapnel. Cuts opened up on Felix's face, and Pit cowered beneath a lifted wing. A bloom of iridescent green fire engulfed the remains of the island, and Felix whipped his head backward. Behind them, perhaps half a mile away, was a colossal ship that looked merely gigantic due to the distance. Dark sails and a black flag featuring a white hand with ten fingers flew high from their mast.

Faster! cried the Maw.

Felix didn't need the encouragement. He poured more of his Mana into the control orb and the sloop shot off.

"Full speed ahead! Catch the bastard!"

Captain Nokk paced at the helm of his ship, the *Hippocamp's Fury*, venting his spleen on all and sundry. He'd been interrupted during a very important meeting with several nubile guests, only to be told that his promising new recruit had gone missing. Moreover, the boy had killed three of his men and stolen food from the larder, unseen and presumably laughing at Nokk the entire time! And *then* they had the audacity to tell him that the bastard stole a ship! One of *his* ships! Who would do such a thing! Stealing another man's property! Preposterous! Outrageous!

Nokk fumed, just barely able to contain his rage and not rip his favorite tricorn hat into pieces. "Faster, you mangy curs! My left nut could sail this ship better'n you!"

Screams could be heard down below, but Nokk grinned to hear it. It meant more fuel was being added to their fire, and soon they could push the *Fury* that much faster. His men, dirty and irascible to the last, cursed and shouted at each other as they loaded up the ballista with more Manashot.

The stone spears weren't much to begin with, but once infused and launched from their deck-mounted siege weapons, they'd take down just about anything without a ward. Nokk had destroyed his share of settlements with these weapons, and his new flagship boasted twice as many as normal. He was unstoppable, as long as they kept pace!

"Faster!"

He couldn't let the boy get away, not when the scum had lied to his face. Once or twice a day to use that lightning storm spell? Lies! The freak was pumping enough Mana into that sloop to cast such a spell a half-dozen times, at least!

"I'll catch him, and that dumb bird of his! I'll chain 'em to the *Fury* for the rest of their days!"

No one double-crossed Captain Nokk.

Not when Nokk was gonna double-cross first!

SILENCE

The pirates' flagship was gaining on them, having suddenly surged with Mana in the last few moments. Other than feeling it loom closer, Felix couldn't pay it any mind. His entire focus was absorbed by the thickening rock field all around him. He consulted the map as they jostled about. If the dotted shapes indicated rock islands, then it was going to get worse before it thinned out.

Hopefully we'll even make it that far!

Felix strained himself, pushing more and more Mana into the Control Node and devoting his attention to bobbing and weaving through the maze of shifting rocks. A few times, he attempted dual casting Reign of Vellus to shove aside an impeding formation, but it was extremely difficult to also maintain Mana Manipulation. It also ate away at his Mana, more than his regeneration could bring back, so Felix couldn't afford it. He could only focus on speed.

KRAK!

KRAKOOM!

Stones burst into shimmering green flame all around them, but Felix had them moving too erratically for the pirates to draw a bead on them. The floating islands were as much an impediment to the pirates as to Felix, but where he had to dodge and evade them, the flagship plowed through. The weight and bulk of the ship rammed the stone formations aside, though the hull was taking a beating. Felix could only hope it would get too damaged to continue, but he wasn't even sure how these ships operated. Was hull integrity a concern?

Apparently not; the question answered itself as the pirates put on a burst of speed, crashing through the islands and cutting Felix's lead in half.

They're burning them up to catch us. The Maw stared backward, brow furrowed and teeth bared. *You must go faster!*

"I'm trying! It's too—" Felix cut himself off as he heard the near-musical groan of the Narhollows again. More importantly, he remembered what followed in their wake.

"Hang on Pit! I'm trying something!" The sloop shot outward, banking to port and the swimming pod of Narhollows. Felix weaved the ship up and over, cresting the giant, whale-like Void creatures like a craggy hill. More stone arrows were fired, and bursts of green flame ignited along the flesh of the Narhollow. The beast basically had rock for skin, but that got its attention. It cried out and lashed its immense tail. The Mana that spewed from its tail swerved and jittered, its steady pattern interrupted by the Narhollow's agitation.

Felix banked hard, turning toward the pod's rear and those self-same Mana trails. He didn't care about the Mana, but a lot of other things *did*.

"Brace for it!"

The sloop darted forward, and what seemed to be empty Void turned out to be a mass of angular wings and flashing talons. A flock of Harrowings burst in all directions as Felix drove through them, scattering... except for the tantalizing flare of Mana that Felix released around the ship.

"Come and get it!" Felix yelled at the beasts and vented a large chunk of his Mana through his right elbow Gate. Vapor, crackling and shimmering with light followed behind them like a contrail, and Pit offered him a look of disbelief. Felix just grinned, though it was more rictus than humorous. He pivoted again, this time heading straight for the pirates.

What are you doing? The Maw screamed as it dragged nails down its face.

Felix didn't answer. He was too busy avoiding the green detonations all around him. They were clipped several times, and parts of their sails started to burn, but he pressed forward.

"He's coming this way! Fire at will!" Distantly Felix could hear the pirates shouting and cheering, and more stone spears were launched at them. Taking shelter behind the slew of islands, Felix wove through them until he reached the hull of their ship. He was going entirely too fast, but he knew he could do it. It was just a matter of Willpower... and Alacrity, he realized. The stat was humming, or else he was going crazy.

Pulling hard on the Control Node, the sloop shot upward, the hull of his ship scraping loudly against the flagship. Felix burst into the cleared Void above the ship, which he saw was named the *Hippocamp's Fury*, and for a moment, everyone just stared. Time seemed to slow down as the sloop arced over the deck, and Felix could see dozens of pirates swarming below to man the ballista. Captain Nokk's forehead veins bulged in fury, and Felix grinned.

He shot off, back into the distance.

You fool! We're in range and in full sight of the ship! We'll be taken down easily! The Maw's eyes were bloodshot, and blood dripped from its mouth, it was so angry.

Then behind them came the sound of a thousand furious mouths screaming in shrill hunger. A wave of angular darkness descended on the pirates as the Harrowings flowed over them.

"Hah! The Voidbeasts feed on Mana, remember?" Felix laughed and fed the sloop more Mana, urging them further and faster. "I just gave them a new target!"

Behind them, the *Fury* was swarmed by Tenebrils and Harrowings, their mottled bodies clogging the decks and rigging. Felix could hear panicked screaming, and then the *thump-hiss* of something being shot off into the air. The pirates had shot off brilliant purple flares, and these arced high above them, drawing a good amount of the Voidborn away from the ship.

Felix sniffed and tasted the tang of Mana even as his eyes identified it as some sort of mixed type. It drew only a few away, as more piled onto the ship from the darkness. Something about Felix's Mana was too tasty to deny.

He grinned into the dark, and his vision abruptly flickered with gold and blue sparks, heavily diluted by an amount of dark, near-black crimson. Pain built up in his head and core, like heartburn and kidney stones wrapped up in one, before an audible trilling assaulted his senses.

New Skill!
Manaship Pilot (Rare), Level 1!
You've proven your mettle through a trial by fire in the hostile Void. You are now able to utilize Manaships with a greater degree of finesse and efficiency! Accuracy increases with Skill level, Mana exchange rate decreases with Skill level.

"Huh," Felix said, half dizzy from the pain.

Faster! Faster! the Maw urged.

Felix glanced back, just in time to swerve to port. The green cannonball still hit them, though, shattering through the hull and main mast and sending the three of them careening into the black.

Pit screeched in fear, clinging to the deck, and Felix dumped all the Mana he had left into the sloop. The ship wobbled and rolled, nearly bucking the lot of them, before it gathered an unwise amount of speed and shot off into the Void.

CHAPTER FOURTEEN

"This is the best we can do?" Cal asked, raising an eyebrow.

"You wanted out of sight, what better place than the Dust?" Yan said, scratching at his goatee. His bald head shone in the early morning sunlight, reminding Cal of the wretched heat to come that afternoon. "No one will come bug us here. They'd rather not get their heels too muddy."

Cal tilted her head in acknowledgement and pushed open the door ahead of her. The corrugated iron creaked like a pensioner's joints, and a veritable rain of rust crackled off its surface, but at least it opened. Inside, the warehouse was wide open—some might even say cavernous—though it looked like there were a few sectioned-off areas in the rear.

"Walls have some holes, and the roof leaks, but all that can be patched up easy enough," Portia said in consideration. She put her hands on her hips as she and others followed Cal into the building. "This is… not the worst."

"Your words are like honey on my heart, dear," Yan said with a broad smile. Portia snorted and turned back to the others.

"I think it's—I don't think that's the right saying," Kelgan said, stroking his beard in thought.

"Looks like there's space for me to set up shop, too. Could do some good here in the Dust while we're at it," she suggested.

"Hmm," Cal said noncommittally. She walked in a slow circle amid the dust and scattered leaf debris that dominated the space. After the Tribunal's judgment, their group had been cut loose from the Guild and left to fend for themselves. Some of the survivors were allowed to stay on, and those who had fallen ill during the return trip were still being given medical attention by the Healer's Ward. All of Cal's closest friends and allies, however, were sent packing with only the armor and weapons on their backs. There was little else to do but rally together and figure out their next step. "I'd rather not get the Guild's attention, Portia," Cal said, and the pixie-haired woman scowled.

"Blight the Guild and their attention," Evie said. Her young voice was thick with a bitter vitriol that was so familiar to Cal; it was the same poison that coursed in her veins, after all. "Why should we listen to them at all?"

"Because they control this city, kid." Harn grunted as he walked into the warehouse. "You gonna burn down the house you're still livin' in?"

"Maybe," Evie grumbled.

It had been two weeks since the sentencing, two very long weeks that Cal had spent talking to Elders and fighting to get her people out of "observation," whatever that was. Since then, they'd moved to a tiny inn in the depths of the Dust Quarter, the poorest of the four sections in Haarwatch, until Yan had made this discovery.

"It's larger than the Owlshade Inn, at least," Cal allowed. Yan puffed up his chest and looked between Portia and Kelgan. "But it needs work. Work we aren't gonna be around to appreciate later. You know the plan: we do some hunts, run some board tasks, earn enough silver to take the first caravan outta town. That's a couple months, at most, so make the fixes we need, but no more than that. Yeah?"

Her crew—friends, the lot of them—gave her a variety of salutes and nods before scattering into the open space. Yan, Trendle, and Vivianne followed Portia into the back area, presumably to find space for her "shop," despite Cal's objections. She merely rolled her eyes; the Dust could do worse than a healer setting up in the worst area of town. Bodie, Karp, Kelgan, and Harn all started shifting debris from the central area, their Strength and Endurance making short work of it all. Evie... she lingered near the door, staring back into the haze that had started to build outside.

"Why are we running, Callie?" she asked without turning.

"You'd rather fight?" Cal asked. She had dreaded this question from the start.

"Of course I'd rather fight," Evie said. Yet the heat Cal had expected was absent. The girl just sounded tired. "Maggie... she would've fought. She started hating the Guild, by the time—"

"Maggie did fight, that's why we were able to get outta the Foglands at all." Cal walked closer and lifted a hand to put on Evie's shoulder. She hesitated, though, and dropped it. "But there's a time to fight and a time to retreat and gather your strength. Going against the Guild might ease my anger, but it won't bring her back, Evie."

"We could try!" Evie said, spinning to face her. There were tears in her green eyes. "We could do more than sit back and take their punishments! They stripped her, Callie! They took everything she'd ever worked for, and wouldn't even let us have a funeral. They wouldn't even let us take her body."

Evie's voice fell to a whisper at the end, but a blaze of prickling fire had already burned across Cal's neck and scalp. Pain gathered in her throat, an ache she'd been repressing for weeks now.

"We'd die before we made it through the second floor of the Eyrie, kid," Cal said softly. This time, her hand rested gently against Evie's shoulder. "I know, I tried, the day she was taken away from us. Silver Rankers pushed me back, four of them." She sighed, heavy and exhausted. "They don't let us go, even in death. Silver meant she could opt out, but now Mags has no rights."

"So, they just get to boil her down for her Essence Draughts? And that's it? End of story?" Evie wiped at her eyes furiously, as if she were mad at them for leaking.

"We have to make the best of what we have. What Magda gave to us. That's you, me, Harn, everybody she sacrificed her life for. My job is to make that sacrifice worth it, to keep *you* safe. Cause we all know she'd come back from the grave to kill me if anything happened to you."

A ghost of a smile flitted across the girl's face, and Cal caught her glancing at her neckline. Cal reached down and lifted her triangular locket, twin to the one Mags had given her a long time ago. That she'd only just returned, right before she died. Cal ignored the burning in her eyes and squeezed Evie's shoulder, once.

"We have our memories, yeah? They can't take that away from us."

"Let 'em try." Evie bared her teeth. Cal felt a sad, hysterical laugh bubble up, but she held it back.

"For now, we get stronger. Focus on developing your core. Harn told me you're close to the Visualization Stage." Cal smiled gently and pulled Evie into a hug. The girl stiffened slightly before melting into the embrace. "You get there, and you'll get to come with us on hunts. Sound square?"

"Square," Evie sniffed.

"Alright. Let's go check on this ruin, then."

―――――

Atar studied the tome before him, tracing the shapes inked on the page with his left pointer finger, while his right etched them in the air before him. Orange Mana flared, lingering just long enough to complete a simple sigil, though Atar refused to activate them. The Elder's study was not the place for such hazardous experimentation.

No, the mage was merely getting acquainted with the sigaldry in the books before him, as he had been doing for the past fortnight. Elder Teine had provided Atar with a number of books—twenty-nine, to be exact—calling all of them required reading. Only then, he was told, would he be considered educated enough in the bare fundamentals. He was working his way through the twenty-eighth at the moment, and it was both tedious and faintly humiliating to be reviewing the basics of his favored art.

Atar considered protesting—he had studied sigaldry extensively under his master—but he ultimately kept quiet and accepted his new lot in life. He was no longer a prized pupil, and had once again started at the bottom of the social hierarchy. In fact, there were a large number of apprentices under the Elder. They ranged in rank from Tin to Bronze, with the more advanced Guilders having a far greater involvement with the Elder's works, a fact that made Atar seethe with jealousy.

"Move aside, Untempered swine, you are in my way."

Atar looked up incredulously to find a slight woman in an ornate dress embroidered with thread of gold and draped with a crimson stole of such exquisite make that only a fool would not recognize her station. A minor noble, by his eye, one dressed to impress others in a way that had little to do with aptitude and much to do with the depths of her pocket. Her face was small and pointed, and her eyes too big. No Vessilia with her dark beauty, but attractive nonetheless. She stared at him with those too-large eyes, unblinking.

"Well?"

"Well, what?" Atar asked.

The girl huffed a breath. "Pathless take you—move. This is my favorite seat."

Atar looked around him, noting the abundance of seating in the Elder's study. It was a massive hall, filled to the brim with books and plush armchairs and beautifully appointed desks, all designed to study the fascinating knowledge held within. While large enough for dozens of apprentices to work within, was still restricted to a chosen few, and at the moment only Atar was present. "I am an apprentice, just as yourself. There are plenty of seats to take that are not currently occupied, Miss...?"

"Miss?! Listen, you Tin Rank child, I am Lilian Knacht, first daughter of the Ore Lord, Octavius Knacht. Apprentice Tier and Iron Rank member of the Protector's Guild. My father has bought people for less than the cost of your pathetic battle robes." The girl flicked a hand and curled her lip. "So shoo, you are not welcome near me."

Atar's olive complexion reddened the longer the girl spoke. By the end of her little speech a vein was throbbing visibly along his neck, and his jaw clenched so hard he was liable to break a tooth. Never had he been so disrespected! Not even that hooligan Felix had dared to speak to him in such a way! Just as he opened up his mouth to lambaste the idiot girl child, he was interrupted, yet again.

"Lilian, knock it off," said a genteel voice from across the room. A man followed after it, one with dark brown hair expertly slicked back into fine waves above his slightly pointed face. He wore a doublet and trousers whose make, much as the girl-child's, suggested minor nobility. They were devoid of thread of gold and instead only formed to his slender body in a way accentuated by the dark blue half-cape over a single shoulder. A silver-hilted rapier poked from his left hip, likely an ornamental weapon of some design. "You've already been warned off for frightening the new apprentices. Don't let it happen again."

The girl-child turned meek, though Atar knew her fangs were merely hidden. "Of course, cousin Alister. I was simply explaining to this... desert boy that he had sat in our spot. The light, you see, is perfect here for perusing the Elder's exquisite collection."

"Naturally. But there are chairs aplenty for all of us," her cousin said. Alister, apparently. "Let's simply sit and introduce ourselves properly."

Alister was older than his cousin, though the resemblance was unmistakable once it was called out. They both shared the same pointed nose and slender chin, even if his eyes were a touch smaller than the girl-child's. On her they were strange, a doll's eye on a Human, but on him they were... not unappealing.

"Sit? Blind gods, yes," muttered a third voice, this one gruffer. A boy stepped around a leather armchair, roughly the same age as Lilian, perhaps seventeen or eighteen summers and built like a plowman. He flopped down into the nearest one, letting his bulk skip the chair backward. "My legs are aching after all that formwork."

"That is because you wield earth Mana like someone doing manual labor," Lilian said in snide derision. She folded herself neatly in a chair flanking her cousin and glared daggers at Atar again. "*Why* exactly are you still here, Tin Rank?"

Atar bristled. "The study is open to all of Elder Teine's apprentices, bar none."

"My cousin is... impatient," Alister drawled in his urbane accent. "But she has a certain aversion to manners."

The girl-child drew in a sharp breath that made Atar smile.

Alister smiled back. "I heard her introduction, so I shall follow. I am Alister Knacht, first-born son of Albert Knackt. My associate here is Dabney DeLane, second-born son of Rodric DeLane."

"A pleasure," Atar managed, meeting Alister's handshake with his own. He was right. Minor nobility within Haarwatch, which meant they were country bumpkins compared to the true world-shakers from the Interior. A measure of confidence suffused his limbs. "I am Atar V'as, former apprentice of Sig'nyh Kel'lyv, Grandmaster of the Desert's Fire."

Alister whistled. "Grandmaster, you say? And you're in Haarwatch?" The young noble gave him a considering look. "Please don't be offended by my asking but, why?"

Atar turned his grimace into a thin smile. "To advance my knowledge, my Master sent me to apprentice under Elder Teine. He had a great many good things to say about the Elder's prowess."

"He certainly is quite remarkable," Alister agreed.

The thick lout snapped his fingers and leaned forward. "Now I remember! Atar V'as! You came back from the Foglands!"

Lilian gasped, and Alister's attention sharpened. "Truly?" he asked.

Atar shrugged helplessly, the book in front of him a scant barrier from their inquisitive stares. "It is true."

"Fascinating," Alister said, his eyes sparkling. "I do believe we sat at the right table today."

CHAPTER FIFTEEN

High Elder Fairbanks considered the city from his high vantage atop the Spire. Here, at the very tip of the Eyrie, the highest point in the entire Territory, he could see over hill and dale and into the very heart of his domain. In his more fanciful moods, he liked to imagine his realm as an actual Domain, with the Guild as the Domain Core that kept everything in its proper place. A clock with a great many cogs, each perfectly set and secured so that the machinery of war continued without abatement.

Haarwatch. It was a solid city. A place of purpose, to protect the Heirocracy from the beasts that threatened its borders. It was even built atop Ages-old ruins and sported some few defenses harkening back to those halcyon times.

Like the Wall. It was a relic of the Lost Race that built Haarwatch's precursor city, used even now as foundations for the very tower he was standing within. It was built of solid orichalcum, a metal so rare that the Heirophant once considered dismantling the Wall for her own use. But its defensive capabilities were too useful, and it proved a hardy bulwark against the endless waves of chimera that attacked from the Foglands. That *used to* attack.

Fairbanks leaned over the edge of his balcony, his Adept Tier eyes as sharp as any raptor, and saw the forest. The Foglands, bare of any fog at all. It had been weeks since the fog dispersed, but still he was not used to it. He felt strangely naked, defenseless despite all their protections. Which was why the Guild was sponsoring teams to enter the Foglands and cut it down.

Let's see those chimera take us by surprise now, he thought with a bit of vicious glee. *Without their fog, without their tree cover, they are but clay targets to my battalions of Guilders. And eventually, our foothold will expand. The time for Haarwatch to grow has come at last.*

For too long, his city had been in an immobile war between monsters and men. Now they could press the attack and reclaim land that had been lost to fog for Ages. The riches they had unearthed already would fuel that expansion, as well as many other things for Haarwatch. More than enough to push to become one of the Hierocracy's premiere border cities, and to even garner further resources from the Protector's Guild Head Branch.

He had worked hard to bring business and riches to his people, to extend the city into the mountains and delve deeper into the earth for the ore that sustained so many of his nobles. He was a Lord in all but name. Gold Rank granted him a political position similar to a Baron, but it was not a landed title, nor a System-granted one. The Heirophant only let rule those who were indispensable politically or economically garnered true landed rights. As it was, it was his Guild branch that held the Provisional Authority over the Territory… and that only extended to the city itself.

However, even now resources from the Foglands were piling into the Guild coffers, swelling their vaults with power—both figurative and literal. It was the dream, finally real.

The scheme they had hatched so many months ago—based on Eliza DuFont's questionable intel—had failed. They had intended to gain the Foglands as their Territory by virtue of a little known Hierocratic law: if a force takes possession of a land, creates a bastion and defends it against all comers for six months, they gain a provisional hold on the land itself. There were bylaws and stipulations to that occupancy, but they were easily smoothed over. No, the greatest threat were the monsters and dizzying fog itself, which had proven too much for their people.

And then, by some stroke of luck, that bitch Magda had handed the Foglands to him on a silver platter.

Hmph. One good thing before her deserved death. Fairbanks had never liked the common-born Aren nor her loudmouthed sister. *A pity that little assassin DuFont had hired wasn't able to kill them both.*

Though her original plan failed, it was DuFont who he had to thank for their good fortune. She had hedged her bets and set loose a Sworn assassin on the Silver Rank team, ensuring Magda's death and recovering the Dayne girl. He was willing to overlook DuFont's questionable methods as the results spoke for themselves. It only resulted in a few deaths, after all, and of those only the traitorous Magda had any real worth. The rest were Bronze Rank trash, destined to never rise above their limitations. The loss of Calesca and Harn to the Tribunal ruling was a blow, but they weren't trustworthy anymore. That damned Magda had gotten in their ears. Turned them against their better interests. Against the Guild.

Against him.

"Knock knock," said a smooth baritone. "It was unlocked, so I did myself the courtesy of walking in."

Fairbanks turned from his view of Haarwatch to look at the new arrival. He was younger than the High Elder, and though his silvery hair and goatee suggested otherwise, they both had the flawless skin and features that came with enough advancement.

"Uldred. I'm surprised to see you outside your little warren," Fairbanks said. "I've heard you've been enraptured by a new project."

Elder Uldred Teine smirked as he crossed the High Elder's chambers. "You know how it is: time slips away from you when you're uncovering the mysteries of Creation."

"And have you? Uncovered anything?"

"You speak of the reason for the Fogland's sudden surcease of fog?" Teine ran two fingers over the surface of Fairbanks' desk, bobbling the floating, scripted lamp. "No. Other than the fact that Magda entered the Labyrinth, was accosted by many Frost Giants and died, little is known. Our... source, of course, is somewhat suspect."

"Calesca."

"Just so. But she claimed there was a vault or some such below the earth. I have two teams on their way to inspect it, but they haven't yet returned." Teine waved his hand, as if swatting an annoying fly. "But nevermind that. It is the least exciting news I have brought to you, High Elder."

"Oh?" Fairbanks walked to his high-backed chair and sat. The chimera leather was as soft as any southern silks, supple and tough after the alchemical baths used to treat it. "What new discovery could so excite my Elder of Spirit?" He gestured for Teine to sit as well.

Teine sat, but the nervous energy in his bearing forced him back to his feet almost immediately. "It is the injured and ill survivors. They are not improving."

"I would think that an issue for the Healer's Ward," Fairbanks said.

"Mhm, and you would be right, under standard circumstances. But I've had the opportunity to examine several of the survivors. They range from Humans to Elves to Dwarves and Orcs. Even a few Goblins, if you can believe it," he snorted.

"The Guild is welcoming of all Races," Fairbanks recited.

"Sure it is." Teine smirked before switching gears. "The survivors. Yes. All of them, regardless of age, Race, level, or Temper have... something swimming through their channels. At first, I thought it was debris from a recent advancement, or some sort of core ailment, but no. The longer I have examined them, the more certain I've become."

Fairbanks waited a beat, while Teine stared at him with wide eyes and a wider smile. "Well? Are you a mage or a street magician? Quit with the dramatics and spit it—"

"It is Primordial Essence."

Fairbanks shot to his feet immediately, flaring his Spirit and forcing Teine backwards along the floor. The Elder of Spirit grunted and fell to his knees, unable to withstand the pressure of his power. Even his robes flattened.

"Speak swiftly and with extreme caution, Uldred," Fairbanks forced out. For the first time in too long his heartbeat hammered in his ears and he even felt sweat begin to bead along his neck. "Have you touched the Essence? Has it spread?"

Teine struggled to lift his head, gasping out his words. "It is… inert!"

Fairbanks hesitated, reducing the pressure of his Spirit. "What do you mean? Primordial Essence doesn't go inert. It is an infection, a plague that wipes out entire nations! And you are… toying with it?"

Teine struggled from his knees, still under the influence of the High Elder's immense Spirit. "I—I have tested it in every way we have. Every piece we have found in a survivor is completely and utterly inert. As if—as if it's devoid of a Mind or Spirit."

"The Body without the animus of Mind or Spirit," Fairbanks mused. "How is that possible?" His Spirit retracted fully, and Teine took a deep, measured breath. "The Primordials are nightmares from the darkest of Avet's pits. You are too young to recall the one that ravaged the East, but if you weren't, you would know what you are suggesting is unimaginable."

"Ah, but it *is* imaginable," Teine said. He coughed twice, and his voice was a bit strained. "It is happening, now. And we are in a prime position to use it to our advantage."

"Advantage?" Fairbanks' mouth twisted at the idea. "How

could a terror from the dawn of Creation be an advantage to us? Kill the patients and burn their bodies."

"No no, listen!" Teine's face was urgent and his left eye twitched. "They are inert! There is no spread! Which means we can test the Essence we have extracted—"

"You've already extracted the Primordial Essence? And nothing happened?"

"Yes. That is what I am telling you, High Elder. With this, imagine the Essence Draughts we can brew! Imagine the benefits to our own advancement! To the Hierocracy itself!"

"Don't patronized me, Uldred. This is not for the Hierocracy. They would burn you for even suggesting such a thing." Fairbanks drummed his fingers on his desk. "If it is inert as you say… then yes. This is an opportunity. One for the Guild, and the Guild alone."

Teine bowed, his earlier intensity suddenly absent. "As you say, High Elder. As you say."

"What do you need to begin?"

Teine smiled.

CHAPTER SIXTEEN

Manaship Pilot is level 10!

Felix's ability to steer and provide power to the sloop increased with every passing hour, yet the ship's integrity degraded fast. After roughly half a day, Felix wasn't so much flying the ship as he was nudging it as they coasted through the frictionless Void.

Mana Manipulation is level 24!

+3 WIL
+4 AFI
+6 ALA

His mental reserves had long since been dredged. Felix forced his Mind to hold together just enough to keep gliding slowly through the dark.

Help? Pit offered. He was currently tucked tightly against Felix's side, ears back and nervously watching the dark.

"Dunno how, bud. Not like we can get out and push," Felix muttered. Currently, a fist-sized piece of bone was outpacing them as it floated past. "It's be nice if you could fly, though. Wings and all. You sure you can't?"

Pit stood and flicked his ears. His wings spread out, russet and black plumage a match for his fox/raven aesthetic; he flapped them, once, twice, three times. He lifted perhaps an inch with each flap, but it was clearly too much for the tenku. He collapsed to the deck, panting. A plaintive whine echoed across their bond, and Felix ruffled the bird-dog's head.

"Hey, good job anyway. That looked really hard."

Pit chuffed in self-pity, which turned out only to be a ruse for more pets and food.

"No more, bud. We have to ration what's left of the food, or else we'll starve," Felix said, pulling the burlap sack away from his greedy friend. "I don't think I need as much food as I did before, and you definitely don't need any more any time soon." Felix looked up at the Maw, floating near the broken mainmast. "Why don't I need food as much anymore?"

The Maw rolled an eye down at him, altering her hovering to better see Felix. *You're Tempered, are you not? What use is mortal sustenance as you proceed down the path of immortality?*

"Immortality—That's what Tempering is?" Felix said, with a raised eyebrow. "I thought it was just strengthening your stats and… stuff."

And what would you call it as you pursue perfection in Body, Mind, and Spirit? What name would you use when you reached said perfection? The Maw held out its hands, chipped and broken fingernails spread wide. *Immortality. It is the endless fox the hounds of the finite have long pursued, yet so few come close enough to even see their prey. Most fall, never having caught even the barest hint of its scent.* It scoffed. *Pathetic.*

Felix ignored its aggressive rhetoric. While the Maw was fearsome and had almost killed him only a few short days ago, he had grown used to its toothless anger. Just so long as it didn't try and touch him again, Felix could happily ignore the ghostly Primordial. Most of the time.

And as usual, the Maw only half-answered his question, but

Felix could tease out the meaning himself. He'd Tempered into Apprentice Tier as he fought against the Primordial originally, and that had apparently changed his Body enough that hunger and thirst bothered him far less than normal. He checked his Temper Formations.

Body: Moving Mountain
Mind: Godeater
Spirit: Dawnwalker

His Body made him denser, faster, and stronger, while his Mind further enhanced his Willpower and cognition. His Spirit... was a mystery, at least to him. Other than being a function of magic and part of his core space, Felix had little idea what the Spirit even was. He looked up at the Maw, who had returned to gazing intently into the dark. Was it even worth it to ask?

He was tired, and his head was killing him. His Mana was scraping the bottom of the barrel, barely kept above twenty percent by his regeneration as the sloop pulled more and more from him for less and less effect. He was so tired he hadn't even been able to work on his Mana Gates, and was likely leaving a trail of Felix-scented Mana like chum for sharks.

Felix fumbled out the map, which had been well worn in recent hours. Estimating their position—and unsure if the map was to scale—Felix plotted their course, such as it was.

So if these lumpy shapes are floating rocks, then that was behind us by about four hours. We left at this angle, I believe, so that would put us... He tapped the map. *Right in the middle of nowhere.* There was nothing noted on the map anywhere nearby, not an outpost or town, and even the rocks had dwindled away. *We're lost.*

Even if they were near a marked settlement, there was no scale on the map. The distances were essentially meaningless and could be hours or weeks away. Maybe farther. The Void, as the Maw consistently pointed out, was way bigger than anything he could conceptualize. It felt like outer space, if space had no stars or planets, but had air. Or something like it.

What *was* he breathing?

Felix groaned. So many things, so many mysteries. He'd gone from the beginnings of understanding the Continent to here, a place that made less sense than everything else put together. Chased by pirates.

Pit chuffed once, twice, and headbutted Felix's legs. The dog-sized tenku rubbed himself against Felix before sitting down at his feet. Felix smiled.

At least he had a cool dog.

"What's he doing?"

"..."

"Ugh, you're the worst," Bridgven moaned quietly. "There's a sound ward up and everything! Can't you break your vow of silence once?"

The slender Elf ignored her, wholly focused on the spyglass they were using. The two of them were huddled atop a cutter, a small single-masted ship similar to the sloop they watched. The only difference was that theirs still functioned. They'd been ordered after the Mana-filled wretch after he'd given them the slip in the rock fields.

"He's talking to himself again, huh?" Bridgven muttered. Celat nodded, and the bard snorted. Quietly. "Already got the Void-madness, eh?"

Celat gestured, their long, thin fingers forming shapes almost too fast to follow. "Okay, sure. Maybe he's talking to the dog... bird... thing. That's still weird."

Bridgven sighed and ran a hand through her white hair. They were coasting at a considerable distance, ordered to observe and report for some reason known only to Captain Nokk. They were even running sound and void wards, effectively keeping them hidden from the eyes of an Apprentice Tier.

The biggest problem was that it was burning *boring*. The Half-Orc couldn't even play on her mandolin; too loud, she'd been told in a series of curt gestures. Too much for the wards to hide.

"Ugh, just wake me up when he does something interesting," she said before nestling back onto the bench. She tucked her long coat around herself and tipped her hat forward, mind set on sleep.

Celaat said nothing. They simply watched.

And waited.

Felix was half dozing, Pit's big body nestled awkwardly in his lap when something screamed.

He jolted awake and slammed his arm into the Control Node, hard. Eyes squeezed shut, he hissed out a low, pained breath before gathering his wits. "What the hell was that?" He scrambled to his feet and looked over the low railing. Around him was the Void, endless and featureless. Unchanged from before he fell asleep. Except...

"Is it darker?" he asked.

Indeed.

Felix jumped and his hands swung before his Mind caught up with him. The ignition of bright green Mana lit up the sloop, but his Corrosive Strike slid right through the Maw's body. It looked at him, decidedly unimpressed.

Are you finished?

Felix didn't quite stumble, but the lack of connection made him shuffle his feet in a series of half steps. It was an improvement over his old body, which would have had him falling flat on his face. Felix regained his center and scowled at the Maw. "Were you *trying* to scare me?"

Oh, did I scare you, poor boy? It cooed, condescension writ large across its stolen features. *Were you afraid it was a voidbeast, come to take you in the night?*

"Shut up," Felix snapped. "I heard screaming. What was it?"

The Maw regarded him for a long moment as their boat coasted listlessly. Then it raised an emaciated arm and pointed one of those too-long fingers.

We have touched the edge of liminal space.

"I'm sorry?" Felix looked where the Maw was pointing. It was where he thought the Void had somehow darkened, as imperceptible as black on black might be even to his increased Perception. "What's liminal space?"

Transitory. Neither here, nor there. You should be familiar, as you've traveled through it before. Many, many times.

"I think I would remember that," Felix said.

The Maw fixed him with a squint. *You traveled in liminal space when you were brought to the Continent. I doubt your mortal Mind held onto much of that journey. More recently, you floundered through the boundaries of that insufferable neighbor of mine.*

Felix blinked. "The Archon? You mean—?"

The acid sea and monsters within were the defenses of his Domain, a place of power. I was quite surprised to see you manifest your Will as you had. The Maw chuckled. *Then again, Unbound do not pay heed to the rules as written.*

Felix's perfect memory flashed back. The sea that wasn't, the segmented horrors in the water, the waves that threatened to topple him. He had made a ship, a boat crafted from nothing but his Willpower, as that place had operated under strange rules.

"So this is a Domain in here?" As far as Felix understood, Domains were basically the same as dungeons in games back home. The Archon's place under the mountain was one such place. "Then whatever is inside can enter the Void, too? Why are you touching it?"

They had drifted closer to the patch of darker shadow. The Maw dragged its hands through it, and the Void shimmered.

No, idiot child. The Domain is locked by its own laws. The sheathing of voidstuff is merely a border between realms, one that keeps a Domain separate from the Realms. Nothing from the Domain can leave, nor can anything from this side enter. Not unless the sheathing is broken, and to do that one would need far more power than you—or I in this state—might muster.

It looked repulsed by that fact. Weakness did not agree with the Primordial.

"Grimmar. The duel for the ice shard," he looked over his shoulder, half expecting it to still be there. Just like his hooked sword and notebook, it was left behind. "That was also in liminal space? Grimmar *called* it the Void."

Grimmar was a simple creature. Born and bred for violence and naught much else. It clucked its tongue. *Your duel was within a liminal space, one made for such contests. But all* liminal spaces are drawn from the Void.

"All—" Felix paused. He thought on the Sworn's Memory and others, where the world seemed to shatter around him. "The Memories I take… in some of them, I've been in a dark place that breaks into some of the most insane imagery I've encountered."

Indeed. A representative model of your victim's Memories. The Maw paused from toying with the shimmering dark to smack its lips appreciatively. *Delectable. How I miss the taste, already. That Harrowing you ate was lacking in history. Leaves the flavor a bit hollow, I find. But yes, all liminal space. Where the Mind of Creation touches upon its Body and Spirit.*

"The Mind of Creation? What Body?" Felix tried to keep his frustration banked as the Maw was finally offering up interesting information. "That Sage, Old Mungle, he said the Void was the place *between* Minds. Said it was made of the gods' own Minds."

Mm.

"So the Body is… the Continent?" Felix asked.

The Corporeal. He learns. Slowly.

Felix clenched his jaw at that. "Then what's the Spirit? Is it —" his own Mind groped at his recent memories. "—is it the Desolation I've heard about?"

The Maw looked at him, its claw once more passing through shimmering voidstuff. *Desolation. A fitting name for it. Yes. The Spirit Realm, the Ethereal is a confluence of all things. A maelstrom of energies left over from Creation. The pirates had a shell made of it's energies. A feat I had not—It is an unwise power to dabble within.*

Felix thought on Nokk's words, on the sigil that supposedly created a shield of Desolation energy around the pirate base. "You're afraid of it," he accused, and the Maw recoiled. "It can destroy even the Unending Maw, can't it?"

The Maw bared its teeth at him, flat and human-looking. It leaned forward, looming above Felix like the monster it was. Then it stopped. *Feeble, moronic Felix Nevarre. You worry on my destruction when yours is far closer. Beware. They come.*

The shimmering dark erupted around them, and out of it came dozens of writhing Tenebrils.

"Whoa!" Felix leaped back from the railing as the tentacular voidbeasts burst across them. He deflected their wild, barbed limbs, dropping two with hastily thrown punches. "I thought you said nothing could come out of the Domain!"

I did. The Maw said, now suddenly atop the foresail. *They did not come from the Domain, however. They came from the sheath itself.*

Perhaps the Primordial said more, but Felix was too inundated with mottled gray voidflesh to hear it. Bursts of purple-white and green-white Mana shot from Pit's position, Frost Spears and Wingblades slicing into the horde with abandon, yet they did not stop. The things swarmed as if possessed, latching onto sails and railing, lashing anything within reach. They focused mostly on where Felix stood.

On the Control Node, he realized. *The Mana.*

"Pit! Get down!" Felix shouted. "*Reign of Vellus!*"

A 360 degree burst of electricity and force erupted from him, hitting everything in a range of about thirty feet. The Tenebrils were hurled backward, many of them slammed into the mast and deck, while more were simply flung back into the Void. Without thinking, Felix pulled the cutlass from his waist and slashed outward.

"Gaaah!" He screamed, clutching his own arm, half expecting it to be a bloody mess. He dropped the sword in anger and frustration. "That Skill's broken, idiot!"

Mantle of the Long Night!
Influence of the Wisp!

Felix let his Mana burst around him, feeling it churn up from his core and out of the Gates in his elbows, hands, and feet. The purple-white Mana of his Mantle surged first from those Gates, whirling around him in a visible cloud of mist that immediately coated the deck in a layer of ice. Immediately following that came a pulse of vibrant violet and orange Mana from the base of his skull.

Fire Within is level 36!

You Have Enthralled Tenebril (x32) for 5 Seconds!

Their bodies began to burn under the effects of the blue wispfire while the arctic chill of his Mantle sank into their pliable flesh, turning it cold and rigid.
Corrosive Strike!
Corrosive Strike!
Felix lurched forward, his acid-infused fists driving through one and then another voidbeast. Their bodies squish-shattered into lifeless pieces on the deck, colliding with the railings and masts as he mowed through them all.

Pit didn't slacken either, and soon jagged icicles and ripples of wind tore through even more.

It was all over in thirty seconds.

Unarmed Mastery is level 26!
Corrosive Strike is level 27!
Influence of the Wisp is level 27!
Mantle of the Long Night is level 15!

"Haah...haah." Felix took several deep breaths, watching the creatures for any sign of movement. When nothing seemed to be twitching, he looked to his Companion. "You okay, bud?"

Pit nodded before preening one of his wings. The poor guy was covered in their dark blood.

"Maw! What the hell?" Felix shouted into the sails, but he couldn't see the rawboned Primordial.

You cleaned them up quite nicely, it said. Even though he was half-expecting it, Felix still started. The Maw grinned. *Though I admit, there were less than I expected. The Domain's defenses must have stopped quite a few.*

"Defenses...? No, you know what, I don't care. You almost got me killed. Why didn't you say things could enter and exit from the Void?" Felix demanded.

Did you sustain injury? The Maw looked at his right arm. *One you did not do yourself?*

Felix clutched his arm, where even now he could see faint bruising underneath his skin. Exactly where it had hurt when he'd tried to use the sword. He scowled at the Maw. He wouldn't have any broken Skills were it not for it's schemes. "You—"

He interrupted himself this time, because suddenly the black on black of the Domain was... gone.

"Where'd it go?" he asked, leaning forward over the railing. Hard as it was to see, he couldn't spot it anywhere nearby.

Domains do not stick in one place, the Maw said, as if it were something every child knew. *Why would they?*

"So it moved here, does that mean it moved on the Continent?" Felix looked at the Primordial's skeletal face, wondering if he'd notice if she lied. "How's that possible?"

It isn't. Don't be ridiculous. A Domain may grow or shrink based upon its potency, but it is fixed to is original placement.

"Then where'd it go?"

Domains only touch lightly on the Void. As I said. They sheath it only. The sheath is simply sourced elsewhere. The Maw rolled a hand, as if debating something with itself. *Of course, there are those more... tidally locked with the Void. But they are of uncommon power, and not something you would see in this stretch of emptiness.*

Felix shivered, though it had nothing to do with the ice

melting on the boards. He had enough of voidbeasts and mysterious Domains. He walked back to the Control Node and fed in his Mana, letting the sloop lurch forward.

"You see that?" Bridgven said. "Kid killed a whole flock of Tenebrils like nothing."

Celaat gestured.

"Well sure, they're not as strong as Harrowings or Nightvipers, but they're tough. You see those Skills?" The Half-Orc shook her head, marveling at the taste of Mana in the not-air of the Void. "He's been piloting that sloop for hours, and he still had enough to fight off all those voidbeasts."

Their own ship slipped in Felix's wake, leaving plenty of space between them. Bridgven bared her teeth at the dark.

"This kid's too strong to be a new arrival. And how he's handling that ship? He's working for someone." She tightened her hands on the Control Node. "We gotta find out who."

CHAPTER SEVENTEEN

Unarmed Mastery is level 27!
Dodge is level 26!
Physical Conditioning is level 24!
Manaship Pilot is level 15!

Felix wasn't sure how long he'd been piloting the sloop. He'd stopped counting the times he'd reached Mana fatigue. His regeneration, while slowed, still had enough to bring him back from the edge again, and again, and again. Now that Felix was aware of his Gates constantly releasing and taking in Mana, it was impossible to ignore. The thinness of the Void was like trying to breathe on top of a mountain. He couldn't even devote the mental energy to focusing on fixing them as he danced on the edge of exhaustion.

They had been attacked two more times by roving void-beasts. A smaller flock of Tenebrils and a full on murder of Harrowings—he'd ruled that group nomenclature as the most appropriate. If there was ever a creature that deserved it… regardless, they had killed or driven them off. Left with little Mana to spare, Felix had instead focused entirely on the physical while Pit supported him with magic and the occasional Rake or Bite.

Skill levels had grown, though not as much as he figured they should. That anemic quality of the Void felt like he was starving for System energy, whatever it was that fueled Skill and stat growth. What little he'd accomplished was likely only because he'd been a blood-drenched rag by the end of each of those fights, covered with more cuts and rents than ever before. Pit fared a bit better, but the monsters had targeted him almost exclusively. No doubt because Pit had more available Mana than Felix by that point.

Pit's Wingblade is level 20!
Pit's Frost Spear is level 18!
Pit's Poisonfire is level 14!

Pit had grown a bit as well, though neither had gained another level. Which, in his addled state, Felix considered almost funny.

Could I even gain a level in this place? His Mind spun, teetering on the edge between wakefulness and sleep as the featureless Void slid inexorably past. Felix clamped down on his thoughts as he clutched the Control Node, marshaling them to this Very Important thought. He'd gained three levels when he'd arrived, but that was part of a Quest. What—

Something crunched ahead of him, and his ship lurched and sent him sprawling forward. That was all he knew for a period of time, as the pain in his Mind sent ripples of agony up and down his spine.

—*listen for once, you idiot child.*

Felix blinked bleary eyes up at the Maw, who was floating in front of him. Or was that above him? How long had he been on his back?

Ugh. Mortals. Even Unbound are pathetic. Look!

The Maw pointed to the distance, but as he sat up, Felix first only saw the rock formation he'd run into. It was tall, going at least twenty feet higher than his ship's deck, and extending about the same distance below. A single, large symbol was carved into a rough-hewn side, a swirling shape that he couldn't parse. The monolith bobbed from their gentle impact, like a buoy.

"It's a rock, Maw," Felix groaned and held his head. Mana deprivation was sending pulses of pain in a straight line from his core to his head.

It's carved, you clod! That means mortals are nearby. Now we have to find out where, and perhaps you can navigate us out of this Blighted place.

Felix grunted and settled back against the low railing. "Is that a sigil?"

A glyph, actually, the Maw said with a tilted head. *Right. You have touched on their construction. Sigils of the Primordial Dawn. How... humorous.*

Felix rolled his eyes, wincing at the effort. Either the Maw was going to share something, or it wasn't. Either way, he refused to rise to its bait. "If it's a sigil—or a glyph—" he added with a groan. "Then it's part of some sort of magic, right? So why is there no Mana in it?"

An... astute observation. The Maw floated toward the monolith and ran its intangible fingers across the glyph. *Were it active, it would glow with the living light. The Void has drained this array.*

Felix fought against his aching Mind and Body and forced himself up. Once he started moving, the pain was a bit easier to manage. "So, if it's drained, then someone should come to refuel it, right?"

The Maw froze and turned back to Felix with an odd look. *That is not... an absurd idea.* It floated through the stone only to emerge seconds later. *One that has merit. The repository is empty, but not entirely. We have but to wait.*

It was a measure of Felix's exhaustion that he felt neither annoyance or glee at the Maw's surprise. Instead, he sank against the railing and let himself drift away.

"Ahoy the ship!"

Felix jerked away, though this time he managed to keep relatively still. He stretched his Perception outward, and could barely make out a figure in the near distance. He turned, just his head, careful to move slowly until his eyes cleared the edge of the railing.

A small...dinghy? Probably a dinghy, it floated out in the black. It was around four feet long and barely half that wide, enough for a single person to fit inside. The person inside was a Korvaa, one of those birdlike people, and what plumage could be seen beneath his plain trousers and cloak was brown and a mottled off-white. Wings hung from his back, but were obscured by his dark frock and wide collar.

He held a long pole in thin, clawed hands, with which he navigated forward. The pole was made of voidbeast bone, just as the dinghy, and had a strange organic pouch growing from the top. Each movement sent a soft ring of undifferentiated Mana spiraling outward, propelling the small craft forward a few feet at a time.

Do not mention pirates, the Maw insisted. It was hovering just behind Felix, and he twitched at the proximity. *He will doubtless overreact.*

"Ahoy the ship!" he called again, his wide, hooked beak snapping off the words. It was a curious, sharp sort of accent. "Is anyone still alive?"

Felix put up his hands, slowly. "Yes, ahem, yes we are alive!"

The Korvaa pulled up, their own craft knocking gently against the monolith. "A Human! What are you doing way out here? There isn't a Human settlement for a hundred leagues."

Felix smiled and ducked his head. "Bad luck, I suppose. I got on the wrong side of some pirates. I barely made it out of there alive."

You idiot!

Voracious Eye!

Name: Bateo

NICOLI GONNELLA

Race: Korvaa
Level: 32
HP: 1127/1127
SP: 643/994
MP: 434/0
Lore: Korvaa are highly intelligent and agile, gaining bonuses to both at each level. They are known for being relatively physically weak compared to many other Races, though they are stronger than Humans and Gnomes.
Weakness: More Data Required
Strength: More Data Required

Zero Mana total?

Deception is level 8!
Deception is level 9!

"Pirates!" Bateo squawked, and Pit perked up from his own nap. "Molt! A chimera!" The hawk-like Korvaa looked at Felix with wide eyes, his beak agape. "I can tell you've quite the story to tell, stranger."

"You don't know the half of it," Felix muttered. "I've been fleeing on this stolen ship for… days? A long time." He shook his head, clearing the cobwebs of his long, delirious sleep. "I'm lost, and I could use some help."

Bateo was quiet a moment, tapping his clawed fingers on the gray bone of his pole. Felix didn't miss that the hawkman's eyes landed on Pit more than a few times. Bateo let out a soft, helpless sigh. "I think—I think you should come with me."

"Come with you where?" Felix asked.

"To Echo's Reach. You must see the Conference."

―――

"What? What?" The Half-Orc batted away an insistent nudging and grunted. "Leave me be you blasted Elf!"

The nudging persisted.

"Alright, fine! What?"

Celaat was pointing into the distance and Bridgven was forced to push herself up onto her elbows to see over the railing. A league or so distant, the boy was being... towed away by a—was that a Korvaa?

Celaat gestured, and Bridgven groaned. "How should I know? Korvaa are rare anywhere you find 'em. Doubly so in the Void. Captain'll be ecstatic to find another."

Celaat frowned and pointed after them.

"Why are we waiting then? Let's go," she grunted and took the helm. The ship flared as her Mana trickled into it.

Silent as the Void around them, they followed.

CHAPTER EIGHTEEN

Felix looked down at his bound wrists. "Is this really necessary?"

Bateo chirruped a nervous laugh and fixed him with a single golden eye. "I'm quite sorry. But yes. It is. The community would absolutely lose their pinions if someone in a pirate vessel was allowed in without… assurances."

"I see." Felix tested the bindings, pulling slightly at them. They were made of some sort of braided leather. Out of habit, he tried to Analyze them.

Voracious Eye.

Name: Voidleather Bindings
Type: Handmade Good
Lore: Made of voidleather which has been cured for several cycles, the final product is extremely durable and comparable to tempered iron, only more flexible.

Agh, stupid Maw Skill. Felix was trying not to use it. Each time he did, it felt like the damn creature won a little bit more. *Stupid Maw.*

The Primordial had all but disappeared when Bateo had

hitched up his boat, and wasn't replying to his attempts to talk. That would have been a great development if it actually had left, but Felix knew it was simply hiding. He had been so afraid of the Maw when he'd been trapped in its vault, but now—stripped of most of its power and ability to really hurt him—Felix just felt annoyed.

He pulled at the bindings again, and they flexed slightly, enough that he was confident he could rip through them if he had to—it was the only reason he stayed bound at all. Pit, on the other hand, remained completely free.

"And they trust my friend?"

"The chimera? Of course! Why wouldn't they?" Bateo looked fairly appalled by the suggestion. "He's a chimera, and more importantly, a Tenku. Molt, but bindings on him would be extremely inappropriate."

Pit preened under the praise, and Felix was once again left with more questions.

"Well, what—"

"Ah! We have arrived!"

Felix looked ahead and saw... nothing. Yet, just as he opened his mouth to ask, the Void around them rippled like heat haze. The empty space before them was immediately filled with one of the most remarkable things he had ever seen.

"Welcome to Echo's Reach, Felix Nevarre," Bateo said with a wide gesture.

A series of floating rocks were piled between and atop one another, forming a complex network of islands connected by what looked like chains. Small craft, similar to Bateo's rowboat, floated between the islands. Felix spotted dozens of homes, all of them made of gray voidbeast bone. The shapes of the homes were rough and eclectic, with high sloping roofs and sprawling layouts. All told, the settlement was triple the size of the Ten Hand's makeshift castle.

Bateo poled them toward the settlement with greater enthusiasm. Soon they were descending down into the center of the complex, passing by several floating islands before he realized they were aiming for the largest of all the rocks seated in the very center. Resting upon the isle was something akin to a town hall, three stories high and fitted with the first windows he'd ever seen in the Void. A couple Korvaa in voidleather armor and bone spears lazed by the front steps, their wings tucked tight by their sides. They both scrambled to attention as they took note of Felix's arrival.

"Oorah, ooro? What goes, Bateo?" said one, his plumage a distinct black, blue, and white that reminded him of a magpie. "You have a... prisoner?"

"Good cycle, Hepset. I found this one lost and injured at the wardstones. He brings with him a tale for the Conference." Bateo made a brief shrug of his shoulders, which seemed similar to an informal bow of sorts. He also brings—"

"A Tenku?" cried Hepset, his dark eyes wide enough to make out the whites around them. A feat considering the iris took up nearly the entire surface. "Molted fury! You bring a— right away, right away! You! Go! Tell the Conference, and I will bring them up!"

The other guard scurried up the steps, disappearing into the portico to the sound of slamming doors.

"All this fuss. Aren't you special?" Felix murmured to Pit. The chimera threw his head back, beak up, before nuzzling against Felix's leg.

"He—the Tenku touches him? Is it under compulsion?" Hepset asked Bateo. Felix frowned but held back any words. For now.

Bateo wobbled his head, a sign Felix took for indecision. "You know I do not have Analyze. They get along, and the Human seems calm enough. This is what I know."

"Ooro. Of course. Of course." The big bird gestured to them. "Come."

Hepset led them up the stairs and into a wide, shadowed portico. There should have been no shade, as everything in the Void seemed to be lit by a sourceless light, but there it was. In fact, Felix realized the pirates also had their rooms and docks drenched in darkness that shouldn't have been possible. The answer, it turned out, was revealed to his Manasight: hidden in a panel was a small light-gathering array, which was actively absorbing the light in a set radius.

Fascinating.

Hepset led them through door after door, from foyer to antechamber to a short hallway filled with bright orbs that hovered motionless near the ceiling. Felix knew where all the light was being shunted, at least. They stopped before a large door, built wider than Felix was used to, but of standard height and made entirely of wood.

"Brace yourself, Human," Hepset said to Felix. "You will stand before the Conference of Echo's Reach. It is understandable to tremble before their might." He shoved open the doors, and Felix's eyes went wide.

A large, circular room dominated the entire floor. Thin columns held some sort of observation area along the rim of the chamber, while the left and right walls were floor to ceiling windows. Real windows, furnished with glass. Beneath them, bone slabs shone with polish or lacquer or something, so that, as they began walking, Felix's hazy double stared back up at him. Hepset led them into the center of the room, stopping several yards before the semicircular table at the far end. Four birdfolk stared at him with varying avian expressions that were all rather difficult to parse. What struck him as interesting was that each looked like a distinct bird species back home: an owl, a hawk, a raven, and a peacock.

"Lords of the Conference, please allow this one to announce the arrival of Bateo of the Rim." Hepset bowed in a stiff, formal way. One of his wings even extended outward before curling back in. "And with him is his prisoner, a Human."

Felix felt a faint pressure against his senses, as if a giant, unseen hand were pushing at his shoulder blades. Bateo and Hepset both fell to their knees, while Pit and Felix merely shared a second of confusion. The pressure kept on, trying to shove them down. *When in Rome...* Felix and Pit slowly kneeled.

"Hail and well met, Bateo of the Rim," said the peacock, his voice deep and resonant. "You have done well to bring this intruder to us immediately."

"As is my duty, Grand Detachment," Bateo said, providing them with his own winged bow.

"Just so. And this... Human. We have heard tales of pirates. Do we believe the vile creatures are after him still?"

"No, Grand Detachment. There was no sign of pursuit in the wider Void," Bateo said.

"Hmm. We have also been told he is accompanied by a Tenku." His tail quivered behind him, a fan of eyes just as a normal peacock might have. His flinty stare wavered just slightly as he beheld Pit. The tenku must have sensed Detachment's mood, as he dropped his head and let out a warbling growl. "How do we know it is not an illusion? Have you Analyzed this man?"

"No, my lord. Neither Bateo nor I possess such power," Hepset answered from the floor.

"Very well. Knowledge?" The peacock turned his blue head to their right, and a Korvaa with a round, almost fluffy head bobbed it in acknowledgment. The owl-like Korvaa reached out a clawed hand.

"Analyze. Analyze."

Felix felt something wash over him, a ripple of heat and song that coiled against his skin before snaking down into his Mana Gates. He tried to fight it off, but the force ignored him, questing down into his core space before rebounding the way it had come. He could feel it brush against Pit as well, though it was far fainter. Despite the lingering sense of violation, all of it happened in a fraction of a second.

Is that how it feels to everyone?

Fire Within is level 37!

The owl *quarked* in surprise. Detachment tilted his slender head at Knowledge. "What do you see?"

Knowledge's huge eyes blinked rapidly, and his beak clacked soundlessly for a moment. Then he gathered himself, and his feathers smoothed back. "Level 25, strong of Mind, Body, and Spirit. His Race, however, is... unknown."

Unknown? Felix fought to keep the confused frown from his own face. *But my Race is listed as Nym, just with an asterisk.*

"Unknown? To you, Knowledge?" The hawk bobbed her head in surprise. "What is it called?"

"You misunderstand, Quest. It is not that I am unaware of his Race, it is simply Unknown." The Korvaa pushed his hands forward, and every member of the Conference looked down at the empty air. He had shared his Analyze screen. "I've not seen such an occurrence in my life, though I've heard of it happening. My boy, how did you end up here in the Void?"

Felix felt six sets of eyes on him like a physical thing (guard and Bateo included), and he cleared his throat as he considered exactly what to say.

Do not mention Primordials. They will kill you. The Maw's voice drifted on the breeze, but its body was nowhere in sight. *Disobey me at your own peril.*

The contrarian in Felix wanted to shrug off the creature's advice, but he felt a certain... danger in the Conference's gaze. *Caution wouldn't be the worst path*, he reasoned with a nervous twist in his gut.

"I was exploring an ancient ruin and found a relic. I... fell. The relic transported me here, best I can tell." Felix tried to keep to the truth as best he could. He wasn't even sure it was considered Deception, and sure enough, his Skill didn't resonate at all.

"Hm, not the tale of derring-do I had expected. Were there monsters?" Knowledge asked him.

"Oh yeah, a lot. Frost Giants, actually."

"Hmm hmm," Knowledge hummed to himself. He clacked his beak twice more as he thought. "Perhaps the stress and the nature of this relic affected you. Fascinating."

"That is neither here nor there," said the hawk. Her voice

was light and airy, but there was an edge Felix could sense. She was dangerous. "What of the supposed Tenku? You have left us waiting."

"Oh. Oh! Fallen coverts, but I am sorry," Knowledge ruffled his feathers again and swiped more invisible objects at his compatriots. "Yes, the chimera is true. Before us is a Tenku."

The room went quiet for a long few minutes as the Conference traded silent looks. Felix assumed they were communicating in some way, but he had no idea. They could have simply been shocked, and they were that as well. As he'd been gathering, a Tenku was a big deal, apparently.

Detachment was the first to break their silent communion, and he cleared his throat loudly. "Honored Tenku, we welcome you to our humble community. How may we be of service in your journey?"

Pit let out a confused warble and looked at Felix.

"No need to involve the… Unknown in this," Detachment said. "It is your needs we are most concerned with addressing."

"Um, Pit can't talk with words," Felix explained, but received only annoyed stares. "We're bonded, so I can understand him, but I don't think—"

"Bonded?" Quest asked in alarm. "You *bonded* a blessed Tenku?"

"Preposterous!" Detachment squawked. "Ridiculous. No chimera would take on the Spirit of another, let alone a creature so base."

"Hey—!"

"Guards! Remove the Unknown from our presence!" The peacock flapped his wings, and out of side doors came three more Korvaa dressed in voidleather armor. They rushed him as a colorless Mana surged around their frames. Felix took to his feet and broke his bindings with a swift flex. Lightning danced along his channels.

SKREEEAAW!

A shriek pierced the chamber, and the guards stumbled to a stop. Pit had leaped forward, his huge wings spread wide and beak open. Felix repressed a gasp as cords of harsh energy burned through Pit's core.

Pit's Cry is level 25!
Congratulations! Pit Has Reached Apprentice Tier With Cry!
He Gains:
+10 STR
+10 VIT
+10 INT

Pit's Cry faltered as the stat boosts took effect, yet no one moved, guards nor the leaders behind their elevated table. Bateo looked between Pit and Felix with a clear expression of wonder.

"He saved you," Bateo whispered.

"Perhaps," said a new voice. This was the raven-like Korvaa at the far end of the semicircular council table. "Perhaps he saved us." The Korvaa tilted his head and regarded Felix with a single gray eye. "But it is clear that to attack one is to attack the other. Yes?" This time he turned his gaze to the others in the Conference.

Knowledge bobbed his head again. "Wonderment is correct. We have been too hasty!"

"And there is no coercion here?" Quest asked harshly. "No befuddlement of the Tenku's senses?"

"None that I can sense," Knowledge affirmed. "The Honored Tenku is free of all Status Conditions or afflictions."

Detachment gritted his beak, clearly unhappy, but inclined his head to the guards. For their part, they recovered from Pit's attack and stumbled back out of the room. "Then you can stay. For now."

"Tell us what the Honored Tenku wishes of us, if you please Mister Nevarre," the raven named Wonderment said, spreading his talons palms-up on the table. "If it is within our power to give, we will be happy to accommodate you both."

Felix licked his lips and lowered his hands, only belatedly realizing they were still up and ready for battle. He looked at Pit, and waves of anger, mistrust, and annoyance flowed between them. "We wish only for a place to recover, and for repairs to our ship."

"Very well. This we can manage. As the pact mate of the Honored Tenku, this Conference accepts your request for sanctuary. But," the peacock said with a raised finger. "Our little community is both hidden and modest. What bounty we have must be earned, and you must do your part to support the Reach."

"Sure, I can understand that," Felix said, pushing his suspicions out of mind.

"Excellent. Then, we have but to find a place for you. Clearly, the Honored Tenku will need to remain with us in the center of town, while the strapping Unknown may attend his… duties."

Felix didn't like that idea and had opened his mouth to say so when Wonderment let out a cawing laugh. "You think they're separated so easily, Detachment? Fool. Can't you see our Honored guest's hackles rising already?"

The birds looked at Pit, who had set his feet once again and was just as annoyed as Felix.

"Look, I'll pitch in, if that's what you need. But we're not being split up, for any reason, okay?" Felix knew he could take at least a few of them in a fight, and put as much threat as he could into that statement. However, pain immediately lanced through his Aspects, nearly sending him to his knees.

Goddamn broken Intimidation Skill!

He recovered, but Wonderment noticed. The others were too busy discussing his fate again.

"It is decided!" The peacock wailed into the chamber. His eyes looked victorious, while the owl and hawk looked worried and annoyed respectively. The raven seemed utterly disinterested. "We will ask a volunteer to take you and the Honored Tenku into their home! I submit—"

"I will take him," Bateo said.

Felix looked at him in surprise, as did everyone else. Detachment spluttered.

"Bateo? Are you sure?" Knowledge asked with concern. "The Tenku is, of course, above reproach, but this Unknown is simply that. An unknown element."

"I'm sure," the hawk-like ferryman and ward-lighter met Felix's gaze and nodded. Felix nodded back. "For the Reach."

"For the Reach," echoed the Conference. And that was that.

CHAPTER NINETEEN

"Why'd you stick your neck out for me?" Felix asked as soon as they were on their way again. "The tension in there, you could cut it with a knife. Why mix in?"

"Allow me to ask you a question in turn, Felix," Bateo said as he poled them away from the central island. They were all three crowded into his small rowboat while Felix's sloop was carted off, presumably to be repaired. "Could you have broken your restraints at any time?"

Felix nodded.

"Why didn't you?"

"You said it was important to make assurances." Felix shrugged, causing the rowboat to wobble. Pit fell into him, and he secured the Tenku around his neck and chest. "Whoa, sorry."

Bateo evened them out with another movement of his pole. He laughed nervously. "That you listened to me at all is telling, Felix. You could have killed me, I can tell. Just as I suspect those guards would have had a hard time putting you down. You allowed yourself to be bound, and every time you spoke, you chose the path of lesser suffering, even when they wanted to take the Honored Tenku away from you."

They slid between islands, and it was clear it was the equivalent of evening. People were out and about, but most were inside their homes. A few other craft similar to Bateo's were being pushed around, though the faster ones were piloted by decidedly younger Korvaa. Many of them wore colorful scarves that streamed behind them.

"The Conference spoke true," he continued. "That you have formed a mutual pact with an Honored Tenku speaks well of you and your true nature. Chimera are creatures of Harmony, after all."

They rode in silence for a while after that, both thinking their own thoughts. Felix's revolved around the number of revelations he'd had that day, namely that there were entire peoples that venerated chimeras. After spending so much time with Harn and Magda, he'd figured chimeras were universally reviled due to the defensive illusion on the Foglands. It made them look like abominations, even if they were just a big puppy.

Pit nestled closer, curling around Felix's legs as he tried to sleep again.

Echo's Reach and their rulers were strange. Clearly, they were on guard against pirates and other violent creatures, and Felix couldn't blame them for their caution. After what he'd seen with the Ten Hands, if anything, they weren't being cautious enough.

"What do the wards do?" Felix asked.

"The outer wards? They're a repulsion for voidbeasts."

"Voidbeasts? Like all of them?" Felix asked. Would it keep the Whalemaw out? They clearly did nothing for people.

"In general, but our main concern are Harrowings. They prey on our livestock and cause all manner of chaos," Bateo said. He poled beyond the last chained island and off into the greater dark. "You've likely encountered them, no?"

Felix nodded. "And the inner wards? They screen you from sight?"

"Something like that," Bateo said. "I can't say much on the inner defenses. We Rimfolk only take care of the outer wards, and even then, it's typically left to the strongest of us. Which means me."

Strongest? At level 32? How low-leveled are the rest of them? "Are the folks in the center stronger?" he asked.

"Some. The Conference Leaders, absolutely. In levels and core formation, they're head and crest feathers above anyone else." Bateo gave him a sideways look. "Why do you ask?"

Felix shrugged. "Like I said, I ran into the pirates. They were something else entirely."

Deception is level 10!

"Aye, I believe you. We've stayed out of their sights for many centuries now, no matter the roving gang." Bateo made a circular gesture with a talon. "Hallah's grace that we remain so."

The blackness of the Void slipped past them, and Felix was left to his thoughts. Those thoughts lingered around strength, as had his words. Before they had left the Conference chambers, Felix had risked using his own Voracious Eye. What he got back was a smattering of details that didn't make much sense.

The leaders all had levels in the forties true enough, but they felt weak in a way Felix couldn't put a finger on. Moreover, they all had zero Mana capacity, which as far as he understood was impossible. Willpower and Intelligence governed your maximum Mana, and he'd never met anyone with zero in those stats, let alone multiple people.

All in all, it left him a bit cold. There were too many things that didn't add up, and Felix couldn't be sure of where he stood. Wonderment, at the very least, seemed to like him.

I'll take what I can get.

After a while in the black, they came to a series of stone islands easily as large as the ones in the center of the settlement. There were only three, held together by those same chains that Felix recognized were made of braided void leather. Atop the three islands stood a series of odd structures, the largest of which looked remarkably like a farmhouse, albeit one on high stilts. The design and general aesthetic made Felix think of some sort of elaborate tree house.

Or was he just thinking that because they were bird people?

They landed in short order at the base of the farmhouse, and Felix quickly recognized pens and cages containing the shadowed forms of some sort of beast. Bateo *was* a farmer, but owned less produce and more livestock.

"Welcome Felix and Honored Tenku, to my home," the smallish Korvaa gestured and let his wings spread outward. "It is a small farm by the measure of such things, but it is enough for me."

There was a squeal of delight from up above. "Papa! Papa's home!"

The clatter of talons on bone stairs and a rapid, hummingbird style flapping of wings followed the voice, until a fuzzy lump tackled Bateo. A second and third soon followed, along with joyful screaming and a gaggle of giggles. Small birdlings clung to Bateo's body, their wings beating so fast they were a blur, while Bateo laughed in delight.

"Girls! Where in Avet's name—oh! Kili, Nell, Jain! You'll strangle your father like that!" A rounder Korvaa with similar hawk colorations as Bateo stepped out of a door on a higher level. "Dear me, you're finally home! And—with guests."

"Yes, beloved, the Conference Lords had questions for us both," Bateo said as he carefully set the three Korvaa children back down onto the ground. They clung to him like velcro, however, and merely wrapped around his legs instead of his arms and neck. Bateo sighed, happily. "It has been a long day."

"I would say so! You've not set foot on this farm since before cycle-break," the female Korvaa said in a tone that sat comfortably between annoyance and relief. She walked down the winding steps, one wing spread slightly to keep her balance as she hoisted two other children on her hip. Like the others, they all looked to be vaguely five or six years old, but Felix had no clue. "And here we are, end of cycle nearly in sight."

"Ah, beloved, you know I'd have been home sooner if I could've," Bateo began, but his wife cut him off with a gentle hand on his cheek.

"When the lords call, we answer," she said before turning her delicate beak toward Felix. "And who is your guest?"

"Beloved, this is Felix Nevarre, a wanderer who has recently been lost in the Void. Felix, this is my wife, Estrid."

Felix extended his hand and the woman looked at it with a tilted head for a brief moment before grasping it. They shook. "Nice to meet you, Estrid. Your husband did me a solid, letting me stay here, and I promise not to be a burden."

"Stay? Bateo," his wife said with a gasp.

The farmer yelped and quickly gestured to Felix's side. "And this is Pit, an Honored Tenku and pactmate to Felix."

Estrid's gasp turned from annoyance to pure joy. "What? Oh my pinions, it's true."

Pit smacked his beak and blinked blearily at the woman, his bright golden eyes still sleepy. When Estrid's hand came out to touch him, he simply leaned into it and accepted the soft scratches along his crest.

"Bright day, but this is a blessing," she said. She looked up at Felix and her eyes glimmered with unshed tears. "How?"

"That, I think, is a story best told over dinner," Bateo said.

Felix smiled. "That's the best thing I've heard today."

Dinner was a long affair of shouting children and interrupted conversation. Felix had come to learn that folks that had Tempered their Body needed less food than usual, but that didn't stop their appetites. Both Estrid and Bateo said they were in the upper reaches of Apprentice Tier. Course after course were carried out from the kitchen, each one featuring meat, meat, and more meat. What little there was in the way of vegetables were mushroom-like fungi and anemic-looking tubers. Bateo explained that they threw both the *paroo* and *cnop* on the third island, but yields were typically small. Unsurprising in a dimension without a sun or soil. Felix was amazed he was able to grow anything.

The meat, of course, was voidbeast meat. Unlike the pirates' gamey and tough preparation, this was extremely tender and flavored with various sauces. Unable to restrain his curiosity, he used his Voracious Eye and saw it wasn't Harrowing as the pirates had served, but Tenebril.

Estrid noticed Felix's clear enjoyment and snorted at the snuffling sounds coming from Pit. "I'm glad to see my food is appreciated," she said with a fond smile at the tenku. She looked back up to Felix. "The both of you eat like you've not seen a meal in years. What happened to you?"

Felix didn't entirely know how to answer that, so he started at the beginning. As always, he edited out being Unbound and Nym, as well as the more sensitive topics. He spoke of the Frost Giants, of the ruined city of the Geist, of the Labyrinth and… a heavily redacted version of what he found within. It ended with the same story he told the Conference, of an accident with an artifact. The Void and the pirates came next, along with hordes of voidbeasts that all wanted to eat him. And then his escape and fortunate encounter with Bateo.

"And that brings you up to date on my history," Felix said.

"You've lived a remarkable life for one so young," Estrid said. "Tragic that it ended with you here."

Felix couldn't help but agree, but he was working on fixing that. He shoved the last piece of meat into his mouth and couldn't help a pleased groan. "This is so good. I feel like it's bringing me back to life."

Estrid giggled. Bateo had left a minute or so ago to put the kids to bed. He'd already heard the more recent bits. "As well it should. That Mana marinade is a technique of my mother's."

"Mana—" Felix paused and studied the thick juices still left on his bone plate. They shimmered faintly in the magelight above them.

Voracious Eye!

Name: Mana Reduction
Type: Food (enchanted)
Lore: A technique of those that live in the Void, it uses a creature's own Mana stores to flavor its cooked flesh.
Effect: Mana Regeneration +5%

Sure enough, his Mana was ticking up faster than before. Nowhere near his old capability while on the Continent, but still. "Wow. Mana Regeneration increased by five percent."

"It is the only way we can stay ahead of the Void's constant hunger for Mana. Eat the bladders of voidbeasts and take on the unfiltered Mana they've collected." Estrid raised a feathered eyebrow. "But you've an Analyze Skill? That's rare out here. So many have focused on Skills that keep them alive."

"I've found information has kept me alive more often than a better way to punch something," Felix said.

"Oh I don't mean offensive Skills. Those are mostly useless in the Void unless you're a Rim Hunter. No I mean Farming, Husbandry, or even Butchery. Things that keep a homestead alive through the lean times." Estrid shook her head, and the feathers along her neck lifted in agitation. "Not that there is anything but lean times. And it grows leaner by the cycle."

"We will survive," Bateo said as he came back in. He put his hands on his wife's shoulders and gave her head a peck. "The hatchlings are tucked away, dreaming sweet dreams."

"If only we could share those dreams," Estrid said as she leaned into Bateo's taloned hand. "The Void is harsh, and it only grows more desolate. Dreams would be nice."

"We will survive," Bateo repeated. "Our farms provide food, the Hunters protect us, and the Conference looks continuously for a way home. As always."

"A way home?" Felix asked. That certainly perked his attention, and even Pit poked his curious head above the level of the table.

"The true purpose of the Conference is to look for the pathway that led us here, once upon a time." Bateo settled in his chair at the head of the table and his wings flexed, like a tired man stretching his arms. "An Age ago or more, our people traversed the Passages betwixt Realms in order to flee a terrible enemy. The enemy was wily, however, and used its eldritch might to curse us. The Passages failed us, and the Void took its due. None of those who fled our home still live, but the tale is passed down generation after generation, so that we may never forget and never keep seeking a way back."

The Korvaa smiled, an expression that hinged open his beak and stretched just the corners of his mouth. "Who knows how much is true, but the Conference uses the knowledge of our ancestors to verify it. One day, we will all be free." Bateo slapped his knees and stood up again. "But until then, we've sleep to take. Tomorrow is a busy day, and I'll have you with me if you don't mind, Felix."

"Oh, no that's fine. Like I said, I plan to earn my keep." Felix stood up and thanked them both again for the excellent meal. Estrid waved off his words, but her eyes were delighted. Bateo led him out of the main level, up several flights of stairs and into a small attic. It wasn't much bigger than his studio apartment back on Earth, but at least there was a nest of blankets and pillows on the floor and a large window along one triangular shaped wall.

"It's not much, but Estrid has given you what we could. Rest well. I will wake you just before the new cycle begins." Bateo nodded to him and significantly deeper to Pit, before turning to leave.

"Bateo?"

"Hmm?"

"Thank you. From both of us."

The Korvaa ducked his head and scratched a shoulder. "You are… very welcome."

CHAPTER TWENTY

Though he had a bed and privacy, Felix found it difficult to sleep. It wasn't that Pit snored loud enough to wake the dead, or that he didn't trust Bateo—not entirely, at least—but mostly it was that he'd slept a lot on the sloop while they were drifting. It hadn't been the most restful sleep, but it reset his internal clock all the same. So, as the hours ticked by, Felix got to work.

The first few hours were devoted to the painful job of closing his Mana Gates. His two palms were done, and over those two hours he'd managed to close not one, but both elbow Gates. It hurt like hell, but he did it. Felix was still getting the hang of opening and closing them, or keeping them closed as needed, but his proficiency grew at least a little. By the time he was moving down to his right foot, he almost felt like he knew what he was doing.

Of course, that was when the Maw reappeared.

"Where have you been?" he asked, eyeing the listless way the Primordial was floating through his cramped room.

Investigating.

"Investigating what? Tenebril farming?" Felix half-laughed.

When the creature didn't respond right away, he grew even more suspicious than normal. "Investigating what?"

Do you not find it curious, Felix Nevarre? That the one you found you, who engendered a meager speck of trust within your breast, that one was he who took you in? How outlandish. Those birds are plotting, and this one, this farmer *is in on it.* The Maw sneered. *Him and his tiny brats.*

Felix snorted a relieved laugh. "Bateo and his family are the least of my concerns," he said as he stood from his nest of blankets. The room spun, just a little.

You've used too much Mana. Your stores are low.

"They're climbing fast enough," Felix said. "Faster than anyone else out here. Did you know that most of them have no Mana total at all?"

Mhm. The Void has poisoned their core spaces. Not completely, but enough that it leeches any Mana they dare try to absorb.

"Bateo said he was born here, and that his people have been looking for a way out for an entire Age." Felix toyed with the rough spun blanket.

A likely story. If it were true, then they've never had Mana at all, except what they steal from these beasts, the Maw said in disdain.

"Don't you do the same thing? Isn't Ravenous Tithe literally that?"

We secure the power of our enemies and turn it against them. That is the prerogative of the predator over the prey!

"Mhm," Felix said absently. It was a measure of the weirdness in his life that he was able to respond so casually to an insane Primordial that had been grafted onto his soul. Yet he couldn't quite help it; whenever the Maw devolved into rhetoric about "predators" and stuff, he kinda zoned out.

Deep Mind is level 31!

Felix jolted to his senses and cast a suspicious look at the Maw. The creature was floating near the triangular apex of the ceiling, inspecting the pale, lifeless bone of its construction. It had lapsed into silence. Had it done something to trigger that Skill level? Felix brought up the Skill's description.

Deep Mind (Epic), Level 31!
You have delved deeper into the mind than most, traveling upon a dark confluence of truth and perception. Increases Resonance per Skill Level, increases potency of mental Skills by a moderate amount per Skill Level.

No clue what makes it stronger, other than mental... duress. Felix thought on his first meeting with the Maw, where his Bastion of Will and Deep Mind kept rising in level the longer it spoke. At the time, it was toying with him attempting to befuddle him and lure Felix into agreeing to be its Vessel. And now...

Now I am a Vessel, just not how it wanted. I have to assume it's gonna keep trying to take control. He looked at the Skill description once again. *And I have to assume that it did* something *to provoke that level.*

Felix took a breath, and with an awkward twist of his Perception, he fell inward. Into the dark space just below his rib cage and above his navel.

His core space.

It emerged from the darkness, a burning star set upon the black. His core. It was a blue-white star of flames and crackling lightning, immobile in his center but whirling nevertheless. Farther out were bright patterns of light in varying colors and sizes and intensities, each strung out in concentric circles around his core. Each light, a Skill. He had never seen them all so clearly, likely due to his increases in Fire Within. He fell until he hovered just before the enormous, raging inferno, just out of touch of his nearest Skill. Armored Skin, it turned out; not the one he wanted.

Where is it?

The distances were fuzzy, murky even, not resembling the Void so much as a brackish lake filled with grit and debris. His core itself was the clearest, the most defined, as were those Skills closest to it. Felix peered at them.

Stone Shaping. Influence of the Wisp. Unarmed Mastery. Every Skill I Tempered into Apprentice Tier—that I used in my Formation—they're the closest ones. He drifted toward them as they floated sedately within his miniature solar system. *Higher leveled Skills are closer too, like they're... getting more sustenance from my core.*

Felix looked around, peering through the murk and found one of his newest Skills: Abyssal Skein. It hovered in the middle distance, twisting on itself like a maze. As a Rare Skill, it was a decently large pattern, complex certainly, but it wasn't its rarity or level that made it strange. It was a Void Skill, his first, and it seemed to... drink in the dark. Felix squinted, for all that he was within his own vision, but the particulars of Abyssal Skein's pattern were impossible to parse. It flickered, almost vanishing before resettling in its former position.

Felix turned away, unable to bear looking at it any longer.

Is that what happens with everyone's core in the Void? It grows strange and... glitchy?

He'd have to ask Bateo, though he suspected the birdman likely wouldn't answer. It seemed the sort of thing people would keep close to their chest.

Felix pivoted away from Abyssal Skein and caught sight of another disconcerting pattern: Acrobatics. Unlike Abyssal Skein it didn't glitch, but it did spark, like exposed live wires. The pattern of the Skill was disrupted, severed almost, as if a series of claws had torn through it. Looking at it was painful, like a visual migraine, and Felix quickly averted his gaze. Others were out there, ten others that had been damaged by the Maw.

Anger and fear pulsed through Felix, both impotent in a way he'd grown uncomfortably used to—there was nothing he could do about them. Not unless the birds knew something about fixing broken Skills.

Thanks to having a considerable Will, Felix was easily able to force himself away from that line of thought. It wasn't productive, not at the moment. He returned to his original purpose. *Deep Mind, Deep Mind, where are you?*

As if it heard him, the Skill pulled into sight, closely followed by his Bastion of Will. Both were patterns of exceptional size, not the largest—that honor belonged to Etheric Concordance—but of considerable complexity. They also both dealt with the Mind and were as good a place to start as any.

Okay. Deep Mind. Does it look different? Would I notice? Felix thought as he drifted closer to its folding whorls of light. Pulses in regular rhythms shot down the pattern, knots of light that were followed by the barest of humming. It was a song—a vibration, really—as much as a shape, flaring to a crescendo when he activated his Skills. That process was automatic, though, a thought trigger pumping Mana through the Skill, his channels, and out into the world through his Mana Gates. Only recently had he started following the pattern, altering it slightly with a few of his Skills. *Deep Mind is a passive Skill, reactive. So, can I follow the pattern? See why it changed?*

It was worth a shot. The perception that was "him" in his visualized core space floated closer, until Deep Mind took up all of his vision. It loomed like an actual planet made of textured ribbons of light, hollow but huge. Felix grasped at his Affinity, the Harmonic Stat that was all about sensing the music that seemed to underlay the world.

Affinity - Affects empathy and connection with the Harmonies. Confluence of Vitality and Perception.

At only 60 points, it was far weaker than most of his Primary Stats. At first, he heard only the omnipresent hum— the only thing he could perceive this close to the Skill—but as he tested the parts of it, it began to resolve into something steady and deep. Dark, full tones rolled beneath a glissando of lighter notes, hinting at… secrets. Felix couldn't explain that thought and didn't try, he simply listened. Followed the pattern.

Until it stopped.

He'd reached the center of the Skill, of the etchings all around him. Light pulsed and traced in a kaleidoscopic display, but there it did not touch him. There was a profound silence there, insulating, empowering. Felix felt... more. If he focused, he could even see beyond the Skill, out into the dark of his spinning core. All the gunk and flotsam that drifted in the hazy shadows between Skills and his burning sun came into sharp relief.

Fire Within is level 37!

Oh jeez. Gross. He recoiled from the sight of the brackish debris, and at the same time felt a tight pull on his being. Space rushed around him, and he was suddenly outside Deep Mind again.

Deep Mind is level 32!

Confluence of truth and perception, huh? Felix was of the mind that the rarer Skills got, the more obtuse their function became. Which... made sense. Harn had said the Beginner Tier of power was easy to muscle through by simple repetition and training. Apprentice Tier was harder, requiring a deeper understanding of one's Skills. So clearly, he'd just learned something. *Sure wish I knew what, though. I can't—Oh.*

Felix looked at Deep Mind again, and at the dark around it. Dark that so resembled the Void outside. Was that intentional? If his core space was created subconsciously, how did he know to add in the Void? Coincidence or not, his Deep Mind was trying to parse something about his space, and maybe even about the Void itself.

It's pushing against the Void? Since it's passive, maybe it's always running in the background then, always trying to delve deeper.

Deep Mind is level 33!

Delve for what though? A secret—?

What are you doing, Felix Nevarre?

"Ahh!" Felix shouted internally and externally as he rapidly oscillated between the real and the envisioned worlds. The Maw loomed over him in both, entirely too close for his comfort. "Back the hell up!"

The creature fixed him with a gimlet eye before tilting itself backwards. Felix leaped to his feet and took a step backward for good measure.

"I don't ever want you that close," he panted. His pulse thundered in his neck and temple, and Felix fought to rein back his emotions. "Understand?"

Were you within your core space? The Maw floated down until it was only inches above the attic floor. *I could hear the vibrations. It was... disconcerting.*

"Good to know." The Maw clearly didn't care to listen to Felix, so finding things that discomfited it were the next best thing. "I'll make sure to try it again when you're being a pain in my ass."

Petulant child. I am trying to help you.

"You have a funny way of helping, Maw. I was looking at my core space. You interrupted."

The Maw scoffed. *Your core space. You envisioned a strange, floating dance. It is inscrutable, an emptiness littered with detritus. A pathetic attempt.*

"That's outer space. Sorta. It's a solar system."

A what?

"A solar... You know the sun? It has—where I'm from, it has planets that revolve around it."

Madness, the Maw scoffed. *No wonder your planet is so broken. That it would produce Unbound is a marvel that I cannot answer. All revolves around this world, from the stars in the heavens to the shuddering depths of the Realms. We are held aloft by the Will of those that came before, the Primordials of the Dawn. What holds* your *pathetic marble in place? What prevents it from hurling into the Void?*

"Uh, gravity?" Felix said, nonplussed. He tried to keep track of the crazy the Maw spewed, but it was getting a bit much.

Gravity... what is this? The Maw's face twisted. *It has the taste of more nonsense.*

"What? No, it's a natural law," Felix said. "Been a while since physics class, but anything with mass creates its own gravitational pull. So if you get something big enough, like a planet, then it has its own gravity. It's why people on the Continent don't fly off into the sky as the planet spins."

And you say your Earth slings around your sun? How does your ball of mud not dominate the star? It is not the path of the greater to dance for the lesser.

"Uh, well. The sun's a lot bigger than earth. It can fit like," Felix felt the memory surge into his Mind, fully formed, of a scientist with a bowtie explaining a great many things. "One point three million Earths inside it, if it were hollow."

That is indeed large. Suspiciously so. Why would the sun not destroy your Earth, with it in its thrall?

"So because it's so big, it has a lot of gravity. The sun holds the earth and a bunch of other planets in orbit around it, and the opposing forces create paths that the planets travel on. At least, that's my understanding of it, and I guess that's what I drew on when I made my core space." Felix scratched the back of his head. "It was all instinct, really, just ideas on top of one another and then bam: there it is."

How... fanciful, the Maw said, but the derision in its voice had faded. Instead it was staring into Felix's midsection as if dissecting him. *Then you must embrace that idea. Turn your errant madness into power. Your core space, and your progress in the Visualization Stage relies on the potency of your Mind. Lucky for you, you have your Fire Within, which is a Skill designed to aid such growth.*

"Really?" Felix considered the pattern for Fire Within that floated through his core space. "That seems convenient."

It truly is not. You fought tooth and nail for that Skill, nearly dying beside that waterfall. That you latched onto the fledgling flame of your core was an inspired choice... and an astounding stroke of luck. Embrace that luck, use the fruits of it to your advantage, and seize what lies before you.

Felix glanced at the Maw, noting its stolen features were twisted into an uncomfortably intense expression of rapture. Its words, in turn, felt less like good advice and more like the guidance of a wild cat on the hunt.

Don't give me that look, Felix Nevarre. You are as much a killer as anyone.

Felix frowned. He had killed, but only when there was little other choice. The Continent and the Void had rarely given him other options. What he didn't like, however, was the look of satisfaction on the Maw's face. Like it was proud of him.

Your core space, inferior though it is, has… potential. You must clarify it, however. It drew itself up until the Primordial looked down its nose at him. Its voice reverberated with a dire promise, with temptation that picked at Felix's heart. *Only I can aid you there. Only my Ages of experience will catapult you into the realms of power that is your destiny.*

Bastion of Will is level 43!

"No thanks," Felix said simply. The echo in the Primordial's words cut off mid-thought, like someone had cut its mic. The creature's odd spell defanged, the Maw's face cycled through disbelief and then smoldering outrage. With a smirk, Felix dropped back into his core space. It had given him an idea.

His descent was rapid this time, a mere blurring of his surroundings, and Felix was there beside his burning core. His Bastion of Will was in the closest orbit, being so highly leveled, and without pause, he dove into its twisting pattern.

Unlike the others, his Bastion was special. Perhaps the construction of his core space affected its appearance, for as he passed into the Skill, it was as if he were truly entering the atmosphere above a planet. Gray skies and low, scudding clouds swirled around Felix as he descended. Below spread a field of gray grasses, rocky mountains, a dark forest, and a green, steaming sea. And in the center of it all, a squared fortress that had seen better days.

Felix landed atop the lone, central tower. It was square-shaped but listing slightly to the side, Tower of Pisa style. The battlements that surrounded the inner bailey were ragged and broken in several places, and several of the crenelations had been sheared off. The place had suffered extensively during his fight with the Maw, when he attempted to resist her takeover. That struggle had transferred to his Bastion when the acid seas had risen, carrying horrors to his walls. Now the water had receded, though not entirely back to its original place. The damage had stopped, but there hadn't been any healing. The earth itself was ruptured, the grass dead between gaps of exposed loam.

His Bastion had just protected him from another manipulation attempt by the Maw. How many had he missed because his mental fortress was in disrepair?

The air whined slightly, distorting with a pale crimson as the Maw manifested. A strain of atonal chords speared across Felix's senses, enough to make him recoil against his tower. The Maw's thin body stumbled slightly as his Skill's gravity suddenly affected its immaterial form, and it hissed in displeasure. *Remarkable that you didn't lose this Skill as well. You see what I did, just by stepping into the domain of your Spirit? The damage I was able to wreak? While I am a peerless power, even lesser beings can achieve the same with enough Will, Intent, and potency. You have but to seek clarity. In all things.*

Felix looked the Maw up and down. "How do I do that?"

You strengthen it, reinforcing it with your Spirit and Mind and Body.

"Hm," he said, noncommittally. Inside, he was already planning, flipping through plans that formed in his Mind. Angles against the monster in his brain. "I see."

The Maw opened its mouth once more, perhaps to press its point, but suddenly closed it. Instead, it simply watched him.

This is going to be difficult, he thought.

CHAPTER TWENTY-ONE

Felix's attempts at repairing his Bastion of Will went poorly at first. He hopped down to the broken inner bailey, an area dominated by a grassy field that had been ripped by what looked like massive claws, and set about moving the massive blocks of stone. The smallest were three feet across, while the majority were all six foot square blocks of dark granite. Lifting them was awkward and difficult, both because getting a grip on them was almost impossible, and also their weight. It was only his overconfidence in his Strength that he even tried, but while he might be able to punch them apart, given time, lifting them in one go was an effort in sweat and exhaustion.

All in all, it took him four hours to move thirteen blocks from the inner bailey up onto the outer walls. That included building a rudimentary staircase using the less uniform stones, which wasn't the best plan. He fell seventeen times, nearly crushing himself three times, and tore a muscle in his left shoulder that hurt like hell. But Felix didn't give up, and his Endurance let him continue long beyond the time a normal human's body would have died from exhaustion.

The blocks were set upon the battlements, roughly shoved

up against one another in the absence of any sort of mortar. Felix wiped sweat from his brow and surveyed his work. The wall was fixed... ish. At the very least, one of the four walls no longer had a gaping hole in it—just a number of much smaller holes. The sky was still gray and the grass still dead, but maybe the wind smelled a little sweeter. Maybe.

You are going about this incorrectly, Felix Nevarre, the Maw interjected. It had been lingering near Felix the entire time, but he'd chosen to ignore the Primordial's unnerving gaze until it decided to attack him. Now he looked at it with all the weight of someone who had sweat through their shirt, was lightheaded, and was very hungry. Ravenous, even.

"I don't need your advice, Maw."

Yes, you do. If you plan to achieve anything, you need me. Alone, you are nothing.

"Nothing? If that means being alone, without you? I'll take it," Felix snapped, before tuning the creature out altogether. He checked his Bastion's level, but it remained the same. Unchanged despite his work. However, he did have a few other notifications.

+1 STR
+1 END
+1 AGL

Interesting.

It wasn't exactly a surprise; he had learned weeks ago that the higher his stats rose, the more effort was required to improve them through resistance training. So until he could, like, bench press a car somehow, he was limited—

Now that's an idea. I'm too tired now, but later I could—Wait... what am I thinking? This isn't reality. This isn't my real body. Flexing his Will, Felix returned to the Void, expecting to see his changes dissipate... and yet they did not. His shoulder even ached exactly where he'd strained it in his Bastion. "What?"

Confused, Unbound? The Maw said, and Felix didn't even have to look at it to know it had a smug grin on its stupid face. *I could enlighten you, if you wish.*

"Hard pass," Felix said with a scowl.

Then be prepared to never know, imbecile. Stagnate in your ignorance!

Felix ignored it. Instead, he put his supposedly impressive Tempered Mind to the task, calling up everything he knew about Skills, core space, and his Aspects.

What is core space? Harn and... and Magda didn't really talk about it, he thought. *But they also mentioned Tempering was kept a secret from many trainees in the Beginner Tier, or at least the specifics. Would they also keep the nature of core space a secret, too?* He snorted. *Who am I kidding, of course they would. Everything is a secret technique or hidden training plan to get stronger than the other guy.*

He just had to consider Atar for proof of that. The guy was stuck up and useless in a physical fight, but he'd developed his Skills and Aspects in a way that supported his impressive firepower. What Titles did he have that helped that out? What was his Born Trait? Secrets on secrets.

Felix shook his head and abandoned that line of thought. It led nowhere useful. He returned to the original question. *What is core space?* Then a memory resurfaced, a conversation with the Maw. *It's a confluence of my Aspects, all of them combined together, just like the Mana Gates. Body, Mind, and Spirit all exist in the core space, which means... which means each one can be affected? Even in imagined training?*

Felix tapped his lips for a moment before closing his eyes. He didn't cast himself down into his core space, but instead put together a daydream. Pure fantasy, all in his head, he thought of fighting against Skinks back in the Foglands. After a second, he backtracked and made it voidbeasts. They were less scary.

Yet, no matter how he fought or what Skills he used in his daydream, there were no improvements, no stat increases. He felt no strain when he lifted a mountain in his Mind's eye. It wasn't real.

So...my core space is real? Everything that happens there is just as real as what happens out here? He huffed a surprised laugh. *How? That's insane.*

He was pretty sure the answer was "magic," but that was annoyingly non-helpful. His eyes flicked to the Maw, and its stolen face looked at first troubled before settling back into disdain.

Felix very nearly dove back into his core space, intent on checking a few other things, when he knew that Bateo needed him. There was no voice, no build up of call and response, just a sudden and unquestionable knowledge that the hawk-like Korvaa was downstairs and waiting. For a moment, Felix even felt a light twinge of need, as if his own voice was telling him to get up and walk down the stairs. That ended with a flare of Willpower and Alacrity, his Harmonic Stat for mental feats of strength. Whatever Skill was being used on him cut out, hitting the wall of his Will and folding like a paper airplane.

Though it failed, Felix was not a fan. It wasn't a particularly strong coercion, but anything that touched his Mind was off limits. He'd reserve judgment, for now, but if that happened again, they were gonna have a talk.

"Pit? You gonna wake up, bud?" The tenku merely grunted melodically at him and rolled over, even going so far as to extend a wing over his face. Felix snorted, but stopped short of a real laugh. "Oh, I'm sorry, your highness. I'll let you take your rest."

If he were being honest, Felix was a bit more tired than he expected. His head was even a touch dizzy, but that could have been because of a number of things. Pushing his discomfort aside, he made to stand up, but found his legs as wobbly as a newborn foal. Tremors shook through him, setting his muscles trembling under the modest strain. "Whoa, whoa... why... why do I feel so weak?" Felix asked in an unsteady breath. His eyes found the Maw's again, and this time it had a sneer ready and waiting for him.

Do you still not need my aid, Felix Nevarre? Or would you rather rely on your own... Strength?

SILENCE

Felix glowered at the Primordial and forced himself to his feet. It was painful and difficult, but he did it. He felt at his bond with Pit, but the chimera seemed entirely fine, if sleepy. No trace of the weakness Felix felt. Pride and stubbornness managed to fuel Felix's walk out of his room. He even made it down the first flight of stairs before his knees gave out completely.

What the hell is going on?

Felix had started to panic. His stats were unaffected, he had no Status Condition, and his Health and Stamina were both only a few points shy of full. Nothing was wrong with him, except he felt weak as a newborn baby, and his pulled muscle was a white hot pain that took all his concentration to withstand. His Body, Mind, and Spirit felt sore and strained, his core space—

It feels… empty?

Dipping down there for only a moment, Felix realized the grimy darkness between his floating Skills was somehow *less*. It made no sense, since it was basically just trash-filled nothing in the first place, but the feeling was potent just the same. Everything else seemed normal, save that one of his Skills was flickering with a fitful light.

Ravenous Tithe. The Skill I learned when the Maw stole my Gourmand Title and Lessons of the Past Skill. When my Godeater Mind took a bite out of the Primordial itself.

Ravenous Tithe (Epic), Level 2!
Consume completely an object or creature which you have claimed and can physically touch. Uses Mana to power conversion. Chance of gaining Skills and/or Memories from target if applicable.

The Skill itself looked as if it were going to blink out at any moment; a neon light on its last legs. If Felix wasn't mistaken, its pattern almost looked like it was reaching out. Attempting to grasp the darkness around it and… do something to it. Sparks gathered at the edges of his vision before a notification snaked across his senses.

Ravenous Tithe is level 3!

A wave of sound rushed from the murky depths around him, traveling horizontally as a brilliant tide of colorless energy. It swept through his Skills and Felix, leaving them untouched as it proceeded to strike the ball of flame at the center of his core space. The sun flared and bubbled, releasing scorching prominences of blue-white flame before a ring of golden-azure light exploded outward. The new light soaked into his core space, all of it directed right at his Ravenous Tithe Skill. Its grasping pattern pulled at the light, hungry for it, until it was consumed entirely.

Just like that, his legs regained their strength and his skin ceased tingling. He was fine.

Somehow.

Great. More mysteries. Felix groaned. Ravenous Tithe was providing him a sort of energy, and likely... that came from eating monsters, like the Harrowing. *Did I just not have enough of it left after learning Abyssal Skein? And it just*—Felix's eyes widened as some combination of Intelligence and his Apprentice Mind snapped the puzzle together—*it used my own power to fuel my growth. Which is why I felt so weak!*

Felix put his hand to his head, considering the implications. There were quite a few, but ultimately it meant that he had to eat. And more than just breakfast.

Felix furrowed his brow at the stairs. *But first, we talk to Bateo.*

If Bateo had been surprised at how long it had taken Felix to come downstairs, he didn't show it. The farmer was sipping a steaming cup of *saf*, which was the local approximation of coffee or tea. Felix passed on a cup after sniffing it nearly burned out the inside of his nose. The food, however, he more than happily devoured. Again, it was a lot of voidbeast meat, but this time mixed with a decent amount of the potato-like *cnop* until it was basically a sort of hash.

It was very good.

Status Condition: Mana Regeneration II!
Mana Regeneration II - 10% boost to Mana Regeneration for the next three hours.

Huh. That'll be useful. His Mana ticked ever closer to full.

Health: 860/864
Stamina: 871/873
Mana: 1311/1458

Felix almost felt normal, a far cry from his Ravenous Tithe-induced weakness just minutes before. It was a relief.

"Come, Felix. You might only be here until your boat is fixed, but until then you'll need to know how things work," Bateo said. He beckoned him out onto the large, covered porch. There they could see over all three islands that comprised the Korvaa's farm. The two smaller islands floated lower and were chained to the central "home" island they stood upon, and the raised nature of the house meant they had quite the vantage point. "Before you is all my family has built over the course of generations. The lower island contains the pens and grazing grounds for the voidbeasts, while the higher has our limited crops and storage."

"What about the cages I saw beneath the house?" Felix asked.

"Those are for any wild voidbeasts we might find," Bateo said with a wistful look in his eye. Korvaan expressions were difficult to read, but Felix was warming up to it. Lacking a truly flexible mouth, it had a lot to do with posture, feather "fluffiness," and their eyes. "The wards aren't perfect. Nothing that relies on Mana is in the Void. So, we lure new stock when we can. Tenebril, Skeeling, or even the smaller Vroll are easy enough to capture if they come around."

"If they come around? I've seen packs of the Tenebril out there," Felix said. "I'd think you'd see more than a few if you're placing out food for them."

"Predators are picking off more and more, and—" Bateo let out a sharp squawk. "Harrowings. They're the bane of any voidfarmer. They strike from the dark, invisible until they've already slaughtered half your herd." Bateo shook himself, ruffling the feathers around neck and shoulder. "Come, come. I'll show you your duties."

Those duties were to first check on their crops, which apparently required a lot of attention. The potato-adjacent *cnop* and mushroom-like *paroo* grew in neat rows atop the second island, which covered an expanse the size of a Little League baseball diamond. Not massive compared to Earth farms, but more than impressive in the Void. At first, Felix was utterly confused how anything was able to grow on the barren rocks of the Void, but the answer was both remarkably simple and confusing: the System.

Bateo possessed a number of Skills that would have made Earth farmers drool: Summon Water, Humus Among Us, and Encourage Growth. The first did just as it said on the tin, and was able to manifest water from nothing but Bateo's core and channels. Using it and two spare Manabladders to recharge his Mana, Bateo was able to water all of his crops as efficiently as any irrigation system.

The second Skill, Humus Among Us—apart from having a name that made him laugh—would somehow break rock down into nutrient-rich soil. The last was more esoteric, at least as far as Felix was concerned. Bateo explained it as using his Mana to gently coax his plants to grow more efficiently, even without any sunlight.

Not that mushrooms need sunlight, if I recall correctly, he thought. *But potatoes do... right?*

SILENCE

"My truest dream is to plant a tree," Bateo said later. His eyes almost glittered at the thought of it. "I've heard so many tales of the Continent, of the sun and winds and water from the sky. But trees always captured me." He laughed. "It's a bit silly to you, I imagine."

Truly idiotic. Why reach for what cannot be? This creature is a fool.

Felix grinned, ignoring the Maw. "Not silly at all. I think a tree in here would liven it right up."

"I wouldn't even know what to do with it, truth be told." Bateo shook his head, chortling. "Ah, dreams. They're good to have, even if they don't make much sense."

Bateo couldn't really answer his questions on how his Skills worked, except the one about rocks. If he was turning it all to soil, wouldn't the island eventually erode? Turned out that the farmer would regularly go and collect floating stones in the Void and bring them back to be crushed and spread out among his fields. Simple.

After seeing Atar conjure fire from the air, something like Summon Water shouldn't have shocked him, but it did. It also answered the question of where fluid came from in the endless Void, and how anyone was still alive.

Bateo paid a lot of attention to the crops, fiddling with the levels of water and soil before using his remaining Mana to reinforce the fungi and tubers. Felix did very little except watch, his own Skills not a good fit for the task. Now, if the farmer wanted his crops violently ejected from their island, Felix was the man to do it. He had a feeling that wouldn't be appreciated, though.

From there, the two of them went and checked on the livestock, and the Maw trailed listlessly after them. A low murmur of complaints came from its withered throat, but Felix tried his best to ignore it entirely. Instead, he focused on the Tenebrils. Lots and lots of Tenebrils.

"The trick is to not let them sense your fear," Bateo explained as a half-dozen barbed tentacles roamed over his extended hand. He had pushed it through a small flap built into the access door. They were as gentle as lambs, not even dimpling the birdman's skin. "Or, in your case, your Mana." He offered for Felix to put his own hand into the flap, but the Nym hesitated.

"Hm," Felix hummed skeptically as Bateo pulled his hand back. "I've had some run-ins with Tenebril. They were more than happy to tear me apart to get to my juicy Mana center."

Bateo trilled a laugh and tilted his head back in revelation. "Of course. You still have your native Mana composition. They likely find it far more appetizing than my own."

"I'm sorry, what?"

"No no, there's no reason you would have known of this," Bateo said before releasing a small arc of Mana vapor from his left palm Mana Gate. It sparkled, white light streaked with a variety of colors. "I have never had a true core. I was born in the Void, which means I was born Manaless. The only source of Mana has been the bladders of voidbeasts, as you've seen me use several times now. And voidbeasts—"

"Have undifferentiated Mana," Felix said, biting the inside of his cheek. "So if your core isn't… how do you use those earth and water Mana Skills?"

"Voidbeast filter Mana from the things in the dark. Other beasts, the Void itself? It is unknown how. But the Mana they collect has many types within it. Elemental potential, we call it. We learn at a young age how to harness the pieces we need to meet our needs."

"So, the rest, the bits that aren't the type you need?" Felix asked.

"They are wasted, sadly," Bateo admitted. "What the Void does to us… we are broken sieves. The Mana will always escape us to be eaten by the Void itself."

"And I have that to look forward to," Felix said, gut sinking. "Joy."

"Not for many years, Felix. The record of my great-great grandsire says he retained much of his core well into his second century. But it will come," Bateo paused and seemed to consider his words. "The Void steals into us quietly. It breathes through our Gates, into our channels with every Skill and spell. It cannot be stopped."

Great.

"If you're born here in the Void, how do you get Skills at all?" Felix asked.

"A tithe of System energy is born with every hatchling, even here. It is enough to nurture us for a time, enough to expend on learning a few necessary Skills, and perhaps to advance a bit before it is gone, though our core is always a false one." Bateo's voice was wistful. "I still remember the heat of it. I imagine that is what the sun feels like."

They continued to check on the Tenebrils while Bateo continued to explain the relative unresponsiveness of the System in the Void. It still functioned, clearly, but advancing Skills was rare and difficult, and learning new Skills was all but impossible. Another topic that the Conference was working on an answer. Each time they were mentioned, Bateo's voice lifted, and he mentioned the strides they had taken toward escaping the Void.

"One day," he said, and those two words had such hope.

Once the enclosures were mucked and Tenebrils fed, they moved onto repairs of the outbuildings and checking on a few arrays Bateo maintained to keep his stock of butchered meat and stored crops clean and preserved. Those, as everything else, required Mana to be provided. Unlike his own reserves, Bateo couldn't just pour out a Manabladder onto the array and refill it. Instead, he filled the reservoir of the pole he'd used in his little boat, then used its sharpened end to transfer Mana into the small arrays.

Felix found the arrays particularly fascinating. They looked like classic magic circles from Earth fiction, filled with circular lines and rings of squiggly runes. *Sigils,* he reminded himself. A few he could even identify, such as *cold, heat,* and *light,* though he had no idea how they worked or functioned as a greater whole. When he asked his host, Bateo only shrugged.

"These were built by my great-great grandsire. Most of the arrays, including the one around the settlement, were built back then. The knowledge and Skill for such things has sadly died away. The best we can do now is maintain them."

So it was with many things. Maintenance and upkeep. Washing and cleaning and mucking. The Void actively broke things down, turning rock to dust and dust into *nothing*. It didn't happen overnight, but in tiny increments that were easy to overlook, so repairs were constant and neverending.

It was labor-intensive, but Felix almost enjoyed it. Having reached the First Threshold with his stats, lifting and scrubbing and moving items even Bateo struggled to budge wasn't hard so much as time-consuming. Yet, Felix found himself with an abundance of time. He was stuck in the Void, not in immediate danger (if you didn't count the Maw's constant talking), and had plenty to eat and drink.

It was almost like a vacation.

At the end of the day, he would rest for a few hours at complete ease. No sudden monster attacks, no immediate doom. It was... nice.

Felix decided he could get used to nice.

CHAPTER TWENTY-TWO

The Crafters' Quarter was a wild cacophony of wagons, screeching avum, and hollering porters. Goods moved across the cobbled streets like Mana through channels, and Atar found himself hard-pressed to cross some of the busier thoroughfares. He was carrying a pack atop his battle robes, and it threatened to overbalance him with every step. Not to mention the pressing crowds as everyone and their grandmother apparently had important business with the various crafthalls. Someone had even tried to pickpocket him. Him!

Damn common, Untempered trash, he griped. As he came to the corner, Atar looked up at the street signs once again to gain his bearings. *Potter and… Dyemaker's Way, yes here we are,* he thought. *It should be a block centerward.*

Everything in Haarwatch was described as either toward the center or toward the various walls. Folks rarely relied on the cardinal directions, for whatever reason, but it was an easy enough system to understand. Rustic and idiotic, but simple. The Eyrie loomed at the center, after all, visible from all Quarters with very little effort. Nothing about Haarwatch had impressed him, save for the Eyrie itself. Compared to the

Archive and resources within the Guild tower, the rest of the city was as interesting to him as different varieties of mud.

In fact, Atar wouldn't have been caught dead in any of the city Quarters, were it not a direct request from Elder Teine. His Bronze Rank assistants required reagents and materials for their various unnamed experiments, and Atar soon learned that it was the job of lowly Tin Ranks to fetch said materials. So, he had swallowed his pride and followed the hierarchy of authority, eager to please his new teacher. That had lasted for approximately three days, until the constant fetching had turned from onerous responsibility to rage-inducing futility. The requests never ended! Now, he was delivering as well as procuring supplies like some sort of common messenger!

Atar grunted in annoyance as another musclebound porter jostled him. At the very least, his trips were usually restricted to the Crafters' Quarter, the nicest section of the city after the noble's Sunrise Quarter. He hadn't been sent to the Wall or Dust Quarters, which were far less pleasant-smelling, and that was even considering the tannery three streets wallward from the fire mage.

Trade was booming in all Quarters, however, and the press of people did nothing for the stench. Materials were flowing into Haarwatch as never before as teams of harvesters had begun denuding the forests at an impressive rate. Monster cores abounded, rare herbs, flowers, fruits, even precious stones found in ancient dens beneath the forest were uncovered every day. It made getting the Elder's supplies that much easier, at least.

He trudged another block, sweat soaking his robes, before he reached his destination. A thin, wrought-iron sign proclaimed it the residence of *Mr. Bartleby's Pottery And Lampworks*, and he groaned in relief. His pack was cutting into his shoulders, and Atar was half-certain he was going to have blisters. He stepped into the narrow stone edifice with the jangle of a tin bell.

"Welcome and well met, young sir!" A man looked up from the front desk, dressed in a clay-splattered apron over a simple tunic and trousers. Khellish design, if Atar's eye wasn't mistaken. Well out of date. "If you are here for our ceramics sale, you are just in time! We have—"

Atar crossed the small room and tossed his bag atop the thin counter. It hit with a solid *thunk*, and a number of vases and bowls jumped.

"I am not interested in your ceramics. I've come on behalf of the Elder of Spirit for the Protector's Guild." He began opening his pack and unloading eighteen small sacks of heavy sand. Each one was labeled with a glyph, which was a series of sigils joined into a singular pattern. Usually, those were control nodes of an array, but this was simply the seal of the Elder of Spirit. "I am to pick up supplies in exchange for these reagents."

The portly man wiped his hands on his apron and picked up one of the sacks with reverence. He licked his lips and opened the ties. Within, the sand was a vibrant, shimmering hue, somewhere north of green-purple. "Yes." He tightened the ties again. "Yes, of course. Wait a moment."

The man set down the sack and disappeared into a back door. He was gone just long enough for Atar to massage some of the strain from his shoulders, and when he returned it was with a faint, chiming clatter. The back door opened and the portly man carried a large crate that looked at least three times as heavy as the pack filled with sand. He set it down on the floor next to his counter, and dozens of glass bottles glinted within.

"Reinforced potion bottles, just as the Elder requested," he said with a tap on the side of the crate. He beamed with pride. "Impervious to casual abuse and able to survive a fall of over thirty strides."

Atar stared in disbelief, which only made the potter beam brighter.

"It is impressive, no? The best work in Haarwatch! I've the Elder's seal to prove it!" The man kept talking, droning on and on, but Atar wasn't listening.

I have to carry that?!

He was a sweaty mess by the time he reached the Eyrie once more. Thankfully, he no longer had to enter through the always-busy main entrance, and his Tin Rank medallion allowed him access to a few of the external doors on the Crafters' side of the tower. Still, he had to slog through crowds that only increased as the day wore on, leaving the fire mage battered and bruised by the end of it all.

The bottles, on the other hand, were unharmed. Even after Atar dropped them from exhaustion.

Burning... bastard wasn't... completely lying, Atar thought with a grunt. But of course he wasn't. The Elder of Spirit had contracted him for these potion bottles and wanted them durable, so durable they would be. Else there would be... consequences. Atar shook his head. *No one wants...to be on the bad side of Elder Teine.*

He'd heard a few stories of Guilders that came up against Teine, and it was never a happy ending for them. Atar could admit much of it was likely hyperbole, but if even a fraction of the punishments were true, the mage never wanted to cross his benefactor.

Atar struggled up the last of the steps to the lift. Though the Tin Rank doors weren't nearly as busy as the main entrance, they were still congested with low-level idiots all on various assignments for Guild credit. He had to muscle his way through the crowd and take his place in line for the lift, because of course there was a line. It was a magically powered automatic ascension—a design only the Guild had access to—why would anyone want to take the stairs? Especially when *some* people had to climb to the tenth floor.

Atar swallowed. His legs felt shaky just thinking about it. His Stamina was barely above two percent full after his exertions. There was little chance he would endure a march up so many flights. He reined in his patience and waited.

If nothing else, the wait allowed his abysmal Stamina regeneration to bring him up a touch. He even had a nice seat with his crate of bottles. It let Atar's mind free up. He found himself wondering what his teammates were up to.

Since they had met, Alister, Lilian, and Dabney had joined forces with Atar. These particular fetch quests were even split up among them for greater efficiency. They were expected to be done at the same time, but Atar hadn't anticipated his troubles. Alister and his troublesome cousin were likely finished a glass ago, and Dabney… well, he at least was likely still lost among the warrens of the Dust Quarter. Dabney was something of an idiot.

Another stroke of luck, I think. Atar shoved his crate another few feet as the line moved. *Alister and Lilian are likely out to eat at that tavern he's always inviting me to.* The minor noble had invited Atar to the place on Chandler and Lapidary a handful of times, even suggesting they ditch his cousin and that bumbling hanger-on. Atar was tempted. Yet as… fascinating as Alister was proving to be, Atar's first priority was the job. Advancement above all else.

I need to get to Apprentice Tier. I'm so close!

Teine handed out Essence Draughts of increasing rarity to those who accomplished his tasks with the greatest diligence and skill. Those who did not, those who failed him, were swiftly drummed out of his inner circle. Which was why Atar was working so damn hard, exhaustion be damned!

He achieved the lift, eventually. Atar had no clue how it worked, and his usual curiosity was barely piqued by his ride. He couldn't get distracted. It rose swiftly, almost too swiftly, and before he could believe it, Atar was at the tenth level of the Eyrie. The wrought iron gate opened up onto a wide corridor with serpentine inlaid stone floors, austere white walls, and a preponderance of bright magelights tethered to the sconces along the ceiling.

He exited to find a number of thick, wooden benches and a single desk right outside the lift. An Elf in curiously wrapped robes sat behind it, quill scratching rapidly at a number of sheets of parchment, so fast his hand was a blur. The Elf was named Qellyn, a Bronze Rank, and was one of Elder Teine's mostly highly trusted aides. Qellyn looked up at Atar as he struggled off the lift with his crate.

"Be careful not to scratch the floors. They were just refinished last week."

Atar let out an unseemly grunt and leveraged the crate onto one of the nearest benches. Panting, he turned to the aide. "G-good afternoon. I am Atar V'as, Tin Rank, and I've come with a requisition for Lot 4117."

Qellyn's hand stopped only for a few moments, long enough for him to gesture down the hall with his quill. "Down the corridor. First blue door on your left. Through there, follow the hall until you reach the sixth intersection. Wait there." The Elf returned to his paperwork without another word.

Atar, who had done similar jobs before, knew not to ask questions. That wasn't his right, not yet. He took a breath. *Soon*, he promised himself. *Soon they'll all be following me.*

END +2
STR +1

He followed the aide's instructions to the letter, though it took him far longer than it should have. However, he did earn two whole points in Endurance and a single point in Strength for his day of agony. It was small compensation, but Atar would take what he could get. Once at the final intersection, Atar sat down to wait and recover more of his Stamina.

Time passed. At least a glass, and no one had come for him or his supplies. But that was the way of it. He was at the mercy of those higher-ranked, and they were all busy, especially here in Teine's domain. There were so many research projects ongoing, but the main priority were the tests being performed on those survivors from the Foglands. All voluntary, of course. In the early days, even Atar had gone through a battery of examinations by the Healer's Ward, and while he had received a clean bill of Health, not everyone had.

Those who hadn't were quarantined for a time while their Health recovered, but something was still off with all of them. The details were never explained—not to him—but the survivors were so thankful to be back home, they would accept anything short of death, Atar imagined. What they had seen, the giants and the monsters in the fog... he shuddered. *He* still had nightmares, and Atar had been relatively unscathed.

"UUUAAAAAAAAAHHHHH!"

A horrible, heart-wrenching scream tore through the hallways and set Atar's own pulse pounding.

Wha-what was that?

Whoever it was, they were hurting terribly and... and it sounded close. Atar looked at his crate of bottles, his bundle of contribution that would grant him that much more credit toward earning his next set of Essence Draughts. Toward working more with the Elder directly. Atar bit his thumb, torn between responsibility and a burning, terrible curiosity.

No one has come by in so long. I've got time. He stood. *I've got time.*

Atar crept down the halls, which were less well-lit than the main section near Qellyn. He hadn't a Stealth Skill, but he managed well enough. Robes didn't make much noise, not even his hardened battle robes. Two lefts and a right had him outside a room where the screaming continued to come from, and he discovered why he'd been able to hear it at all: someone had left the door ajar. He stood just beyond the angle that he could see anything, knowing it was the last moment he'd be able to feign any sort of ignorance. Atar burned through that feeling and crept forward.

His eyes widened.

Through the open crevice of the door, a man was begging to be killed. Three figures stood over him, their faces and bodies covered in curious suits of cloth and leather that left no skin exposed. Not even their Guild medallions hung on the outside, which made identifying them impossible. The man on the ground, however...,Atar recognized him, though it took some doing. Corum Bettle, a low-level scribe they had saved from the

Foglands. Atar had helped the man several times on the journey back, as he'd been less adept at physical exertion than the mage himself. Now, Corum was writhing on the stone floor, covered in his own blood and screaming.

"Kill me! It's taking—!" Something was wrong with his mouth. It wasn't the right shape at all, and it made his words sound clunky and tangled. "Please! Please! I just want to see my family! To let them—to know," he whined. His mouth filled with fluid that he hacked onto the ground.

What sort of test is this? He couldn't believe the man agreed to… whatever this was. The three Guilders only stared at Corum in silence. *I-I don't want to know. I shouldn't be seeing this.*

Corum's eye snagged Atar's own, and the man turned in terrible, bloody hope toward the door.

Blight! Atar scrambled backward, no concern for stealth, and hurtled down the hall. He heard the door pull open behind him, but he didn't stop, taking turns at random until he reached a door that wasn't locked. He slung it open and dove within, closing it behind him and throwing the latch.

Fool! Why did you do this? Atar knew he'd stepped far beyond himself at that moment. Things were happening that he should never have seen. *Hopefully they didn't see me or Analyze me. I don't think—*

For the first time, Atar realized he was in another stark chamber, though this one was filled with a series of cots. At least thirty, and—he stifled a gasp—they were all occupied.

Highest Flame, what is wrong with me? I just had to wait with the crate!

Swallowing, Atar scanned the room. Everyone was asleep. It was late afternoon, so he had to assume they were all sedated in some way. If they were all as Corum was, then a soporific would be a mercy.

Good. I can hide here a moment before I slip back into the halls. Even if they started looking for someone, they wouldn't search forever. He shook his head. *This is bad.* Even if he went back to his crate, there would be questions. What if someone came for the potion bottles, and he was nowhere to be found?

Damn my curiosity! Atar was having trouble breathing. He looked wildly around the room, foolishly hoping for a solution to his problem. His eyes settled on form after form, all of them breathing slowly and regularly. All of them... except one. It wasn't moving at all.

Analyze!

Atar's eyes almost fell out of his head. *Magda? Why is her body here?*

He took a few steps toward it, close enough to notice the number of arrays built into the metal gurney her body was placed upon. Preservation arrays and a few others he didn't recognize. *What are they doing with her body? And why would it be here, with the sick?*

"You are not supposed to be here," said a cold, sharp voice.

Atar whirled toward it, hands clutching at his robes. Yet instead of an angry Guilder, he found a strangely pale man wearing some sort of medical robe. He stood near a disturbed cot, and clearly he was a patient who had woken up. Atar didn't recognize him from among the survivors, though.

"I, ah, I am here on official Guild business," Atar said, quickly flashing his medallion. "I'm inspecting—"

"No," said the patient in his strange voice. "Guilders wear protective equipment. They fear infection. You wear nothing."

Atar's mouth dried out instantly. *Infection? From what?*

He tried to smile and managed something like a grimace. "I am simply resistant to infection, so I don't need the protection." He coughed. "Go back to bed, and I'll be out of your hair soon enough."

The man (or was it an Elf?) looked at Atar without inflection save vague irritation. "You must leave now. You are interfering with the Great Work." Then, without further prompting, the strange man turned and climbed back into his bed.

The mage didn't need further encouragement. He held his breath as he went back to the door, unlocked it, and carefully opened it. He opened it only as much as required to slip his slim frame out, and shut it after him. Only then did he take a deep, steadying breath.

You absolute idiot! He had to get back to his crate. Atar started backtracking, carefully peering around corners for any Guilders out in the corridors. There were a few, though none were wearing the full-body suits he had observed, and all disappeared into various rooms along the maze of halls. It took him another quarter glass, but Atar found his way back to his crate eventually. What's more, it was still there, chock full of glass bottles.

"Highest Flame, Urge of That Which Burns, thank you," he muttered to himself as he ran his hands over the crate. Now he only had to wait for—

"Tin Rank!"

Atar froze, his back stiffening into icy stone as a hand clamped onto his shoulder. The mage was pulled around, directly into the face of a Bronze Rank he recognized. Okar, a bearded giant of a man, with access to materials and projects an entire level above Atar's own. Not inner circle, but closer. He stared into Atar's face with something like rabid fury on his face.

"Where were you just now?" he demanded. "This crate was left unattended!"

Atar sputtered. "I was just curious, so I walked down the hall a bit. I—" he flinched as Okar brought his face within a fingers width of the mage's own. "I-I just walked. I saw nothing!"

Acting is level 22!

Okar's wild eyes settled, and his teeth hid behind his lips again. The fury abated, just far enough that Atar saw something that shocked him. The man was *afraid*, though certainly not of him. "Forget anything that happened. Forget me and this entire afternoon. I'll take this crate and your credit." He put a thick finger to Atar's face. "If I hear even a whisper that we had this conversation, then I will find you. And you will not like what follows." He shoved the mage backward into the wall hard enough to shave a few percentages from his Health. "Understand?"

Atar nodded, hiding both his grimace of pain and surprise.

"Then get out. Now."

Atar ran.

CHAPTER TWENTY-THREE

Dragoon's Footwork!

"Faster, Lady Dayne!" Darius called out. "Channel the very wind into your steps! Let it flow through you!"

Vess moved—a step here, a turned foot there—complicated footwork that both drew the eye and misled it by turns. It had been the downfall of many monsters in the Foglands, but Darius saw through every feint and stride, always appearing where he was least expected. Pushing.

"Is *this* what these Guilders have been teaching you?" he shouted. She whirled and struck three times in rapid succession, but the tip of her silver spear failed to find purchase. "Pathetic!"

Darius kicked at her, forcing her back, but she went willingly. When fighting with a spear, distance was her friend and ally. In order to keep that distance, she had to keep mobile no matter what. She burned her Dragoon's Footwork and kept to her kata, the Seven Steps of the Dragoon. But against the Hand, her kata was useless. It was a technique he had fought against his entire life. Again and again, he broke her footing and soured her thrusts, allowing her to achieve nothing more than glancing blows.

"You aren't trying hard enough! Where is your Mana?" he growled. His greatsword was a blur as it deflected every strike she attempted. "You are so close to Apprentice Tier, and yet you are worse than when your father let you leave!" His massive greatsword wove through the air, mesmerizing in the freedom of its movement and scraping loudly against her armor with every strike.

"You're too close! Mind your feet!"

CLANG!

"You're over-extended! Guard high!"

SPANG!

"You aren't paying attention! Focus!"

"Enough!" Vess shouted. She bared her teeth. With an opponent like the Hand of the Duke, the only real tactic was to bleed them dry.

Spear of Tribulations!

Six more identical spears manifested around her, each six feet long and made of what appeared to be silver chased with golden designs. It was the one Skill that had truly risen above the rest, and she was tired of this. All at once, the spears launched themselves at Darius. The man danced between their strikes, letting the spears stick into the ground while he advanced on her. Vess smiled and hurled the last in her hand, but he batted it away.

"You will have to try better than—"

"Seven Tribulations!" she shouted.

Every single spear erupted into a maelstrom of violently decompressing wind, and Darius was thrown forward. Not hurt, but off-balance. Vess kicked up a training spear from the ground, tossing it into her hands and propping it against the earth as the Hand fell. He stopped himself, barely, before the spear would have pierced into the soft underside of his jaw.

"I win," she said.

Darius only smirked, before driving his head down upon her training spear, and obliterating it against his skin. Vess gasped, and when the Hand pulled back, his neck was unmarred and unharmed. He laughed.

She hated him.

"You gave up your best weapons to make a kill shot with an inferior tool. That's not winning," he scoffed. "That's choosing how to die." He straightened up fully, looming over her in his full armor. He held his greatsword in a single hand, a massive hunk of enchanted steel that weighed as much as a teamster's wagon, and flexed his grip. "This place has made you weak, Vessilia. Excise what foolishness they've taught you. We must start anew."

The man paced backward, setting distance between them once again. "We will attempt this again, until you understand exactly what you must. Reject the cowards that dragged you into the Foglands, those who populate this very tower. Their insipid Wills are the dross you must let fall as you rise." He thrust his greatsword forward. "Begin."

Spear of Tribulations is level 15!
Grace is level 24!
Dragoon's Footwork is level 28!
Pierce the Sky is level 23!
+2 STR
+1 VIT
+1 PER

"Blighted Night," Vess cursed as the cuts along her left arm and leg were sutured closed. She was seated atop a padded bench amid the lush finery of her chambers in the upper reaches of the Eyrie. The Spire, they called it, reserved for Elders and visiting dignitaries.

"Your Grace," said the healer in a scandalized tone. "I understand that this hurts, but I would ask that you refrain from blaspheming."

Vess felt her cheeks heat, darkening the skin across her nose. "My apologies, Matron Kelsys."

The elderly healer smiled in sympathy and patted her knee. "Oh, I've heard much worse from my patients. Doesn't make me like it, but I understand. I'm almost done."

A few more passes of her Mana-reinforced needle, and the sutures were drawn closed. A quick application of salve and bandages finished the treatment. Matron Kelsys stood and cleaned her hands in a nearby basin. "There we are. I suggest avoiding use of both arm and leg for at least six days, but I know that is impossible for you Guilder types."

Vess waved her hand. "That will not be an issue. I am to work on my Vitality, so I shall be recovering naturally from my wounds." She took a breath and smiled up at the healer. "I will remain abed for at least a short while."

The healer clucked her tongue and began gathering her supplies. "While I approve of taking a rest, I do not condone such methods to force one's Vitality score higher. It has only limited benefits. Far better to secure an alchemical bath, your Grace."

"I am aware, Matron Kelsys. Thank you for your concern."

The old healer knew a dismissal when she heard it, but it didn't stop a final *'tut'* before she stepped out of Vess' apartments. The moment the door clicked closed and the silencing ward enacted, the Heiress of Pax'Vrell fell sideways onto the bench, groaning in pain and frustration.

Darius had not let up in his "instruction" for over four hours. Every muscle she had was sore, battered, or bruised. And some in worse condition.

Vess had thrown everything she had at him, but nothing put a dent in the man's impenetrable defense. Not even her Spear of Tribulations, a new yet powerful addition, had proven enough to turn the tables. Concentrating, she pulled Mana from her core and out of her left palm. The Mana Gate flexed open, and green-white air Mana poured out. It shimmered as it formed into a six-foot-long silver spear. It had heft and weight, just as a real metal spear would, but she was able to move it faster than any weapon she'd ever wielded.

Simple and powerful. Her newest Skill was an evolution of her former Spear Mastery, retaining all of its old benefits while allowing her to conjure seven weapons out of thin air. Moreover, it let her explode those same weapons in a spectacular detonation of air Mana. In practice, that meant she shredded her wooden targets with ease.

Against Darius, it had merely pushed him a little.

She growled in frustration at the memory. Every use she'd attempted, he had either evaded or easily withstood. Vess was fully cognizant of the disparity between them. She was barely into her second decade and Apprentice Tier, while Darius had ten years and two advancement levels over her. *The man is an Adept Tier. Of* course, *you would not land a blow on him.* Especially not without a single complete Tempering to her name.

She'd put in the work these past three weeks since the trial. Constant combat trials against the Hand, against Wooden Golems procured from the Guild, ceaseless fighting and sparring. She had pushed her stats to a new ceiling, earning point after point from brutalizing her physique and reflexes. It all came to a head with her Skill Evolutions.

Evolving her primary Skill—Spear Mastery—has always been the plan. Since a young age, Vessilia Dayne had been tutored by the greatest of warriors for a singular purpose: to take up the mantle of the Dragoons. An order of hunters and aerial combatants, the Dragoons had served the nation before the rise of the Hierocracy, when it was a series of warring states plagued by the constant threat of flying predators. The dragons may be gone, but their lesser kin were still a threat to the scattered populace. It was her order—her Mother's order—that kept those smaller communities safe.

The Spear of Tribulations, Pierce the Sky, and Dragon's Descent were all core Skills of the Dragoons, and all of them were only ever earned in the last gasps of one's Beginner Tier. For many, Skill Evolution was a legendary, uncanny occurrence that would strike once in a generation. For the Dragoons and those societies like it, it was a matter of course. Resources and specific training regimens had long since been detailed, Titles to be acquired and avoided, all of it designed to elevate the newest generation of Dragoons.

That said, it did not mean it was easy. Most aspirants failed on their path toward Apprentice Tier, and even more fell short of the proper Skill Evolutions. It was a journey that few could even begin, detailed tutelage or not. In the past three weeks, she had evolved no less than four Skills, thankfully preserving their levels, and pushed them so very close to Tiering up.

She brought up her Skills.

Body:
Acrobatics (C), Level 20; Grace (C), Level 24; Heavy Armor Mastery (C), Level 18; Small Blade Mastery (C), Level 11; Unarmed Mastery (C), Level 9; Dragon's Descent (R), Level 22; Pierce the Sky (R), Level 23; Dragoon's Footwork (E), Level 28

Mind:
Analyze (C), Level 20; Oratory (C), Level 25; Diplomacy (U), Level 22

Spirit:
Elemental Eye (R), Level 19; Gaze of the Unseen Hunter (R), Level 9; Wyrmling's Call (E), Level 10; Spear of Tribulations (L), Level 15

Her training had her focused as few others. Commoners would find their Skill lists filled with redundant abilities or counter-intuitive pairings. A Dragoon was forged differently, and while it was nothing like the slew of Skills Felix owned, it was a respectable array of abilities.

Used to own, she corrected herself with a hitch in her chest. She had heard that he was not listed among the survivors. In fact, none of the local Guilders had heard of him or anyone similar to his description. That was but one oddity that kept her up at night. Magda's trial. The location of Evie and Atar. Of Harn and Cal and their team. She'd been forbidden to contact them, all but isolated in the Spire atop the Eyrie, where servants met her every need and provided her with everything she might desire. Everything save freedom.

Vess wanted answers, and she'd used her sleepless nights as a way to get them. She spoke to servants and caretakers in the halls, piecing it all together from castoff rumors and weeks-old news. She knew Elder DuFont was somehow involved, that she had hired the Sworn agent to find and retrieve her. The why on that was easy enough to guess—her father would have made hell for the Guild had she died in the Foglands. So, DuFont had sent someone to shadow Magda and Harn, to retrieve the heiress when things went wrong.

Moreover, Vess found out that DuFont greenlit the territory-staking operation in the first place. The entire reason why Magda had arranged her illegal rescue mission. She followed that thread as far as she could, but the Sworn has disappeared. There was nothing connecting the Elder of Acquisition to the Sworn save dim rumors and her own guesses, or even that the Sworn had been engaged at all. Her repeated attempts to have the High Elder listen to her had failed. He was constantly "too busy" to have an audience with her, but she booked an appointment for weeks later. When that time came up, it was inevitably shunted ahead by several weeks. This, she could tell, would continue without end.

"Siva's Silver Chords!" Vess cursed. She was sick of *thinking*. Sick of the powerlessness that accosted her, so unlike how things worked in Pax'Vrell. Back home, while at the mercy of her tutors and trainers, she was Heiress to the Duchy, and her word was something very close to law. Not even Darius Reed could gainsay her in the seat of her power.

Vess' mouth filled with a sour taste as she thought on that odious man. They had once been close, had even been promised one another as children, but that felt like another life. She had delved deeper into the Dragoon's training, and he had joined her father's elite champions. To think on who they once had been... it stung like touching a burning stovetop. She recoiled. The Chosen Hand no longer cared for her, only her father's Will.

Darius is right about one thing, though. I need to get better. Stronger.

Physical training out of the question until her injuries healed, that meant working on her core space. Vess grimaced at the thought, but quickly admonished herself. The process was... unpleasant, true, but it was remarkably beneficial. So, with the help of her conjured spear, she climbed to her feet and hobbled across her apartments and to one of the massive, floor-to-ceiling windows that dominated the eastern wall. As the weather warmed across the city, she left them open for the cooling breeze they provided.

Without hesitation, Vess hobbled across the casement and out onto the ledge beyond.

She wore loose-fitting robes, white and green as her chosen element, the one with which she built her core. They whipped about her as Vess stepped out into the wind, but she let it guide her, flexing her Will upon the ambient Mana in the air so that her movements all but clung to the thin walkway. It was but one application of her Seven Steps of the Dragoon, but as all katas, was less a Skill and more of a technique. She was not a master of the Seven Steps, that required multiple Tempers, but the greatest masters were said to be able to land atop a leaf in a hurricane.

As it was, it took a good chunk of Vess' concentration to maintain her footing on the stone walkway. The path extended from the side of her building, connecting the corner of her section of the Spire to a flying buttress that jutted out into the thin air. They were thousands of strides into the air, nearly a league, and Vess had to fight to keep her nerve. One step, one improperly turned flow of air Mana, and the Heiress of

Pax'Vrell would be nothing more than a stain upon some nobleman's garden shed far below.

She marshaled her Willpower and trudged forward regardless, pushing herself until her heartbeat slowed and her limbs steadied. She reached the end, where the buttress was surmounted by a small ridge. It was here that Vess stopped and sat, robes billowing in the ceaseless breeze.

The wind swirled again, but she shifted just enough to keep her spot. Up there, amid her chosen element, it was a touch easier to visualize her core space and channels. Any advantage was to be seized upon. She let the air Mana ebb and flow, pulled into her Gates with every breath. Her long, dark hair whipped up into the air, and Vess followed the motion, closing her eyes and letting herself *rise*.

The Dragoon's called it Ascending the Steps, and it was one of the twenty-two movements that would lead her to the very peak of power... eventually. For now, she had barely cleared the second Step. Her core had been established, her Mana channels carved, and now before her rose the malformed ridges of a mountain range. A mountain range that was supposed to house her core, Skills, and the potency that grew with every Skill level and Temper.

She had been called a prodigy by her tutors, all because she had a grasp of her core space that few did. Even when her core was no more than an errant breeze, that breeze wrapped around the misshapen prominence before her. When she had arrived in the Foglands, that breeze had become a steady gale that fueled the Skills that let her fight so explosively. Yet months later, Vess found herself only a half-step further along her path.

Prodigy, she scoffed.

Vess focused, leveraging her Willpower and Intelligence on the hazy landscape before her. The mountain sharpened, ever so slightly, the rocks gaining striations to their forms, and the wind gaining the slightest of edges. Beyond her core space, Vess felt the insistent press of the Continent's wind, and pulled that in with her. The air thickened and intensified until the tiny plants and grasses that had taken root around her trembled with their insistent passage. The mountain beneath her grew, finger spans at a time, but it grew nevertheless. Soon, she would be ready to build her Temple atop it.

Time passed.

Wind surged and Mana flowed, and Vess put all she had into her working. Years of training kept her still and steady, her concentration never flagging nor failing as the glasses tumbled into the next. Strenuous as it was, Vess found a certain measure of peace in the slow build of her space. There nothing was hidden from her, and the next step was always clear. Layer, sharpen, *rise*.

But the world was not to be ignored for too long.

"..do you mean?"

"The Elders cleared the entire level. We were relocated to the eighth floor, and fast, too. Apparently they needed room for those sick survivors to stay."

"They're still sick? It's been weeks since they got back."

Vess fell from her mountain fastness as the words reached her. Opening her eyes, she leaned back and peered upward. Three stories above her, the Inner Ward extended beyond the normal confines of the Spire. It was the elite training area of the Protector's Guild, meant only for Bronze Rank or higher, and only if you could earn it. Voices drifted on the wind, carried to her ears by virtue of her Perception and the Seven Steps technique of guided air Mana.

Survivors? From the Foglands? She stilled herself as the conversation continued.

"...something about restricted access. She couldn't find out what's on the tenth floor," one said, their voice sharp and crisp.

The other was deeper and more gruff, like some guardsmen she knew back home. "Strange. I heard Elder Teine was taking charge of them, too."

"What's the Elder of Spirit got to do with sick Guilders? That's Elder Regis or Guilder Ty'lel's concern."

"No clue. His people came in and swept the Healer's Ward

without answering any questions. The Alchemist was right pissed."

"I bet."

There was the clash and clatter of swords on armor, as well as the muffled thump of feet on dirt. Vess focused, pulling all she could from the snippets.

"...transport... to the 'staging ground,' whatever that means."

The sharp voice tutted. "I'd stay away, if I were you. Teine has a reputation. Don't care for much aside from mages, and noble ones at that."

"Hah! That ain't us," the gruff one laughed.

"Not a bit."

The conversation drifted away, either lost on the breeze or because they moved farther away. Vess wasn't sure, but it could have easily been because her mind was racing.

What do the Elders want with the people we saved? Her mind reflected back on the enervated and despondent survivors she had rescued. They were a people who had seen horrors under the fist of the Frost Giants, and worse down among the Labyrinth. *What more could these iniquitous, felonious Elders want from them? What blood could be squeezed from a stone?*

Vess' hair was a dark banner against the light stone of the Eyrie, and her Spirit, Untempered though it was, ignited with frustrated conviction.

By Avet's black teeth, this at least will not stand.

―――

Several stories higher, within the Inner Ward, a lone woman with ochre skin and blue-green hair stood casually against the boundary wall. She could still sense the form of the heiress atop her perch, though she soon made her way back into her chambers. Sigils, dull and lifeless, ran beneath the woman's fingers along the wall. With a twist of her Will, the sigils flared with light and went active once again. The sound of the howling wind was all but cut off.

Let us see what you do with that information, your Grace.

"Archivist Zara? Is there somcone out here with you?" Another woman stepped off a wooded path, garbed in a thick brigandine with a bronze medallion around her neck.

"No, of course not," Zara said. "Just me."

"Ah. I thought I—nevermind. Are the privacy wards repaired?" the Guilder asked.

"Yes," the Naiad replied while adjusting her glasses.

"Oh thank the Pathless," she breathed. "Sorry for asking you to come all the way up here. But with Teine's people all busy on his mysterious tasks, capable inscriptionists are hard to find."

"Not a worry. It was a simple repair."

"Simple. I can't understand how you mages think sometimes," the woman said, marvel evident in her voice. "It's all a bunch of squiggles to me."

"Magic is the same as anything, really." Zara gave a shark-toothed smile. "It's all about listening, then choosing how to act."

CHAPTER TWENTY-FOUR

"Can't get me!"

"Ahh!"

"I wanted to be it—aiii!"

The high pitched squeals of the children mingled joyously with the musical barking of one Rottweiler-sized tenku as they chased one another through the fallow fields. All five children were about, Kili and Nell running faster than the rest, while Jain, Pol, and Kor were giggling around boulders. Felix watched them as Pit raced after one, then another, grabbing them by their belts or trousers and carrying them triumphantly back to a larger boulder they'd designated as safe, or as they called it, High Rock. They were unruly, all of them barely past potty-training age were they Human, and rules were things for someone else to follow. Regardless, Pit's beak was split open in a panting grin, and their bond was alight with unreserved delight.

It soothed Felix's soul to see it.

That is your Affinity at work.

Felix was perched atop the peak of the farmhouse's roof, and he glanced to his right where the apparition of the Maw hovered soundlessly. Its pale yellow dress still rippled in a phantom breeze, as did its lank black hair. The face of Lhel, once Nymean researcher and mage, stared at Pit and the kids. It kept talking, unprompted.

Your Affinity is your connection to the Realms, and all that lies within them. Even here.

"My Affinity," Felix said. He pulled up his Harmonic stats.

Harmonic Stats
RES: 103
INE: 88
AFI: 62
REI: 60
ALA: 143

They were impressive numbers, all told. Aside from Resonance (RES) and Resilience (REI), which directly affected his mental and physical regeneration, he was fairly uncertain about the lot of them. Alacrity (ALA) supposedly governed "feats of the Mind" while Intent (INE) was how Felix interacted with the world at large, both of which were vague enough to mean almost anything. Affinity (AFI) as a connection to the Realms was something, though. In fact, the manner in which the Maw was bound to him related to Affinity, according to his Cage the Beast Title. Was that how he'd remove the parasite?

He'd have to keep that in mind.

The days—cycles, as they said—had passed much as they had the first day. Felix lost track of the time after a while, but it hadn't been terribly long since he'd arrived in Echo's Reach. A few cycles at most. He spent those cycles doing "hard" work that rarely made him sweat, and learning the ins and outs of farm-living in the Void. They were also eating meals at the Korvaa's table, Mana-enhanced and all, which meant Pit was growing in strength the more he devoured. With how diluted the harvested Mana tended to be, it wasn't much, just a point here and there, but it added up.

Whenever he wasn't helping Bateo, Felix was either practicing his Skills, attempting to clear his Mana Gates, or rebuilding his Bastion, one stone at a time.

It was slow going on all counts but his Mana Gates, but even that was only to a point. He'd managed to free up both feet and knees, and now that he could open and close the majority at will, it felt as if he could breathe for the first time. Before, closing a single Gate felt suffocating, but with practice, he'd learned to tolerate closing all of his Mana Gates, if only for a few minutes at a time. The Maw suggested folk on the Continent typically held their Gates closed at all times, unless they were trying to regenerate their Mana. Felix doubted he'd ever be able to get to that point, but the improvements were promising.

Yet he still had one Mana Gate left: the one just below his skull. The Maw had warned him repeatedly that clearing his skull Gate was tricky, but Felix had paid it little mind. The others were difficult and painful—like performing a root canal on himself, except all over—but his Pain Resistance at least blunted a large chunk of it. But the skull Gate proved beyond painful, igniting his nerves in electric agony with every attempt. Maybe it was because the Gate was near his brain, or some more esoteric reason, but he'd barely put a dent into the accumulated "rust" around his final Mana Gate.

Instead, he focused on his Bastion more and more, and he soon discovered the reason for his weakness a few cycles prior. The effort and "training" he was doing within his Bastion was drawing on his personal stores of energy, namely his Aspects. Mind, Body, and Spirit, they'd been drained of what little they had to spare. If he wanted to repair it properly, far as he could tell, Felix would have to get more energy from somewhere. In the Void, a desert of System energy, his options were extremely limited.

Can you sense their emotions yet, Felix Nevarre? Not just through your... Companion Pact, but in the air. A taste on the wind.

"There is no wind," Felix said. He didn't mind being intentionally thick when it came to the Primordial's lectures. "You're awfully chatty this morning."

The Maw looked offended. *Am I not allowed to share my infinite wisdom with those barren of it? This is for your benefit. All that I do, now that we are stuck together, has been for* your *benefit.*

"Mhmm." Felix kept his disbelief from his face, though it was a close thing. "And what do you want for that help?"

Want? I merely want you to survive long enough to escape this wretched place. The Maw's mouth twisted, like it had bitten into a lemon. *To have your core remain unaffected by the insidious* nothing *here.*

Felix narrowed his eyes, but couldn't keep the surprise from his voice. "Why do you care?"

I have already told you. We are one, much as neither of us want it to be so. The greater your power, the greater I become in turn. Helping you is helping myself.

"And what happens when you get powerful enough?" Felix asked. It was a question he'd dreaded asking, but it had to be said, if for nothing more than setting the stakes. "You try to take over my body again?"

The Maw regarded him for a long moment, silent. Its gaunt, stolen face was pinched, as if he'd actually hurt its feelings. *They way we are bound, you will always outstrip me in advancement and power. I… I am at your mercy, Felix.*

Felix locked eyes with the Primordial, staring down bluegreen orbs. If it was true, it was great news. *And I'd be a fool to believe even a part of it.*

Below, a door slammed open.

"Eyas! Suppertime! Come an' get it!" Estrid's voice was loud, powered by her Apprentice Body, and the children pivoted on the spot at the sound. With a series of excited *whoops* and cries, the children ran to the edge of the farming island and leaped off.

Felix's gut clenched at the sight, but each kid had wings that snapped open, carrying them effortlessly to the central island. Pit followed, mimicking their feat, and Felix was surprised to see the tenku achieve it easily. More joy floated through their bond, and Felix's worry transformed into indulgent joy.

"That means you too, Felix!"

Ignoring the Maw, Felix grinned to himself and leaped down.

Supper was less involved than breakfast or lunch, featuring light fare and hot cups of a bitter sort of tea. Estrid was a firm believer in "food is fuel," and knew the mornings and afternoons often held the most laborious of tasks on the farm. Laborious for Bateo, perhaps, though Felix hadn't found anything too onerous. His physical stats felt like he was doing everything on Easy Mode.

Still, it was damn good food. And though light, there was plenty to eat, which he knew wasn't the usual state of things in the Void. If nothing else, he appreciated the three square meals he'd been receiving at the farm.

"So, how long have you been here?" Felix asked during a lull in the feeding frenzy. "You said you were born in the Void?"

Bateo dabbed a rough woven cloth at his beak. "Yes. Most in Echo's Reach were born here. I am..." Bateo paused and tilted his head up to the right. "I believe I have lived over one hundred thousand cycles."

Felix almost choked on his tentacle casserole.

"That's... that's like three hundred *years*," Felix said in a strangled tone. He pounded at his chest, dislodging the hunk of food before continuing. "You look like you're in your prime, still."

The Maw had said the pirates were something like two hundred years old, at least. They were almost all grizzled and haggard, evidence of a hard life or something more? Or maybe his viewpoint was skewed. Most of the pirates were humanoid, and Bateo was more of an avian.

Bateo's crest feathers rose a little, and a smug smile tilted the edges of his beak. His wife rolled her eyes. "Thanks for that. Now he'll be insufferable."

Bateo laughed, and so did Felix, caught up in the birdman's good mood.

"It's the voidbeasts, you know," Bateo said after a bit.

"What is?"

"Our longevity. I'm sure you've noticed we're not particularly high-level, yes?"

Felix nodded. "I had wondered about that. It's because of the Void?"

"It is. The System does not reach us here, not in the same way it supposedly does on the Continent," Bateo explained. His voice had a wistful tone when he talked about the Continent, like a man describing a fairy tale. "Skills and levels stagnate after a while, just as our core spaces change the longer we take in the thin dregs of Mana. Long ago, our ancestors realized that eating voidbeasts and their Mana bladders meant living longer, fuller lives out in the black." He slapped his chest. "We're hardier, and our Bodies adapted. Now we push on, our cores evolved to live in this place, cycle after cycle."

"Sounds lonely," Felix said before he could stop himself. He winced.

Bateo only smiled, however. "I've my Estrid." He took her hand in his own, and they shared a long look. "And the children. It is enough."

"Mister Felix, please tell us about the Continent!" Pol begged as dinner wound down. He and the other little hawks all crowded near Felix with wide eyes and hopeful expressions.

"Oh yes!" Kili agreed. "I want to hear about monsters!"

"No!" said Kor. "Monsters are scary."

"Okay, no monsters," Kili said. "Tell us about the sun!"

"Yes! The sun! The sun!"

A chorus was taken up, and Felix couldn't stop himself from

smiling at the grubby little birds. Out of the corner of his eye, he could see Bateo and Estrid both smiling over their cups. Unwilling to disappoint such an eager audience, Felix cleared his throat a bit nervously.

"Alright then, how about I tell you how Pit and I first met?"

"Yes!"

"The Honored Tenku? Please, yes!"

A second chorus supplanted the first, all of them exhilarated by the idea. Even the parents leaned closer as Felix started weaving his tale. He wasn't a storyteller, so he stuck to the facts—more or less. Starting in the Bitter Sea, he navigated his way across the Foglands, fighting monsters the size of their house and emerging unscathed every time.

Yes. Just the facts.

They were the perfect audience, despite Felix's stumbling narrative. They *oohed* and *ahhed* in all the right places, shivering in fear when the Seven-Legged Orit emerged, and cheering in righteous anger when Felix recounted its ignoble death. Sure, the story was a little more PG than before, with Felix actually fighting the beast off with his former sword in grand fashion, but it made for a better tale.

Just as he finished the retelling, Pit bobbing his head in pleased agreement, Felix noticed most of the hatchlings were nodding off. Without another word, Bateo stood up and calmly ushered them up to bed. "When I return, I'll have more tales from you, Felix!"

The Unbound watched them go with a smile, climbing the stairs one sleepy leg at a time.

Pathetic. Can they not climb the stairs under their own power? Must they rely on this elder creature to provide for them? The Maw sat near the ceiling, looking down its nose at the retreating family. *Felix. You must leave this place, or else you'll end up just as weak-willed as these hatchlings.*

Oh my god, shut up! Felix glared at the ceiling, projecting his thoughts with all he had.

"Felix?" Estrid still sat across the table from him, and she briefly looked up at the ceiling before fixing Felix with a steady gaze. "May we speak?"

"Um, sure," Felix said. At the very least he was happy to ignore the Maw. "What's up?"

"What are your plans?"

"My plans?"

Estrid ruffled the feathers along her neck and shoulders, the equivalent of an uncomfortable shrug. "You surely don't intend to spend the rest of your days here, on our tiny farm, do you?"

Felix leaned back in his chair, and the bone creaked under his considerable weight. "Well, the original thought was to get my ship fixed, gather some supplies, and head back out there."

Estrid frowned. "To do what? Die in the black?"

"Find a way back. To the Continent," he said.

Estrid's frown deepened. "I know you've only just arrived in the Void, strange as that is, and you've more hope in you than most. But... escape is a fool's dream, Felix."

"Bateo seems to think it's possible."

"I love my husband. More than anything. But he's a fool, through and through." Estrid shook her head, and her feathers seemed a touch duller. Dingier. Her eyes, unlike Bateo's, were ringed by bags and a certain darkness he could feel. "I love that my husband believes. That he listens to the old stories and hopes for a way out. It drew me to him, long ago."

"How did you meet?" Felix asked, hoping to divert the subject.

Estrid laughed, a short little chirp. "Blasphemy, if you would believe it. I was set to devote myself to Noctis, and Bateo accidentally set fire to the Temple."

"Whoa," Felix said with a laugh. "How's setting a building on fire an accident?"

"When a dozen Manabladders get punctured at once, many unexpected things can occur," Estrid said. Her voice was fond, but also tired. "He was carting a shipment for the Conference, and a chance accident with some skimmers sent him crashing into the Temple. He was so agile and strong, moving aside the priestesses and securing what bladders weren't too far gone. Lost half his crop and won my interest."

"Wow," Felix said with a chuckle. He never knew Bateo had it in him. "Temple of Noctis, huh? I've heard of a Temple of Vellus in the Void, but not Noctis."

Estrid gave him a strange look. "It is not a true Temple. The Void would never allow such a thing to exist. The divine would be sucked away into the nothingness around us." She sighed, which sounded much like Pit's own noises. A whistling tune. "But yes. I was a devotee of Noctis for a long, long time. Goddess of the Night, Time, and Truth itself. Fitting for this place, which is eternal night, though no mythical stars or moons shine on us." A bitter note entered Estrid's voice and she glanced at Felix again. "Noctis was the beloved of Vellus, you know. Goddess of the Storm, of the Tide, and Blood itself. When Vellus was Lost to Ruin, it is said Noctis cried enough to create the Bitter Sea."

"Really," Felix said. "Vellus was Lost, too? What does that mean, exactly?"

No one had been able to explain it, not really. Magda and the others had tried, but he always felt like he was missing some sort of cultural touchstone to understand what they were talking about.

"It means Ruin took her, ripped a goddess from the heavens and cast her into Desolation. Or so the scripture tells us," Estrid shrugged. "Not even the gods can survive Desolation, though they reside within the Ethereal."

Felix's mind flashed back to the wards around the Ten Hands' fortress. Desolation magic, Nokk had called it. Estrid snagged her stonecrafted mug of tea and held it in her hands, letting its paltry warmth waft over her.

"I understand sadness like that, Felix. It's what drew me to the goddess. The Void is a realm of despair, and only the foolish avoid its eventual sting." She smiled again. "Only when I met my Bateo did I feel happiness, and again when each of my littles hatched. Motes of light in the dark, the only stars I'll ever see."

"There has to be a way out," Felix insisted. "I know it."

"I'm glad you believe that," Estrid said. "But I cannot. Your tales are powerful and strange, speaking of alien lands and things we've only ever heard of in our oldest legends. I even felt myself get lost in them, just for a moment.... and I cannot let Bateo chase that dream any more than he already has."

"What? What do you mean?"

"You're a kind person, Felix. My Bateo sees that, trusts that. I know that if you asked, he'd follow whatever lead you may discover in the hopes that an exit could be found." Estrid shook her head again, and the stone cup hit the table hard enough to slosh her tea out. "We need him. *I* need him to be here."

She reached out, placing her clawed hand on Felix's own.

"When you leave, do not tell us."

Felix hadn't a clue what to say to that, for all that he sensed Estrid's earnest sincerity. The pain behind her eyes and twitching feathers. "I—"

"Raid!"

Bateo's voice rang out into the stillness of the Void, loud as his Body would allow. Alarm shot through Felix, seizing his fight or flight response.

"Voidbeast attack!"

CHAPTER TWENTY-FIVE

Felix was out the door in a flash, Pit right behind him. Bateo had climbed out onto the roof, likely out of his children's window, and was pointing toward the beast pens.

"Thrice damned Harrowings! Let go of my stock!"

With a piercing cry, Bateo launched from the roof and literally flew toward the smaller island. Felix could see at least a dozen black shapes flitting against the buildings there, though their forms were lost once they maneuvered in front of the Void. Felix focused, flaring his Voracious Eye and Manasight. He could sense their presence easily enough, but only when he chanced upon them. His Manasight, however, was ineffective. But it didn't matter. The things were tearing into Bateo's pens, trying to eat the tamed Tenebrils, most likely.

Not if I can help it.

Felix burst into a run, Agility and Strength surging together with such easy grace it felt beyond natural. He leaped, and the power within sent him catapulting up off the central island and into the emptiness of the Void. He soared through the air like a gold medal gymnast, though his stats marked him as well beyond any human from Earth, and Felix landed in a crouch at the edge of the next island.

Wrack and Ruin!

With a grunt, Felix hurled a dark orb of concentrated acid at the nearest Harrowing, hitting it squarely in the back and melting through its entire body.

You Have Killed A Harrowing!
XP Earned!

Three Harrowings broke off from the flock, turning and angling for Felix's head.

"Careful of their claws!" Bateo shouted. "They'll drain you of Mana in no time!"

"I know!" Felix shouted back, dodging the first two, but receiving a jagged slash across his chest from the third. The blue bar that represented his Mana in his vision shortened, dropping by about ten percent. Felix hissed in pain and unfurled a tendril of shadow Mana. The Shadow Whip snapped out, wrapping around the Harrowing's angular beak, and Felix hauled back. The voidbeast flew through the air, unable to resist his Strength, and smashed directly into the jagged stone island next to him.

You Have Killed A Harrowing!
XP Earned!

Brilliant Mana surged and shot out in all directions as its Manabladder ruptured like liquid fireworks.

Gah!

The liquid Mana, dense at first, sublimated into a vibrant, rainbow vapor. Instinctively, Felix breathed it in.

Ravenous Tithe!

The power of the Harrowing pulled inward through his Mana Gate at the base of his skull and into his core space. It collected there, roiling with energy above the crackling blue flame of his core.

Further Bloodlines Have Been Found. Processing 3%

"Damnit!" Felix growled. Every time he used that Skill, his Bloodline progression increased. What would happen at one hundred percent?

Felix wasn't given time to worry about it, as the other two Harrowings came in for the kill.

Reign of Vellus!

A cone-shaped blast of lightning and force sent them both careening to either side of him, while visibly whetting the appetites of those nearby. He could almost feel their hunger, like a pain in his own gut as the entire flock pivoted toward him.

"Shit."

Shadow Whip!
Shadow Whip!

Two more inky tendrils launched from either palm, slapping into the disoriented Harrowings and latching on. With a fierce tug, he yanked both of them toward himself. They flew true and fast, giving Felix barely enough time to drop the Shadow Whips and conjure his Corrosive Strike.

Corrosive Strike!
Corrosive Strike!

His fists, propelled by his Strength and the voidbeasts' momentum, punched straight through their center mass. It was a clean hit, but still a chance claw raked against his thigh, draining more Mana. Luminous liquid splashed outward from their fatal wounds, vaporizing into the dark.

You Have Killed A Harrowing (x2)!
XP Earned!

More came for him, and Felix pinged six before he lost count in the flurry of jagged claws and sharpened beaks. Reign of Vellus smashed into them, disorienting them enough that they didn't see the orbs of concentrated acid that tore through their ranks. But the spell cost a lot, and despite the effects of his meal, Felix's Mana wasn't regenerating as fast as it usually did. The Harrowings advanced, and Felix met them, fist against claw.

He did well, all things considered. Talons raked against him, stealing his Mana, but he gave them crushed wings and shorn claws in retribution. Felix was tempted to pull the cutlass at his waist, but the memory of his broken Skill and the pain that followed was enough to rely on his fists alone. In fact, he had to be careful even when dodging attacks not to engage in anything the System viewed as acrobatics. He'd felt the burn of that broken Skill several times as he'd evaded the lethal talons of his enemies.

But there were far more than just a dozen Harrowings. More and more kept coming from the dark, invisible until they attacked, lost among the crowd once they swirled about him. His Health started dropping almost as fast as his Mana.

The Maw was screaming. *Run from them, you fool! This farm is not worth my life!*

"Shut up!"

A rallying cry shook through Felix's Spirit, closely followed by the snap of outspread wings. Spears of ice whistled passed, so close he could feel their chill, and Pit swooped after them.

Pit used Cry!
Harrowing (x3) Are Stunned For 4 Seconds!

"Yes!" Felix eyed his Mana. He had enough for this at least. *Influence of the Wisp!*

You Have Enthralled A Harrowing (x6)!

Four seconds was an eternity in a battle, though it was only nine of many. Regardless, Felix joined his friend and got to work. Frost Spears and Wingblades ripped gaps in the Harrowings' formation, and Felix flowed into them, fists flying with all the power he could muster. Magic and claws and strength of arm met the bestial might of the Void and did not falter. Less than a minute later, bodies scored with wounds and drenched in ruptured Manabladders, Felix and Pit stood victorious.

You Have Killed A Harrowing!
XP Earned!

Felix idly accepted his notifications, noting that he'd neither earned a level or increased his Skills at all. The energy from the System felt thinner than ever. Yet, the roiling cloud of stolen power above his core space was lively and thick with sizzling energy.

"Felix! Are you alright?" Bateo flapped down from the second level of the enclosure barn. His clothes were a bit torn, and the crooked knife he carried was dark with blood, but the Korvaa looked perfectly Healthy. A quick Voracious Eye confirmed it.

"I'm fine," he said. The pain of his wounds was already dulling into nothing, though his Health regen wasn't anything like his Mana regen.

"Still, come into the house. Estrid'll get you patched up."

Felix insisted they check on the farmer's cattle, so with some prodding, they turned to inspect the barn and enclosures. There weren't many points of damage, just near the front gates where the stench of the Tenebril was strongest. It was what called out to the Harrowings in the first place.

Wait, Felix paused. Looked back at the front gate. *Smell?*

Voidbeasts didn't have a smell. Aside from the heavily seasoned cooking he'd experienced, little else did either. Even the funk of his sweat-stained and grimy shirt was heavily muted by the deadened nature of the Void. He sniffed again. For some reason, Felix was smelling the Mana the creatures exuded.

His gut rumbled again, and Felix clenched his jaws. He had a feeling it wasn't because he needed more food.

"Goddamn Maw," he whispered.

"Everything alright, Felix?" Bateo asked, and Felix waved the question off. He stood from his inspection of a door joint and massaged his lower back, right below his wings. "Unf. Those beasts get worse every time I see them."

"I thought the warding kept them away?"

"Usually does." Bateo frowned. "It shouldn't have failed yet, not so soon. I'll need to contact the Rim Hunters. They are the ones meant to hunt these beasts down before they get so far." He looked at Felix's wounds, still oozing blood. "Come. Let's see Estrid."

Estrid wasn't happy to see Felix hurt, though she was clearly happier that Bateo hadn't suffered any injuries. She patched him up—and his clothes—with exceptional skill and speed, though her needles weren't able to pierce his Armored Skin and high Vitality. They made do with simple salves and bandages made from the same rough material as all their clothing; a cloth woven from the above-ground stalks of the tuber-like *cnop*.

Fully bandaged and more or less decent, Felix stood as Bateo made to leave. "Are you heading to the Rim Hunters now?"

"Yes. They need to know."

"Bateo, I do not want you out in your skimmer in this," Estrid said. "Who knows if more Harrowings are out in the black, waiting for the first bit of Mana that pokes its head out?"

"If I don't tell them, then we risk this happening to another of the farms," Bateo said. "Or worse, the school yards in town."

That caught Estrid up, and Felix took the chance. "I'll go. Pit and I can handle the Harrowings if we see any, and I," Felix threw a glance at Estrid. "I'm less needed here."

"That's false, Felix. You've proven to be a deft hand at farm work," Bateo said. He too looked at his wife and sighed. "But I see what you mean. Very well. I don't like you risking yourself for me and mine, but I'll not fight the wind."

Bateo pulled a rolled up piece of leather off a rack next to the wall. Felix had noticed the rack previously, but hadn't given it much thought. Now he realized the leather scraps were scrolls, and writing adorned the voidbeast skin.

"Here. This is the path to the Rim Hunter's lodge. The way is simple, but the Void is nothing if not treacherous."

Felix and Pit departed shortly after that, taking the scrap of voidleather along with them at Bateo's insistence. Though Felix could have redrawn it himself from memory, he didn't argue. The old farmer and his wife cared, that much was certain, and he didn't want to shoot that down.

In his short time on the Continent, Felix had noticed a state of fear gripping its denizens. The few non-monsters he'd met were under unusual circumstances, but Felix got the impression the world he'd landed upon was not one of kindness and mercy. It was one where strength mattered above all else, and that... that made him sad.

Bateo and his family were different. He'd accepted Felix quickly, coming to his aid at the array marker and again at the Conference Hall. His family had welcomed him into the fold, even with Estrid's confessed fears. In a lot of ways, they reminded Felix of home. The Void was a far cry from Fort Lauderdale, and their bone-built farmhouse was not the colorful stucco of his childhood home, but the warmth of their household was undeniable. His mother looked at her kids the same way Estrid did, warm and a little fearful of what terrible new things they might get into.

It made Felix very homesick as he skimmed into the Void.

That collection of codependents is noxious, Felix Nevarre. You should leave this place.

Felix rolled his eyes. The little skimmer—the dinghy from before—fit Felix and Pit comfortably, but the Maw didn't need to ride with them. It opted to float menacingly at the corner of his eye, gnashing its stolen teeth in muted rage.

"The moment I take interpersonal advice from you is when I know I've made a wrong turn," he said.

The Maw scoffed. *You trust them so much. What would happen if they found out you've a Quest to leave the Void?*

"I'm sure many do," Felix said. "It can't be that uncommon of a Quest."

Quests are rare. You know this. None here have such a Quest, or any Quest. This is a place beyond the System, no matter what the farmer *says. More importantly, a Quest suggests a solution, a true way out, hmm?* The Primordial smiled, and as always it was worse than its grimaces. *What would that Conference of birds do if they found out?*

Felix didn't answer, but he didn't have to; they both knew how it would end. The Maw laughed. An ugly, cruel sound.

Echo's Reach would tear you apart.

The way to the Rim Hunter's lodge was fairly straightforward. Bateo had taught Felix how to read the navigation markings on his maps, which, like the other map in his possession, were all the dotted lines and odd notations. Because the Void was a 3D space, it didn't simply use cardinal directions, but more complex and arcane methods that measured pitch and something called "yaw." It didn't make a lot of sense to Felix, but he had the basics down.

The trip was silent, save for faint seething from the Maw. Felix considered telling her off, but didn't bother. It was a waste of energy. The Primordial wouldn't change, couldn't by all measure, and only wanted one thing: to be free.

That makes two of us, he thought with a snort.

Once they had passed a series of oblong-shaped islands,

barren except for a small watchtower made of bone, Felix got the idea that something was definitely wrong. There was no one at the watchtower, despite Bateo's insistence that they never left it unmanned. Felix continued past it, unchallenged by Rim Hunter or beasts, and followed the map the rest of the way.

What he found was chaos.

CHAPTER TWENTY-SIX

"From above!" Felix shouted.

A tide of Tenebrils flowed through the dark, arcing up and over the lodge to slam down into a grouping of severe-looking Korvaa. They weren't fools, either, and all six of them leaped outward and raised heavy bone shields. The Tenebrils came down, a cyclone of lashing tentacles, and the barbs on their ends caught and gouged the walls of the lodge and the shields both. But no one died.

"Pit!" Felix shouted, and burst forth. His friend replied with a screech.

Tenebrils Are Stunned (x13) For 2 Seconds!

A swath of void-squid locked up in fear of the tenku's voice, but there were plenty more that flowed over their brethren and attacked the Hunters.

Shadow Whip!

Shadow Whip!

Two tendrils snapped outward, and Felix spread his fingers to grip nearby islands. They were still a dozen yards away from the fight, and he meant to change that. He hauled back, stretching the slightly elastic whips and unleashed lightning as he jumped.

Reign of Vellus!

Kinetic Mana blasted him forward, Shadow Whips focusing the shot, and Felix flew bodily into the fray. He hit the column of Tenebrils, some still stunned and smashed several to pulp with just his bodyweight.

You Have Killed A Tenebril (x2)!
XP Earned!

"A Human!" one of the Hunters said. "What's he doing here?"

"Bateo's pet!" said another. "Don't mind him! Fight off the squids, you slackjawed idiots!"

The Rim Hunters exploded outward, carried forth on wings and dark streamers of some Skill. Felix, meanwhile, landed heavily among the still swirling Tenebrils. He'd rung his own bell a bit in the collision, but he shook it off and flared his favorite ability.

Reign of Vellus!

An electrical storm slammed outward in all directions, by turns frying and hurling back any Tenebril within thirty feet of him. Only a few hit rocks or the lodge, while more were sent spinning into the dark. Off to the side, a spray of yard-long icicles snapped through the Void. The Frost Spears stabbed into several Tenebril, but most managed to wriggle off their pinning strikes. As masses of writhing tentacles without a solid body, they were hard—but not impossible—to hit in such a way.

He just needed more spears.

Stone Shaping!

The island he was on, containing a lodge and two outbuildings, burst upward as the surface melted into goo before rapidly reforming into one, two, three dozen spikes of stone. Pit did not relent either, as Frost Spears and Wingblades followed.

You Have Killed A Tenebril (x17)!
XP Earned!

Felix almost expected the thunderous approach of energy signifying a level up, but the System was silent. Instead, he felt a sudden ache in his bones, like a hole had opened up inside of him. That energy that roiled above his core fell, fed into the blue-white flames before rolling outward in waves of golden-blue light. The light hit his Skills and murky core space like a breath of frigid air and the sizzle of burning metal. It was pain, but also pleasure, as he felt himself become just the tiniest bit *more*.

Stone Shaping is level 26!
Shadow Whip is level 27!

Felix stumbled, taking two slashes across his chest and face. He felt that similar, shaky weakness he'd had previously in the farmhouse. A Tenebril hit him, and he fell, rolling from the force of its attack. Pit shrieked in alarm.

Eat them, you fool! Don't let your pride kill me! The Maw floated above him, its entire body twisted inward, as if it were trying to tear its own guts from itself. *The Grand Harmony cannot find you here, Felix Nevarre! That is a hunger you must embrace!*

Felix tossed his head, ignoring the Primordial's ravenous frustration. He steadied his arms and stood.

"No. I can do this." He lifted his bare fists, scratched and bloody. "I can do this."

He threw himself back into battle. There was plenty to be had.

The Hunters put up a good showing, though Felix's Eye said none were beyond Apprentice Tier or level twenty. Still, they were strong, and the light weapons they used were very effective on the agile voidbeasts. Polearms mostly, but a few wielded thin, thrusting sabres and targes that they handled with exceptional skill. They moved like Harn and Magda, for all that they were far lower in level, and any Tenebrils that fled Felix's field of spikes were mopped up in short order.

Fight over, Felix fell. Pit was at his side immediately, helping him stay upright, but it was more than exhaustion clawing at his foundations. It was his Ravenous Tithe, greedily grasping at the Essence and debris-filled darkness of his core space, only there was no Essence left. His core had consumed it to push his Skill levels up, and Ravenous Tithe was gnawing at him instead.

Shit. I don't have a choice. The voidbeasts were still venting Mana from their bladders, a haze of shimmering, liquid light that hid him from the Rim Hunters. *I—I just need a little.*

Ravenous Tithe!

Felix's hands wrapped in the nearest plumes of Mana and felt a suction from within his channels. The Mana and several of the beasts themselves were sucked from the air, pulled into his mouth in a sharp whirlwind before pouring through his wide-open skull Gate. The hunger pangs quieted, fading, as his core space filled once again with sparking clouds of power. Some of them sank into the dark, strengthening it, he thought, but the rest pooled in agitated swirls of fog atop his blue-white ball of flame.

Further Bloodlines Have Been Found. Processing 4%

Felix gritted his teeth. What would happen at a full hundred percent?

"Hey, you alive over there?"

A Korvaa with a wide scar across his beak leaned over Felix, squinting down at him. He had golden eyes and brown coloration, along with a sharp crest of feathers atop his head. His severe look broke into a grin when he saw Felix move.

"Damnation, you fought like a Demon of the Void!" He squawked out a laugh. "You could use some lessons on aiming, though."

"He about splattered himself against the lodge, is what ya mean!" Another Rim Hunter, similarly colored, said from close by. Felix climbed to his feet, bracing against the pain he expected, but finding his Aspects hale and hearty. Aside from a few scratches—and the wounds he took earlier—he felt great. "Never seen a Human fly, but damn if ya didn't try your best!"

A round of rough laughter flowed through the Hunters. Felix saw that they had all survived as well, not even bearing any wounds. At worst, Felix could see a few destroyed shields and savaged armor, all of which was made of void bone.

The scarred one, named Ulin, shook Felix's hand. "Thanks for the help, though. Can't imagine it felt good to burn so much Mana on a spell like that."

Felix wasn't sure what he meant, until he realized that the Stone Shaping he'd cast had deformed half the island into a series of vicious spikes. "Ah, well, there were a lot of enemies. I couldn't let you all handle them alone. Not when I came here to report another attack."

The jovial, just-survived-a-fatal-encounter atmosphere vanished in an instant. Ulin looked at him, golden eyes sharp. "Another attack? At Bateo's farm?"

"Beasties are gettin' bold, attacking us here."

"Other places, too..."

"Yeah, Bateo's livestock was attacked by a flock of Harrowings," Felix said. "We fought them off, and wanted to come tell you."

Ulin nodded, his crest of feathers flexing in a very intimidating way. "Good you did, lad. We'll have to find out why." He put out his clawed hand again, and Felix took it. "Our thanks, again. And to you, Honored Tenku."

Pit chirruped, and the Rim Hunters bowed low to him. He perked up and tipped his beak into the air, haughtily.

Eat it up, lil pig, Felix sent.

"Next time though, you'll owe us a new wall," snickered one of the other Hunters.

Felix gave them a wan smile, and the two of them departed, though not before using Stone Shaping to smooth out his jagged spikes. More or less.

He found his abandoned skimmer easily enough on the not-ground below the rock islands. Luckily, it hadn't been broken outright when he'd catapulted off its top, and he could still feed his Mana into it. All the while, back at the lodge, the Hunters had entered and returned quickly, more fully decked out in protective gear and weapons than before. A hurried conversation took place, and it was clear they either didn't notice him or didn't care he was still around.

"We head to the farms, check on them before we move inward. The Conference hasn't shown up on our doorstep, so we can assume no one's died. Leastwise no one important. But keep it snappy! Split into two groups and move fast!"

"Aye!"

The groups split, the distinct snap of wings unfurling as the nearest group glided down to their own skimmers.

"That Human... his Mana was strong. Too strong."

"He's fresh, they say. Void hasn't diluted his core yet." The familiar voice of Ulin waved off the concern. "He'll be just as us in a century. If he lives that long."

"Hah! The way he threw himself at those voidbeasts? The boy's mad."

The voices faded as their skimmers disappeared beyond some islands, and Felix was left to ponder their words in sudden silence.

Dilute?

He checked his core, which conversely felt full of fire and curiously empty. Tinges of that weakness was washing against him, but it was far less than before. And fading, as the nebula-like cloud of monster energy swirled above his burning core. Other than the strange nature and effects of his Ravenous Tithe, his core space felt much the same as usual.

"Maw, is the Void diluting my core?" he asked.

There was a snort from within a rock formation before his inescapable enemy poked its head out of the solid stone. *Not yet. These poor prey animals? Yes. Yes it has.*

"How can you tell?"

Their Skills, boy. They are but shadows of true Skills, washed out remnants of abilities the Void has long since corrupted. The Void breaks down all, eventually. Their consumption of voidflesh is but a stalling tactic that will only delay the inevitable. When they die, they will leave nothing behind, not even dust.

"And it takes time. Everyone's been saying that. But why do I feel like it's hitting me already?"

The Maw shrugged. *You are Unbound. The way you interact with Creation is neither known nor predictable.*

It was less comforting than he wanted, but Felix had to accept it. His life had become a series of wild encounters and strange developments. His body changed; his mind did, too. Felix's chest hitched, and he consciously flared Meditation. Slowly, his breathing smoothed. The agitation dwindled until it was manageable.

His considerable Willpower did the rest.

"Let's get back."

They took the skimmer the long way round this time. Felix was also concerned about voidbeast attacks. He hadn't even met any of the other folk around the town, but no one deserved to be attacked by those monsters. Since the Hunters were combing the Rim, he started heading inward, toward Echo's Reach.

And, he added to himself. *I can see more about this Ravenous Tithe thing.*

The Primordial was messing with something. Already had. But what did that mean for Felix? What other bloodlines were found, and what would happen when it was done processing? Could he use it to his advantage? The Skill clearly pulled energy from his enemies, their entire body, it seemed, and he could utilize that to supplement his fading connection to the System. Right?

Pit trilled a concerned note at him. He was crowded into the back of the dinghy and nudged Felix's calf with his beak. *Caution.*

Felix smiled and let out a breathy sigh. "You're right. I just... what if we can't get out, Pit? Do we resign ourselves to living for hundreds of years in this... nothing? As much as I like Bateo and Estrid... And then on top of that, we fade out, and the power we've worked hard to claim just—poof? Goes away?" He shoved more Mana into the skimmer, and the dinghy scooted ahead, faster than before. "We have to get outta here."

Pit nodded in agreement, and warm comfort extended across their bond. It was a nice counterpoint to the endless dark.

Fifteen or so minutes later, Felix came across the nearest home sitting atop a lone rock fragment. Dark shapes flitted near the roof, and Felix's Perception could pick out a group of Harrowings scrabbling at the chimney, as if trying to force themselves down it.

"Pit, we're going in," he warned before pouring more Mana into the skimmer. The Control Node whined as the skimmer shot off, far faster than it was intended to go, and Felix guided it like a missile toward the neared voidbeast.

Wrack and Ruin!
Corrosive Strike!
Corrosive Strike!

Starting with a volley of his ranged acid spell, Felix lobbed it into the amassed horde. It zipped through the Void and hit like a cannonball, sending the Harrowings tumbling into the dark.

You Have Killed A Harrowing (x2)!
XP Earned!

Again that squeezing sensation, denying him the experience the System claimed he had earned. He gritted his teeth and put it out of his mind as he skimmed close enough to slam two more Harrowings from the sky.

The last four were easy to mop up, using a combination of

Shadow Whip and Reign of Vellus to turn them all into meat paste and oozing, sublimating Mana. It was over in a handful of heartbeats, and he hadn't even left his boat.

Pit let out an annoyed chirrup.

"Sorry, next time I'll leave more for you," Felix said. "Not like we're getting anything from them, though."

Felix watched the bodies begin to smoke and sizzle, far faster than it happened on the Continent. They mingled with their own vaporizing Manabladders, black smoke and rainbow mist co-mingling.

"Amazin', lad." An older Korvaa had emerged while several much smaller and curious heads peered out of the door behind him.

"It's Bateo's Human!"

"The Tenku! Bevvi, you see? You see?"

"He killed them all?"

The Korvaa hushed the excitable hatchlings and gave Felix an apologetic smile. He had long, dark claws and several scars on his neck where the feathers didn't grow in. "Thank you. And you, Honored Tenku."

Pit nodded to them regally, and Felix had to suppress his smile. "We saw a few packs of these beasts out and about. Be careful. The Rim Hunters are catching what they can on the outskirts."

He nodded. "Aye. We'll make sure to stay indoors tonight." He reached out and clasped Felix's wrist. "I've little ones in there and… we thought the beasts would end us. Take this. As thanks."

The bird man tried to pass a tray of food on Felix, but he shook his head. "No, please keep it. This should only last the night, but I'd rather you not lack food because of me."

"Are you sure?"

"I'm fine." Felix patted his belly, flat and taut though it was. "Bateo feeds me plenty back on the farm." He smiled at the old Korvaa and half-waved at the little ones.

Then they were off.

Town safe? Pit asked after a while.

"Not sure. It's why we're checking." Felix looked back, but the old Korvaa's home was lost amid the increasing jumble of stone islands, most of which were uninhabited. "Voidbeasts could be hiding in any of these islands."

No, Pit sent. Impressions of blank darkness thrummed across their bond.

"Yeah, I don't see them either," Felix said. "Alright, I'll keep moving forward, and you tell me if you spot them, okay?"

Pit gave a determined little nod, his big golden eyes narrowed in concentration.

Okay.

CHAPTER TWENTY-SEVEN

When Felix saw the ring of chained islands denoting Echo's Reach, he let out a relieved breath. Clearly the voidbeasts hadn't made it that far, at least from the direction Felix was approaching. Felix hadn't caught sight of any, and Pit said everything smelled normal. He decided it would be good to at least cross the island chain before heading back to Bateo's.

Just as the last time he'd been in town, it was evening. Korvaa of all shapes and sizes were about, lingering on their islands or gliding between the large chains on some sort of errands. Everyone was dressed in robes or cloaks, cut and belted in such ways that the drapery didn't interfere with their wings or limbs. The types of birdfolk differed despite their similar clothes, from ravens to owls. He even saw a woman who resembled a dove. It seemed the Korvaa as a people varied wildly in appearance.

No smell, Pit said. *Good.*

Felix smiled and ruffled the tenku's head. "Hell yeah, it's good. We're a great team, you know?"

Pit hummed in delight at the scratches. *Great team. Yes.*

Giggles and shouts rang out as a succession of kids zipped

by the nearest island. Each of them held a glowing pole and was aboard their own skimmer, though it was little more than a flat board of bone. Felix and Pit paused their progress, watching the kids do loops and barrel rolls around the islands, much to the annoyance of their residents. Angered hoots and squawks followed the children.

It reminded Felix of when he was a kid, wandering through abandoned houses. A development called Wayward Oaks had suffered the brunt of a hurricane, and the developer, likely out of money, had simply dropped the project and left the area. So a large, six-block area crowded with half-filled foundations and the shells of houses became the playground for every kid in the neighborhood. Some were skaters and potheads, looking for places to do tricks and get high. Others were just kids, inhabited by the primal urge all kids had to just break stuff. There was plenty of stuff to break inside half-ruined developments. They'd almost gotten caught a time or two, when cops would patrol the area, but Felix had always gotten away.

Watching the young Korvaa slip by on their weird skimmers hit him harder than he expected. Nostalgia, mixed in with regret, was a familiar concoction he'd brew back home in his tiny apartment. This was that, mingled with a sense of loss that Felix thought he'd come to terms with—back when he said goodbye to his mom.

"Ah, shit," he said. His throat tightened and everything felt too much suddenly. He had the Willpower to force the feeling away—had done so repeatedly since arriving on the Continent—but he was tired of it. He let the feeling spool out from his chest and throat and behind his eyes, a burning ache he hated as much as needed. "I'm so far from home, bud."

Pit trilled comfortingly and pressed up against his back. A wing extended up and just barely over his shoulder, while his back rumbled with Pit's deep breathing.

Etheric Concordance is level 27!

SILENCE

A chunk of his stolen power was siphoned away and into his core flame. It was spat back out, now a golden-blue light that surged into the Skill that formed their bond. A soothing melody, barely heard, caressed Felix's being. It took what Pit was doing and somehow amplified the warmth and comfort on offer.

"Thanks, bud," he said after several long minutes. The melancholy hadn't gone away entirely, but it felt manageable again, even without Willpower. "We should get moving."

Felix reignited his connection with the skimmer's Control Node and pushed more of his Mana into it. He had less than before he'd left the lodge, but more than when he'd left the farm. His natural regeneration was still able to pull in enough Mana from around him to restore him at a relatively fast rate, but Felix estimated it was operating at fifty percent efficiency.

And that rate is dropping with each passing day—cycle, whatever.

It reaffirmed his need to leave the Void. No matter how comfortable it was living with Bateo, this place was a death trap. To that end, Felix angled his skimmer toward the town center. Bateo had told him that the Conference leaders were in charge of finding a way out of the Void. Surely they would have *something* by this point? The real question was whether they would willingly share it with him, the "Unknown."

But he had a plan for that.

No less than ten minutes later, Felix was hovering near the Conference Hall and watching as the guards sat around and rolled dice against the stairs. The cursing was loud and often. Every few minutes though, one of them would leave the front steps and trudge upward to do a circuit in the Hall itself, before inevitably returning and kicking off another round of swearing.

I could come in from behind. But… no. Felix flew around the central island. *There are guards here, too. The only approach is to walk right up and pretend I'm supposed to be there. I've got Deception at level 10. Hope that's enough.*

Felix and Pit flew down and landed at the edge of the central island. The guards immediately stopped their game and stood up, hands going to shields and spears as he approached. Felix held out his hands in a gesture of peace.

"Hey there. How's it going?" he said. The guards stared at him, stone-faced. Felix didn't see the magpie-colored Hepset, and instead the majority were all burly-looking eagles and a single reddish-colored hawk. Or was it a falcon? "Nice night, huh?"

The guards just watched him, their faces stone. Except one, who sneered at Felix. "What does the Unknown want here?"

"Wasn't the Unknown banished to some piss poor farmstead?" said another.

"Oho, true! He was. So what's he doing here, bothering us?"

Pit stalked forward, but Felix held him back with a hand on his shoulders. He then plastered a smile on his face in spite of the wave of anger that came from his Companion. "I've just come to speak with one of the Conference leaders, if they're available."

"Conference—You think one of the Lords is going to make time for *you*, guano stain?" The sneering one laughed, a squawking screech. "You're not even worthy of the Honored Tenku's attention! Why don't you shove off into the Void, so we can give your better the glory he deserves."

The jerk guard's pronouncement was met by a wall of laughter and jeers. It took all his Willpower to wrestle the combined annoyance and rage from Pit as well as himself. It would be so easy for him to destroy them. He'd just killed three flocks of voidbeasts, more or less alone. These guards stood no chance, not against his acid and fists.

Not against lightning.

Yes. Destroy them. A voice whispered to him. *How dare they oppose our Will!*

Felix let the sparks fade from his fist, and the Skill within his core space slowly hummed into silence. He hadn't even realized he was grasping at Reign of Vellus. Felix shot a look to his side, where the Maw was hovering with a look of vicious satisfaction —a look that morphed into disgusted disappointment.

Pathetic.

The guards, fully unaware of how close they came to death, pressed forward. They carried their spears with a casual arrogance, utterly confident in either their power or numbers. Or both. Felix realized few people had the Analyze Skill on the Continent, and it was likely fewer still had it out in the Void.

"C'mon, Unknown. Do something. Anything." The sneering one opened its beak wide as his crest lifted in clear aggression. "Give us the excuse."

"What is happening here?"

The guards swept around, and the sneering one gaped up at the Conference Hall. "Lord Wonderment!"

A dark, raven-like Korvaa stood atop the steps, decked out in dark robes stitched with white and silver thread. It accentuated the almost blue-black coloration of his feathers and pale gray eyes. Those eyes pierced the guards with an imperious sensation, one that Felix felt the barest wash of, for all that he wasn't the target. The guards trembled, and several fell to their knees.

"I'll ask again. What is happening here?"

"S-sir, the Unknown wanted to-to enter the Conference Hall. To speak with one of you," the sneering guard stuttered.

"And why was I not made aware of this?"

"I-I thought, I thought that—"

"That you thought at all is a problem, Guardsman Rhys. You are to guard and to relay to us when we have visitors and precious little else. Do you understand?" The pressure the Conference Lord was exerting increased by the smallest margin, and Rhys finally fell to his knees as well.

How'd he do that? Felix wondered. He felt a similar alarm from Pit. *What if he turns that on us?*

When those pale eyes turned to them, Felix managed not to flinch, but the pressure he had tasted did not follow. Instead, Wonderment smiled and beckoned to them both. "Come,

Honored Tenku and Felix Nevarre. You are welcome to speak with me in my offices."

Felix spared the guardsmen a glance, but none of them dared to even look in his direction. All were staring resolutely at the ground. Felix and Pit mounted the steps quickly and found themselves following in the sweeping wake of Lord Wonderment. They quickly followed.

The Maw, however, had disappeared again. *Where'd it go this time?*

The three of them traversed the outside of the Conference Hall before heading to a large side door. All of which was made of well-polished voidbeast bone, carved into images of stylized wings. The door opened soundlessly, and Wonderment led them through a series of well-appointed chambers, until they reached a set of even more impressive doors. These were also made of bone, also carved into wings and talons and the silhouetted images of many bird people gathered close under a series of clouds and seven moons.

"Seven moons. I thought there were only six?" Felix said as the doors opened to admit them into a plush office.

Wonderment looked at him over his shoulder as he walked to his large desk across the room. "Seven moons for the seven gods. Well, the seven that matter, anyhow." He tilted his head in surprise, beak slightly agape. "Don't tell me you're not familiar with the gods."

Felix waved a hand, perhaps a little too hastily. "No no, I know about them." Vess had given him a rundown on the gods once, though he had to grasp at the memory with his Born Trait. "Noctis, Yyero, Siva, the Twins, and Avet. Those are the ones I know."

Wonderment chuckled. "I see. That makes sense. I doubt many places teach about the Lost Goddess." He gestured to a chair. "Please sit."

Felix did. "Lost Goddess?"

"Mm. Lost Ages ago to the Ruin. They say her wife, Noctis, wept tears enough to fill an ocean that day." The raven sighed, almost longingly. "To have someone love you so much. It is a romantic tale."

"Lost to the Ruin," Felix muttered. *Even gods were susceptible to this Ruin thing? Damn. What was it?* "Wait, is the Lost Goddess named Vellus?"

"So you have heard of her. They say her moon fell from the sky the moment she was taken, but we Korvaa have long memories and ancient traditions. We try to keep the truth alive."

"Can't argue with that sentiment," Felix said. "There aren't many out here who think the truth is all that important."

"You speak of the pirates, yes?" Felix nodded and Wonderment continued. "Your ship tells the tale that it once belonged to the Ten Hands, is that right?"

"It is. I like to think of it belonging to me, now." Felix said.

"So it does. Speaking of, that is why I had wanted to speak with you. I was even planning on coming to visit you on Bateo's farm in the next day." Wonderment smiled and spread his hands. "Your ship is nearly fixed. I'm told it will be finished in the next few cycles."

Pit chirruped happily, drawing a warm look from the raven-like Korvaa. Felix felt a thrill at the words. He'd be able to leave! His stomach dropped in the same instant, thinking of Bateo and Estrid. It was... confusing, and rather than deal with that viper's nest of emotion, he drew on his well of suspicion.

"Thank you for that, but why tell me yourself? Don't you have messengers for that sorta thing?"

"We do," he admitted. "But you are a notable guest in our tiny village. I simply wished to speak with you in person without the... august personages of my fellows."

Felix laughed, but kept it at that. A thought occurred to him. An idea that, if it didn't work, would make breaking into the Hall later a much harder prospect. But he had to try.

"I imagine you're curious about Pit and me, right?"

Wonderment didn't nod, but his eyes glittered, and a faint smile crossed his beak.

"I'd be willing to tell you more about our bond, if you'd be willing to let me see your records."

"Records?" Wonderment asked archly. "What, pray tell, do you wish to find?"

"A way out."

Wonderment paused and considered Felix, from the bottoms of his battered shoes to the top of his shaggy head of hair. It made the man acutely aware that he hadn't showered or shaved in a long while, though either his Tempering or the Void itself had neutralized any smell.

"The goal you seek has not been found. Not by us, nor any others. If it had, would we still remain?"

"I get that. But what if you're missing something?"

"Missing what?"

Felix shrugged. "I don't know. But I can safely say I have a... different perspective from everyone else here."

Wonderment considered him again, drumming his fingers on the top of the desk. He did it for so long that Felix feared he'd ruined his chances at seeing those records, but the raven Korvaa suddenly slapped his hand down on the desk and stood.

"Come with me."

CHAPTER TWENTY-EIGHT

Wonderment gripped an empty candleholder—of all things—and gave it a solid yank. The candleholder tipped, audibly engaging some mechanism that swung open a panel between bookshelves. The raven gestured into the open doorway, which was well-lit with a buttery yellow light.

"After you."

Felix and Pit walked through, senses stretched outward for any sort of threat, but the hallway was simply that. It was well-made, just as the rest of the Conference Hall, lined with small magelights in sconces set regularly down its length. Interspersed between those lights were small tables or chairs—small pieces of furniture—each and every one made of well-polished wood. *Actual* wood, according to his Eye.

"Where'd these come from?" he asked Wonderment as he stepped up next to Felix.

"All in good time," was the response. The Korvaa led the way down the corridor, his taloned feet clacking against the void bone flooring. They passed room after room, all closed doors, all made from a mixture of wood and bone. Where had it all come from?

Felix and Pit followed the tail feathers of Lord Wonderment for at least five minutes, passing from the corridor into several smaller chambers, all of which had wood or simple metal items within them. A sitting room had a platter of silver cups and some sort of chaise with silk throw pillows. Silk! They slipped through some sort of kitchen, dark for the evening, and Wonderment pushed back a heavy-looking island in the center of the space. It shifted with a slight grating noise, revealing hidden tracks built into the floor, as well as a secret door leading down. A single heave opened the door, and Felix saw a set of stairs leading down into darkness.

"Follow me, Honored Tenku and bonded Companion." Wonderment led the way down the stairs.

"Maw? Isn't this where you tell me not to trust them?" Felix muttered. Yet the Primordial was curiously silent. He turned in a full circle, searching for it, but it was gone. *Doubt it's for good. Pit, what do you think? Trust him?*

Pit shrugged and followed the Korvaa down into the dark. Felix reluctantly stepped after, pushing his thoughts at his friend. *If he murders us, I'm blaming you, then.*

The stairs led only a short way down, no more than twenty or thirty feet, though it was filled with shadow Mana. Felix's Manasight couldn't quite parse what was in the room, as the shadow Mana did a great job obscuring it all. And perhaps that was the point, considering the amount of secret doors they'd just gone through. There was a spark of ghostly golden light, and the shadow Mana was suddenly banished as a series of manalights formed along the vaulted ceiling.

"Whoa. What—What is this?" Felix asked.

They were in a room that Felix could only describe as a crypt. There weren't any bodies lying in the many alcoves, or even graves; instead, it was *filled* with the most astounding level of trash he'd ever seen, filling up an area easily as large as the width of the entire Conference Hall.

"This is the flotsam and jetsam we have collected over the years. Much of it brought over from the Continent, but some are from far stranger origins." Wonderment walked up to the pile, picking up some sort of spoked wheel, completely made of wood. "Please. Take a look."

Felix's eyes widened as he took it all in. It was trash, broken and mostly useless, but there was a *ton* of reclaimable wood. Which explained the Hall's furnishings in the back areas. Pit nosed through a mound of the stuff, and a few pieces cascaded down the chest-high pile. Felix gasped. Sitting on the ground was a pair of miracles: a worn toilet plunger, and a water-warped copy of *Xtreme Dirt Biking* featuring a blonde woman in a bikini standing next to the eponymous vehicle.

He picked up the magazine with shaking fingers and flipped it open. The pages were mostly a single mass of water-sealed paper, but near the back, it opened to an advert for some sort of energy drink. It depicted a long beach, a summer sunset, and people lounging in the sands. It reminded him of home so viscerally it was like a punch in the gut.

Stupid emotions. Felix stifled a laugh, feeling a giddiness in his chest. If he started laughing, it'd end up hysterical real quick. Flaring Meditation helped him center himself again, at least. He held up the magazine. "Where did you find all this?"

"Ah. One of the picture books. Remarkably lifelike renditions of all manner of folk. Mostly Humans, however." Wonderment's wings flapped, and he did a sort of assisted hop over another mountain of debris. There, the Korvaa pulled out stacks of other magazines from a carved nook. "We've found many of these, strangely enough. We aren't sure why there are so many...*varieties.* Regardless, to answer your question, all of this comes from a hole in the Void, where the Ethereal Realm bubbles through into ours. There is a darkness there, something more than the Void, but as the Ethereal presses into it, *things* emerge."

"Ethereal?"

"Mhm. An old name, to be sure. Just as the Void was once called the Cognitive Realm." Wonderment shrugged and placed the magazines back in their cranny. "No matter. You may know it by another name: Desolation."

Felix recalled Nokk speaking of Desolation. "I thought the Desolation were holes in the Void that ate up everything around it?"

"That is true. But all things require balance. The Ethereal also ejects bits of dross with every cycle. We dredge the area around the nearest hole to Desolation regularly, and sometimes we find wheat among the chaff." Wonderment flapped his wings again and executed another assisted hop. He landed a few feet away from Felix and Pit. "Once, we had hoped that it was the answer. A way back. If the Desolation released things, then surely one could enter it and survive. Or, so was my predecessor's theory." He spread his arms wide, palms up. "His attempt at just that is why I now have this position."

Felix swallowed. His Mind flashed back to the sight of voidbeasts being disintegrated by the pirates' Desolation shield. Wonderment handed Felix an object approximately the size of a magazine. It was a folded piece of vellum, actual vellum according to his Eye, inked with a series of strange diagrams on the outside. Felix opened it, and the item revealed itself to be a map of the Void.

"This is the extent of our knowledge. Nearby settlements, dangerous areas, we've marked down what we could. Take it with my blessing, as poor recompense for helping the Rim Hunters."

Felix glanced up at the Conference leader in surprise.

"Oh yes, I received word from the Hunters shortly before you arrived." Wonderment smiled—or as close as the bird folk could come—but it was a sad thing. "I wish I could offer you more. A way out… I have wished for nothing more my entire life. But there is nothing."

Wonderment let out a soft, musical note, and a sense of exhaustion poured over Felix.

"There is no escape from the Void."

"I appreciate your discretion. For years, we've trawled for materials and kept it a secret. The wood is useful, luxurious even, but we've not told the Reach." Wonderment sighed. "It would only lead to discontent and futile arguments."

They had left the contents of the trash crypt behind and made their way back around to the front offices in the Hall. Here, everything was made from void bone, leather, and the odd piece of coarse, woven fabric. They stopped, just at the edge of Wonderment's office.

"Yeah, I, uh, it would be pretty cruel to dangle hope in front of people like that," Felix said. His hand lingered on the door, tapping at it unconsciously. His mind was filled with a worrisome weight.

"Indeed. Your ship is located at the Rimward docks and, as I said, will be repaired shortly. I will send word when it is ready." Wonderment sat at his desk once more, and his raven-like face became suddenly professional and aloof. "I wish you good tidings, Felix Nevarre. Honored Tenku."

Felix nodded wordlessly and opened the door, only to find the peacock features of Grand Detachment staring in the face. Or rather, staring at his chest, as the Korvaa was considerably shorter than Felix.

"*You*," his deep, resonant voice laced with suspicion. "What are you doing in these offices?"

"He was my guest, Detachment, and just leaving," Wonderment said from behind. "If you allow him to do so, we can begin our meeting."

Reluctantly, the big blue bird shifted out of the way to let Felix pass. He did so, stepping quickly. Both he and Pit exited the Conference Hall far more rapidly than they had entered. Apart from annoyance at Detachment's tone, Felix was in a bit of a daze. He couldn't believe that Echo's Reach had *nothing*, not a single clue on where to find an exit. He unfolded the map he'd been gifted—a copy, he'd been told—and admitted it hadn't been a huge loss.

I could cross reference this map with the one I got from that pirate cook, Felix mused to Pit. *If we're lucky, maybe there's something both groups missed.*

Pit chirped and sent back the sensation of utter trust and confidence. Felix chuckled, mood somewhat lifted by the magic of bird-dog loyalty. He scratched the tenku's ears, and they took off in their skimmer.

It took another half hour or so to get back to the farm, but when they did, Felix immediately noticed something was off. Bateo was on the front porch, wrapped in a cloak and hefting a heavy pack while Estrid fussed about him.

"Why do you have to go back out there so soon?" she was asking him.

"Dearest, we've been over this," Bateo said kindly. Then he noticed Felix's arrival. "Felix! You've returned! I trust you found the Rim Hunters."

"I did. They said they were moving out and patrolling the Rim before moving inward." Felix climbed the steps of the porch three at a time, Pit right behind him. "What's going on?"

"You see? The Hunters are out and about. It's perfectly safe," Bateo said to Estrid. She simply sniffed reluctantly. To Felix, he said, "The wards that keep out the voidbeasts are drained. One of my neighbors saw the nearest one and told us. It has to be why the voidbeasts got into the area." He hefted his odd staff, the one with the organic-looking pouch attached. A pouch Felix now knew contained a whole bunch of Manabladders. "I need to refuel them again."

"I'll go with you," Felix said immediately. There was no chance he was gonna let the guy go alone, but he refrained from saying why. He looked at Estrid before making eye contact with Bateo. "I want to help."

Luckily, Bateo was quicker on the uptake than Felix. The hawk's eyes widened before he nodded in understanding. "O-of course. But… the skimmer is a bit much with you and your Companion, at least for speed."

Felix picked up on that, at least. He was concerned about his family. "Not a problem. Pit can stay here. Keep an eye on things while we're gone," Felix said. "Sound good to you, Pit?"

Pit chirp-barked, earning pleased looks from everyone. He was more than willing to protect Bateo's family, and it resonated through their bond. A fierce urge to protect and a willingness to help. Felix patted the tenku affectionately.

Estrid sniffed again, but this time it was a noise that conveyed all her fear and aching worry for her husband and family. Felix wasn't sure how he could tell that from a sniff, but he was certain of it. Bateo folded her gently in his arms and outspread wings. His wife replied in kind, her lighter coloration standing out sharply against Bateo's.

"Come back to me, you fool," she whispered.

"Always, my stolen priestess," he whispered back. The exchange was too soft for others to hear, but Felix found his Perception to be a bit of a curse in that regard. Still, he looked away and tried to focus on anything else.

Which was why he was surprised when hands grabbed his shoulders and pulled him down into a hug. Estrid held him tightly. "You keep him safe, Felix."

"I will," he promised.

CHAPTER TWENTY-NINE

Felix and Bateo were off again, the skimmer shooting off into the dark on Felix's Mana. The farmer was surprised at their speed and seemed concerned that Felix was wasting his Mana, but Felix had waved off his concerns. He had the Mana to spare—at least for now.

It also meant they made good time, reaching the first monolith in short order. While the interior wards were closer—the ones that hid Echo's Reach away from sight—they were also apparently fully functional, according to Bateo. The first monolithic ward stone made Felix gaze in concern at the wider Void beyond.

"It almost feels like being at the edge of a deep, dark ocean," Felix said. "As if your town is safer than out there."

"It usually is," Bateo protested. He had begun tracing the glyph that dominated the ward stone, his staff moving in slow, careful patterns. "The greater Void is a nightmare that never ends. Here, at least we have family and friends."

"You're not wrong," Felix said. He turned to focus on Bateo's process. It was pretty interesting, akin to writing with a fountain pen. The Mana held in the staff's pouch was released by Bateo's Will, and it traveled down to where the staff touched the monolith. After a handful of minutes, he was done.

"Why did they run out so fast?" Felix asked.

Bateo hesitated, running his talons across the stone's grooves. "I don't know. They should last for at least thirty cycles, contained as they are." He lingered, staring up at the monolith. "It is strange indeed, but perhaps... ah, I haven't a clue. But I know we must refill them quickly." He shook himself. "Onward, Felix. Six more to check."

"Aye aye, Captain," Felix said with a mock salute.

They flew in silence for a time. Felix thought incessantly of what he was going to do. Would he take his stolen pirate sloop and wander the Void, hunting for an exit? Maybe he could make returning to Echo's Reach a regular thing, like a supply run or something. *It'd be nice to see Estrid and the kids in the future.*

"Felix?"

"Hm?" Felix broke from his musing and saw Bateo's face quirked in an unfamiliar expression. Guilt and concern, maybe.

Bateo took a breath before speaking. "Those pirates you said you escaped... how long were you with them?"

"A couple days. Why?" Felix asked.

"Some of the neighbors have been spreading rumors, I think. About you." Bateo seemed almost embarrassed to be sharing the information with Felix. "They say you were a pirate, too."

Felix laughed. "What? That's dumb."

Bateo grinned. "That's what I told them. You've told me too much, and done the same amount to help me, that I'd be a real fool to believe some beak-creakers."

Beak-creakers. That's a fun expression. Felix grinned. "Don't worry. I'm the farthest thing from a pirate there is—"

Danger, starboard side.

Felix recognized the acerbic tone of the Maw just as he saw a dark, hideous form loom out of the black.

"Down!" Felix screamed as he sent their skimmer into a

dive. Bateo squawked in surprise and lost grip on his staff while Felix's hand on his cloak dragged him downward.

Teeth the size of Felix's arm snapped down on the staff, splashing a burst of brilliant, liquid Mana. A creature followed, flowing sinuously over their position in a wriggle of massive, scaled flesh. The light of the undifferentiated Mana lit it briefly, long enough to see the flash of ribbed fins and jagged spines.

Voracious Eye!

Name: Noctnatter
Type: Voidbeast
Level: 37
HP: ???/???
SP: ???/???
MP: ????/?
Lore: Dread serpents of the Void, the Noctnatter are one of rarest and most deadly voidbeasts to be found in the Cognitive Realm. Using their immense fins like sails, they navigate the gelid absence of the Realm by burning the stolen Mana of its victims. Like the Narhallow, the Noctnatter will trail pieces of its Mana stores behind it in order to lure in other voidbeasts, though in the Noctnatter's case, it is a fishing tactic, and they often eat the Tenebrils or Harrowings that come after them.
Strength: More Data Required
Weakness: More Data Required

The creature whipped about, rolling its slender, eel-like body on itself as it reoriented on them. The ribbed sails along its top, bottom, and sides billowed and snapped as the thrum of Mana filled them. It surged forward, practically unhinging its jaw as it flew.

"Brace!" Felix shouted before slamming Bateo down into the skimmer and pushing out as much Mana as the craft could hold. The Control Node whined, and the skimmer trembled, but it flew. It flew *fast*.

"SKKIIIISHAAAW!"

The Noctnatter flowed after him, twisting like a ribbon in the air. Its face was a series of eyes—three on each side of its skull—and a half-dozen spines anointing its crest. Mana spiraled off of it as it swam, undulating frantically toward them.

Influence of the Wisp!

Enthrall Failed.

Blue wispfire bloomed along the Void serpent's length, but it failed to catch. Felix gasped a desperate breath.

Reign of Vellus!

He narrowed the focus with a pinch of Will, and the expulsion of force sent the pair of them careening sideways... and a bolt of lightning skittering into the Noctnatter's snarling face. It sparked along its crest—static on an aerial antenna—as it briefly went rigid.

The Maw pointed a sharpened finger at the beast. *It hates the lightning! Hit it with that worthless goddess' spell again!*

"Th-that's a Void snake!" Bateo hollered at almost the same time.

"I'm aware!" he shouted at the both of them. "Hold on!" Felix dipped their skimmer forward and up, looping back around the Noctnatter in a move that made Bateo shout and grab onto him. The serpent twisted on itself again, spooling and unspooling in his direction as if it had no bones at all.

Reign of Vellus!
Reign of Vellus!
Reign of Vellus!

Felix spammed the spell while he held the shape of it firmly in his Mind. A tight cone of electrical force swept outward into the black, beyond bright for the inky Void, and slammed repeatedly into the Noctnatter's stupid face.

"SKKIIII—! SKKI—! SHAAAW!"

It seized again, this time the electricity coiling off its crest and stabbing bright veins of blue-white lightning into its scaled hide. Felix twisted the skimmer, hoping to hit it with a second volley, when it snapped its massive jaws at them.

"WHOA!" His Will and Alacrity jerked hard, sending the pair of them barrel rolling up and over the serpent's snout, just barely missing its nightmarish maw. "It was faking!"

"They're very smart! That's what makes them so dangerous!" Bateo tightened his grip across Felix's chest. "Why is it here?"

"With the wards down, it must have wandered in!" Felix shouted back.

"No, they're a deep Void creature! They shouldn't be near us at all!"

Felix didn't have time to ponder that, as the Noctnatter came back around for another try.

It's clearly attracted to the skimmer's Mana output, but if it's as smart as Bateo says it is, then it already recognizes us as a nice meal. How do we shake this thing?

Rip it apart! the Maw was screaming. Her flat, yellowed teeth flashed in the light of Felix's kinetic lightning. *Shred and rend and tear, Felix! You are the apex predator!*

He tried to shrug off the Maw's strangely encouraging words and cycled through his many Skills. Acid punches and orbs did little, only splashed against its hide ineffectually, while there was no stone around them to shape. Influence of the Wisp didn't work, and his Mantle slid from its body like a cool mist. What's more, Felix noticed its Mana total was increasing as the fight went on.

It's absorbing my spells! Felix snarled wordlessly.

Shadow Whip!

A near-invisible tendril of shadow Mana snapped from Felix's outstretched palm, manifesting directly from his Gate, and slammed into the serpent. Strength flared, the strike setting the Noctnatter back, hurling into its crested skull like a falling I-beam.

"Hah! Take that!" Felix shouted triumphantly.

The Noctnatter spun, its flat tail slicing through the air quicker than even Felix's Perception could follow. Felix twisted the skimmer and ducked, but the very edge of the appendage rammed into his friend's chest. With a tortured, wet exhalation, Bateo was hurled from the craft.

"Bateo!!" Felix flared his Will and dropped, but the damned snake was faster. It swooped toward the falling Korvaa, jaws wide. "No!"

His Mana flashed, a quarter of it vanishing into the Control Node on the skimmer. Felix plummeted, faster than he'd ever moved before, so fast that the skimmer itself exploded beneath him. He screamed in pain as heat and fire scoured his nerves, setting his broken resistances to vibrating within his core space. Felix clenched his teeth and cast through the pain as he fell at speeds way higher than terminal velocity.

Reign of Vellus!

Angled behind him, the blast of kinetic lightning shot Felix down faster. He impacted the Noctnatter's gaping, lower jaw, headfirst into the slick meat of the floor of its mouth. Its jaws snapped closed as Felix's sheer weight slammed them both into the not-ground of the Void.

Reign of Vellus!
Corrosive Strike!

Lightning lit up Felix's body as he poured more and more Mana into the spells. The lightning skittered, absorbed, but then started charring the green-pink meat of the Void serpent. Before it could recoil, Felix hurled a single fist straight up. Acid seared through the roof of its mouth, too much too fast for it to absorb, melting its soft flesh and letting his fist burrow straight up into its skull.

Wrack and Ruin!

Dark acid flooded from around his forearm, far more potent than his Strike. The majority of it pooled above, eating rapidly through whatever amounted to a brain the voidbeast had.

**You Have Killed A Noctnatter!
XP Earned!**

"Damn," he panted. The air was hot and wet, and it *stank.* "Gotta get outta here."

Felix hesitated for a second but… what sort of Skill could he learn from the creature? It was only a point of Bloodline progression, after all.

Ravenous Tithe!

The serpent dissolved into dark smoke streaked with a thousand multicolored lights. It swirled as it gathered, before streaming into Felix's mouth and through his skull Gate. He breathed it in, but it kept coming. And coming. The creature had been huge, after all, and it was absolutely *packed* with stolen Mana. He took so much that it felt like his core space was stretched and distended.

Further Bloodlines Have Been Found. Processing 7%

Felix dropped several feet, stumbling as the monster turned to insubstantial smoke around him. He peered at his notification and frowned over the terrible roiling inside him.

The bloodlines advanced by three percent this time, he noticed. *Was it the amount? Or the strength of the monster?*

There was a groaning from close by, and Felix's eyes widened. "Bateo!"

He spun toward the sound and found the Korvaa crumpled on the invisible, slightly bouncy not-ground of the Void. One of his wings was bent at an odd angle, and his arm was clearly broken.

"Oh my god, Bateo are you—do you need help?"

"Get—get my pack," he gasped through the clearly excruciating pain. "Bandages and—and a tonic."

Felix hurried to do so, quickly finding the farmer's pack half strewn across the Void. Finding the tonic and bandages was easy, however. The tonic was a faint shade of pink and the

Mana within it extremely small, while the bandages were similar to what he'd used on Magda, at the end.

Clenching his jaws against that little blast from the past, Felix hustled back to Bateo and helped staunch his bleeding. The bandages sizzled and tightened, fusing his skin shut with an application of undifferentiated Mana.

"There, that should hold you over for a bit, but I'm gonna have to carry you," Felix said.

"Where's—hssshhh!—where's the skimmer?" Bateo asked.

"It uh, the monster destroyed it," Felix said with a wince.

"Damn voidbeast," Bateo muttered.

"Well, well, well. What has happened here?"

Felix winced again, but for an entirely different reason this time. He recognized that voice, and sure enough, above him hovered the brilliantly plumed form of Grand Detachment. He stood tall upon an impressively ornate skimmer. Beside him, also on their own transport, was the owl-like Knowledge, followed closely by five of the Rim Hunters.

"Looks like a voidbeast attack," one of the Rim Hunters said. He thumbed his beak, considering. "Only I don't see no voidbeast."

"Already burned away," Felix said. He fought to keep anything from showing on his face. "It was a Noctnatter."

"A Noctnatter!" A Hunter whistled. "They never come here. Not ever."

A few of the Hunters were giving Felix a sideways look, as if they didn't believe him. The peacock Conference Lord regarded him with a steady stare and smirk.

"My lord, why have you come out here? It is far from the Reach, and dangerous," Bateo said. He had muscled down the pain, but his limbs shook with the strain of bowing. Felix wanted to grab him and straighten him up. No amount of manners were worth aggravating his injuries.

"We have come here," the peacock Grand Detachment declared. "Because we were told that someone had sabotaged the protection array."

"No!" Bateo said. "I—I had thought it strange they would run out of fuel so fast, but sabotage?"

"Indeed! Someone sabotaged our array and then led the voidbeasts in, distracting our Rim Hunters, before guiding more of them deeper into Echo's Reach itself!" The peacock thrust his blue arms outward, his wings and impressive fantail following. Dramatically, he stabbed at Felix with a clawed finger. "You! You were the only one capable of such a deed! The only one in the right places during all of it!"

Felix's gut dropped. "What?"

"Don't try to deny it! We have multiple witnesses saying you were at the head of a column of voidbeasts as they came into town. That you stretched out your hands and they descended on our village like beasts to command, same as you command the Honored Tenku!"

Hard looks and white-knuckled grips met Felix's astounded eyes as he swept them across the Hunters and Lord. At his side, Bateo sputtered.

"That is all nonsense! Felix has been with me! For days on end. How would he have time to slip away and sabotage the array?"

Detachment smiled, and it was a sharp thing, meant to cut. "You sleep, Bateo. All of us do. How easy would it be for him to slip out into the dark while your household slept? How simple to drain the array? After all, we just saw him drain a voidbeast dry."

Felix clenched his jaw as the Hunters spoke up. "Yeah, he just... he ate something as he approached. I seen it! All smoke and lights and he, burn me, he ate it!"

"Felix?" Bateo asked. His voice was pained, but he was steady. Felix couldn't lie to him.

"Yeah, I ate the voidbeast. It's a Skill," he started, but was inundated with jeers and angry cries from the Rim Hunters.

"He admits it!" Knowledge, the snowy owl said. "Profane! Disgusting communion with the monsters in the dark!"

Small-minded peons, the Maw hissed. It had swum the depths around them all like a shark, drawing close enough to touch the Korvaa. *They seek to place their troubles on you. And someone among them is telling lies.* The Primordial spun about the peacock features of Grand Detachment. *I wonder who.*

Felix kept a grimace from his face, but only barely. His Voracious Eye pinged the Rim Hunters as capable, and perhaps he'd be able to fight them, but the two Lords were strong. They had likely advanced themselves well beyond others, relying on access to Manabladders and the like to push themselves further. However it was done, Felix knew he couldn't face all of them, not together.

"I did not do anything to your array, and I've not led any voidbeasts into town," Felix said. "I've been on Bateo's farm my entire time here, and only left to let the Hunters know about the monsters. They were already facing them by the time I arrived!"

"Or they arrived ahead of you, chased from behind by your tricks!" Detachment sneered at him, much as he was able with a beak. "You are a stranger, and you've already enslaved the Honored Tenku to you. Who else would do such foul things to our fair community? Who else, but the one I found *conspiring* with Lord Wonderment just today?"

"Conspiring? Detachment, you did not mention this," said Knowledge, his feathers fluffed in alarm. "Wonderment is in cahoots with this stranger?"

"He must be! What else would they speak of? Why else would he show him the crypt?!" The peacock whirled on Felix again. "You see our treasures, boy? Is that it? Do you work for the pirates you say you 'escaped?'"

Felix ground his teeth. It was clear now. Nothing he said would stop their accusations.

"Fine, then I will leave—" Felix began, but was cut off by the raised weapons and screeching laugh of Grand Detachment.

"Leave!? You are *banished*! Never to be welcomed among our homes again!" The peacock gestured at the Rim Hunters, who closed in on their skimmers, blades held forward. "We claim your ship, junker though it is, and all you have left behind."

"This is unreasonable, my Lords," Bateo stuttered. "I do not believe any of these charges against my friend. He has only been a help!"

No one paid the injured farmer any mind. Knowledge, the mild-seeming owl, instead smiled viciously at Felix. "And the Honored Tenku will stay with us. It will do him well to be severed from your despicable enslavement."

"Pit is not enslaved!" Felix shouted, his frustration turning to furious incredulity. "He is my friend and Companion, System-bonded! You can't keep him from me!"

"He will be saved from you, *boy*, whether you like it or not," Grand Detachment spat. "Hunters. See this *thing* out of our home."

The Rim Hunter's faces were heavy with anger and no little bloodlust. Whatever else the Lords had said, they bought it, hook and sinker. "Aye. With pleasure."

Felix had little choice. Either leave or risk his life fighting. The latter tempted him, but it was the Maw's words that convinced him otherwise.

Kill them, Felix. Rend their flesh and eat their Essence! Show them the cost of opposing us!

Much as he pained him, Felix gritted his teeth and let them march him at spear point away from Echo's Reach, the farm, and Pit. Out into the black.

CHAPTER THIRTY

Atar paced outside the Elder's study, deep in thought and unable to come to a decision. His soft, suede boots whispered against the immaculate stone and intricately woven rug, but his eyes were blind to the wealth on display. The same two thoughts fought against one another in his mind, unable to quiet until one was victorious.

I am a Guilder. I am apprenticed to the Elder of Spirit and set to learn his esoteric sigaldry methods. I have responsibilities and a duty to follow the orders of those more learned than I... Atar ran his hands through his blonde curls, dragging portions into a deep disarray. *They have Magda's body! They're testing it. Are they testing it the same as the survivors? Highest Flame! What were they? Those teeth!*

Round and round his thoughts circled, mimicking the steps he made. He was aware of the hushed details regarding Magda's dishonorable discharge from the Guild. Her rights and Rank had been stripped from her posthumously, and that meant her body was fair game to extract Essences. The Draughts she had used to Temper herself to Apprentice and Journeyman still existed within her core, and though it was difficult to do, most could be retrieved by a proper Alchemist. And they had Aenea

Ty'lel, the best Alchemist in Haarwatch; the best in any of the neighboring Territories, he'd heard.

Except, when Atar did some digging, he'd found that Ty'lel had never been sent to the tenth floor.

So why do they have her body?

He came to a stop, his fine boots clicking against the stone floor between rugs. Atar swallowed and quietened the spinning of his core. The roiling flame churned, half-formed, and he breathed. Once. Twice.

"Blood and ashes," he cursed. "Where's my damn quill?"

He had a message to send.

Evie sat on a rafter, well above the floor of their makeshift home. It had been weeks, and while scrap furniture and piecemeal tables had been brought in, it did not feel like home. Magda and her had spent years in hovels, literal holes in the wall with only a thin blanket and the threat of violence to keep them safe. Looking down, she regarded that past fondly, with a faint smile.

She knew it wasn't fair. Callie was doing all she could to provide for everyone. She was pushing hard, doing six or seven jobs a week on the Hunter's Boards. But the monsters were getting more unsettled, just like the people of the city. Stronger beasts kept showing up, and in greater numbers. Most of the Board jobs were for Tier I beasts, but reports of strong Tier II monsters lurking in the Foglands were spreading. Unfortunately, there was some truth to it. High Tier I creatures had begun lurking in packs near the city, often assaulting the Wall and spreading even more unrest through Haarwatch.

So, while getting more jobs was easier—who wanted to risk themselves against powerful beasts?—but completing them became much more of a trial. Callie, she knew, was scrambling to make do and add to their coffers.

Evie spat over the edge, watching her spittle fall the hundred feet or so to the swept stone floor. She wondered when the silvers would pile high enough. How soon would they leave Haarwatch altogether?

The city surely hadn't done her any favors, but Evie was loath to leave the last place Magda's body had been left. Or leave Vess, for that matter, though the heiress had screwed them over during the trial. The rational part of Evie recognized that Vess' hadn't a chance, not with the Elders stacking the deck against the survivors. The less rational part of her was still pissed, though.

Didn't make her want to leave it all behind.

Avet's dark eyes, I even miss Atar. That's how Evie knew she was off-balance. Still, they'd lost a lot, and Evie wasn't keen on losing more.

"Evie!" Bodie shouted from below. The musclebound man, nearly dark as an Orc, waved at her from the front door. "Messages for the Mistress of Chains!"

Rolling her eyes, she descended from the rope she had secured for that purpose. The spot atop the rafters was her thinking place. "Don't much like that name, Bodie. Thought I told you that."

"I may recall hearing it once or twice." Bodie grinned. "Got you down here fast, though. Can't say that hollerin' for a half glass would've done the same, minus your nickname."

Evie grunted. That was fair enough. She'd been ignoring most of the team the past couple weeks. "You've got messages for me."

"Some." He handed her a rolled-up scroll, twice-bound and almost hot to the touch. "Looks like it's been warded with fire Mana."

Evie took it gingerly, but it wasn't so hot it'd burn. Just felt… uncomfortable. "This it?"

"Mhm, and this… thing," he said. He held up an odd, segmented beetle the size of her hand. Evie peered at it in fascination, and noticed its wriggling legs were all covered in a tight golden script.

"That's a construct," she muttered. "How'd you know it's for me?"

"Keeps tryin' to climb the walls while you were up the rafters," he said. "Here, watch."

Bodie placed the large green beetle on the wall again, and it swiftly pivoted and twisted its antennae. Then, with a buzzing leap, it flitted right to Evie's feet.

"Huh. Curious little thing," she said and walked away. She retreated to her room, tight quarters though they were. She at least had a door that locked. She set the scroll and beetle on her wobbly desk and dropped her chain on her bed. The blades and spikes tore up the blanket, again, but Evie didn't much care. Instead, she leaned forward to inspect the beetle, poking at its back with the tip of one of her throwing daggers.

[Query: Evie Aren?]

"Um, yes. I'm Evie Aren."

[Query: Alone?]

Evie swallowed, suddenly a bit nervous. "Yeah. I'm alone. Why?"

The beetle construct unfolded, its shell flipping up to reveal innards made of odd moving parts and hundreds of inscribed sigils. A greenstone was buried in it, now revealed, and it glowed with a brilliant light.

E-evie? Is this working? It is? All right. Evie, this is Vessilia Dayne. Y-your teammate and, I hope, your friend. It has been weeks since last we saw one another, weeks for the words I said at the trial to be indelibly etched into my memory. I am so very sorry for what the Elders pushed me to say. I am so very sorry for what has happened to you, Harn, Calesca, her entire team, and… and to the memory of your sister.

I am wracked with guilt over it, but this message is not about that. I managed to secure this construct from some of the Inscriptionists here in the tower, though they tell me this will only be good for a single message.

SILENCE

This is about the survivors from the Foglands. They are in danger. Someone among the Guild is doing something terrible with them. I have heard... dark rumors, and I've confirmed half of them. The other half are too vile to even recount, at least in this manner. I am looking to find a way to help them, save them a second time.

I had hoped you would join me. I am ever so much in need of allies... of friends.

Come and meet me at the Archive. Reaching there should not prove difficult to you. Two days hence, at tenth glass.

I look forward to seeing you, Evie.

Vess' voice faded, as did the glow in the green stone. Evie ran her dry tongue over her dry lips, trying to work some sort of moisture into them. It was a shock, hearing Vess' voice.

[Message Delivered]

Without another word, the beetle simply...fell apart. A wash of tingling energies she could barely see fluttered up to the ceiling and stank of burnt air. Evie coughed and waved her hand at the invisible smoke.

"Gods damned inscriptionists," she muttered.

Vess wanted to meet? Evie had no issues with that. She missed the duchess-to-be almost as much as she missed her sister, and hearing her apologize... Evie felt a weight lifting from her. The anger she'd felt wasn't gone, but it dimmed.

In a far better mood, she turned to the other scroll. It was exuding an aura of heat and tiny, phantom flames were licking around the inscribed wax seal. The glyph of the seal was made to look like a stylized A, and she had little doubt who it was from.

Messages from former teammates at the same time. What are the odds?

She cut open the seal with her dagger, and fell on her ass from the billowing clouds of fire Mana that boiled out.

"Blind gods, Atar! What is wrong with you?" Evie climbed back to her feet and stared down at the scroll that had unfurled atop the desk. It was written on thick vellum in a fine, fancy hand she had trouble reading. When she finally parsed it, her face had grown pale, and she found her chain back in her hands.

"Atar," she growled. "You better not be lying to me." Evie wrapped her chain about her shoulders and stalked out of the room, shouting. "Anyone have some burnin' parchment?"

CHAPTER THIRTY-ONE

Two days passed on since Evie had stopped brooding in the rafters. Cal was happy for it, and for the fervor with which she pushed herself into combat training again. It had been lacking in the weeks since their arrival, and Cal finally felt like some semblance of normalcy had returned to their lives.

The jobs continued on as well, though they grew harder by the day. Already, the offers had dried up by half, with too many dangerous beasts pushing toward Haarwatch, few were willing to risk their lives for a few silver. Her team were still taking as many as possible, still turning them in with the regularity of seasoned Guilders. The Elders might have thrown them from their roster, but they could not take away their Skills and years of training. Few could handle the increasing monster hordes as well as her people.

Cal stood atop their small slice of the Dust Quarter, the creak of corrugated iron loud beneath her shifting boots. The sun was rising, a time she loved more than any other. It reminded her of simpler times, when her biggest concerns were crawling out of a tavern or securing her next paying gig.

"Yyero's backside, this district is a hole," Harn muttered.

Cal smirked. "The Dust is aptly named. Few eyes turn to this place, out of habit or disdain."

"Either one's good for us," he grunted. "New jobs got posted. Yan and Kelgan checked the boards last glass, says there's three Elimination jobs."

"Tier II beasts?"

"Mhm. Leader types, heads of a smallish horde, they say." Harn spat over the edge of the roof. His heavy metal boots made almost no noise against the iron. "We'll likely need to bring the heavy hitters on this one."

"Bodie, Yan, Kelgan, yourself, and… Vivianne, I'd say," she said. Then a thought occurred to her. "Oh, take Evie with you. She could use some more field experience, somethin' a bit more straightforward."

"Hm. One problem. Evie—" A shadow swept over them, as if a cloud had passed over the rising sun. Harn stopped dead, and Cal followed his gaze. "What's that?"

"Blood and ashes," she cursed. "Blood and burning ashes!" She gritted her teeth and watched as the shadow pushed beyond the sun and crossed the sky. "What in the Twin's name are they doing here?"

A banner flew from the Manaship's mast, a golden sunburst on a white and red background. Harn growled in recognition. "Inquisitors."

"A whole gods damned Manaship of them," Cal added. She watched as the craft scudded across the air, before docking smoothly with the topmost section of the Guild's Eyrie. "This can't be good."

Harn spat again. "Do we drop the jobs we took?"

Cal shook her head. "No, keep 'em up. Take more if we can. We need the silver to get out. If the Inquisition is here, I don't wanna be." She paused. "What were you saying about Evie?"

Harn drummed his fingers on the haft of his axe. "She can't come with us on that job."

"Why not?"

"Because she's already left," Harn said.
"What?" Cal narrowed her eyes. "Where?"

Evie tried to slip through the crowds and found herself flummoxed at every turn. People were everywhere in the city center, packed to the gills and jostling for position along the main thoroughfare around the Guild tower. The tiered steps leading to the Eyrie were difficult enough to manage on a normal day. She groaned aloud, berating herself for the fourth or fifth time. Evie had expected to hide among the crowd so as not to be noticed approaching the Guild, but the crowds were beyond thick. Now she was packed tight as a priest's wallet, or an Elder's sense of superiority.

The ramps and steps wound, serpentine, around the crown of the city center and were typically crammed with tradesmen and porters moving materials hither and yon. Now, however, it was filled with men, women, and children all watching wide-eyed as the Inviolate Inquisition went on parade.

"Finally! The Pathless sent warriors to save us from the monstrosities!"

"Bah! The Guilders are already handling it," a grumpy voice decried.

"That's not what I hear," someone replied.

"Praise be the Light!"

The Inquisitors marched, all shiny and new in their white and silver armor. Technically, they were only Acolytes, low-level members of the order. Still, the early summer sun glinted off their armaments, near blinding folk, and their crimson cloaks flowed heroically in a steady breeze. Evie had lost track of how many had entered the city. She was fairly sure they were doing loops around the upper streets, just to impress people. She pushed forward, finally managing to enter the square before the Eyrie itself.

"Look! The Inquisitors!"

Cheers went up as someone stepped out onto a hastily erected stage near the fountain. It was packed with more of those redcloaks, though these had fancy swords and more elaborate chest pieces. Many of them didn't even wear the strange helmets the Acolytes did, instead baring their grim faces to the world.

Lotta greybeards, she noted. Wasn't a single higher up younger than fifty, though all of them were physically fit enough to shame most Untempered folk. The benefits of money and powerful Essence Draughts. Evie slipped through more of the crowd, drawing on the weight of her chain to give her some more momentum. Folks started stepping away from her path, and some she didn't even have to jab in the ribs at all.

A tall man stepped out onto the stage, slender save for his bulky armor of white plate. The armor was far more ornate than the others, even the full-fledged Inquisitors, decorated with delicate gold filigree across the pauldrons, vambraces, and cuisses. A tunic edged in gold thread and emblazoned with a golden starburst across the chest finished the look, along with his bright red cloak thrown over one shoulder. A complicated helm was tucked beneath the man's right arm, displaying his hawkish features and graying temples. He smiled out into the crowd, and Evie felt his Spirit wash over her. Over everyone.

Soft sighs escaped those closest to the man, and applause soon followed. The man let it go on a while before raising a hand for silence. It fell immediately. "People of Haarwatch. Countrymen. Loyal defenders of the Hierocracy! I am Lord Khorun Katan, Master Inquisitor of the Inviolate Inquisition, and I have heard from your leaders that trouble stalks your gates. The Foglands, long cloaked in mist and secrets, has unveiled itself… and monsters have come calling."

Mutters passed through the crowd, rippling around Evie like soft waves. She put her head down and tried to ignore it all. She pushed toward the Eyrie, toward the Archive.

"Your pleas for protection have been heard by the light and flame of the Pathless. The Hierophant herself has sent us to alleviate your worries! To cleanse the Foglands of all that is dark, foul, and impure." The man raised his hands, and a shimmering, golden radiance descended upon him from the sky. The crowd squealed and cheered, but hushed a moment later. "We will restore this city and its lands to the faith! The true faith! And all of us shall be blessed by the light!"

At last, the golden illumination spread outward, like a growing stain. Evie gasped as it fell on her like a physical force. It was Mana, she knew, and it swirled above and through the crowd, so thick and potent its streamers danced across her face. Evie spat and flared her own core, weak though it was, and the sensation of dark ice in her veins pushed back the cloying heat. A little.

The one advantage of the Master Inquisitor's move was that Evie could easily slip through the dumbstruck townsfolk. Were she a dipper, a pickpocket, it would have been quite a haul; none struck by that light seemed to have the presence of mind to move, let alone protect their valuables.

But, eventually, the light winked out. Evie stumbled, trapped between several broad-shouldered laborers and washerwomen that roused from their stupor. She glanced at the stage, but the Master Inquisitor was already gone, as were all the others. The Acolytes still marched, but they appeared to be filing out into the city, the massive columns splitting and spreading down every street she could see.

"This ain't good," a Dwarf laborer remarked in a low voice. He was talking to another Dwarf and a Hobgoblin, both wearing the dusty jackets of stone haulers. They eyed the redcloaks nervously. "Inquisition don't just show up to put on a parade."

"What do they do?" the Hobgoblin asked. His skin was almost as red as their cloaks.

"Pathless is all about his three pillars, you know? Strength. Order. Purity. For Strength, you got the Paladins. For Order, you got the priesthood. But for Purity?" the Dwarf nodded at the shining white zealots. "You got them."

"Purity of what?"

"Of the Pathless," the other Dwarf said in a menacing tone. His lip curled beneath drooping mustaches. "They hunt down anyone what worships the old gods."

"Lotta people round here pay lip service to the old gods, not so many are goin' to temple for em," the Hobgoblin pointed out. "So why're they really here?"

"Resources," the first Dwarf said. "Here for the Foglands, right? They gotta be."

Evie shook her head and pressed on, eager to get away from nosy laborers and Inquisitors alike. It took another twenty minutes, but eventually she slipped into the Eyrie and down the marble steps to the Central Lobby. Guilders hustled here and there, lining up at various desks to turn in jobs or receive them. A bustling place, certainly, though it seemed busier than ever, like an overturned ant hill. Countless doors and hallways cut into the sides, leading to meeting chambers and even a communal bath. At the far end were the stairs, sweeping upward in grand arches to ascend the many levels of the Eyrie. Apart from all of that, the lobby's space was dominated by a huge device hanging from the vaulted ceiling, suspended sixty paces up. Made of thick glass, brass gears, and more sand than she'd ever seen, it was a sandglass to beat all others.

"About time you showed up!" a voice hissed from a shadowed alcove. Evie looked over to find Atar, his robes done up all proper and his hair just so. He would've looked almost handsome had his face not been red and veiny. He stabbed at the sandglass above. "You're approaching an entire glass late! I had to duck out of plans with my team for this!"

Evie glanced about. No one was looking at her or him, so she casually walked to the side. "If you haven't noticed, we've got a parade on our hands. Didn't expect that to come, now did I?"

"No one did," Atar said. He shook his head. "The Elders are scrambling. They were not told the Order was coming here until they were docking at the Spire."

Evie chuckled. "Ooh, bet they loved that."

"You damn well know they didn't," Atar snapped. "Everyone's running around in a tizzy. And the Elders..." At this he grabbed Evie's arm, leading her into deeper shadow. "Elders are busy at least. We have to move now, or else lose what little advantage we have."

Evie nodded. "Lead on to the Archive, then."

"Don't you know the way?"

"Can't say as I've ever felt the need to read about stuff instead of doin' it," she said with a shrug. Atar's face screwed up incredulously and Evie hid a smile. The fire mage swiftly led the way to the back staircase and upward.

The Archive was as expansive as Evie had been told, containing more books than she could read in six lifetimes. Or would want to. The two of them entered and ducked quietly past the Archivist at the front desk, and Atar led them into the rear of the sprawling second level. This meant climbing yet more stairs, a task with which Evie was becoming annoyed and had Atar puffing with exertion.

"Thought the Guilders would have you doin' more Endurance work," she said.

"I'll have you know, I've earned six whole points in Endurance and two in Strength in the past months."

"Ooh, you're big time now," Evie snorted. "Harn'll be happy to hear that. He's been wanting to spar against your fire magic again."

Atar's olive skin blanched, and Evie suppressed another snicker. The mage was entirely too easy to rile up. It was almost unfair.

Still fun, though.

"I'd have thought you'd be more serious, considering the situation," Atar said at last.

Evie sobered immediately. "Just get us to the meeting place."

Atar nodded, but she didn't miss the satisfied look in his eyes. *Bastard.*

They passed stacks and stacks of books, with shelves that went all the way to the ceiling. Ladders on little wheels were shifted about curving tracks, and a few times Evie spotted a Guilder moving them around to access some hard to reach tome. It wasn't too ugly, either, well-appointed with thick rugs, tapestries on the walls, and the shelving was carved with a repeated pattern of slanted diamonds. It was fairly empty as well, with only a few Guilders off in the distance. Only once did she see an Archivist aside from the one at the door, and she was rearranging books on a ladder. Had the nicest blue-green hair, though.

Atar brought them to a secluded alcove somewhere in the twisted depths of the Archive, so far back that Evie swore she spotted layers of dust thicker than three of her fingers. There was a tapestry in the alcove, depicting some sort of battle between a huge serpent covered in feathers and creatures made of mountains... it was pretty enough, but it looked ridiculous. Evie couldn't believe someone would waste time making such a thing for some tavern tale.

"Get in," he said, holding the tapestry to the side. Evie's lips thinned but she dipped her head and stepped into the dark.

Night Eye.

The dark came alive in shades of green, showing her a small chamber with a table, several chairs, and some sort of mosaic on the far wall. There was a single other person in the room, and they stood up nervously.

"Evie, hello," Vess said, but didn't manage more than that. Whatever else she was gonna say was cut off by the crushing hug Evie gave her. They embraced for a while, neither speaking, but Evie could feel the weight of the last few months lessening a bit.

Magelights bloomed above them, garishly bright in the space. Evie and Vess both winced, stepping away from one another and deactivated their vision Skills.

"Ah, yes, sorry," Atar said from the door. He latched it closed and locked it with a thick, iron key. "Should have warned you."

"You think?" Evie snapped, rubbing the bridge of her nose and blinking. "Now I'll be seeing spots for half the day."

"I said sorry. We don't have a lot of time," Atar said. "With the Elders in disarray, this may be the moment we need to seize our chance."

Vess nodded. "The arrival of the Inquisition has put my guardian on edge as well, and is why I've been able to slip away so easily. The survivors are on the tenth floor; I only hope their guard slackens during this time."

"It might," Atar said. "Some very capable Bronze Ranks are stationed on that floor. With everything happening now..."

"Tell me," Evie said. Atar swallowed. "Tell me about Magda."

Vess looked between the two in confusion. "What is this?"

"Atar sent me a message the same time you did. He even had some bits about the survivors, too, which is why we're all here." Evie leaned forward, intending to loom but unable to keep her arms and hands still for nerves. "Tell me. You said you have information on her body."

Vess' breath caught, but Evie didn't want to miss anything the mage said. Atar, for his part, looked supremely uncomfortable. He cleared his throat.

"The same rooms they are holding the survivors also hold her body, held in stasis with a ridiculous amount of arrays. I—I thought they were trying to remove her Essences for another Guilder, but I found out no alchemist has been seen on the tenth floor at all."

"Then what do they burnin' want with her body?" Evie demanded.

"I don't know. I don't!" Atar protested as Evie leaned forward menacingly. "I saw her body there, and it sits sour in my gut. The more I found out about it, the more I didn't like it.

Maybe she hadn't been the best to me in the past, but that didn't mean someone should... it wasn't right, is all."

Atar heaved a couple tense breaths, as if he'd just sprinted down the hall. Evie nodded, reluctantly, and Vess' mouth firmed into a disapproving line.

"Then we put an end to it," the heiress said. "Right?"

"Right." Evie grinned through the wet in her eyes, and if her voice was a little thick, well, who doesn't get a frog now and then? "How much of a tizzy are the Elders in, exactly?"

Atar smiled nervously.

CHAPTER THIRTY-TWO

The journey up to the tenth floor was a breathless rush, the three of them ducking into alcoves and side hallways whenever they heard other Guilders on the steps. With everyone scrambling over the Inquisition's arrival, few would have noticed their presence, yet all of three of them were on edge. Evie assumed Vess was nervous because she wasn't supposed to be down there, rubbing elbows with the common folk, but she couldn't put a finger on why Atar looked like a scared goat whenever a boot dropped above.

"What's your deal?" she whispered as they hid for the sixth time. Luckily, the stairs were very wide and heavily decorated. A couple of potted ferns and a deep nook kept them out of sight. "You're jumpier than a fresh dipper on market day."

"Fresh dipper?" Vess mouthed to herself.

"I'll have you know, I'm risking my neck coming down and bringing you up here!" Atar's voice was barely a whisper. It was a black thread at night. "If I'm caught leading the Heiress of Pax'Vrell around, I'll get slapped on the wrist and put on retrieval duty for two months. If I'm caught with *you*? They'll kick me out, sure as fire flickers."

"Kick you out? Over little ol' me?" Evie batted her eyelashes at the mage. "I'm impressed. The Elders didn't want to settle on a death sentence for helping evil Magda's sister?"

"You're closer than you know," Atar grimaced. "No one was happy to hear about Magda—"

"Not even you, Sparky?" Evie asked, certain to keep the edge in her voice. "My sister didn't treat you as you liked, if I recall."

"That is neither here nor there," he breathed. Evie could almost hear the lie on his tongue, but she let it slide. For now. "And it is in the past, too. Look, they've passed us by. Let's go."

"Why would they punish you for seeing me?" Vess asked before he could stand.

"You don't know?" Atar bit his lip, as if debating whether to talk. "The Elders gave a warning. No Guilders are to talk to you, except those they'd already approved. Said it was to ensure you're not bothered during your training and recovery. Said it came from your minder."

"Darius," she said in a dangerous voice. Evie glanced at her with respect. The prim and proper lady sounded like she wanted blood. "I shall take care of that later."

They slid from the nook and continued on. They only had to stop three more times before they reached the tenth floor. At each floor, there were multiple doors leading off the stairwell. It was so large that anything else would have been a waste of space. Atar led them to the right-most door, a plain thing with a panel of copper inset at the base and up to their waists. He motioned for them to hold and stepped within.

"I truly am sorry, Evie," Vess said. Again. "Elder Teine's questions came so fast, I could never quite say the words I wanted."

"I know," Evie said. Her voice was low so as not to carry and she eyed the stairs again. "I was there, yeah? I was mad at you for a bit—more than a bit, truly—but I'm past it. It wasn't fair, not really. You didn't say a word of untruth at the Tribunal."

"Perhaps not. But perhaps I could have fought more valiantly. Said more, pushed them harder." Vess made a frustrated clutching gesture. "Something. Instead I let Darius whisk me away, leaving all of you. Siva's Grace! I have not been able to even send you a letter before now."

"It's fine," Evie lied. "Look at me, I'm fine." It was nice to hear Vess say those words, late as they were. She sniffed. "Agh, you'd think they'd dust in here more often. Clogging up my nose."

Vess smiled at her, wide enough that her dimple showed through. "Indeed."

"Hmm."

The door opened only a few moments later, and then only enough for an olive-complected hand to wave them both in. They slipped through, one after the other. On the other side lay an empty reception hall, filled with soft chairs and well-polished floors. A large desk sat at one end, and hallways opened up in several directions beyond it. Not a soul was there.

"Where is everyone?" she asked.

"Moving," Atar said. "I overheard more speaking on it as they carried out crates of supplies. Everything is moving."

"Moving?" Vess asked. The three had stepped quickly and quietly across the chamber, following Atar's furtive lead. "Moving where?"

"Damned if I know. The Guilders I heard only called it the 'staging area.' Watch your step here," he said.

They all navigated over a series of other crates and boxes laid out in the hallway, but quickly moved on. Down corridor after corridor, following a plan that Evie suspected not even Atar knew all that well. He kept pausing at intersections.

"Are you lost?" Evie hissed.

"No! I'm just—" Atar's eyes alighted on a marking on the wall. Each intersection had them, small brass plates bolted to the well-appointed walls. "Ah, yes, here we are. I was a little turned around when I first came this way, but I remember this corridor. Come!"

They hustled forward again, taking turn after turn, and each time Atar becoming more and more sure of their progress. As they came to the last intersection—according to Atar—they heard voices ahead. Evie swallowed hard, and gripped the chain she had wrapped around her waist. Atar all but slapped her hand away and pointed at a nearby door.

Vess eased the door open, and they vanished inside, ducking low and closing it soundlessly behind them. Voices, people passed beyond the portal, not loud but certainly not quiet, either. There were at least four, all talking at once.

"Well, I think Elder Teine is panicking," said a high voice.

"Panicking? He's downright terrified of the Master Inquisitor!"

"How dare you suggest our master would be threatened by those zealots!"

"Peace, all of you. My, but you go on." Their voices faded a bit as they moved, and as the argument stopped. "Teine wants everything transported below. Everything, and at a quick pace, too. That's hard enough without working our jaws off, claiming knowledge of things we know nothing about. Mm?"

"But what if the Inquisition finds out about what we're doing here? What if they find the bodies?"

"They won't. No evidence is gonna remain. Anything we can't take with us gets burnt. Now move. We're short on time."

The squabbling faded further as they walked off. Evie met her friend's gaze, and she couldn't help her eyes from widening. "Burnt?"

"Bodies? Who have they killed? The survivors?" Vess asked. "And would they truly kill the rest to avoid notice?"

"Of course they would," Atar said in a voice that suggested they were being foolish. But Evie didn't miss the way he worked moisture into his lips before talking. "What I've seen them doing... I wouldn't want that traced back to me, were I involved."

The silence continued for several dozen heartbeats. Evie knew; she was counting. It was a good distraction from the thought of finding her sister's—She closed her eyes and ran her hand across the bladed chain at her waist.

Still, the thought of it bled through, staining her mind. Evie grunted as she stood.

"Enough of this, let's go." She pushed open the door, not bothering to check if anyone was beyond. Luckily, there was no one, but Atar's face was apoplectic regardless. Evie pushed down her worry and kept advancing. "Where to now, Sparky?"

Atar made an annoyed sound in his throat, but it wasn't nearly as amusing as she usually found it. "Here, it's here." He pointed to a large door marked with another copper panel. It looked like any of the other doors, well-made but utilitarian. So why did she feel so nervous?

"We can't stand out in the hallway all day," Atar murmured.

"Hush," Vess said.

Evie barely heard them. She focused on the door, on the faint scratches in the wood, on where the metal had been polished by a hundred hands. She reached out, pushed it, and it opened on greased hinges. Evie walked in, and the first thing she noticed was the smell. It smelled of medicine and cloying flowers, one making the other worse, and underneath it all was a thick odor of rot. Decay. Death.

"It smells of a charnel house," Atar complained. "It wasn't like this before."

"Where is everyone?" Vess asked. She stepped forward, past Evie and gestured to the room. "These beds are empty."

Stuck in the entryway, *that* shook Evie from the torpor she felt. "What?"

Stalking inward, Evie found the same sight Vess did: there were many, many beds in the chamber, but every single one was empty. Linens were tossed about and crumpled, and in many places stained with odd yellow fluids, but there was not a single sign of the survivors. Vess cursed, which Evie would normally have been delighted to hear, but she felt as if someone had stuffed her ears with wool.

Evie spun on Atar. "Where are they?"

Atar held up his hands defensively. "You heard the Guilders! They're moving everything and everyone somewhere else! I didn't—I don't know where! I told you this!"

"Atar," Evie growled, but was cut off.

"Evie!" Vess gasped. "Evie, come look."

Hidden behind a partition, Vess was staring with a hand over her mouth. Evie raced over, the numb feeling she'd labored under dropping, sinking into her legs and toes to become something more, something terrifying. She turned the corner, and her breathing hitched in her chest.

"*Maggie.*"

There, on a bed inscribed with countless lines and sigils of pale green-gold, was her sister. She was dressed in some sort of healer's gown and not her armor. *Of course she wasn't,* she thought. *Where is her armor, though? That was expensive. Took us years of saving to buy the first piece of it. We can't—*

"...Evie?"

"Hm?" Vess was speaking to her, had been for a while. "What did you say?"

"Are you all right?"

"I'm," she swallowed. It was hard to form words. "We have to get her out of here. Help me." Evie stepped forward, but a hand on her elbow pulled her back.

"Don't," Atar hissed. He pointed at the sigils flickering along the raised sides of the bed. "These keep her body in stasis. Keeps it from... you know. But these," he pointed out another set of sigils, all spiraling around each other like water down a drain. "These are protections. Wards against contact and movement. We can't touch her until those are taken down."

"Then take them down," Evie snarled and yanked her elbow from his grip.

Atar pulled out a slender silver pen, but instead of a quill or ink reservoir, it was more like a chisel. He got to work, slowly etching a series of symbols to the side of the complicated array. Evie's attention quickly wandered away from him, flitting back to her sister. She looked as if she was sleeping, just moments from waking. Evie knew that was a combination of a powerful Journeyman Body and the wards, but she couldn't help the treacherous thrill of possibility that climbed her spine.

She's gone. And yet... Her hand reached out, stopping shy of the almost-invisible dome of energy surrounding Magda. *If only she could simply wake up.*

Evie closed her hand atop her chain, letting the hard metal press through her gloves. It hurt, but that was the point. At least it made it easier to think, like when she fought. The burn of muscles and recoil from a blow well-struck, it cleared Evie's mind like nothing else. But here, here she had no foe to fight, no monster to kill. It was just her and the specter of death.

She gritted her teeth and fingered the daggers across her chest, but she did not move from Magda's side while Atar scratched away.

———

Atar placed the last mark of his array down and leaned back to view his work. It was rushed, not as precise as he'd wish, and thus would be less Mana efficient, but it should do. *Yes,* he nodded to himself. *That is a fine array.*

Sigaldry is level 18!
Sigaldry is level 19!

The notification was a welcome surprise, and Atar just about grinned. Only when he caught Evie's drawn face did the happiness drain out of him. He couldn't very well celebrate when they were still dealing with Magda's body. Instead, he focused his Willpower, snagging it upon the starting sigil, and breathed Mana from his right palm Gate.

Invocation is level 14!

The array activated, fueled by his Mana, and as it did, it

sent tendrils of power out into the larger array sequence. The stasis and containment arrays were monstrously complicated, far more so than he could hope to understand in a glass or even a week, but they had the same problem many arrays had: a maximum Mana limit. The Mana from his array surged, collecting and refining before injecting itself into the formation. There was a bright, blinding spark and a whoosh of silent flame before everything went dark.

"There. It's done." Atar let himself smile this time, truly proud of his workaround. Not many could have gotten around the surge dampeners he'd found, especially not someone without an Apprentice Tier Spirit.

Evie's breathing quickened, and she reached out a tentative hand. When she encountered nothing, the hand rushed down to Magda's side, grabbing a shoulder in a fierce grip. Atar looked elsewhere. People crying made him uncomfortable.

Vess was standing a ways away, or she had been. Atar couldn't see her from within the partitioned area, so he stepped out to give Evie some privacy. He found Vess at the door, listening with a single ear.

"What's going—"

"Quiet," Vess commanded, her voice low so as not to carry. "Someone is coming."

"What? We have to get out of here!" Atar also kept his voice low, but it was a close thing. "We—"

The door opened faster than they could stop it, and both Vess and Atar were shocked into immobility. A bulky figure stood there, framed by the threshold, and chuckled.

"If you coulda seen the looks on your faces," Harn chortled. "Priceless."

"Harn?" Atar said in confusion, while Vess greeted him with a bright smile.

"How did you know to look for us?" Vess asked.

"Evie ain't as slick as she thinks she is. Only took a little investigatin' to find the message you sent her, Atar," Harn shrugged and stepped into the room. He looked around intently. "Where are they? The survivors?"

"Gone," Vess said. Harn swiveled to her with an angered grunt. "We do not know where. Only that they were likely moved due to the Inquisition's appearance."

Harn grunted again, this time in sour agreement. "There'll be a lotta that. Reshufflin' the deck now that the pit boss is watchin'."

"What?" Atar asked. That reference had made no sense to him.

Harn opened his mouth to answer—or say something rude, one never knew with the warrior—but he snapped it shut again. He tilted his head. "Someone's coming. Multiple people, at least two, maybe three."

"Noctis' tits!" Evie cursed as she came around the partition. "Harn! No, Atar! Go! Take care of it! Stall them or—or something!"

"Why me?" Atar said, his heart in his throat. "I'm not supposed to be here, either!"

"Because we'll get kicked out the nearest window," she growled, gesturing to herself and Harn. "And she's a Duchess. Go!"

She shoved him, and despite his increases in Strength, he was no match for the girl. "Fine! Fine. Let go of me, you chain-slinging cretin!"

Evie stopped pushing, and Atar straightened his robes. He took a breath and looked at the others. "You all owe me."

He stepped into the hall. It was empty for a stretch, but Atar could hear people coming up from his right, and he moved quickly. Bracing himself, he took the corner and walked headlong into a group of three Guilders. Bronze Rank Guilders. *Burn me. Of course, it's him.*

"You!" snarled the lead, the barrel-chested Okar. "I told you never to come back here again, didn't I?"

"Who's this?" said a woman beside him. Long, intricate

braids hung from her head, and her face had been painted with blue and black shapes.

"Some worthless Tin Rank, Yvette," Okar said to her offhandedly. "One I threatened with bodily harm if he strayed back here again."

"Listen, Okar. Sorry. I just—I got lost again. These corridors are confusing," Atar said glibly. It had been the excuse he'd prepped before he'd ever sent Evie that letter. "Surely, you wouldn't kill me for being lost?"

"He's done worse for less," said a pale haired man with a wide smile. He had several scars over his lips. "Haven't you, Okar?"

In response, the bearded Bronze Rank merely smiled, but it was not comforting in the least. It was a rictus grin, devoid of warmth. A spike of dread sank deeper into Atar's bones. He worked his tongue, drying to dredge up some moisture so he could speak, but terror gripped him hard.

Damn you, Evie!

"There you are!" said a surprising voice. Atar jerked, alarmed to see Alister step from another side corridor. The man threw his arms to the side, letting his blue coat flare dramatically. "I've been looking all over—did you get lost with the last shipment?"

"Wha—I, um—"

"Of course you did," Alister sighed, so loudly it was as if he was questioning why he was cursed with such an incompetent. Atar almost felt angry about it, before he realized what the noble was doing. "Forgive him, Okar. He's a bit of an idiot when it comes to directions. Gets lost so easy."

The bearded Bronze Rank eyed the both of them, from the tips of their shoes to the tops of their heads. His beard twitched and mouth puckered, clearly unwilling to let any of it slide. Yet before he could say a thing, the tattooed woman beside him groaned in annoyance.

"Come off it, Okar. We've shipments to haul, and I don't plan to be here all burning day."

Okar grunted and stuck a blunt finger in their faces. "Get outta here. And don't come back 'til I see an Iron medallion on your chests, eh? Otherwise, I'll gut you, audience or not." He jerked his head. "Let's go."

Atar swallowed as he watched the three Bronze Ranks continue around the corner, heading straight for the room Vess and Evie were in. He only hoped he'd bought them enough time. He'd arranged this to ease his conscience, not add to it.

"Ahem."

"Oh, you're still here?" Atar muttered. "My thanks for the assistance. I clearly had everything under control, but, well, thank you."

"My pleasure," Alister said offhandedly. Was he grinning? "Is this where the illustrious Professor gets to when he can't help the team? Avoiding the Elder's fetch quests?"

"Listen, I—"

He shrugged. "I don't need to know. Easier to tell someone I don't know, rather than lie."

"Oh, ah," Atar stammered. "I see."

"Buuut," Alister said, dragging out the word. "If you want to repay me, there is a tavern over on Chandler and Lapidary. We could go and have a bite to eat or a drink."

Atar sighed, defeated. "...Fine. Just one drink."

"Wonderful." They began to walk away, just as a deep voice shattered the quiet.

"WHERE'S THE BODY?"

Atar started walking faster, pulling Alister's arm away from the Bronze Ranks. "We should leave. Quickly."

Evie panted, winded and shaking from their chancy escape. She risked a peek around the corner, but there was no sign of pursuit, though she heard the sound of muffled yelling further off.

"I think we're good," she said.

"We ain't good til we're outta this tower," Harn said. He shifted the bundle on his shoulder, carefully. Evie kept looking at it and jerked her eyes away. She couldn't think about it, not 'til they were done.

"I can get you down to the Lobby, but from there, you will have to fend for yourselves," Vess said with a grimace. "I am not... *allowed* outside of the Eyrie. The last thing you need is an angry Adept coming to find us."

"Sounds like a real ass," Evie said. "But thank you."

"Of course." Vess took Evie's hand and squeezed. "I am incensed, however, that we could not find the survivors."

More angry shouting came from behind them, this time accompanied by hurried footsteps.

"We haven't the time, Vess. Evie, let's go." Harn pointed the way. "There are servant's entrances along the back route. If we move, we might just make it."

Evie squeezed her bladed chain, letting the pain center her, before nodding. Harn caught her eye.

"You did good, kid."

She grinned, despite herself. "Yeah."

They ran for their lives.

The Envoy had watched the Humans fumble about with the body of the dead one from beneath one of the beds. He had been tempted to interfere, to either kill them or aid them, just to get them out of the way, but his mission was too important. So he had hidden beneath an illusion instead as they had barged into the chamber. He was the last of the "survivors" the Guilders were moving below, and that concerned him enough that he did not need the distraction of some interlopers.

For below them was the very purpose of his journey to the heart of the mortal's city.

In the end, the Envoy did nothing. He rested and waited, senses extended to envelop the whole of the tenth floor. A simple thing, really. These Guilders were far weaker than he had been led to believe. Even a trio of Untempered fools was able to steal away their prized corpse.

The last one, however, the armored one, was dangerous. The moment he arrived, the Envoy had let his Father's powerful arrays flare, hiding him from all senses. He hadn't bothered with the Untempered; they barely noticed anything at all.

When they left, carrying their corpse, the Envoy breathed a sigh of relief. His skin, pasty and entirely too fleshy, it itched. He wished to tear it away, but now was not the time. No. No, it was not right yet.

He stood, letting his illusion of shadows and dusty flooring fall away as he climbed back into his bed and reactivated the simple sigils upon its frame. He closed his eyes just as the other Guilders barged in.

Soon he could begin his Father's plan.

Soon.

CHAPTER THIRTY-THREE

Felix wandered the dark. The Rim Hunters had escorted him to the very edge of their territory, just beyond the ward array, the one they said he had sabotaged. He had tried talking to them, to convince them of his innocence, but none listened. Not even the ones he'd fought with, back at their lodge. Instead, they glared at him with hard eyes and jabbed at his back with insistent spears.

The Conference Lords had followed at a distance as well, close enough to keep him from fighting off the Hunters, and far enough that attacking them was impossible without facing the others. The memory of it made Felix grind his teeth. They had watched him walk for a half hour or so before they took off. Each of them had their own small skimmers, and they were gone within minutes. While the Void had little in the way of landscape, the darkness had a way of obscuring things from too far off. It was unpredictable and strange, as sometimes he could see rock islands miles distant clear as day, while other times something like a narhollow would remain unnoticed until it was a half mile away.

Felix repressed a shudder. Even thinking of a narhollow

made him picture the Whalemaw. He hadn't seen the Whalemaw in a long time, over two weeks now if he had kept the days straight, but the memory of its fluid eyes and jagged mouth... He'd be happy never to encounter it again.

I told you it would come to this, Felix Nevarre.

Bad enough he had to deal with one Maw.

"Shut up," Felix groaned. He adjusted his path as the next monolithic ward stone came into view.

You should have killed them, as I suggested. Right now, you would be digesting their Essence, taking what you needed from their Memories and Skills. That is the way things must be, here at the edge of all things.

Felix ignored it still. They hadn't stopped sniping and complaining since the Rim Hunters had begun their march, and it showed no sign of slowing down.

What shall you do now, Unbound? How shall you find your way in this bleak landscape? A cruel laugh bubbled up from the thing. *Even your Companion is gone. I say good riddance. That thing was a pest, and a danger besides. Guardians of Harmony—pfah!*

"Shut your damn mouth, for once!" Felix snarled, too angry to care how loud he was, or that lightning discharged from every single one of his Gates at once. "You leave Pit out of your ravings, or I'll—I'll go find the Whalemaw and throw myself down its throat."

Pfft. You haven't the stones.

Felix bared his teeth. "Remind me again, who was it that killed themself to stop you before?"

The Maw paused, its stolen face snapping out of cruel revelry. Thin brows tugged down above its sharp nose. *You wouldn't dare—*

"Why wouldn't I? I've done it once, and nothing has changed since then. So watch yourself, or we'll both find our ends in a maw of a different kind."

The Maw went quiet, so much so that Felix wanted to look and make sure it was still there. It had a habit of disappearing for days at a time, though he didn't know where it went. But no—it didn't matter. Felix kept walking. It was all he could do.

He walked for days—cycles, whatever. Moving between monolith ward stones was an achingly slow process on foot. Even running would have only halved the time, somehow. Manaships and skimmers followed different rules than the physical, apparently. They moved far faster than they should, owing in some small part to their Control Node and Mana engines. Or however they functioned. Felix wasn't really sure, and no one could explain it.

He still had the map from Wonderment, though the one from the pirates was stashed in Bateo's farmhouse. So was Pit. The maps weren't a concern—he'd glimpsed them recently enough that he could recall them in exacting detail—but his Companion was. In the days that passed, despite his attempts to reach out through their connection, he had not seen or even felt Pit.

He could access Pit's Status sheet, though, and a vague warmth in his chest, but their shared sensations and communication was entirely absent. A feature of the Void, he suspected. He knew Pit was alive and unhurt, but still he worried. He had walked, and sometimes run, trying to gain an angle that put him closer to Bateo's farm without crossing the ward, but nothing had happened yet. The connection hadn't faded or grown any stronger, which meant Pit was alive, well, and unmoving.

What've they done to him?

Felix bounced to a stop, the slightly giving not-surface of the Void pushing back at him. He felt lost. With the maps in his head, he could puzzle out the directions to another settlement eventually, but without Pit, why would he try? And even if Pit were with him, if he could somehow sneak into Echo's Reach and steal Pit back out, what then? Live in the Void forever?

I still have the Quest. Escape The Void. Felix snorted, bitterly. *But no clue how to do it. Best I can figure is to break into Echo's Reach, rescue Pit, steal my sloop, and blow outta there. Would I survive the attempt, though?*

Felix had tried to stave off his frustrations by working at his last Mana Gate. The pain of it was a good distraction from being chased away like a rabid dog. Still, it was a long process, and not nearly half done by the time he'd received the message.

**You Have Finished Digesting Your Target's Mana!
You Have Gained A Memory From A Noctnatter!
Would You Like To Review It Now?
Yes/Yes**

Felix felt his eyes light up, a curious sensation he hadn't experienced in a while. Not since Shelim, he was sure. Worry and anger tingled at the edges of his Mind, but excitement dominated.

The world went gray... more gray, at least, and even the Maw stilled until it was a cadaverous statue. Then, everything rippled, moving inward from the unseen horizon, until the ripple was miles high and like to throw Felix straight into the sky. Yet, as it reached him, the ripple cracked and shattered into ten million motes of incandescent light.

He was somewhere else.

Some*thing* else.

He swam through the dark, his body powerful and unstoppable. An apex predator without rival in the black. Prey scattered before it and he could taste their fear, their despair.

He reveled in it.

But now, new prey had come. Rare prey, those that hid behind the dead, that rode their corpses like foul monstrosities. Fins of skin and hide of bone, they rode at him over and over, him and his brothers. His sisters. His kind stayed close together, hunting as one, but the Dead Riders separated them. Stabbed at them with claws and teeth that drew precious Life from them. Struck them with violence they could not fully answer back in kind. With green fire.

He—no, Felix. I am Felix, he realized. He rode within the head of the Noctnatter, one of dozens, all of them harried by a series of Manaships. They were being jabbed at, driven forward like cattle on a ranch. Those who did it were no ranchers, but pirates.

And the flag atop their masts was all the same. A series of bloody handprints on a black background. Ten of them.

Pirates of the Ten Hands, *he hissed.*

The pirates were spurring the voidbeasts onward, and as the noctnatter's senses caught up, he realized clouds of Tenebrils and Harrowings flew on ahead, as if to whet the void serpents' appetites. They all passed a familiar monolithic ward stone at speed, though the pirates hung back to jeer at the voidbeasts.

His fellows kept on, pushing inward, following the delectable scent of prey and of great prey to come. But his noctnatter slowed and turned, hidden by its abilities, watching.

"Alright! That's enough beasties! Circle back!" This was said by a Half-Orc woman with several blades and a mandolin strapped across her back. "More than enough to crack this hideaway!"

Another scoffed. "Hiding from us? Not payin' for us to protect 'em? That'll teach the damn birds!"

"Captain'll be pleased," said a third with a wicked laugh. "So many new Mana batteries!"

All of it made little difference to the noctnatter, save that it swam in loops, hoping to catch one of the Dead Riders unaware. To Felix however, the information struck like a lightning bolt out of a clear blue sky.

Straining mightily, Felix leveraged everything he had. The Memory flexed and shivered around him, until his Willpower shattered it completely and threw him screaming into the deepest Void.

Bloodline Progression is 8%

Felix jerked to his feet, already running.

Felix? What are you doing? Finally taking vengeance? The Maw's voice was hopeful.

"They're in danger! All of them!" Felix said as he pumped

his legs as hard as he could. The Void flew beneath him, faster than he'd ever moved.

Who is? From what? The Maw laughed. *This entire Realm is a death trap! What more could—*

"Pirates! They're coming!"

CHAPTER THIRTY-FOUR

Felix! Stop!

He didn't listen, bounding across the ground faster and faster, he pressed all he could out of his Skills. Relentless Charge carried him forward in a flash, and he chained them together over and over, pushing himself until his Mana hit the halfway mark. Then he ran some more, desperate, feeding some of the Essence into his crackling core. It washed back outward, lighting up his Skill pattern.

Relentless Charge is level 13!

Even that took the lion's-share of the nebulous Essence he held within his core space, so thin was the System's influence. But Felix didn't care. He pressed on, until the miles disappeared and the second ward layer loomed close by.

That was when the air rippled ahead, and a Manaship a bit bigger than his sloop ripped toward him. It's dark sails and broad bone beams shone with Mana, a vibrant life that animated the ship as men and women dressed in coarse leathers screamed obscenities into the black. They noticed him at the same time Felix saw them, and the ship took a wide turn, bringing four ballistae to bear on him.

"Fire!" a voice cried out, and four bolts the size of spears exploded forth, lit with a terrible green light.

Reign of Vellus!

Felix dumped his Mana into the Skill, spending almost a quarter of it on the cast. A sphere of omnidirectional force slammed outward, slapping the Void with a sound like thunder as lightning chased after it. The wave of kinetic Mana hit the ballista bolts and stopped them dead.

"Well, if it isn't the Mana-freak!" said a feminine voice from atop the forecastle. A Half-Orc woman stood there with white hair, dark green skin, and eyes as sharp as the cutlass at her side. A mandolin was slung at her back, but she didn't seem in a mood to play it. He recognized her: Bridgven Parsdattir, the bard from the Ten Hand's fortress. "Just who we've been lookin' for! Reload!"

"Why are you here?" Felix cried out, barely able to keep his temper in check. Faced with an entire ship filled with pirates, he couldn't let his anger make the decisions here. He counted at least seven aboard the ship, with more potentially inside.

"We tracked you, fool! You think someone can steal one of Captain Nokk's ships and get away with it?" She laughed, delighted. "I will say, setting the voidbeasts on the Captain's flagship was inspired. I may write a song about it!" She grinned, and her tusks gleamed in the light of green flame. "Fire!"

Relentless Charge!

Felix vanished from his position, easily evading the ballista bolts and running toward the hull of the ship. *They can't fire at me if I'm on their ship, right?* More pirates pointed and called out, tracking him.

"He's a slippery one! Keep him in your sights, boys!" Bridgven shouted. "First one to pop him gets their pick outta the loot we took, eh?" A raucous cheer went up among the pirates, and Felix snarled.

"What've you done?"

"Plundered your little nest of marks!" Bridgven cackled, firing her own light crossbow at him. The bolt missed and flew off into the Void. "And oh, great goddesses of old! What riches we've taken! Our ships will never run dry, boys!"

"Plenty of birds to fuel 'em!" someone shouted and laughter followed.

Felix bared his teeth.

Relentless Charge!
Relentless Charge!
Relentless Charge!

He zipped through the air, chaining each Charge so that he fairly rocketed up and into the side of the ship. He hit so hard it tilted, throwing off the aim of several arbalests, and was only just able to catch hold of the railing. He pulled himself up with a single yank, vaulting ten feet into the air before landing in a deck-splintering crouch.

"How'd he do that?"

"I don't care! Kill him!" Bridgven yelled.

Shadow Whip!
Corrosive Strike!

The first two were snared by his split whip and hauled off their feet. A single, punishing acid punch put them both into the deck, splintering it further. They did not get up.

"You little—!" Another pirate hurled himself at Felix, and this time it was an Orc the size of a linebacker. He caught Felix at the waist and heaved backward... yet Felix was unmoved. He was too heavy. The look of confusion the Orc gave him before Felix clocked him would have been hilarious in any other situation. Now, however, Felix simply moved on.

There were plenty more pirates to go.

Pirates came at him in waves from every direction, two or three at a time, bearing cutlasses and pikes. Pale washes of Mana flowed from their channels, but it was weak. All of it was weak compared to Felix's own abilities. Skill after Skill buckled under Felix's own, and Corrosive Strike, Shadow Whip, and Reign of Vellus took a hefty toll on them all. The last to come at him had a metal hook tied to a rope that he whirled about. He was fast and dangerous, even better than Evie, but not faster than Felix. He caught the hook in his bare hand and yanked, hauling the pirate into the main mast, where he just about cracked it with his skull. A heavy stomp ended him for good.

Then it was just him and the Half-Orc. She held her cutlass out, but Felix's Manasight could see her gates swirling with unreleased energy. "Who are you, eh? You're not some nobody that got sucked into the Void. Who're you runnin' with? Blade Eels? Three Skulls?" She pivoted as Felix advanced on the forecastle, bright green Mana swirling on his own fists.

"Who?" Felix asked as he closed the distance.

"Pretend all you like, but I know a con when I see it," Bridgven snarled. "You came to our home with lies and a sob story, all the while you were ready to fleece us." Suddenly she laughed, and Felix got the impression that she wasn't entirely sane. "I can respect a good grift, some solid misdirection. But now you've killed my crew. Now you've made me mad."

Mana swelled in her off-hand, thicker by far than her crew, and she made as if she were pitching a ball at him. Felix tensed, ready to dodge, when his Perception flared up like a klaxon. Desperate, he leaped straight up, almost Willing himself higher as a scything blade of silvery Mana swung horizontally through where he had stood. Felix, holding onto the lowest shrouds, gaped below. Even if he had dodged where he'd planned, it would have sliced him in half.

Bridgven laughed. "I told you! I love a con!" The scything blade twisted and shot upward.

Reign of Vellus!

Just as the scythe sheared through the void leather rigging, his blast of kinetic force sent Felix sideways, into the main mast. Felix rebounded off it and fell, hard, onto the deck twenty feet below. Boards burst beneath him. Felix scrambled to his feet, ribs and back a mass of agony, and ran across the deck.

The Half-Orc laughed again, sounding more and more unhinged. "Don't run away! Stay awhile!"

Her scythe followed him, slashing and stabbing in turns, stopping just shy of cutting through rigging and bone-shaped railings. Felix barely kept ahead of it, bounding from railing to rigging to main mast again. He tumbled without thinking, and felt every nerve ending seize all at once. Felix fell like a sack of grain, just beyond the mast, gasping in excruciating pain as Acrobatics tried to activate.

The Half-Orc's scythe missed him by bare inches, unable to get an angle on him from the opposite side of the massive main mast. Distantly, he heard her snarl in annoyance. "Get up! This is no fun if you don't fight back!"

The agony did not let up, despite his wishes, searing his skin and arms and every muscle between. It felt as if a thousand blades were stabbing into his core, and each stab sent waves of pain rolling into the rest of his body. Heavy boots thudded on the deck, pulling his eye. He saw Bridgven slide to a stop, now on the other side of the mast. She scoffed, and that mad gleam in her eye had redoubled.

"Fine! Stay still and die!"

Felix threw his mighty Willpower against the savage pain in his core, and drew enough control to push against the main mast with his legs. He skidded backward like a hockey puck, so fast he fetched against the railing with the sound of splintering bone.

"GAHH!" The impact was more than enough to jostle him from his tormented core, and Felix lurched to his feet. He gasped, panting for breath, as Bridgven rounded on him. Her scythe hovered in the air above her. His Mind whirled, Perception flared for something, anything. *Damnit, I hope this works!*

Influence of the Wisp!

Blue-white wispfire ignited across the Half-Orc's chest, flaring along all of her limbs, an echo of the fire on Felix himself. Yet even as it lit, it died and flickered out.

Enthrall Failed.

But it was distraction enough. Felix ran, not for his enemy, but laterally, toward the main mast. Bridgven swung, but at the last minute pulled short, unable to damage more of her precious ship. Felix couldn't even muster up the amusement to enjoy it. He leaped, straight up.

Reign of Vellus!

At the apex of his leap, which carried him up thirty feet easily, he sent a focused beam of force directly above him. Felix's entire body was forced back *down*, slamming into the deck of the Manaship. He'd learned he'd grown in weight and density since earning his Apprentice Tier Body, and now he relied on it. The entire deck pitched to starboard, and the Half-Orc pirate was thrown from her feet, her balance utterly broken.

Wrack and Ruin!

Reign of Vellus!

Felix ran up the near-vertical deck, propelled by the spark of lightning and thunder behind him, rocketing up at her with all the strength he could muster. Bridgven snarled in surprise as they met, her eyes wide and manic, too fast, too close to avoid him...

He slammed the orb of dark acid straight into her solar plexus. His fist followed it, until both emerged in a shower of viscera that revealed destroyed flesh and bone in equal measure.

You have Killed Bridgven Parsdattir!
XP Earned!

The deck rolled in the opposite direction, slamming hard into his feet and knees, sending him sprawling like a sack of meal. Gamely, he grabbed onto a dangling line of void leather, and was flung about like a child's toy, smashing into the deck as the Manaship fought to find its equilibrium. When finally the ship settled, Felix was wrung out and more than a little battered.

"Oough," he elocuted, rolling heavily onto his back atop the heaving deck. "Unbound's number one weakness: big ass ships."

Felix spent some time on his back, but eventually leveraged himself into a sitting position. He gasped at a pain in his ribs—it felt like one of them had cracked, but not broken. He couldn't be sure. Felix stood. Bodies were all around him, many tossed against the starboard railing during his maneuver, and he scanned them nervously. Manasight flared, checking the masts and sails for anyone still lurking, but neither his Skill nor his Perception caught anything at all.

He'd won.

Aside from that bit at the end, you did well. Very well.

Felix jerked his head up and saw the Maw hovering above him, its lank hair drifting in a non-existent breeze. It smiled with delight.

Such excellent violence. You'll make a fine Vessel, yet.

"Don't get your hopes up," he snapped. Felix looked about. "I will take *this* vessel, though." Quickly, he descended the steps into the areas below decks. He swept his Manasight through the area, looking for more pirates, but found no one else aboard ship. At least, no one until he reached the rear most section, where he could hear a set of soft, pained cries.

The door was locked, but Felix put his shoulder to it and tore it off the hinges completely. It flew through the air, only barely missing a set of complicated machinery that could only be the Mana engine running the ship. Set in the center of that engine, however, was a... a person.

"Oh no," Felix gasped.

According to his Eye, he was a Dwarf named Svengard, but he responded to nothing Felix said or did. That is, until Felix came close enough to see just how closely he was bound to the engine array. Void bone spikes were driven into the Dwarf's chest and arms, along with a complicated series of void leather bindings, each inscribed with complicated sigaldry that extended deep into the guts of the machinery.

"Kill... me..."

Felix flinched back, horrified. The Dwarf's eyes were

clouded over, but they still tracked Felix. He tried repeating it once more before the Dwarf was too exhausted to go on.

"God damn it," Felix muttered. "I'm not gonna kill you."

Then you will be draining him to power this ship?

"I'll pilot it myself. I've got the Skill and the Mana to spare," Felix said, still grimacing at the Mana engine before him.

Unless you remove him, that will not work. It is designed to pull Mana from one placed here, first. The Maw was suddenly atop the engine, pointing at a particular line of script. *Says so, right here.*

Felix clenched his jaw, unwilling. Then without warning, a shrill cry stabbed through Felix's Mind and Spirit. His back arched with the intensity of it, and sense memories flashed through his head in a hectic rush. Then it was gone, and Felix was gasping for breath.

Pit. He turned and left, pounding up the stairs at speed. *PIT!*

So, you just leave him there to rot? The Maw kept pace with him as Felix leaped off the deck of the Manaship, setting it slowly tilting again in his wake. *Not very heroic and noble of you, Felix Nevarre.*

"I'm not killing him, you psycho! And Pit's in trouble!" Felix gathered his Stamina and Mana, and activated Skills that set him flashing forward atop a wave of lightning.

Reign of Vellus!

Relentless Charge!

He approached the second ward again, this time at speed, and flashed through its defenses. He watched the Void ripple, revealing dozens of stone islands in eyeshot, many of them linked by braided chains. More importantly, he could see Bateo's home in the near distance.

The farmhouse was a pyre, blazing acid-green in the dark.

"No," he whispered, before pouring more of his Mana into his Skills. His channels fairly screamed, torn raw by the flush of power, until he all but crashed into the side of the island. Felix rolled with the impact, hurtling himself forward and Charging across the two outer islands.

Relentless Charge!

Felix all but flew through the Void, flashing ahead regardless of his Stamina and Mana. He landed heavily atop the still burning island, gasping and panting. Felix pivoted, taking it all in. The pens, the fields, all of it was torn apart and ruined. The farmhouse—the farmhouse! He could feel the heat from where he stood at the edge of the island, and it stabbed at his skin like a thousand daggers.

"Bateo! Estrid! Kids!"

Disregarding the pain, Felix stumbled up the steps three at a time. The building was burning hot the higher he ascended, screaming against his nerves and shrieking within his core space. Felix spasmed but pushed onward, bellowing as loud as he could.

"PIT! ESTRID! BATEO!"

He struggled to the top of the steps, half-blind from the pain. His chest felt as if it was ripping in half, but Felix didn't—couldn't—stop.

"PIT!"

Inside! Hurry!

Felix gasped, instantly regretting it as the heat surged into his throat and blazed across his nerves. He fell, screaming to the floor. Slowly, agonizingly, he forced himself forward, through the thin bone panels of the door as fire bloomed all around him. The kitchen was more or less intact, but flames had consumed the upper stories and dropped portions of it down from above.

Where are you?

Here! Hawk hurt!

A warmth in his chest pulled Felix, distinct from the nightmare of pain around him, and he turned with it. There. Pit struggled with a large stone beam that had fallen down across the living area. At first, Felix feared his Companion was trapped, but then he saw another figure next to the tenku, and this one wasn't moving at all.

"Bateo!" Felix limped to their side, hissing as the heat redoubled and flames licked at his boots. His Aspects screamed in agony, and he could feel his Health draining with every second he remained. "Pit! What happened?"

Attack! Stolen! Hawk hurt! Hawk trapped!

Each word was a stab at Felix's brain, but the tenku was scared and injured. Felix activated Voracious Eye through his half blind vision... and saw Bateo still had some Health remaining. They could save him.

S-stone Shaping!

The Skill stuttered as it activated, bombarded with the waves of furious vibration from his Heat and Fire Resistance Skills. But Felix flared it bright, forcing it beyond the interference, pouring Mana into his channels and out of his palm Gates. Dusty brown Mana sank into the stone beam, melting it into a sloppy goo that Felix clumsily shaped away from them all. He spread it about, smothering what fires he could with it, while Pit got under Bateo and began dragging him out of the house.

Felix followed, burnt and haggard, tripping across the boards and down the rickety stairs. The three of them kept moving until they were well clear of the blaze. Pit and Felix both slumped to the stone, exhausted.

Fire Resistance is level 20!
Heat Resistance is level 22!

The pain of both flared again—a jagged, brilliant pillar of agony—before it collapsed on itself, and chunks of his Essence store was torn away once more.

"What," Felix said with a cough. "What happened?"

Pit trembled, and Felix realized the tenku had their burlap sack of belongings tied around himself. He sent a series of sense memories similar to what had been in his terrified cry earlier. Images of ships, multiple ones, sailing into Echo's Reach and laying waste to everything in their path. Of people marched onto the ships at spear-point, wrapped in chains.

"Felix..."

Snapped clear of the sense memories, Felix took a shaky

breath. His core still felt like it was splintering, but it wasn't so bad this far from the heat and flames. To his side, Bateo was awake.

"Hey man, hang on. You're hurt, so don't strain yourself," Felix said, but the Korvaa didn't listen. His wings were burnt up and his left side was… it was bad. Felix tore his eyes away from it, trying to only focus on his friend's bloody face.

"Felix… they took her. They took my Estrid. And the hatchlings, oh gods." Bateo tried to cough, but only convulsed. His eyes were too bright and too wide. "The pirates took them. You… you have to save them. Felix!" His hand gripped Felix's own with a startling strength. "Promise me!"

"Save them? I'll tear the pirates apart to find them, Bateo. Don't worry about that. Worry about getting better, yeah? Pit? Do we have any potions? Bandages? Anything?" Felix felt panic pulling at him, but he refused to give in, Willing it away as Pit shook out a number of things from his bag. Yet when he turned back, the Korvaa's hand had fallen loose. Bateo was still.

"No, no, not again," Felix said. He heard a plaintive note to his voice but couldn't help it. "Bateo…"

Voracious Eye...

His Health had dropped to zero, as well as his Stamina. The Korvaa had died with his eyes open, hand reaching out, grasping for him. Felix stumbled back, unable to look at the farmer. His friend.

Why? Why couldn't he live? He had a family—Felix hesitated, following the man's grasping hands, reaching toward the black. Not toward him. Toward his wife and kids.

"I'll kill them all, Bateo." Felix's vision narrowed. "All of them."

Pit barked and pointed his beak in the direction of Echo's Reach. More green fires blazed in the distance, yet Pit's memories said the pirates had already fled. Felix grimaced but turned away from the sight.

Stone Shaping.

He couldn't leave his friend just sitting there. The rock

beneath Bateo softened and swelled, pulling his body down into its embrace. Above the spot, Felix crafted a rudimentary pillar, then extended branches to either side, thinning and splitting them. He added wide bits to the ends, shaping them into pointed ovals. At the end, panting with the effort, Felix had made a small stone tree. It wasn't very good.

Bateo would've loved it.

"Pit, can you run?"

Yes.

"It's a short distance. Let's—let's go."

CHAPTER THIRTY-FIVE

The Manaship tore into the dark, listing to the side no matter how Felix jostled it. Some of the rigging had been severed during his fight with Bridgven's crew, and the rest were pulling the sails askew. It was also far, far bigger than the small sloop he'd stolen before and only his prodigious Mana capacity allowed him to pilot it at all, especially since he didn't have anyone hooked up to the engine.

He could have hunted for a craft in the burning remains of Echo's Reach, but they hadn't the time. When Pit and Felix had made it back to the Manaship, he quickly went below, intent on pulling the Dwarven slave off the array, no matter how disgusting he appeared. Except he found the man already dead with a smile on his lips.

Felix shook himself from the memory of it. Behind him, the Maw chortled.

Manaship Pilot is level 17!

Felix funneled what Essence he could—*that's what the Maw*

called it, right?—into his core and Skill. He needed all the advantages he could get to pilot the huge ship alone.

Death follows you, Felix Nevarre, like a faithful hound. You must learn to set it to course ahead. To hunt.

Pit growled at the Primordial, though it was spoiled by him sliding several feet across the deck. *Silence, Enemy!*

"What he said," Felix shouted. While there was no wind, the creak and sway of the Manaship was plenty loud, and the thrumming song of the engine—he could hear it through the Control Node—it was a constant, low scream in his ears. "Brace yourselves! We're coming to some rocky terrain!"

Islands the size of men began to litter the Void, and there was no way to avoid them. They floated at all heights so that they hit masts and sails just as easily as the bowsprit. More and more impacted them, slowing them only slightly, still too small to even dent the hull or dimple the sheets. Yet ahead the way thickened, the islands coming in heavier and heavier formations.

Felix had been flying in the general direction Bridgven was headed before they'd stopped for him. If the pirates' map was accurate, then he was heading straight back to the Ten Hands' fortress. He had to catch them before they got that far. He may be strong and fast, but he held no illusions that he'd be able to take on an entire fortress. Not to mention that Desolation-fueled forcefield.

Briefly, he contemplated flying up above the worst of the rocks, avoiding the chaos and damage he was headed toward. Yet, to do so, Felix knew he'd have a good chance of missing the pirates in the chaos of the stone fields. Another island collided with the hull, jarring them hard. Felix was jostled at the Control Node, his ribs aching, but he pressed forward, scanning the horizon.

Questions burned in his mind, questions without answers. Why were people flung into the Void? To wither and die in this hellscape for no reason except that they were in the wrong place at the wrong time. Or was there a reason?

The Maw said he was summoned, and so did that Geist. Vvim. Why? For what possible purpose would anyone bring *him* across worlds?

See! Enemy! Pit's screeling cry was hard to miss, and the joy and righteous anger across their bond impossible to subdue. *Ahead!*

Beyond the stones, three ships the size of his own were cruising through the rock field far steadier than Felix himself. They weren't moving fast, which was a spot of luck, because now the rocks were jamming into his ship hard enough to throw him off course. Felix buckled down, applying all the levels he had in Manaship Pilot to the task.

Piloting the craft was a matter of Willpower and Alacrity, at least to do so directly. The Mana engines seemed to drain poor souls of their Mana and Willpower, leaving them husks, and the pirates freely able to pilot without strain. It was the dirtiest of cheats, and Felix felt his blood go hot just thinking of it. Then again, his blood had never settled, not since he first saw the voidbeasts the night before.

Let us crush them beneath our heels! It is their Fate to die, and our Fate to sup upon them! The Maw cackled, long and hard, doubled up in the remaining shroud lines.

Am I a slave to fate? Felix snarled, and so did Pit. *No. I chose this. A free Maw or a clean death, and I chose the latter.* Maybe he ended up on the Continent because the Maw needed a Vessel, or some wizard somewhere summoned him. He was in the Void because he chose *not* to do that. Felix was a defier.

He would defy until the end.

If fate is real, I'm not gonna wither away and die piecemeal. He laughed, and Pit let out a piercing screech of dark joy. *If I'm gonna die, I'm gonna make it everyone's problem.*

Felix checked his Mana. After everything, he still had a bit over seven hundred points of it left. Enough to reach and handle the pirates, he hoped. Refusing to give himself time to doubt, he focused his Will and Alacrity through the Control Node. The entire ship bucked, hard, before the streamers of green-gold energy thrummed through the decks and up into the sails. The ship lurched forward, bashing another huge island out of the way to the sound of splintering bone.

C'mon! Closer!

The Manaship swayed beneath him, shuddering with every careless impact. Felix pressed onward regardless. The planks beneath his feet vibrated, everything did, as the engine below hummed higher and higher. Ahead, the enemy ships were moving quickly as well, but not nearly as fast. Instead, some sort of ward shoved the stone island away, clearing their path.

Closer!

The sound of cracking bone and crashing rock became constant as Felix's ship accelerated still more. He was moving a lot faster than the pirates, but the ship wouldn't last much longer. Already, bits were shaking loose from above, raining down on the deck along with chunks of broken rock.

"Maw! How far can you travel from me?" Felix asked.

The Primordial was beside Felix suddenly and without warning. Its eyes were intense pools of wild greens and blues, without pupil or whites. Suspicion crawled across its face. *Why?*

"I need you to tell me if the ship, that ship," Felix pointed with his free hand at the rear-most pirate ship. "Does it have captives? How many?" He thought a moment, then added, "Better yet, tell me for all of them. But that one first."

What benefit does this favor gain me?

"I won't kill us by crashing this ship straight into one of those islands," Felix pointed off into the distance, where the rocks grew so large they rivaled large hills for scale. Far bigger than anything in Echo's Reach. "This isn't a compromise, Maw! If you can do it, do it!"

...Fine. But you owe me.

The Maw, sour-faced and scowling, zipped out of sight. Far, far faster than their ship was moving. Felix held onto the Control Node, watching his Mana drain away faster and faster, and hoping. Hoping he wasn't too late.

The Maw reappeared, popping into existence beside him so suddenly Felix was almost thrown by the ship's latest collision.

The rearmost vessel only carries a few captives, fifteen. The majority of them are within the two flanking it. Close to three hundred split among them, and all of them are held in the lower holds, beneath the foremast.

"You're useful!" Felix said from between his gritted teeth. "Imagine that! Pit! Be ready!"

A screech answered him. His friend had his claws in the deck and his wings outspread.

You will not survive this lunacy. There are at least a hundred pirates per ship, and they all have their long-range weaponry. You will be obliterated before you ever get close enough!

Felix ignored its manic worry and increased the pace, racing up to the trailing ship. The pirates finally noticed him, and a number of flaming green arrows arced through the Void, landing amid sails and decks. Green flames spread from them as if the ship were made of tinder, the sails flashing away in a sheet of verdant fire. He did not stop, but poured all his Will into the ship, all his Alacrity, for it to move *faster*.

His ship crashed into the rear of the next, demolishing his prow and tearing open the aft. The bowsprit, already half-torn apart, pierced through a Human manning one of the rear ballista. Felix and Pit jumped at the moment of impact, their Strength and wings respectively carrying them over the shattering bone and raging green flames. They landed with a grunt, just behind the mizzenmast, only just avoiding an accidental tumble that would set off his Acrobatics Skill.

Which meant he didn't see the cutlass aimed at his neck until a Frost Spear took the pirate through the throat. The Hobgoblin clutched at his red-shaded skin, stabbed through with purple-white ice Mana, and a heavy shape knocked him to the ground. Pit bit, once, and the pirate went still.

"Good job, bud," Felix said. His ear perked up. More pirates were coming down the deck, at least six of them. "I'll take the left, you take the right?"

Pit nodded, and they both took off. Felix leaped the railing leading down from the quarterdeck, his fists lighting up with blue electricity as he came down on four grizzled pirates. They snarled and shouted, their own Skills igniting the air, but Felix hit the ground and released a pulse of kinetic lightning.

Reign of Vellus!

All four of them were thrown backward, their Skills misfiring or washed away completely. Felix advanced, not giving them a second to recover. Corrosive Strike claimed their lives, one after the other, until none remained.

"Assault! To arms!"

Felix narrowed his eyes and took a running jump, vaulting the barrels lashed to the center of the deck. He landed amid another battle, Pit versus eight pirates. The tenku was holding his own, his Wingblades dangerous in such close quarters, but more grubby fighters were stomping up from belowdecks. They had to hurry.

Influence of the Wisp!

You Have Enthralled An Unknown Pirate (x6) for 3 Seconds!

All but two of them froze, washed in the same blue-white flames that limned Felix's outstretched arms. Power ate at them, though they couldn't scream, and Felix hurled an orb of dark acid at their gathered mass. Wrack and Ruin tore through them, sizzling through armor and limbs, while from the other side, a forest of Frost Spears stabbed forth. Before the Enthrall could lapse, every single one of them were dead.

Pit shrieked in triumphant fury.

"Look sharp," Felix said to him. "More are coming."

A wave of new combatants ran up the nearby stairs, all of them bearing swords or short spears. Behind them, a familiar Ogre stumped up onto deck, his heavy muscles barely constrained by the canvas jacket he wore. It was the same one who attacked him back when he first met the pirates. He sneered at Felix, cracking his knuckles as green fire raced across the rigging. "Leave the Human! He's mine!"

The other pirates rushed around Felix, attacking Pit instead, and a storm of wind and ice began. The Ogre paid it no mind, instead sizing up Felix. He grinned, baring broken yellow tusks.

"We meet again, little man," the Ogre said. *The Ram*, that was his name. "I was promised another shot at you, and I aim to take it here."

"Then take it," Felix snarled. He moved before the Ogre could react, shattering the deck beneath him as he slammed into the creature's midsection. Ram tried to bring his arms down, to slam Felix into the ground, but the Unbound's fist met Ogre gut before he had a chance.

Corrosive Strike!

Reign of Vellus!

Felix's eye burned, washing his vision with blue light as his two fists met the Ram's gut. Acid and lightning charred his clothes and armor and flesh, cooking him and peeling him, just as the kinetic Mana engaged with Felix's enhanced Strength. The Ram folded, and the six hundred pound Ogre broke.

You Have Killed Stiilgar "The Ram" Raamstell!
XP Earned!

The Ram fell bonelessly to the deck, his eyes already glazed over in death. Felix frowned. He didn't have time for this. A glance at Pit showed him the tenku was doing fine, and had in fact lit himself on fire. Poisonfire burned through the chimera, fouling the strikes of the pirates around him as he shot off blast after blast of air Mana.

Influence of the Wisp!

You Have Enthralled An Unknown Pirate (x4) for 3 Seconds!

I'm going below, he sent to his Companion, as more than half of the pirates froze in place. Pit only screeched in satisfaction.

Felix jogged down the stairs, moving fast. So fast, in fact, that he just barely missed being bisected by another pirate's hooked axe.

Relentless Charge!

He flashed ahead, bearing down on two more pirates and punching them in the face almost simultaneously. They hit the opposite wall hard enough to break their necks. He spun, spotting the axe-wielding Dwarf looking at him with fear. He dropped the axe and lifted his hands in defeat. Felix bared his teeth.

"Where are the captives?"

The Dwarf pointed a shaking hand to his left. Felix followed the motion, seeing a bone door banded with iron. A rare commodity in the Void. In his moment of distraction, the Dwarf charged, ax swinging upward to rip into Felix's chest.

He didn't miss it, not this time. His Perception caught the movement before the Dwarf took two steps, and his Agility and Strength made slapping the ax aside easy. The Dwarf's thrust went wide, and then terribly. Felix grabbed the haft of the weapon and drove it into the pirate's face.

**You Have Killed An Unknown Pirate!
XP Earned!**

Felix didn't notice the message pop up, because the moment he shoved the ax, it was like he had been felled by an arrow to his brain. He screamed, shaking the loose pieces of bone all around, releasing waves of unformed Mana from his channels, Mana that scorched and froze and crackled with latent electricity. His channels burned, his core space trembling as Ax Mastery tried to rip itself apart.

It lasted only seconds, but it felt like an eternity. He heard a distant screech, but not until a feathered head tucked under his armpit did he realize it was Pit. The tenku quivered under Felix's weight, making cooing noises to him all the while.

Eventually he stood, still shaking. "Th-thanks, bud."

Pit chirruped, and disappeared back into the fray. Felix stumbled to the iron-banded door. He tried to shove it open, but his limb twitched hard, and his entire Strength slammed into the thing. Bone splintered and iron screamed as the lock was sundered and the door ripped off its hinges to fly into the room.

Felix heard gasps from within, but he couldn't see any pirates. He shook his head, fighting to clear his thoughts. Inside, only six Korvaa were chained up with void leather bindings. He looked, desperate, but none were Estrid or the kids. A seventh was at the far end of the chambers, his body lashed instead to a complicated series of metal and sigaldry. The Mana engine.

The others first, he told himself. He hurried to the bound villagers, tearing apart their bindings with his bare hands. "Go. Up the stairs."

"What—what are—you're the Human!" a red-plumed Korvaa gasped. "You're in league with the pirates!"

"Do I look like I am?" Felix snarled. He moved down the line, ripping more of the bindings. "This is a rescue. Go, everyone. Up the stairs."

"I don't take orders from you! I—"

"Father! Please! Let us run!"

The crimson-plumed Korvaa gave Felix one last disgusted look and fled through the broken doorway. Felix heard them gasp in dismay as they stepped out there, but he couldn't waste more time on them. One last thing to do on board.

He rushed to the Mana engine, and the Korvaa lashed to it. The birdman gasped in agony, and Felix recognized him as Lord Knowledge. The snowy owl-like Korvaa looked at him without recognition, as if everything was being pulled inward. Drained by the ship. He wasn't so far gone as the Dwarf from earlier—he'd probably survive being removed. Felix gritted his teeth and tore the lashings apart with his bare hands. They sliced into his skin, but it was only a faint sting through his Pain

Resistance. The whole ship tilted as the Mana that had coursed through its planks evaporated into the Void. Freed, Knowledge slumped to the ground, almost catatonic.

Groaning in annoyance, Felix picked him up and dragged him out, thanking his luck that Korvaa were so light. He pulled him out of the cells and up the stairs, finding the villagers huddled together near Pit, who stood atop a pile of corpses, licking a shallow gash across his foreleg.

"You good, Pit?" he asked, depositing the weakened Knowledge into the hands of the villagers. "Any troubles?"

Your enemies are coming, the Maw stated. Felix jerked around, following the Primordial's pointing finger.

The two other ships were turning around, likely to investigate what was happening. They hadn't fired on them yet, but that was only a matter of time. Felix eyed the distance to the closest one. He wasn't going to give them the chance.

"Pit, protect them. I'll be right back."

He took a running leap from the deck, tipping the whole of the ship and throwing the villagers on their butts as he took to the Void.

Relentless Charge!
Relentless Charge!
Relentless Charge!

He chained his Charge, flitting through the Void like a comet, until he smashed into the deck of the next ship.

Reign of Vellus!

A full, circular blast of his power sent the astounded pirates flying back as the ship tipped dramatically. A few even died, their bodies crushed into masts and the swords of their allies. Others rushed from below, only to fall sideways as the ship bobbed as if on stormy seas. Felix was on them in seconds, his Agility and Strength too much to deny.

Then there was only silence.

You Have Killed An Unknown Pirate (x32)!
XP Earned!

Felix staggered back, dizzy from Mana and Stamina loss. A pressure was building up somewhere around his middle, as if a heavy force was trying to press down on him or into him. A burning light that was trying to reach Felix through the Void. *It's all the System energy... it's still being blocked by this place.* It was painful, but he could manage it.

Your Mana is too low! You'll run dry before you accomplish anything! You know what you have to do, Felix Nevarre. The Maw wasn't even near him, yet he heard its words with perfect, disgusting clarity. *Take their power, child!*

Felix cursed, watching the vapor waft from the corpses around him. Mana, right there. And all he had to do was give up a little bit more of what was him. He closed his eyes, dizzy with Mana loss. He had no other choice, not now.

Ravenous Tithe!

The nearest corpse burst into luminous black smoke, all of which speared toward his mouth before flowing into his skull Gate and channels. Essence, and more importantly Mana, flooded his core space.

Felix grabbed the Control Node, channeling the power before he had time to think on it. It sank into the ship, spreading a limited sort of awareness across the vessel. No one else was aboard. Felix maneuvered the ship until it was slightly below his previous, now-burning craft. "Pit! Get them on!"

Pit nudged the Korvaa, none too gently. They got the hint, and soon they spread their wings and glided down to his new deck. Felix was fairly certain the spread of green fire on the former vessel was a deciding factor.

Once they were all aboard, he pulled away from the other ship, now half-consumed by flames.

"You and you!" Felix pointed at some Korvaa. "Go free the other villagers below, but stay down there! It's gonna get chaotic up here for a while." Felix powered down the ship's engines, something that was just a matter of Willing it to happen. Hopefully that'd save whatever poor soul was attached below. He hadn't the time to free them, not yet. "I'm leaving you in charge,

SILENCE

Captain Pit. Keep them safe. I haven't checked the hold for Estrid yet."

Pit chirped in confirmation as Felix ran off the deck. He leaped and Charged straight up, angling for the ship they had just abandoned. It was damaged, already catching fire more and more completely, but Felix didn't care. He used it as a run up, leaping off the edge and Charging across the Void.

This time, however, the pirates caught him with one of their ballista bolts, and he tumbled down. Felix grunted in blinding pain, too stunned to properly react, and his already-speeding body was deflected. Momentum ruined, he became a cannonball of dense, Tempered flesh, one that collided with the lower decks. He tore through the bone planks, sprawling outward into a familiar room.

Mana engine, he realized. *What..unf..luck.* Gasping with pain, his Health down by ten percent, he shoved his left hand into the strange machinery.

Ravenous Tithe!

The whole ship went still, its power torn away and sucked into his Mana Gate. He barely had time to process the scintillating flood of power that poured into his core before the far door smashed open. More pirates were coming, but as the ship lost power, the deck pitched, tripping them, and that was enough for Felix. He jolted forward, hands lighting up with green Mana and fingers held out in a flat blade.

Corrosive Strike!

One after another, he drove his hand into and through the pirates. They crumpled, screaming with hoarse voices and foul-smelling breath, before they went silent forever. He didn't stop, even when he reached the captives, even when he saw Estrid watching him with wide, terrified eyes.

He killed them all.

"Felix?"

He gasped for breath, his three-ship marathon catching up to him, but he didn't meet Estrid's gaze. Not yet. He kicked a sword to her. "Cut yourselves free. All of them. Come to the top deck when you're ready." He straightened up and walked to the locked door, iron-banded as the other ships were. "I'll clear out the rest."

He released the lock and opened the door, coming face to face with three more pirates rushing down the steps. The leader was a heavy-set Human with three missing teeth and an eyepatch.

"Who the hell are you? Where're my men?!"

Felix didn't answer. Actions, he found, spoke louder than words.

Wearily, Felix piloted his newest ship toward the last, fueling it with his curiously topped-off Mana. Absorbing a ship's worth of power was apparently good for the resource pools. Still, the buzz in his thoughts didn't alleviate the Stamina drain or sheer exhaustion after that protracted fight. His ship bumped up into the other, and the former captives streamed onto the still-powered vessel, reunited with many of their friends and families. He'd even managed to rescue the two Korvaa lashed to their Mana engines.

Felix recognized some of them, but not many. He'd spent much of his time on Bateo's farm, not in the village. Pit chirruped at him, barreling into his knees and nearly bringing Felix to the ground. He reached down and scratched him behind his tufted ears.

"All good here, Pit?" Affirmation came through the bond. "Good. Then I've one last thing left—"

Yes. Rid yourself of these hangers-on, feed them to your hunger, and we can be on our way. The Maw flickered into existence next to him, and her gaunt face leered at the assemblage of Korvaa. Annoyance burned at him, but he ignored its violent desires. Felix was too tired to deal with the Primordial after everything else.

Felix scanned the crowd. There were so many Korvaa on the deck of the Manaship, all of them talking and crying and holding one another. Felix felt something prickle at the edge of his awareness, but he couldn't identify it, other than it wasn't any sort of incoming danger. He did, however, notice the Maw's attention focus on him before moving back to the crowd. He narrowed his eyes. His Bastion hadn't shuddered, and his Deep Mind remained inactive; the Maw wasn't doing anything that he could tell.

My Affinity, again? Felix swallowed and silently begged the universe. *I don't want to feel this. Please.*

Yet the feeling only grew as he moved through the crowd, searching now for his final task. He dreaded it, loathed it, but he had made a promise. He found Estrid leaning over some barrels, talking softly to her children. *All of them, thank god.*

Estrid met his eyes, and that feeling went from a tickle to a sudden flood of strangely distant song. A song that was terrified but was fluted with the golden tinges of airy hope. And as Felix approached them, he heard the song turn. The fluting disappeared, replaced by a dark, mournful dirge. Felix almost gasped, and did in fact stop, rooted to the spot. *She knows,* he thought. *Oh man, she knows.*

There was a flash of feathers, a rapid rustle of cloth, and Felix flinched back. He feared her more than pirates, more than voidbeasts. But all he felt was the soft, warm embrace of her arms and wings. "Estrid?"

"Thank you, Felix," she breathed, her voice thick. Her large eyes were bright with unshed tears, but the puffiness there suggested they weren't her first. "Thank you. For the hatchlings. For all of us."

"I—" Felix's words died in his throat, but he pushed them out anyway. "I found him. In the house. It was on fire, Estrid. We—we pulled him out but—"

Bateo's wife closed her eyes in a long, slow blink. Her beak, short and slightly curved, pressed up against Felix's sternum. "I know. I know what you're going to say, and I hate that I do."

"His—his final words were to ask me to save you," Felix said through his own blurred vision. He managed a smile, somehow. "I keep my promises."

"Papa?" A small voice piped up from behind Estrid. It was Jain, the smallest of the hatchlings. "Mama, where's Papa?"

"Oh Jain," she said as she knelt. Estrid wrapped her daughter in a tight hug, one that was soon joined by her other four children. Kili and Nell, at least, seemed to know what had happened, and their faces were a mixture of shock and gut-wrenching loss. Pit let out a sharp, warbling cry and dove among them, spreading his wings over the children. The children clutched at him.

"He—Bateo put himself between the scoundrels and the eyas," someone said from the side. Felix recognized one of the guardsmen, the one that looked like a magpie. "I was already chained. I saw it. He didn't even hesitate."

"Hepset," Felix said to him. "I'm glad you're okay."

"Doesn't matter what I am. I flinched, let 'em torch the Conference Hall." The man's face was screwed up part way between a frown and grimace. "Ooro, were I half the Korvaa Bateo was, I'd have stood my ground."

"Don't be stupid, Hepset," Estrid snapped from below. Carefully, she disengaged from her children, though they still clung to her hips and legs. "You'd be dead, and for no good reason. The Hall can be rebuilt." She looked at Felix, seemed to see *through* him. "It wasn't your fault, Felix. Bateo... Bateo made his own choices. What you did... it was impossible." Tears came down again, but she was smiling. "I don't know how, but you saved us all."

God, she's comforting me. For some reason, that wrenched his heart more than anything else.

It had gone quiet all around them, and Felix realized all of the Korvaa were looking at Estrid and the kids. And him. Even as Felix noticed that, someone raised their voice in a wordless cry. First one, then another took it up, until all of the Korvaa of Echo's Reach were shouting and clapping. Their wings rustled like an oncoming storm, but their voices were a song of joy and relief and grief all wrapped into a piercing cacophony.

"You!"

The word was hurled like a weapon, and the hate and inchoate fury behind it slapped into Felix's chest. His Affinity recoiled, pulling back into himself like it had never existed. Felix saw Grand Detachment, the peacock himself, struggle forward through the crowd. "You brought all of this down on us! I should have had you killed when Bateo brought you to us!"

The crowd, just so jubilant, was set to murmuring. Felix saw some hard looks pass between several Korvaa. Lord Detachment sneered at him. "You and your *pet* disgust me! You were in league with them the whole time! The pirates! The voidbeasts! All of it!"

"Hold a moment, Detachment, hold," said a calmer voice from the opposite side. It was the raven-like Wonderment, his hands palms up and spread wide. He had a nasty gash along his scalp that someone had wrapped with the scraps of a shirt. "We've all been through a lot, Molt, but I won't say we haven't. But you're saying crazy things."

"Crazy? Is it crazy that this Unknown wandered into our homes, and the pirates followed after? Is it *crazy* that the wards were taken down, that voidbeasts attacked the farms, distracting the Rim Hunters so that the pirates could attack?" Each statement was spat out by the peacock, his tail spreading further and further. It was ratty and missing several feathers, but still impressive. "Do you deny that these things happened?"

Wonderment frowned. "They did. But the—"

"But nothing! *He* made it happen! He did! I know it!" The peacock was screaming now, and the murmurs only increased in frequency.

Felix felt a cool rage rise in his breast, an urge for violence he'd barely satisfied attacking the pirates. *It would be so easy*, he thought. *So easy to just kill the bastard.*

You risked everything for these... creatures, the Maw hissed at him.

They pay you back in suspicion and distrust. They are not worthy of the lives you reaped to save them. None of them.

Yet he fought off the urge, leveraging his Willpower as his Bastion hummed along. "I don't care," he said, to everyone. The Peacock bristled, and Felix focused on him. "Say whatever you want. After this, I'm done with you and your town."

Detachment scoffed. "And where will you go? Back to these pirates you've killed? Your allies?"

Felix laughed, and it wasn't calm or sane at all, he was afraid. He caught Estrid's eye. "I promised Bateo. I'm gonna kill them all."

The crowd went silent, but Felix didn't care any longer. He turned and strode to the port side of the Manaship, easily hopping back over to the other. "If you take turns, you'll be able to pilot that ship back to your home, or wherever you're going."

"We'll take care of it, Felix," Estrid said. The concern in her eyes almost broke him, especially because he knew how torn apart she felt. "Felix. Come with us. There is nothing for you out there."

"Go, Estrid. Take care of the kids, and run from Echo's Reach. It's not safe anymore. I—" Felix cleared his throat, flaring his Will and steadying his thoughts. "I've a task to complete."

CHAPTER THIRTY-SIX

The Harrowings flew silently, perfectly hidden from their prey as they wheeled through the Void. Their flesh was one with the nothing around them, their eyes as inky black as the Void from which they were born. Their minds were clear, only concerned with food, blood, and *Mana*. The truth of their existence was infallible: eat or be eaten.

Closer they flew, gliding without movement, their talons poised to strike instantly. The small, strange things that squirmed upon the rocky surface had no chance. Their form was vivid against the darkness, writhing worms of unusual construction, but they leaked Mana at a tremendous rate. The Harrowings gathered, nearly a thousand of them now, a deadly, invisible tornado of restrained violence just waiting to be set loose. The flock leader drew closer and shrieked. That was the signal.

The Harrowings dove. The worms, however, stretched out toward them as if embracing their death. Wing after wing, the angular predators found themselves bound to the writhing tendrils, unable to escape. A low, almost echo-like groan shook the air and knocked the last few to the rocky ground. Tendrils snaked out and captured them, too.

Then the ground opened up, and teeth bigger than any of them emerged from the sundered earth. Shrill screams tore through the black before being silenced by the closing jaws of a mountain. The Corrupted Narhollow fed.

But it was not enough.

The flesh and Mana the anemic Harrowings provided were... adequate for alleviating the constant pain of its Need. A hollow had bored through its center, an emptiness that was never filled, a Need never truly met. It fed on everything it could, even the rocks that littered the endless dark. Yet despite its constant pain, it grew stronger with every passing cycle. Its flesh was less rocky than before, and more of the red tendrils had burst from its once impenetrable hide, even as huge scales formed in patches along its massive length. The creature knew it had been altered, though it barely remembered life before the Need had found it, before it had become one with the essence of eternity.

Even now, in the dark corners of the beast's mind, a discordant whisper sent soft susurrations across its being. The whispers promised things, concepts that the beast did not entirely understand... but it was growing. Learning. From that learning, it discovered the purpose of its Need, and the ache in its immense, unending belly called out for one thing.

The boy.

He carried what it Needed. What it Desired more than food, or drink, or Mana. An ineffable burr upon the Void, a piercing chord that should not be in the black, one that resonated so clearly with itself. He had vanished many cycles ago, consumed by the dark so completely that the beast feared its Need would never be met.

Then, though it had moved many leagues away, it felt it. The boy had stepped back into the dark. Its Need swelled as the beast tasted the boy's Mana.

With a keening groan, the creature banked and began the long process of turning around. It had no choice.

It must eat.

Felix found his new ship to be better than the one he'd taken from Bridgven, and it responded to his Will far easier. He settled against the Control Node as he left behind the dwindled residents of Echo's Reach, refusing to look back any longer. It hurt too much. Better a clean break—as clean as could be managed, at least.

The Manaship shot off into the dark, pushing through the shifting rock islands at speed. He knew the direction to head, because the former captain of the ship had provided Felix with some upsetting intel. After some coercion, the man had told Felix that Nokk was headed their way. "To personally oversee the destruction of the town and the capture of some mage," he had said.

"Destruction? Why? Why would he do this?" Felix had demanded. The captain had only given a mad laugh and spat at him.

"Captain Nokk will end you! Or he'll let his lieutenants face you instead! You'll not survive against a one of them! Bridgven alone could kill you in an instant, her spectral scythe—"

"She's already dead," Felix had growled. The captain had boggled at him, his mouth working silently. "And so are you."

So now Felix raced against time and distance, pushing the Manaship forward and considering the beginnings of a plan. He looked back, this time over the stern rail, where a thick tendril of rainbow-tinged white Mana was streaming out behind them. Felix adjusted the flow through the Node, dialing in the aperture as he wove among the floating islands.

"C'mon, work," he muttered.

The Mana came from the ship's reserves, located at the lowest deck, where a series of artificial Mana bladders stored a chunk of Mana to help supplement the ship's movements. He had discovered them by accident, through the Control Node, and had spent some time cursing that he hadn't found them earlier. Still, he had soon crafted an idea.

Felix tweaked the aperture again, releasing a touch more of the reserved Mana into the Void behind them. It lingered, floating among the stones like a serpentine trail of rainbow light. Frustrated with a lack of progress, Felix added a touch of his own power to the mix, threading a ribbon of shifting, sparking light into the flow. It was obvious to any who saw it, Felix's Mana being thicker and more vibrant, and immediately, there was a response.

Harrowings and Tenebril emerged from the stones around them, the creatures slipping between cracks of rock like hibernating bears in spring. They followed after the ship, only a few so far, snapping at the trail of liquid light.

Again, you vent your Mana! You are putting us—me—in danger. I will not have it!

The Maw was again in his face, pressing its skeletal hands at Felix like a fishmonger chasing a thieving cat. Affinity or not, Felix felt nothing from the Primordial; he wasn't sure if that was a bad thing, however. Madness glinted in the Maw's pupil-less eyes, almost as strong as the hunger that dogged its every feature.

"Get over it, or get out of my head."

The Maw snarled at him, its face less Human—or Nym— than ever before. *Why do you do this?!*

"I'm done running. What happens if they follow me to another settlement, or another? More people dead? Or maybe they just catch me when I'm tired and sick of the chase. Run me into the ground. No. I'm going to them. This is ending today, one way or another."

That pirate captain had told him the flagship's course too, before his end. He knew where Nokk would be… it was just a matter of reaching him.

Setting the hounds to course, indeed, the Maw murmured, its snarling visage fading back to a considering one. *And what then, Unbound? Let's say you survive. What happens next?*

Felix didn't answer its question, only stepped on the gas.

The longer he drove, the more the Manaship Pilot sang to him. It was a murmur of knowledge that had been somehow stuffed into his brain by the System, dim as it was out here. The idea of it made him uncomfortable, but Felix couldn't deny that it was useful.

Moving a ship the size of his new one—a galleon—took an exceptional amount of Mana and Willpower. His Alacrity, which Felix had assumed had a supporting role in the manipulation of a Manaship, turned out instead to be a major factor. Something tickled his brain, telling him the effort to move a galleon should have beggared him, draining his impressive Mana pool to nothing in less than a few miles. But Alacrity was his Harmonic stat for "feats of the Mind," and it proved to be a force multiplier. By his rough estimation, every point in Alacrity reduced the amount of Mana needed and increased the effect of his Will on the ship.

Ultimately, it meant he was fine. He could pilot the galleon for days at a moderate clip, or half of one at its highest speed as he was now. Up ahead, he could see the mountain, called the Horn on both maps. It was small, but growing fast as his galleon ate up the distance. Faintly darkened by the Void stuff around him, it was far less concealed than it would have been by a thick fog.

Felix glanced behind him, counting the shapes in the dark that fought greedily over the galleon's trail. *It might be enough. Maybe.* Pit cried out from the crow's nest, and Felix adjusted their course. *First, we climb the mountain, then we end this. One way or another.*

"Man the ballista! I'll not be taken by surprise!" Captain Nokk shouted to his crew. They leapt to obey, pulling pins and adjusting the massive crossbows on their tracks. It was an ingenious addition, the tracks, allowing the ballista to be moved up and down the deck with relative ease. He needn't worry about turning broadside on an enemy, instead moving his weaponry to the fore or aft to accommodate their targets. "I want green death rained down on him the moment you see this putrid village!"

I'm coming for you, Felix, Nokk thought with relish. He fingered the puckered scar a Tenebril—no, *Felix* had given him. *You thought you could hide, but no one gets the better of Captain Nokk!*

In the distance, the Horn loomed, a massive stone formation, likely the biggest in their area of the Void. It was still leagues away, but appeared larger than his own fortress. The various pirate crews used it as a point of navigation, with a few folks even trying to hold it as territory a century back. Nokk could still see the pieces of their fortifications, crumbled to shards of bone and twisted leather higher up the mountain. For it was mountainous, bigger than many peaks Nokk had seen on the Continent. It was a place of meetings and departures; many a raid had first gathered here before haring off after their foes. From here, a proper privateer could find his way to just about anywhere, and when they returned, their holds would be fat with loot.

He laughed, and the Nixie didn't care that it sounded a little mad. After the damage that *boy* had done to his flagship, Nokk was pissed and eager for revenge, but he did not discount the riches these birds seemed to possess. While the Nym had gotten away in the chaos of their last encounter, he had sent two of his best to track him. And track him they did! To some village, one that dared to hide from *him!*

Nokk scoffed at the thought. Already his men would have raided the village, taking more meat for their engines and leaving it little more than a pyre. He was early awaiting the haul. Still, Nokk would not be truly satisfied until he saw the terror in that boy's eyes as he lashed him to the *Fury's* Mana engine. *And by Avet's broken teeth, I will!*

"Captain."

Nokk twisted, his gray face flushed with the prospect of certain victory, and grunted. "What do you want, Veris?"

His second was a sensible woman, Dwarf or not, and she'd never interrupt him for useless drivel. She squared up next to him, her handsome face marred by the geometric tattoos she'd laid down. "Captain, Celat is in a mood."

Nokk noticed for the first time that his silent, Elven assassin was following Veris. The Elf's fingers fairly flew, flickering through shapes and signs too fast to catch. Nokk had never bothered to learn handsign. Had enough trouble with common script, and no desire to complicate his life. This is why he had subordinates: they did the learning for him. "What in Avet's black eye are they saying now?"

Veris followed Celat's hands and facial expression with increasing tension. "Celat says Bridgven should have been back by now. The village is not far, perhaps a dozen leagues from the Horn."

"Ah, which has just crested the horizon," Nokk said, adjusting his tricorn hat. His gray skin stretched into a broad, sharp-toothed smile. Celat glanced at his teeth once, nervously. That others found Nokk's smile disturbing only pleased him more. "If the woman is not back within the glass, then I'm done waiting. I want this boy and his allies to burn, and I mean to see it myself."

"Aye, sir," Veris said, lowering her eyes.

Captain Nokk walked away from her with a satisfied grunt. It was always good to remind others that you were their better. It prevented them from getting ideas. Captain Nokk knew his people well, and a firm hand is what they craved, despite their whining. He'd spent three hundred years as captain and not a single mutiny.

"Voidbeasts! Starboard side! Two leagues away!"

Nokk followed his barrelman's pointing fingers, and just

barely, he could make out the roil of black on black. Movement for sure, but he questioned whether they were coming closer or not.

"Aye, they are, but they look to pass below us," came the answer. Veris was again at his side, peering into the dark. Those tattoos of hers shimmered faintly, enhancing her eyesight. "Not a one is takin' a different path. Strange, that."

"More's the pity," rumbled a voice. Korm Rocksplitter, an Ogre and Nokk's strongest arm stood from the nest of weapons he had been cleaning. The Ogre was twice as tall as the Captain, but his eyesight was far worse, and he squinted into the black like a man struck blind. "I need somethin' ta kill."

Nokk patted the Ogre on the thigh—the highest point he could reach comfortably. "You'll get your chance, Korm. You've only to be patient."

"Shoulda gone with the bard. Least she's seein' action," Korm muttered. Nokk decided to let it pass. The Ogre was his ace in the hole, all his lieutenants were, so a little leeway now and again wouldn't hurt anything. "I ain't patient."

Nokk shook his head, but understood Korm as few did. He, too, was a man of passions. Fine foods, riches, pleasures of the flesh, all these things were the draw that kept Captain Nokk breathing each day. Even in the Void, there were spots of light. For Korm, that was violence, pure and simple.

Wouldn't mind a touch of blood myself, Nokk thought as he grasped the hilt of his cutlass. *Soon enough.*

They lay within the shadow of the Horn, though the term shadow was misleading. Every exterior of the Void was equally lit by a sourceless light, bright as day without casting a single shadow. Interiors, however, were not. They required magelights and torches to see beyond the darkness. It was a quirk of the Void that Felix barely thought of any longer, and he hated it. So, instead of cooling their heels in the dark cast by an enormous mountain, Felix wedged their Manaship behind a jagged outcropping beneath the Horn, like the stone roots of a massive tree. And then they waited.

And waited.

Time enough to think on the choices that led him to such a place: poised on the edge of violence, ready to take on who knew how many Void pirates. He snorted at the idea. *What a life I'm leading. Imagine if I hadn't gotten on that yacht, if I hadn't gotten into that fight.* This time, his snort was contemptuous. *The Void sucks, but so did working for ten dollars an hour. At least here I've got a dog.*

Pit preened, catching his thoughts. There was little that did not pass between them anymore. A consequence, maybe, of Companion Pact becoming Etheric Concordance. Felix scratched the chimera's cheek, just below his ear, and his hind leg began to slap against the deck.

They're here, the Maw stated. It swirled down from on high, passing through the downswept crags like a ghost. *The flagship and six others, each the same size as yours.*

"Right," Felix said with a swallow. Pit growled, his hackles rising, and he pawed at the deck. He was ready to fight, but Felix had never questioned that. He was less sure of the Maw. "Don't interfere."

I wouldn't dream of it, Felix Nevarre. It smiled at him, but there was an ocean of animosity in its swirling eyes. *You seem dead set on this course of action, common sense be damned. Just don't die, Vessel. I have uses for you yet.*

"Encouraging," Felix said, his lip curling. "We'll see."

When Felix turned away, he could almost hear the creature's teeth grinding. It was childish, but he enjoyed it regardless. He placed his hand on the Control Node again, focusing his Will.

Forward. Faster.

Mana thrummed from his core, sparking and flaring, a thunderflame that twisted through his channels and burst from his right palm. The Node soaked it up, driving it down into the Mana engine, setting its strange sigaldry into fervent motion. The galleon bucked, leather sails snapping taut with unfelt winds while the rigging strained against the pressure of it all. The ship dipped forward, down and around the stone outcropping, and then up, up the side of the Horn.

Faster!

They rocketed upward, nearly vertical, tearing through the Void as fast as he'd ever gone. The entire galleon was shaking almost as hard as the other had through the rock field, but it was working. Distantly, he heard the screaming cry of the pirates. *We've been spotted!*

Instead of stopping or swerving, he forced the ship to move faster.

Faster!

"Captain! Attack from below!"

The call was confusing at first, but Nokk leaned over the railing, expecting to see a gaggle of Tenebrils coming for them. Instead there was a Manaship—one of *his* Manaships—and it was racing up from below fast enough to ram them apart. The ship was still a half league out, but it was rising *fast*.

"Positions men! Battle comes!" Veris shouted. Nokk however, was squinting into the dark, trying to make out the lone pilot.

"It's *him!* The treacherous Nym!" Captain Nokk gripped the railing hard enough to crack it. "Kill him, kill him! Korm!" A stomp beside him, and the Ogre was looking, too. The Ogre's eyes were crazed and his teeth were bared. "You will get your fill of battle, Korm! Our prey comes to us now!" Nokk looked at his crew, his skin aflame and feverish. He didn't care. *He's here!* "Artillery! Reposition!"

"Repositioning!"

The *clank-clank* of the ballista moving filled the dark. His men rushed, shifting all of the ballista forward, through hinged railings, and over the edges of the deck. Until they pointed *down*.

Nokk held back a gleeful laugh. "Fire at will!"

Green flame ignited below them, and the simultaneous twang of eighty drawstrings was a concerto of sublime construction. Nokk capered a little dance before thrusting himself half over the railing.

"Reload! Fire again! And again! Fire until there's *nothing left!*"

They approached the enemy at speed, and were more than halfway to them before a volley of green flame bolts dropped to meet them. Somehow, they had fired *down* at him, despite being oriented the entirely wrong way. They fell well short of his ship, but Felix gritted his teeth. He hadn't expected that, and doubted they'd miss a second time. "Pit! Behind me!"

Growling and reluctant, the tenku scrabbled behind Felix's body. The deck was pitched at such an angle, only his claws were keeping him from falling. Felix had a death grip on the Control Node, leaning his body all but parallel to the deck itself.

This is idiotic! Why are you charging them directly? the Maw shouted at him.

"Because we only have one shot at this!" Felix growled at it. "And talking is considered interfering!"

The pirate fleet swiftly altered its position, all seven ships rearranging themselves, the smaller galleons dropping elevation as a crew worked its sails and engine. They weren't in position to fire on him—*thank god*—but they would be soon, and he still had the *Hippocamp's Fury* to worry about. There was a resounding *twang-pop* over the creak of his ship, when suddenly the Void between him and the pirates was utterly filled with green fire. Bolts the size of spears dropped like burning stones, trailing tails of curling fire as they plunged down toward him.

"Brace!" Felix bellowed. "Pit! Converge!"

White light flashed just as the first bolt ripped through the mainsail. The leather burst alight, and the halyard above was shattered in twain by the explosive impact of three more.

Faster!

The ship shook, the hum of engines now a scream, a shriek, a banshee's wail that was almost louder than the field of flames that engulfed the prow of his stolen ship. Bracing against the Control Node, Felix hurled himself free of the craft with an almighty leap... but not before he gave one final command.

Below, the vast remainder of the ship's stored Mana dumped behind it. A brilliant rainbow haze of sterile, undifferentiated Mana bloomed below, kicking the ship violently upward. Felix's legs were hit, and his body sent careening up into the Void...

...into the sights of the *Hippocamp's Fury* and its multitude of ballistae.

"*FIRE!*"

Spears wreathed in a verdant inferno descended, too fast, too many. Felix could only pull at his core, at the Skills that hung within him.

Reign of Vellus!

Relentless Charge!

Blue-white lightning shot ahead of him, a cone of kinetic lightning that bent the ballista bolts askew. But not all. Two hit his arm and chest, driving the wind out of his lungs and pain deep into his flesh. Even through Pain Resistance.

Relentless Charge!

Relentless Charge!

Relentless Charge!

He gasped out the last, his channels spinning Mana to join with his Stamina as he blurred upward again and again, serpentine to avoid the volley of vile spears that sought his heart. But it was too far, and there were too many bolts. His Perception caught the glint of several ships coming around, broadside to him, their own weapons leveled.

Pit shrieked in frustration, pain, and worry. Felix echoed him, spinning through the Void, no closer to Nokk's flagship. He couldn't stop there. He had to reach the *Fury*, no matter what. Another bolt struck him in the lower back, and the volleys from two separate galleons were loosed. But he refused to let it end there.

He *refused!*

Without knowing what he was doing, Felix reached for the ship above. He Willed himself, as he would a Manaship, he Willed himself to *move*... and it was so. With a blurring of vision, Felix shot upwards faster than ever before, faster than Relentless Charge and Reign of Vellus combined.

Bastion of Will is level 44!

Energy spiked within him, a vicious pain, but Felix hadn't the presence of Mind to bear it. He hurtled—fell, almost—straight up toward the *Hippocamp's Fury*, too fast for the ballista bolts to catch him. His Mind was still focused on the plan, however. Felix released his Mana, more than ever before, trailing from the Gates in his knees and feet until it spread like a widened fan beneath.

The voidbeasts behind him, hidden in the dark, screamed in savage hunger. They raced after him, peeling away from the Manaship with clear reluctance and mounting bloodlust. Green fire rained down on them all.

Wrack and Ruin!
Wrack and Ruin!
Wrack and Ruin!
Wrack and Ruin!

Four orbs of dark acid shot out from Felix's hands, draining a large chunk of his Mana. They hit the hull of the *Fury* and drilled through it, just ahead of his own hurtling form. He braced, but pain still tore at him, jagged edges lacerating his shoulders and forearms. But then he was through, and he landed heavily on the bottom-most level of the flagship.

"Holy shit, that worked," he muttered. Above he could hear the clomp and clatter of boots on deck, and some even closer. He'd breached the forward chamber in the lower decks, and all around him were crates and barrels, and there was only a single exit. "Pit."

A flash of light and Pit reemerged from his Spirit, landing heavily atop two wobbling barrels. Felix pointed to the exit. "Guard the door. Frost Spear anything that comes through it."

Pit chirped brightly and set himself.

While he did that, Felix moved to the next stage in his plan. He crouched over the hole he'd made, laying his hands along the jagged edge that pulsed with a spastic, green-gold light in his Manasight. He could feel it, the power in the craft, but it was muted compared to accessing the Control Node.

Hmph.

Felix rolled his eyes, but didn't even look up at the Maw. Instead, it rotated around him, until its feet were firmly in his way. "What?"

Nothing. You said I wasn't to speak.

"Great, then we're in agreement." He stood and walked around the Maw, careful not to touch it. The thudding above increased, and Felix could pick out shouts from beyond the far door. "Pit, they're coming. I think we're gonna have to fight our way through to the stern. You ready?"

Pit growled in agreement, a revving engine powered by a thrumming bloodlust and anger. Felix hadn't realized before, but the tenku was just as upset about Bateo as he was. He hadn't even considered it.

"We'll make them pay," Felix agreed. "For Bateo."

Hawk! Bateo!

The door ahead slammed open, and chaos unfurled.

CHAPTER THIRTY-SEVEN

A pirate's scuffed boot kicked open the door.
Reign of Vellus!
A narrow cone of blue lightning and kinetic Mana caught the door, slamming it closed again before blasting through it entirely. Beyond, a line of unwashed pirates fell atop one another, the stairs and their fellows fouling their feet. Pit screeched, and several Wingblades flew into the breach.

You Have Killed A Unknown Pirate (x2)!
XP Earned!

Wrack and Ruin!
Felix snarled as he advanced, baseball pitching the orb of acid through the narrow door. The sound of sizzling was closely followed by screams. Three more pirates fell, according to his notifications. Yet more were coming. A lot more.
Frost Spears, Wingblades, Reign of Vellus, and Shadow Whip struck out as the pirates charged forward. Death was their only reward, but still they came. At some point, a few of the larger raiders muscled through their fellow's corpses to strike at

them directly. Pit's Cry and Felix's Corrosive Strike dispatched them as easily as any other. What few Skills the pirates attempted were pale, ghostly things that washed against his Armored Skin or Tempered Body. Time moved at a glacial pace, each spell or blow a slow-motion effort, yet within two minutes, the entire fight was done. Both of them panted, standing amid two dozen corpses and not a scratch on either of them.

Notifications trilled in his ears, but Felix accepted them without much attention. "Pit, you good?" A confirming chirrup. "Then we move ahead. To the stern and the Mana engine."

His plan, such as it was, hinged on reaching the inscribed engine before he was overwhelmed. With the Mana engine destroyed, and the reserves dispersed into the air, the *Fury* would be dead in the water, so to speak. Even if they lashed a hundred pirates to it, the engine wouldn't work if he tore it apart.

He'd worry about the six other galleons when it came to it.

Just outside the door was a narrow staircase. It led up at a steep angle to a wide landing, and the interior was completely dark to his normal eyes. His Manasight, however, saw it all, thanks to the abundant green-gold life Mana that thrummed through the entirety of the ship. The two of them bounded forward, making the landing in two large hops, and paused. Another staircase led upward to a second landing before pivoting again upward to the main deck. The sound of screaming monsters and hollering raiders filled the air, and Felix allowed himself a grim smile. The voidbeasts had arrived.

Just what you get, bastards.

There was a long hallway leading astern, and the two of them took it, fast as they were able.

Doors flashed by, Felix pushing his Agility to new heights in his search for the engine room. Each side portal was ignored, clearly storage or places to sleep for the pirates. A few times, he ran into folks belting on swords and hefting spears as they exited their quarters. These died with barely a whimper, Felix and Pit tearing through them like tissue paper. None of them were Apprentice Tier, and those who were—back at the hold—their Bodies might as well have been made of cardboard and paste for all the protection it gave them.

Near the end of the corridor, a particularly scruffy-looking Human barreled out of their chambers, caught sight of Felix, and panicked. He fled the short distance to the last door of the hallway which, by the smell and sounds, led to a large galley.

Felix and Pit didn't slow, chasing the man around the corner and into a room filled with steam and the sounds of frantic chopping. Yet, as he searched the large room for his quarry, he caught sight of three Goblins staring at him in terror, and a tall woman with ochre skin and sea-green hair. He knew her. *Dahlia, the one who gave us food and a map.* She met their eyes, her large cleaver freezing in place. Felix frowned, feeling... something— She looked to her left—and Felix's Perception caught the sour stink of unwashed flesh.

"Pit! Cry!"

"SKREAAH!"

Influence of the Wisp!

You Have Enthralled An Unknown Pirate (x6) for 3 Seconds!

Pit's Cry Has Stunned An Unknown Pirate (x3) for 1 Second!

Both effects overlapped each other, strengthening their debilitating effect as blue-white wispfire crawled across the kitchen. The small Goblins, their own cleavers in hand, froze among the large Hobgoblins, Humans, and single Dwarf that had only just emerged. The fire ate into them, dropping their Health rapidly, and neither Felix nor Pit gave any quarter. Claws and fists split flesh and broke bones, until only the woman remained.

Felix took a tight breath as kill notifications streamed past his eyes. He looked apologetically between the dead Goblins and the Naiad. "I killed your people too, I—"

"Don't," Dahlia said. "Don't apologize. These would have gutted you without hesitation." She pushed against the bone counters of the galley, looking around. "They'd been lyin' in wait, ever since you started a racket down the hall. Suppose this makes us square, then?"

"Just about," Felix smiled. She had been the one to give them the first map and supplies, the only reason he'd made it to Echo's Reach in the first place. "You need to run. Find a rowboat or skimmer or whatever. Get on it, and don't look back."

Felix sent Pit padding ahead to the double doors at the far end of the galley. Dahlia snorted. "Confident in yerself, huh?" He met her gaze, stare for stare, and maybe something in his own convinced her, because her next words flipped her tone. "How much time do I got?"

"Not much. Move fast," Felix said. He walked past her to join Pit at the double doors. "I'm bringing them all down."

He didn't look back.

The corridors branched twice more, splitting into smaller halls that all fed into odd, specialized alcoves filled with sigaldry. Each was a frustrating dead end, but Felix made sure to put his boot through them anyway. After the fourth one, the Mana in the ship had begun to stutter and flicker, its flow heavily interrupted.

Last one to check, he thought and pushed open the door. Or tried to. It was locked, and heavily at that. If he had to guess, there was a bar across the door in addition to a sparking ward. It flared with each kick and shoulder he attempted, pushing him back just as much as he attacked.

"Damn door!" he grunted.

If you simply... ate the magic of the ward, then you could get in easily.

Felix growled at the Maw's voice. He couldn't see it, but it had to be nearby. "I'm not interested in advancing whatever you've done to my 'bloodline,' Maw."

It appeared then, shrugging through the very door he tried to access. *Very well. Then I suppose he'll kill you.*

"What?" Felix asked, spinning around with scowl. "Who?"

"FOUND YA!"

The ceiling above him was suddenly blown apart, and Felix flinched away from the jagged boards that hit him like sword blades. What he couldn't avoid, however, was the massive hand and arm that followed. It gripped him by the chest and hauled Felix straight upward, bashing him through what floorboards remained.

Screams and shrieking calls became deafening as Felix was hauled bodily to the top deck. His view was dizzying before the hand that grabbed him hucked him against the thick mizzenmast, so hard it sent cracks crazing up the surface of it.

"OUFH!"

"You'll live," the creature that assaulted him said. It was a huge Ogre, easily twice the size of the Ram, covered in heavy void bone plate and bristling with weapons. *Korm Rocksplitter*, he remembered. *One of Nokk's lieutenants.* "But not for very long."

Felix flared his Perception as he took his feet, taking in as much as he could. The upper decks were in utter chaos. Voidbeasts swarmed them, though ten died for every pirate that was torn apart. A few of the pirates ran by, ignoring their confrontation, and Pit was crawling out of the hole behind Korm.

"You seem so sure about that," Felix said. He just needed to distract the Ogre for a few seconds. "I've killed many of your men below."

Korm guffawed, his lantern jaw waggling in amusement. "You think I care about them?" He brought two enormous, bearded axes from his belt, easily clutching them in his hands. "All I want is blood. And your's will do just fine!"

The big bastard blurred forward, his Strength so immense that each step obliterated the deck. Felix stood his ground, hands at his side, and the Ogre's eyes glinted with disappointment.

Now!

A Frost Spear stabbed into Korm's ankles, fouling his pace, and in that moment of hesitation, Felix disappeared.

Relentless Charge!

Felix ducked beneath the Ogre's axes and zipped right back into the hole in the deck, gathering Pit up with him as he did. The tenku hid in his Spirit and none too soon; one of the two axes slammed down into the hole, burying itself in the spot Pit had been. It missed Felix by bare inches.

"Shit!" He backpedaled as fast as he could, away from the door to the Mana engine as the bulk of Korm dropped into the lower deck.

"Fight me, mage! *Fight me!*" Korm began to charge after Felix, his huge frame shattering the hallway as he did. It barely slowed him down. The Ogre Endurance and Vitality had to be massive to put up with the sheer pressure of all that splintering bone, and Felix had no interest in finding out. Not in those cramped corridors.

Relentless Charge!

Along the straight-away, Felix zipped at a blistering pace, bursting through the galley to find it empty save for corpses. Yet the damn Ogre was right on his tail, his Strength clearly enough to keep up with Felix in a direct charge. He had to get out into the open, he realized. *I'm a sitting duck down here.*

"Boom About!"

Felix's Perception screamed at him, and he threw himself forward. A massive club spun out from Korm's grip, held onto by a thick, void leather rope. *Not club,* Felix realized. *An anchor. A fucking anchor!*

He scrambled to his feet, ungainly as anything but shoving with all his might. He lurched forwards and upward, landing atop the stairs just as that anchor came back to shatter the planks below.

Relentless Charge!

Cloudstep!

He shot straight up the stairwell and kicked off a glimmering platform of Mana, pivoting and launching his body the rest of the way up and out of the lower decks. The smashing clatter of the Ogre sounded just below, and Korm erupted from the stairs like a breaching whale. Felix leaped backward, right over the head of several pirates engaged in mortal combat against two Harrowings.

"Stop runnin'!"

"No!" Felix shouted back, flexed his Will, and shot into the air. The voidbeasts were thicker above the deck, and at first they rushed Felix, but he nimbly avoided their slashing claws and barbed tentacles. Acrobatics burned within him, nearly sending Felix careening into a mess of claws before he flared his Willpower and recovered. *Careful, you idiot! Don't get fancy. Just move.*

It was a feeding frenzy upon the *Hippocamp's Fury*, but while that was terrifying to see, it meant the voidbeasts weren't all focused on him. Felix zipped through the rigging, angling himself toward the stern of the ship once again.

But the Ogre was not going to give up.

With a leap that set the huge ship to rocking, Korm launched himself up onto the mainmast, and two spiked axes were enough to secure a place. Felix paled. The Ogre had jumped easily fifty feet, and he was not much farther away than that. He flared his Will and shot between the halyard and the shrouds, only to hear a devastating *crunch* from beside him. An oversized hand closed on his ankle, jerking Felix to a stop, and he snapped his head around to see Korm precariously balanced on the nearest yard.

"Got ya, you little bastard!" Korm's gray, snaggletoothed grin creased his too big face with malice.

Let go!

There was a flash of light in Korm's face, and the bruiser let go of Felix reflexively. He didn't, however, defend himself, and six Frost Spears manifested before Pit's outstretched wings. Each one shot into and through the Ogre's hands, pinning one to the spar and the other to the mast itself. Korm let out a wild animal bellow, but Felix didn't give him a chance to respond.

Wrack and Ruin!

Orb in hand, Felix darted back at Korm, and shoved it directly into his eyes. Flesh sizzled and popped grotesquely, but Felix didn't relent, only pressed *harder.* Korm's scream shifted to a higher pitch as he desperately tried to escape the pain of acid, and the Ogre tore his hands to shreds pulling free of the Frost Spears before falling sixty feet down to the deck.

The *Fury* bucked, knocked askew, and the spar itself started to tip and shear away. Felix panted and traded surprised looks with Pit, who was also flying of his own Will. "Nice distraction."

Enemy.

"Can't... can't argue there," Felix said, his breath catching up with his recovering Stamina. Voidbeasts swooped at them, but he slashed a Shadow Whip and took a gaggle of Tenebrils down.

You Have Killed A Tenebril (x6)!
XP Earned!

But no kill notification for Korm, Felix thought. *How much Vitality does that guy have?*

Felix dove through the rigging and masts ahead of him, a forest of leather and bone. More voidbeasts lashed at him, but he alternated punching those that came too close and pulsing Reign of Vellus. Blue-white lightning crackled and burst above the fight below, one which Felix could tell the pirates were slowly winning. Their Skills might be wan and Void-touched, but they were hardy and bloodthirsty.

Pit screeched a warning, and Felix barely dodged a spear-like arrow from below. Eyes widening, both of them swerved upward, just out of range of an entire volley of bolts, before turning back around. Down on the deck, near where Korm still writhed, a double line of marauders with crossbows had taken a knee, even now reloading with upsetting speed. More bolts came, some the size of normal arrows and a few similar to the ballista bolts he'd contended with earlier. They cut off his path toward the Mana engine.

Damnit! Down, Pit! We have to take care of them first!

Felix followed up the thought with action, swerving wide and serpentine in an effort to elude their aim. His Acrobatics screamed within him, a pain like his arms and legs were dislocating, and it was all he could do to force himself forward by sheer Will. Even so, he felt a number of the arrows jolt into his sides and back, dropping his Health several percentages at a time and ripping his jacket. But he knew if one of them hit him in the throat or eye, or one of those big bolts got him, he wouldn't be walking away.

Shadow Whip!

Finesse abandoned in light of his penalized Acrobatics, he dive bombed the archers, lashing into them with Shadow Whip. Two were bludgeoned into the ground, but three others were caught by the split ends of his Whip. Felix hauled back, dragging their flailing forms up in the air with him before snapping them into the main mast.

"Come down and fight like a man!" Veris called to him, her face marked with all those geometric tattoos. She was the one with the huge crossbow, all wreathed in green flame, same as the ballista.

"You want me?" Felix shouted. "Fine!"

He dropped from the air, speeding toward the crossbowman so hard and fast that none of them noticed Pit swing in from behind. Frost Spear after Frost Spear shot forth, stabbing through the men and even knocking the arbalest out of Veris' hands. She growled in frustration, but then Felix was atop her.

Corrosive Strike!

A single, heavy blow from his fist was all that was needed. Veris' tattooed skull burst like a gourd, and Felix flung himself away in disgusted alarm. In fact, he noticed that many of the pirates had died in a similar fashion, as if their insides had all but hollowed out.

"Holy hell, is that what happens after a few centuries?" Felix asked, for once hoping the Maw would interrupt him to call him a fool, if only to explain. Yet the Maw didn't respond.

Relentless Charge!

His Perception saved his butt again, flaring in warning just as a long dagger slammed into the space he once stood. It hit so hard it punched halfway through the bone plank and hardly quivered at all. Felix snapped his head up, locking eyes with an enraged Elf balanced precariously upon one of the rigging lines. Celat, he remembered, and they looked pissed as they conjured a fan of individual blades.

"Fuck me," Felix hissed. "This is the boss battle from hell." From his side, a few more pirates fired crossbows at them. "Pit! Take them out!"

Pit squawked and ran off, just as Celat flickered, vanishing before Felix's eyes, but not all his senses. Blades showered down on him, slicing him no deeper than papercuts, but strength seemed to bleed from his wounds. Dimly, he could sense a whispering shadow leap at him, and trusting more to instinct than surety, Felix got his arms up to deflect the Elf's final blades. His Armored Skin blunted the hit, but hot liquid still ran down his elbows, and a savage, burning pain jabbed at the edge of his awareness. Pain Resistance blunted the agony, but it didn't erase it. Celat pulled back, so fast that, to everyone else, they were no doubt a faint blur; yet Felix had time enough to snap his hands out and seize the blades themselves.

Celat staggered, halted in mid-step. The ire on their face gave way to befuddlement. Felix held onto the razor edge of Celat's daggers, cutting his own hands. In that split second, just as Celat was letting go of the daggers, Felix thrust his head forward and bashed it into the Elf's face. Blood squirted in all directions, Celat's nose a pulped ruin, and they stumbled backward. Off balance.

Reign of Vellus!

A powerful cone of kinetic force hurled the Elf away from Felix, but a quick Shadow Whip snagged them by the chest. Felix yanked back, hard, and the assassin reversed direction. Right into his fist. It was such a deliberate tactic that Felix was half-surprised it worked, that Celat hadn't reacted.

Reign of Vellus!
Shadow Whip!
KRAK!
Reign of Vellus!
Shadow Whip!
KRAK!

By the third blow, the Elf's bandolier of knives had deformed across their chest, and they were screaming. Celat broke free of the Whip with a final surge of Strength, but Felix was ready. He grappled with the Elf, seizing their arms and chest and squeezing with all his might before lifting both of them up with his Will alone. Celat struggled, bashing their own head into Felix, but he barely felt it at all.

"You're the last, then," Felix snarled. Celat's eyes widened, then rounded in terror as Felix pivoted them and rocketed downward... straight into the deck.

Through it.

You Have Killed Celat!
XP Earned!

It had all happened so fast, so powerfully, that no more than a handful of seconds had passed.

Felix stuttered to his feet, feeling woozy and more than a little Mana drained. He'd used *so much* in such a short time, it felt like his ears were ringing and the boat was spinning. Still, he had a ways to go. Quite a ways.

Reign of Vellus!

Those pirates that had come close scattered, thrown back, leaving Felix to wearily climb the stairs to the quarterdeck, and confront the small gray man that stood there. The Nixie licked his lips nervously before smiling a wide, shark-toothed smile. "Felix. What a coincidence meeting you here."

"You came hunting, Nokk," Felix accused. "You came hunting innocent people!"

That smile grew into a smirk. "Did you think me a liar, when I said we live for plunder? Who'd you think we took?" Nokk unsheathed a cutlass and a narrower saber. Both shimmered with a dusty-brown light. *Earth Mana*. "We take what we want, when we want it! No walls nor beast nor empty Void will stop us, eh!?"

A ragged cheer came from those nearby, the majority of them finishing off the voidbeasts they faced. Streamers of whitened rainbow light rose from all across the deck, tangling with the sails and rigging so that it seemed they sat in a cloud. Nokk pointed his cutlass at Felix and tipped his tricorn hat back with the blade of his saber.

"But you've attacked my crew—my ship!—twice now. That be a sin, Felix. And sinnin' deserves punishment!" Nokk raised his voice. "Men! Don't let this bastard off the quarterdeck!"

All around him, Felix saw the crew stand up and brandish weapons, a wall of flesh and bone and steel to hem them in. Nokk laughed and twirled his blades. "Let's end this, boy!"

The pirate captain came at him fast, his Agility clearly matching Felix's own. Felix dodged, or tried to, taking a hit on the shoulder before he could pivot away. It felt as if he'd been hit by a mountain, and the force of the blow sent Felix skidding across the deck. Right into the wall of unwashed raiders.

"RAAH!"

Scimitars and cutlasses slammed down at Felix, but he deflected or dodged them completely. Nokk might have his speed matched, but his crew didn't come close.

Reign of Vellus!

The crew immediately behind him were blasted into the waist-high walls of the quarterdeck, and several didn't get back up at all. But Felix couldn't spare thoughts for finishing them, because a wave of jagged stone blasted from Nokk. Felix grunted as it clipped him, shaving off more Health and flipping him end over end onto the deck.

"Hah! Never expected *that*, did ya, mage?!" Nokk crowed, his wide mouth filled with a shark's grin. "There's more where it came from!"

The pirate captain spun, his two blades gathering up a pale vapor. It roiled and twisted, turning a faint dusty-brown again, and spears of stone formed in mid-air before flying at Felix faster than arrows. Felix snarled and twisted himself, ducking and weaving between the spears, simultaneously feeding the dregs of his Essence into his core flame.

Dodge is level 27!
Dodge is level 28!

Reign of Vellus is level 29!
…
Reign of Vellus is level 32!

Shadow Whip is level 28!
Shadow Whip is level 29!

The Essence let his Skills take the advances they'd earned, but only so much. *It'll have to do.*

Felix dodged under the final earthen spear, rising before a surprised Nokk and lifting his entire Nixie body with a single uppercut. The bastard flipped backward, long coat flapping and his tricorn hat catapulted into the Void.

"More where that came from, too," Felix muttered.

"Cap'n's down!"

"Get the mage!"

Influence of the Wisp!

Purple and orange Mana vapor rolled out of his channels in a wave, splashing over the first two rows of charging pirates. They froze, to a man, limned in flickering wispfire that rapidly ate at their Health. Those behind them pulled back, burned by their fellows.

You Have Enthralled An Unknown Pirate (x24) for 3 Seconds!

Not a lot of time. Felix trod to the captain, the only pirate not affected. *His Will must be as high as his Agility. Damn.* He lifted his leg to stomp on the man's back, but before he connected, the pirate rolled and slashed at his calf. Felix jerked back in an awkward hop, narrowly missing the blades from carving a chunk from his leg.

"You'll not be rid of me so easy, Felix," Nokk hissed, rolling to his feet. His gray head was bald and covered in curious lines, like scars evenly spaced. "I've not survived so long in the Void to die by your hand, mage."

"I don't care how long you've been here. I'm done with taking shit from people like you." Felix snarled and advanced, his fists up. Nokk went for a thrust, but Felix surprised him. A Shadow Whip formed in his offhand and lashed out, snagging the captain's leading wrist. With a wrench, Felix pulled them close—too close for his swords to be effective.

Corrosive Strike!

The acid punch took Nokk in the chest, driving him down into the deck. But the Nixie was wily. He rebounded, owing to some Skill no doubt, and tumbled backward out of Felix's range.

"Agh! You fight as dirty as any of my crew," Nokk said, though it didn't sound like a compliment. "Just as stupid, too, to let me gain distance again!"

"Did I?" Felix asked.

Nokk raised an eyebrow then glanced down in fear. To his wrist. Where a Shadow Whip still coiled tightly. "Avet's teeth..."

Felix pulled, hard, his high Strength yanking Nokk off his feet once again. The captain flew toward Felix, screaming, but managed to get his swords up between them.

Reign of Vellus!

The kinetic blast knocked the blades askew, while the crackling lightning sizzled along the length of them. Nokk spasmed as the lightning grounded through him, and when Felix punched his right wrist, he dropped the saber completely. The remainder of the kinetic blast flung the Nixie away from Felix once again, except this time, his shadowy tether snapped.

"Damn," he said, but was already chasing after the pirate captain. Abruptly, however, Felix felt a flash of pain and fear. Not his own. He spared a glance around him, almost instantly spotting a point of combat on the far side of the ship, where Pit flew among several pirates with nets and hooked spears. "Pit!"

"Think of yourself, boy! You're facing death now!"

Nokk came at him, his remaining sword positively blazing with earth Mana. He swung at the ground again, sending rising pillars of conjured stone up from the deck. Again, and again, and each time Felix dodged from its path. Yet, he was driven back further and further, corralled, until he could sense the cold steel of the pirate crew waiting just paces away. Felix conjured a Shadow Whip to dash the ring of crew away from his back, but the moment of concentration and effort that took opened him up. He felt a sharp stab of pain as Nokk accelerated and thrust his cutlass deep into Felix's right pectoral.

Felix screamed, the pain overwhelming his resistance as earth Mana poured directly into his flesh. It rampaged there, spikes and boulders that attempted to tear him apart from within. The maw appeared, her—its!—face afraid and furious.

Cycle your Mana, Felix! Use your channels to draw it away! Devour it!

He almost didn't, out of sheer stubbornness, but the pain forced his hand. Felix... pulsed his core, pushing the Mana inside him around his looping channels with increasing speed. The barrage of earth Mana lessened as his own pumped through his body, each loop proving to settle him in some way that made little sense to Felix. He did not, however, eat it with Ravenous Tithe.

"Get off me!" Felix shouted, kicking at Nokk. The Nixie

danced back, his cutlass going with him, and leaving a bloody wound in Felix's chest. He grunted and stood, one hand putting pressure on the injury.

Nokk tilted his head, his victorious smile now a worried frown. "How do you still stand? That should've killed you!"

"I'm too mad to die," Felix snarled, and back in he went.

With his Agility matched, it became a battle of technique and skill. Nokk continuously outmaneuvered Felix, moving in a way that seemed impossible. His feet kept taking complicated steps that somehow reminded him of Vess, different as they were.

"Just. Stay. Still. And. Die!"

Each word punctuated by a slash or thrust, each one barely dodged or deflected by his bare hands. Felix's palms and knuckles were weeping blood at that point, and his Endurance was beginning to flag. He stumbled, his Acrobatics like molten metal in his bones as he fell, impacting an object behind him. Felix's eyes widened.

Nokk grinned and thrust, his sword filled to the brim with earthen Mana.

Felix flared his Will and let it yank him up into the air at the last second. Confounded, Nokk couldn't slow his attack, and it exploded forward. Right into the Control Node that had been behind Felix.

"No!" Nokk spun, murder on his face. "Look what you did, boy! You—"

"You did that yourself," Felix panted. His Stamina was reaching new lows, and his Mana and Health were little better. His hovering stuttered a bit. "It's over. Your ship can't move any longer."

"It ain't over 'til you're dead!" Nokk screamed, and fished two soft objects from his purple leather jacket. *Manabladders*, Felix realized, a half-second before the Nixie hurled them onto the deck. They burst, their Mana splashing upward in a fountain. "Sword of Damocles!"

The Mana joined with Nokk's own pale vapor, spiraling into

a massive stone blade easily the size of the ship's mainmast. It hung twenty feet above Felix for only an instant, before it came screaming downward. Felix fled, Willing himself away, but the sword simply angled itself after him.

"It will follow you until you die!" Nokk cheerfully screamed. His face was drawn and his limbs shaking, but he crowed in glee. "There's no escapin' it! Die, boy! Die for darin' to cross Cap'n Nokk and the Ten Hands!"

The Sword of Damocles hurtled after him, inching closer with every second. It was faster than Felix's Will could propel him, and it was only a matter of time. Nokk was right.

KKKRAASH!

Spinning through the rigging, spars, and masts, Felix led the Sword on a desperate chase. The Sword, however, was not so graceful. It sheared through lines and masts with equal ease, severing sails and dropping tree-sized bones from the sky. Below, the pirates screamed and scattered as first the mainmast and then the foremast fell. The deck shattered, and Nokk was screaming obscenities so foul it made Felix laugh.

It was a wild, hysterical laugh that bubbled up as the Sword bore down on him. If he was gonna die, he'd make it worth it.

He stopped.

Stone Shaping!

As the Sword sped for his throat, Felix reached out his Will and seized the earthen Mana that comprised it. There was resistance, but Felix had nothing left to lose. He threw everything he had at it, every scrap of Will and Alacrity he could manage, until he felt that resistance *pop*.

And then he was engulfed.

CHAPTER THIRTY-EIGHT

Stone Shaping!

Felix dropped from the cloud of earthen Mana vapor, trailing it behind him like a cloak. Down he flew, over the stumps of severed foremast and the limp remains of void leather lines. Pirates scattered from his path, the cloud roiling and crackling as if a storm brewed within. Felix's channels screamed at him, burnt raw and aching, but he held on.

He *shaped*.

He came to an abrupt stop above the mainmast, and from the cloud he hurled massive stone chains, forged in his Mind and Spirit with stolen Mana. The chains spun outward, connected and heavy with large blocks at either end, blurring through the air and shattering pirates and ship alike where they landed.

"Impossible!" Nokk cried, just as the largest chain took him across the chest. He was flung backward into the mizzenmast, spitting up blood and slammed tight as the chain wound rapidly around the thick diameter of void bone. His head lolled, and his cutlass clattered to the ground from limp fingers.

Felix fell too, his Mana almost completely spent, and his

Health not far behind. Pit squawked in terror, apparently having defeated the other pirates with little issue. "I'm... I'll be fine, Pit."

Sense images flickered through their bond, impressions of fighting off several pirates until a mast had fallen on the lot of them. A warm gratitude pulsed between them, and Pit pressed his head into Felix's cheek.

"Thank you too, 'lil man," Felix whispered. "But we're not done yet."

Masts were broken and sails were torn, but he had no idea how important the sails were to a Manaship. He'd rather be certain.

Together, they made their way past the mizzenmast and to the Control Node of the ship. Pirates scrambled in all directions, none of them interested in Felix any longer, for the voidbeasts had made a return. Harrowings harried the scrambling marauders, each trying to defend themselves while escaping the destruction one mage had wrought. Felix would have laughed, had he the energy.

As they got closer to the broken Node, Felix realized he'd done a number in those last few seconds. The chains he'd shaped had torn apart the deck around the Node, collapsing a lot of the deck just below, and blocking access to the engine directly. With what Nokk had done to the Node, piercing it through, it was impossible to issue any commands as normal.

"There's no way I can vent their Mana like this," he muttered. He put his hand on the Node, but it sparked and flashed, sending feedback through his channels that made him hiss in pain. "Damn it. I guess—"

He was interrupted by a deep, terrifying bellow. Felix felt his heart clench, felt everything around him stop as they all looked in the same direction. Up.

A behemoth easily a quarter the size of the Horn itself raced down its immense face. Its reddened, blubbery flesh visibly pulsed—*writhed*—and a single, massive mouth surmounted by crooked yellow teeth was accompanied by a thousand smaller ones, all of them opening and closing with a sense of terrible, inexhaustible hunger. It had been so long since Felix had seen it, he almost hadn't recognized it. Hadn't wanted to.

"Whalemaw," he whispered in horror. That visceral reverberation shot through his guts again, before coiling and leaping back out toward the creature. It pivoted, minutely, its ten thousand eyes widening in glee or fury. He had no idea which.

"Gods have mercy!"

"What is it!?"

"Abandon ship!"

FELIX! RUN!

The shout jolted him out of—of whatever that had been. The Maw was at his shoulder, screaming into his ear. *Idiot! Fool! We'll be consumed! You'll die! For good this time! RUN!*

"Not yet!" He grabbed at the Node again, ignoring the sparks. "*Ravenous Tithe!*"

He had no choice.

The ship rocked, and what sails it had remaining went limp as a *torrent* of Mana was torn free from it. It surged up from the Control Node, stolen from the engine below and whatever unfortunate was powering it. Felix couldn't care, not anymore. He just had to take it!

Pit screeched and converged with him in a flash of light. Yet, not even his presence dented the flood.

It burned through Felix's Gates, searing his channels to charcoal with its fury. A storm unlike anything he'd ever experienced, it was lightning and hot lava, scalding acid and freezing shadow, everything all at once. Dimly, he could feel it collecting in his core like a storm, a hurricane.

Bloodline Progression is 9%

...

Bloodline Progression is 14%

It pressed at him, at his crackling core. His Skill quivered and shook from the might of it all, the potency, and that same pain of broken Skills shuddered across everything that Felix had become. For a brief moment in time, he *was* pain. Pain and nothing more.

Use the power, Felix Nevarre! Use it before it consumes you!

Reign of Vellus!

An orb of blue, kinetic Mana exploded around him, so powerful it shredded what remained of the quarterdeck and sent the mizzenmast tilting toward the fore. Pirates were pitched through the air, impaled with shards of bone or the shattered remnants of ballista. Lightning followed, burning and scoring bone and flesh like, setting a dozen fires in an instant. And still he wasn't done, still his core raged.

Reign of Vellus!

Everything blew out, bones turning to shards too small to see, and pirates torn limb from limb. The sheer force of it hurled Felix up and backward, straight off the ship itself... just as the Whalemaw impacted them mouth-first. It tore past like a freight train on steroids, so huge and so fast, it was more natural force than living creature. An avalanche. The *Hippogriff's Fury* and two other galleons went down in a violent explosion of Mana that swept into Felix even harder than his own Reign of Vellus.

He fell into the black, too overwhelmed to do anything but watch everything be destroyed. Joy or satisfaction didn't find him as he slipped into the dark, just a grim sense of finality.

It was over.

Finally.

And then he clattered headfirst into the bottom of a narrow hull, nearly flipping the entire vessel.

"Ho! You're a heavy one!" cried a familiar voice.

Felix blinked bleary eyes, pain radiating from every inch of his body. Things were boiling inside him, power he'd never felt before that wanted, *needed*, to be expressed. Working his mouth, Felix spoke brokenly. "Who are—Dahlia?"

"In the flesh," the former pirate cook said to him. She was

sitting in back at the Control Node for—was he on a ship? He was. One slightly bigger than his old sloop. A cutter, according to his Eye. Felix groaned the moment he used the Skill though, his core space quivering with the effort. "I'd say it's high time we flee, agreed?"

She didn't wait for him to say anything, instead pouring her Mana into the Control Node. The cutter shot off like a rocket, speeding through the dark, away from the screaming hunger of the Whalemaw.

Felix blinked bleary eyes up at a swaying forest of bone and leather skins. Green-gold energy flashed among them sporadically, but it was only the braided lines that reminded Felix where he was—and who he was running from.

He sat up with a panicked lurch, casting about with his senses, but there was nothing there. Nothing except a groggy Pit beside him and a Naiad at the cutter's Control Node, sweating as she piloted them away from certain destruction.

"You saved me," he said. "Thanks."

"Suppose I did," Dahlia said with a sharp-toothed smile. "You took a nasty spill off the top deck, just before that—that *thing* attacked." She laughed after a while, though it sounded forced. "You're lucky I was still around. Damn ship is a sight harder to move than I expected."

While Felix had laid on the deck of the cutter, Dahlia had put a sizable distance between them and the Horn. He couldn't even see it anymore, and that was a feat, considering its size. He'd meant to stand up, to take over piloting the ship, but he was so damn tired. Pit had laid across his chest the whole while, quivering with his own strain until they both had fallen into a deep slumber.

Now, however, he was awake, and fear coursed through him still. Not panic anymore, but no less strong. "Dahlia, do you have a spare ship? Like a… a dinghy or one of those small skimmers?" He'd seen those hatchlings use skimmers the size of wakeboards just the day before. *Was it really so recently?* "Anything."

"Uh, I don't know," she said and made a vague gesture to the starboard side. "Check there, beneath the rail."

Felix ambled over, his legs stiff from his battle and rest. The slight bucking of the cutter didn't help much. He glanced over the railing, and sure enough, there was a narrow craft with a single mast no thicker than his arm. It was all folded up, as for travel. He grunted.

"Doesn't look like much. How fast can it go?" he asked.

"A fair speed. Meant for small jaunts, though. Somethin' anyone could fuel themselves..." she hesitated. "How much Mana you got, exactly?"

"Enough."

"Yeah, well, don't put too much in. Sigaldry's delicate enough—was delicate—on the *Fury*. Get to somethin' that small, and it'll burn out before too long." She sniffed. "Not that I'm against those pirates endin' the way they did, they just about abducted me to start, see? But that thing... what was it?"

Felix glanced upward and saw the Maw, floating there in its own false breeze. It met his eyes with orbs of swirling blue and green and a worried frown.

"A Primordial," Felix said, and watched as the Maw sneered. "Or close enough."

"A Primordial! Blind gods, we're lucky to be alive!" Dahlia gasped.

"We are. And I need you to take this cutter and fly," he consulted the maps he'd memorized and pointed somewhere starboard and aft. "That way. The creature is chasing me, so staying here is no good for you."

"Chasing you? Why?"

"Doesn't matter, does it? Just get away from me and Pit, and you'll be free of its attention." Felix smiled, but worried it came as more of a grimace. "You've helped us. More than I expected. There's a settlement that way, warded, safe." She leveled a heavy look at him, and he raised his arms defensively. "Safe-ish."

"And you'll take that trash and expect to outrun it? The size that monster is? Are you an idiot?"

Felix blinked at her tone. "No I just figured you'd—"

"Figured I saved ya just for you to get yourself killed? No. Not happenin'. You take this cutter, and I'll have the trash."

"What? No," Felix started, but the former pirate cook whirled on him. She'd produced a cleaver from somewhere, and Pit squawked in alarm.

"I'll be havin' it, aye?"

"Aye, I mean, yeah. Sure." Felix didn't put his hands down until she'd clambered over the railing and slid to the smaller craft's deck. Everything was lashed down and folded, but in a remarkably short time, Dahlia had everything unfurled and chopped the ropes holding it to the side of the cutter. It dropped silently before unfurling its triangular sail with a wash of pale Mana.

"See you around, kid! And you too, Honored Tenku," she said with a sharp grin. "Hope you don't die!"

Banking toward where he'd suggested, the cook sped off. Felix was on his way shortly thereafter. Dahlia hadn't argued too hard about sticking by his side, and he was glad for it. She had left awfully quick after hearing of the Primordial, though he couldn't blame her at all. If he could escape it, he would have done so long since.

His hand on the Control Node meant the cutter passed well beyond its previous speed. Soon, they were among rocky terrain again, though this time they were headed further away from both the Ten Hand's fortress and Echo's Reach. He knew the Whalemaw was coming for him sooner or later, and was willing to bet a whole lot on "sooner."

"Where to go? Where is safe from this thing?" He asked. He hadn't expected an answer, but the Maw spoke up anyway.

The pirate's den is likely secure. That shield of theirs would stop this...Whalemaw cold. Not even I at my greatest strength could dare Desolation.

Felix's eyes widened as his Mind burned. Sparks of memory flashed and connected, fast as blinking, and a series of remembered voices rolled across his senses.

"Seek the tumbled rock, the Temple at the Edge. Hanging at the precipice of Desolation....Please ghost, take me from this place. Take me home, beyond the Lady's gate!"

"It is not a true Temple. The Void would never allow such a thing to exist. The divine would be sucked away into the nothingness around us."

"All of this comes from a hole in the Void, where the Ethereal Realm bubbles through into ours. There is a darkness there, something more than the Void, but as the Ethereal presses into it, things emerge....If the Desolation released things, then surely one could enter it and survive. Or so was my predecessor's theory."

"Mungle, Estrid, and Wonderment. Thank you," Felix murmured.

What are you saying? Have you gone fear-mad already? The Maw scoffed. *I told you not to rouse that beast! It will devour us both!*

"I have an idea," he said and banked hard to port. "You said the Desolation will protect us from the Whalemaw, right?"

If it is smart enough to avoid it, yes. But you cannot be thinking—this isn't the way to the pirate's den. The Maw narrowed its eyes at him and bared its yellowed teeth. *Where are you taking me?*

"I just said," Felix laughed. He felt a bit of hysteria at the edges of it, but there was nothing he could do about that. "I'd suggest not floating too far afield. Desolation's close, after all."

No. No you cannot be suggesting—!

They shot off into the dark.

CHAPTER THIRTY-NINE

Stone island whizzed by them, faster than they ever had, faster than was wise if he were being honest. The cutter was twice the ship his sloop was, and if it didn't have quite the heft of a galleon it also didn't need as much energy from him, mental or Mana. At the speeds they traveled, they were riding the bleeding edge of his Willpower, Agility, and Dexterity, each last-moment dodge and weave taking everything from him to manage. Even so, Felix didn't consider slowing down. The simple thought of the Whalemaw coming out of the dark—from above, below, or behind—instilled enough terror to be reckless.

The Maw didn't care for his speed, fast or slow, but cared very much for the course he was setting.

You head to Desolation, fool. Do you intend to dive into it instead of being eaten by the beast?

"No," Felix growled back. "But answer me this: do Temples to the gods have sheaths over them? Like a Domain might?"

The Maw hesitated, clearly thrown by his change in topics. It didn't even snark as it answered him. *Yes. If it is a true Temple, dedicated and consecrated by a divinity. Why?*

"Wonderment said they gathered objects from the hole to the Ethereal. Said it passed through a darkened part of the Void before dropping rubbish into the black." Felix dipped the cutter under another island, the mast just barely clearing its bottom. He grunted with the strain.

You're saying there's a Temple there. In the Void. The Maw's voice was deadpan, as if it were talking to a simpleton. *Its persistence in the Void would be impossible. The Void would have rotted it away, long since!*

"Which is how Mungle knew about it, I'm guessing," Felix said. "He was a Sage of Vellus. Isn't that like a priest or something?"

Pfah! Sages are to priests as a Grandmaster is to you, Felix Nevarre. That man was not a Sage. A Sage would not be trapped here!

Felix knew what he saw, what his Eye showed him. "He said there was a Temple here, near the Desolation. And within the Temple, Mungle mentioned a gate. He said it like it was an exit, I just didn't believe him."

What sort of gate? No mere Threshold could jump the divide between Realms.

Felix shrugged, but there was iron in his voice. "That's the gamble."

You will roll the dice with your Companion's life?

He didn't even get a chance to answer. Pit simply growled at the Maw and fluffed his feathers and fur. *I follow Felix, Enemy!*

The Maw looked between them and growled, too. *Fie on the both of you, then! Lead us into disaster!*

Abruptly, there was a buzzing hum in the air, a dark reverberation in his skin and blood and mind. A bugle sounded, a million voices raised as one, screaming into the night. A terrible, horrendous bellow that was both too soft and entirely too loud, almost piercing Felix's eardrums. Felix jerked, nearly colliding with an island bigger than his ship. He scanned the dark desperately, but couldn't see anything.

Flesh and fury, it comes! Faster! The Desolation is too close to die here!

Felix did just that, pushing the cutter as hard as he could, but he couldn't help glancing backward. He regretted it as he nearly collided with another island, but then the darkness split behind them and it was all he could do to not gape astern.

Three ships—galleons all—emerged from the dark of the Void, each one partly consumed by green flames and harried by the angular forms of Harrowings. Their prows were beacons of flame and smoke, whirling off behind them like streamers, all but ignored by the men and women writhing on the decks. A stentorian bellow, the same as before, shook them all. The Whalemaw was yet hidden.

"What the hell is this?" Felix asked. "Are they running from the Whalemaw?" Bolts of fire shot after him, falling far short, but the galleons were accelerating far faster than he expected. "And they're firing on us?"

They are changed.

Felix noted the sharp note in the Maw's voice. "What're you talking about?"

As if to answer, a cloud of Harrowings detached from the lead ship, their bodies clear to see in the Void because they weren't black any longer. Instead, they were covered in a crimson sheen that trailed from them like thickened gel and glowed like a bloody sunset.

They've been corrupted by the flesh!

Like lightning, they came at his ship far faster than he expected, reaching the stern within seconds. Felix hurled a Reign of Vellus backward, narrowing the cone of its force, and managed to knock a few into the rocks around them. It was not enough.

"Skreaaw!" Pit cried, freezing several in place with his Skill, before a flurry of Frost Spears shot into the dark. Each one took root in wings and center mass; it was impossible to miss, clustered as they all were. But it didn't stop—wouldn't—until they all died. Felix could almost feel the violence blooming from them like a foul wind.

Wind? He felt it, his horror muted by alarm. The Void

stirred with it, the rock islands moving laterally. *They've never done that before.*

Another ear-piercing bugle shook the air, and the Whalemaw finally appeared, its open mouth wider across than all three ships combined. It was all of his nightmares rolled into one, and the vilest monster Felix had ever encountered. Worse, in some ways, than the Maw itself. The creature belched out clouds of horrid crimson. The thick fumes hit and spread among the ships, coating its people in the same gel-like substance. And not for the first time, either. The galleons were practically dripping with it, a substance that howled in his Manasight. It was sour and vile and tasted of violence and bottomless hunger. Felix gagged.

Primordial Essence! It uses my very Essence to spread itself! The Maw raged at the Harrowings and the hidden, but present Whalemaw. *How dare it do so!*

"Spread itself?" Felix said with a thrill of fear. He risked another look back, in time to see the pirates writhing on the deck, their bodies warping and snapping in ways that reminded him of Grimmar, the Frost Giant chieftain. Horrified, he glared at the thing. "That's what you did with me!"

No, what I did took skill and genius. This is the method of an idiot brute! How dare it abuse my power!

The Harrowings hadn't reached them yet, the now-definite rotation of the rocky islands keeping them at bay. Felix slipped between them all, his cutter taking more blows than he liked with every hard turn or close shave. Without warning, however, a weight crashed into the deck, sending them careening into another island. The cutter's bone-boards screeched and tore before Felix could right it, and when he looked up, it was into the eyes of a bald Nixie.

Except he was covered in crimson Essence that burned like fire atop his skin. Already, strange growths had started, his neck and face writhing with crimson scales and fanged teeth in the wrong places. His eyes burned, bright red, and he rasped a violent cough. "You did this, mage! You've killed me!"

He's infected, too! the Maw shouted, perhaps in warning. *Vile creature!*

Nokk came at him, faster than he ever had before. Pit tried to fire a Wingblade at him, but that sword of his somehow spoiled the spell, deflecting it into the Void. Gasping in alarm, Felix banked the ship hard, causing the boom to swing across the deck. Yet Nokk dodged nimbly around it, his loping form possessed of more Agility than Felix had hoped.

Reign of Vellus!

Blue-white lightning burst forward, catching the pirate captain straight in the chest as he straightened from his dodge. Flung in the air, he somehow managed to slam his cutlass into the cutter's deck, puncturing it easily. Muscles bulged and grew along his one arm, ballooning from his deltoid to his wrist until it looked like a giant's arm had been given to a child. More Wingblades came at him, this time from the side, but that huge arm wasn't even scratched. With a surge of strength, the cutlass came up, and with it a long board of the deck, slapping into Felix's feet and sending him sprawling.

The ship twisted, his hand losing connection with the Control Node as Felix fought for balance. But Nokk hadn't waited and was already on top of him, cutlass free and slashing with abandon. It had taken all of his Agility to dodge the Nixie's attacks before, but now it was like he had become a monster. Faster and faster he moved, until it was all Felix could do to not get skewered. Pit danced in the back, trying and failing to line up a shot.

Shoot, Pit!

I can't! Hit you!

Instead, the cutlass hit him, over and over, glancing strikes on the wrists and forearms, thighs and calves, but they bled just the same. They jolted into rock islands, scraping their way along, and each bump and bash led to another stumble, another cut. Felix and Nokk danced, bare blade against his bare arms, and the pirate was winning.

Nokk grinned as he struck a blow that made Felix stumble

back into the stern railing. His teeth were bloody, while vestigial toothy maws opened and closed around his face and neck. "I can feel it, mage! I can feel what the beastie wants! You! More than anything! I'll bring you to it, dead or alive, and I'll be cured! It promised!" The Maw laughed, and Nokk twitched in surprise. "Who said that? Who's there!"

I did, you fool! Finally! Someone who can bask in my glory!

"Spirit!" Nokk cried, somehow able to see the Primordial.

Relentless Charge!

Taking advantage of his distraction, Felix flashed ahead, hand extended. Bracing as best he could, he bashed the cutlass out of Nokk's grip. Even that simple move, however—when he contacted the sword's hilt—his entire body seized and shook, and Felix fell to his knees. The cutlass went skittering across the deck, and Nokk reared back in fury.

"No! My—I don't need a weapon to kill you, mage!" Nokk screamed incoherently and leaped atop Felix, bearing him down onto the Control Node. The plinth rammed into Felix's back, but it was nothing compared to the agony in his core space or the fresh nightmare of the corrupted Nixie jamming fresh claws into his chest.

Felix screamed.

"Yessss! Scream! Scream like my crew did as you butchered them! As you lined them up for slaughter by this vile beastie!" Nokk's own laugh was too high, too mad. "I'll end you! And-and *eat you!*"

Gasping for breath, Felix pulsed his Mana, pushing it through the ever-open Gate at the base of his skull. It slammed into the Control Node, and the cutter bucked once, hurling everyone up. Felix was thrown from the Control Node almost to the main mast, while Nokk went to the tilting prow. Pit, at least, had taken to the air above, barely keeping up with the cutter's frantic, reckless speed. Nokk clambered to his feet, the crimson corruption around him burning bright, sinking deeper into his channels and core. Felix could almost see it, but Nokk only laughed.

"I feel its power now! I feel it!" The Nixie's other arm ballooned as well, but just the bicep and deltoid, leaving his forearm a malformed stick at the end of it all. "It is making me... so... s-so... hungry!"

He leaped, propelled by a monstrous, newfound Strength—so fast he would have been invisible to a normal Human. Felix, however, had a powerful Perception and noticed more than most. Afforded scant fractions of a second, Felix braced one last time and kicked, straight up. The cutlass at his feet, hooked by his toes, flashed along with it.

Directly into Nokk's heart.

In fact, it hit so hard that the pirate was hurled upward by the lodged hilt, until the sword sank deep into the bottom of a passing rock island. They streaked forward, uncontrolled, leaving the Nixie behind.

Felix! Pit cried, sending flashes of incoming doom.

Relentless Charge!

Felix jolted back to the Control Node, almost missing it in his haste, and slammed his hand and Mana back upon it. He pulled up, hard, and they just barely missed the huge stone island before them, though more and more chunks of the hull sheared away.

"We did it! Holy shit, I thought I was gonna die," Felix rasped through heaving breaths. That fight had worn him out more than all the others combined.

So did I, said the Maw, and he had no idea if it was happy or not. It snarled, hate and hunger clear on its Nymean features. *At least you could have eaten him! That beast took my power, and I'll have you get it back. One bite at a time, if needs be!*

"I'd rather let it eat *me*, Maw," Felix spat. He focused on piloting the Manaship. "The Whalemaw can have your power, so long as *we* can leave."

He could almost hear the creature grinding its teeth at him, but Felix was too tired, too *angry*, to care. He flared his Will, increasing their speed yet again among the shifting stones.

They'd beaten the pirates, and now they'd beat the Whalemaw. They just had to—

Teeth surged from the black, each the size of his ship, and only his panicked burst of speed saved them. A huge maw slammed shut just behind them, the sheer force of it sending the cutter zooming forward. Pit and Felix screamed while they held on as tight as they could, but the Whalemaw flew up, its huge, rocky body missing them as it swam from the depths beneath.

Shaking, Felix scratched the bottom of barrels he'd already thought tapped dry, and *pushed*. The cutter flitted forward, through the stone islands and away, angling toward Desolation… and salvation.

He hoped.

CHAPTER FORTY

The Whalemaw bellowed again as Felix pulled the cutter out of its reach, extending their lead by another hundred yards. It's toothy gob gnashed like a landslide, its incalculable bulk an impossible force sweeping toward them. But they had survived.

So far.

Felix grunted and focused on not passing out. For three hours, he'd been pouring his Mana into the Control Node, pushing the small craft as hard as he could through the dark. The Manaship was far faster than the behemoth itself, but while Felix wasted time and energy weaving through the stone obstacles, the Whalemaw chased, deceptively fast, utterly obliterating any rocks in its way.

The Corrupted Narhollow kept closing the distance, never tiring, forcing Felix to push himself harder than he ever had before. He had eked out a tiny lead in the last twenty minutes, only bare seconds after they'd nearly been bitten in half. But he knew he couldn't keep it up. He was burning out, and his Mana regeneration no longer kept pace with the amount of Mana he'd poured into the ship. It also didn't help that he'd been bleeding from his chest much of the time, his Health regeneration barely able to keep him conscious.

Pit screamed, his echoing Cry launching out at the Whalemaw to no effect. The tenku shot Wingblades and Frost Spears at the thing, but nothing worked. The spells never made it to the beast's hide, fading into useless Mana before being swallowed by the Void.

You'll never beat it. It's… all-powerful.

Felix heard a sigh of longing escape the Maw's rawboned neck. He cast a glance at it, baring his teeth as he saw bony hands almost reach out toward the beast. He blinked, forcing moisture to alleviate his burning eyes. It felt like weeks since he last slept.

Yeah… heard that one before! Felix smiled tightly as the Maw's incensed glare raked across him. *Wasn't true then, and it's not true now!*

Oh yes, your supposed 'victory' over me. How has that been going for you? Been enjoying the sights? The Maw smiled primly and gestured all around them.

This time it was Felix's turn to glower, and he focused back on the turbulent path ahead of them. The Maw was certainly right about one thing: Felix did not feel he had won against it, and he wouldn't, not until he could get rid of it for good.

The Whalemaw roared again, and the sound of more rocks crashing into one another drowned out his thoughts. He pushed on, faster and faster. It was all he could do.

Their ship crashed and banged, sliding through the field around them at a breakneck pace. Already, the sides of the cutter were ragged and splintered, and the sail was all but gone. Only half the mast still stood, the other half sheared off by a close call nearly an hour ago. The only thing keeping it running was his Willpower and Mana. The way the Maw begrudgingly described it, a Manaship used the frame and construction around it to function in the way a normal ship would, but took the majority of its guidance and power from the script core—Mana engine—and control orb. The inscriptions around the plinth and orb were elaborate and confusing, but Felix assumed they were well-made. They hadn't fallen apart yet, unlike the rest of the cutter.

All of a sudden, Felix felt an uncomfortable rush through his entire body. A heady, awful power echoed through him, almost an inverse to the deadening quiet of the Void. It crashed like a waterfall, roaring in the silence. Then the rocks around them opened up, the path clear for the first time in hours. They shot off into the emptiness, and Felix's stomach dropped in mingled awe and horror.

"The Desolation."

A massive hole in the black revealed a blinding white radiance that was everything the Void was not. Heat and sound and life and matter all compressed and crushed into a blinding miasma of utter destruction. The song of it was a strident cry, a never-ending crash that was all noises at once, screaming for his attention.

Felix twisted his head, recoiling from the cacophony, and focused on their approach. It felt as if they had slowed down somehow, though Felix knew he had not. However, the rocky islands around them that had been moving laterally this whole time now accelerated. They rushed in a tightening spiral around the white hole, and where they found the edge, they fuzzed over. He watched as the rocks vanished instantly, as if erased from existence.

Felix gulped.

No! I've changed my mind! Flee from this place, Felix Nevarre! It is better to die in the jaws of that beast than here! The Maw was in a panic, and it spat and snarled at him from inches away. He felt an odd sensation at the base of his skull. Perhaps the Maw had the right of it. Perhaps he should—

"Enough!" Felix flexed Bastion of Will, and the Maw's form surprisingly flickered and vanished for a few seconds. Time enough to focus. To—there! A lopsided orb of pure black, darker than the Void around it and highlighted against the

Desolation. The liminal space... and hopefully a Temple within. "There it is!"

Felix grinned and accelerated. His Mana was draining fast, but it didn't matter. They were almost there!

KRAKOOM!

The rocky islands behind them exploded outward in wild, parabolic arcs as the mountainous mass of the Whalemaw burst out into the empty Void. Its mouths screamed in rage and pain and hunger, and Felix's felt an echo of it all within him, a burr in the air that shook his blood the closer the beast came. The Maw within him called out to the Maw within the Narhollow. They wanted to be one.

"*Fuck!*" Felix dove, just barely staying ahead of the monstrosity. But his eyes blurred and mind felt muddled. His nerves and concentration were shot. He wasn't going to be able to make it. The Corrupted Narhollow swam toward them with the inevitable onslaught of an avalanche, of a tidal wave, a nature-given psychotic, ravenous form. Teeth the size of houses stretched and popped, its jaws pushing outward from its mouth in a grotesque display as it attempted to swallow them whole.

Yes... yes! I feel you! The Maw cackled wildly as it reappeared with its arms spread wide, and Felix hadn't the concentration to banish them again. *I feel your Need! I see now! You only wish to be whole! Take this boy! I need him not!*

Felix snarled wordlessly at the Maw, but then green explosions burst abruptly against the Whalemaw's hide, detonations an order of magnitude greater than Felix had seen used before. The Corrupted Narhollow flinched, its jaws descending prematurely and sending a shockwave of force into the stern of Felix's ship. They were sent reeling.

The galleons had arrived as well, still crewed by those cursed pirates, their flesh now bulging growths of teeth and muscle. They fired again, and this time their shots arced up and over the Whalemaw, blasting near the cutter and fueling his downward spiral.

Felix screamed through his teeth, hauling hard against the Control Node, but his Will was sapped. He tried desperately to regain control of their cutter, but it was impossible. The ship had been too damaged, the hull and mast devastated by debris before and was jettisoning shards of void bone in every direction. Felix gripped hard to the control plinth with his arms and what was left of his fatigued Willpower, commanding Pit to do the same.

Ten, twenty, thirty more shots landed in the Void near him. He felt their heat and their force, hurling them ever faster toward Desolation, and panic crawled up Felix's throat. He barely noticed that more had hit the Whalemaw's fleshy expanse, bursting its bubbling flesh and blasting craters that quickly became terrible, weeping sores. The monstrosity cried out, the rocks all around them quaking in sympathy.

NO! The Maw shrieked as the creature writhed in unexpected pain. *My power! You don't know what lies within that place, Felix Nevarre! You fool!*

Felix bared his teeth and pushed for all he was worth. Every last scrap of power he had, concentration, endurance, everything went toward guiding the ship toward the Temple. The cutter shook and spun, pieces of it shearing off as it hit rock after rock, prow cracking as they rammed into another floating island. An errant blast of the pirates' ballista had them careening in a wild spin.

"Pit! Converge! Brace!"

The black enveloped them, softer and more visceral than he could have ever anticipated. It felt like a hand the size of a mountain combed through everything he was, had been, or could be. His teeth and hair and toenails had been touched as equally as his face and forearms. He felt violated, but it only lasted a second, then he shattered through it all. To his Manasight, it was a hectic blur of colors and odd, circular shapes, there and then gone.

They emerged into a storm. A literal thunderstorm, with clouds and everything, with Felix's nearly shattered cutter slicing through their dark masses. For the first time in weeks, Felix felt the sensation of real air and rain, though it sliced against his skin like iced razor blades.

"What the hell?" Felix gaped in all directions. Lightning danced in the skies, arcing from thunderhead to thunderhead in a dance too fast to predict. "Where are we?"

The liminal space. We've entered the Temple's protective sheath.

Felix's thoughts flashed back to the apparent liminal space around the Archon's Domain, where he'd piloted a ship in a stormy sea of acid. The place could have been the sky above that one, and Felix might have assumed that if the Maw hadn't insisted that liminal spaces are not connected. Sharp, brittle-sounding pops cut through the air, and Felix looked back.

Harrowings had followed, at least a hundred, and all of them coated in the vile corruption of the Whalemaw's Mana. They screeched in furious joy when they saw him before diving in an alarming burst of speed.

Felix gasped and fed a thread of Mana into the Control Node, shoving what was left of his mental strength at the Mana engine below. The cutter shuddered and shook, but it burst forth, speed coaxed from his flagging Willpower.

You Have Entered Into The Domain Of Another. Beware!
It Approaches!

The message flickered against Felix's senses just as a powerful thunderbolt lit up the sky. The clouds, suddenly luminous, revealed a massive, terrifying shape. It appeared to be a serpent as tall as a house and miles long, yet it vanished as soon as the lightning stopped. But Felix's Perception was engaged now, and it drew his eyes, catching bare glimpses of a huge blue-black expanse of scales between the knurled faces of cumulonimbus clouds.

Voracious Eye!

Name: Dark Defender [DAMAGED]

Nothing else came up, only a series of scary question marks. In his distraction, the Harrowings had almost caught up. Burning talons stabbed at the railing, feet behind him. Felix cursed as he drove the ship into a dive. He felt the Harrowings holding on for all they were worth, but the rush of dark clouds and random, crackling lightning made it hell.

He dove, faster.

A massive, serpentine face loomed beneath them, a creature from a primeval nightmare. Blue-black and scaled, its eyes like twin moons flashed.

Felix screamed and pulled up. Up!

The fangs of the Dark Defender snapped shut, seizing the trailing Harrowings in its house-sized mouth. Felix didn't care, he only wanted to escape.

"What the hell! What the hell!" he was screaming, and Pit seemed ready to fall over in fright.

I told you! This is dangerous! There are Guardians!

Lightning surged, and thunder loud enough to shatter the world shook the skies. When he emerged from the clouds and into the clearer sky, he found burning crimson Harrowings waiting for him. They dove upon him, talons slashing.

Reign of Vellus!

The Harrowings were thrown aside as a dome of force and weaker lightning forced them back. Charge broken, Felix sped through them all, not caring a whit that the cutter was being shredded to flinders.

You'll never make it out! Never!

"SHUT UP!" Felix shouted, and he drove the ship forward, toward what he felt was the exit. He was positive when the Dark

Defender rose up through the clouds, its black shape followed by coursing electricity. It coiled through the air and spat a lurid bolt of lightning directly at them.

Ravenous Tithe!

On instinct, Felix reached out and snatched at the bolt, feeling left hand and arm fry and blister as he did so. Yet the bolt shuddered, destabilized just for a moment as blistering potency surged into his Mana Gate. It hit his core, and he cycled it right back out, his Skill already humming.

Bloodline Progression is 20%

Reign of Vellus!

Supercharged by the stolen Mana, narrowed until it was a spear of force no more than three feet wide, blue kinetic Mana and crackling lightning surged. It hit the Dark Defender, snapping its mouth shut and tossing up its head, just for a moment. Just enough time to blast passed it, but not enough time to avoid its retaliatory strike. The end of its tail smashed into the cutter, all but splitting it in half and sending Felix hurtling into a wall of utter darkness.

The dark consumed him.

You Have Survived.
The Challenge Is Incomplete.
Be Wary, Young Nym.

Careening out of the dark, they hit something with a dreadful *crunch*. Thrown from the craft, Felix crashed in tumbling arcs, sending wide cracks spidering across the stone ground. Blearily, he raised his head from the crater he'd formed. Blurry shapes above him twirled and spun, and for a moment, he didn't understand what he was seeing. Then a green bloom of fire ate across the sky, and everything snapped back into focus. It was the Whalemaw, followed closely by the compromised pirates, all of them hurling everything they had at him.

Felix flinched as a ballista bolt of green flame struck true. He charged away, but the strike didn't manifest. Instead it bloomed above, as if against an invisible barrier.

The Domain sheath. It protects us. For now.

The Maw stood wearily atop the rocky island, its gaunt face even more withdrawn and shadowed than usual.

"What's wrong with you?" Felix asked as he gathered himself. With a flash of light, Pit jumped out of his Spirit and alighted on the island.

The Maw didn't answer, but it also didn't float about. That was new and strange.

Felix turned, taking in the terrain around him. Every muscle screamed at him to stop, but Felix didn't have time. His eyes darted around, finding shattered pieces of dark bone and leather scattered all across the tilted stone floor. Pit huffed and puffed, but seemed more exhausted than injured.

The cutter had snapped in half, obliterating itself against a rocky isle, throwing the Nym and Pit free of the wreckage which had probably saved their lives. The majority of the ship had ricocheted off the island and now drifted away in a tight spiral. Felix followed the debris with his eyes, shielding them against the glare of the Desolation. It was extremely close, and the Void seemed... thinner there. Within moments, the remnants of his ship were consumed and... unmade.

"Holy... Pit, I don't know if... if this was the wisest idea."

Pit, exhausted as he was, only snorted in tired amusement.

He could feel a tug on his body, as if the Desolation was trying to drag him into it as well. Pulling his awed gaze away, Felix's eyes were instead drawn to the side, where a set of stairs had been carved into the rock. Pulse rising, Felix looked around him, but only found more craggy stone. He followed the steps as they curved strangely, impossibly around and beneath the island.

The Temple. He was on top of it... or below it, really.

"Pit! C'mon!" Flexing their Will again, Felix and Pit clung to the stone and followed the curve toward the bottom of the island. A broken building laid out before them, cast into silhouette by the glare of the Desolation behind it. Without wasting a second, Felix and Pit flung themselves into its halls.

CHAPTER FORTY-ONE

Howls shook the Void. The Whalemaw's hunger consumed its thoughts entirely, and its great Body quivered with unceasing Desire.

Need! Its Need was escaping!

The Whalemaw bellowed furiously, mercilessly whipping and cajoling its spawn to act. The small creatures, once prey, became part of itself with a breath of its great power. Now they could retrieve the boy, take back what it Needed above all else.

It screamed and screeched, a million voices within its throat, a dissonance upon the Void. It sent its spawn into the black, the darkness which hovered just beside that dangerous, deadly white. It feared the white, a fear that went past knowledge and into its bones, its shifting flesh. The white was its unmaker.

But the spawn did not know that. They swam through the dark, boats of fire and flesh of pulsing red. They swarmed.

It would not be denied. Not in this.

It would *feed!*

With a great lurch, its own Body fought against its Mind, casting off its fears in desperation. Need was all it knew, and its Desire conquered all else.

SILENCE

With all the speed of an avalanche's gradual start, it began to descend.

The interior of the Temple was as ruined as the exterior suggested. Rocks and dust—the major exports of the Void—were in large supply. There were only two things that were strange or interesting about the place: the first, he was upside down, and his hair wasn't falling up. He was holding himself to the ceiling/floor by sheer Will, and it somehow included his hair and clothes. He'd seen weirder things, but the total disregard of physics was pretty wild, despite his circumstances.

And two: the building was cut in half.

After acclimating himself to his shift in perspective, Felix had noticed that the Temple must have been much larger at one point. The main area featured a wide, circular entryway surmounted by a flight of stairs and a lower hallway that would have extended farther... were it not missing. Something had cut through it, severing the Temple so neatly that some of the edges were still smooth and glassy. Bright, Desolate light shone into the Temple, highlighting the pillars and walls and naturalistic rocky formations, all perfectly sliced.

"Just like the Waterfall Temple in the Foglands. The second room looked like this, as if someone had a huge sword and sheared through solid rock." He ran his hand over one of the pillars. Beside them, there was a mural carved into bas-relief on the stone. Moons dotted a sky of clouds and bright stars. One of them was bursting, covered in chains, and dripping something onto the landscape below. A hand reached down, unable to touch the earth, and dozens of folks in robes ran screaming, tearing at their hair and faces. Just as the pillars, most of it was cleaved free of the Temple entirely.

The Maw appeared next to him, dusting itself off as if it were tainted by the room. *Disgusting. Fall or not, a true goddess wouldn't have let her Temple come to THIS.*

Felix half turned to her, torn between wanting to rush ahead and get some answers. He glanced at the sheath around them, but his view of the Whalemaw was obscured by the Temple itself. "Vellus. You talk like you knew her."

The Maw only gave him a withering look. *Vellus.* She spat, though the imagined spittle disappeared before it hit the floor. *Upstart wench.*

"Lost, Mungle said. Lost like the Nym were Lost. Are Lost," Felix corrected himself. He started moving again.

This Temple was pulled into the Void when its master was Lost. Subjected to Ruin, the only divinity to have suffered such a fate. Ah! To have been there to see it! The Maw cackled in glee. *It is one of Ruin's tricks, you see. Not even the gods can survive true Desolation.*

"That's what that mural depicts? The Ruin taking Vellus?"

Vellus...and the seventh moon, Unbound. The Bloodmoon.

Pit gave a curious coo, and his small ears perked up. Reluctantly, Felix tore his eyes from the Maw and glanced at him, and then followed the chimera's eyes back toward the doorway. There was a strange sound, as if the leather sails of a ship were being rustled. The sound grew louder and louder, however, and Felix's eyes widened as he saw a massive trail of vile, corrupted Mana spear across the black. Pit chirruped a panicked warning only moments before *hundreds* of Tenebrils and Harrowings curved around the edge of the island and caught sight of them.

"Run!"

The Temple rocked as it was hit by the flood of Void beasts. Felix shoved Pit ahead of him, heading up the stairs to whatever lay on the second level. Companion out of the way, he unleashed Reign of Vellus. A ring of crackling lightning exploded outward from him, jumping from beast to beast as the corrupted creatures were thrown back nearly twenty feet. Tenebrils dropped by the dozen, but the Harrowings were far sturdier. Felix held it for five seconds before being forced to drop the Skill. The monsters were simply piling against his kinetic barrier; any more, and it would have fallen apart itself. He cursed and ran.

Having tasted his Mana, the Voidbeasts followed.

Felix crested the staircase quickly, remembering to simply relax his Will and fall the majority of the way there. After clamping down again, Felix landed in a crouch atop the second floor, which featured another circular area surrounding a large triangular archway. Both Pit and the Maw were standing in the center of the room, near the archway. The Maw had its hands behind its back, idly looking at the thing.

"What are you doing!"

The Maw gestured. *This is your gate the madman told you about!* It grinned a mad grin, too many teeth showing. *I admit I was skeptical! But it is an exit from the Domain, used Ages past, and it is still connected to the Corporeal Realm. By barest threads, but it is!* The Maw cackled, fully mad and reveling in it. *And it doesn't work!*

"What?!"

Suddenly, the floor beneath them lurched, and Felix found himself smashed face-first into it as the entire island flipped and spun. A titanic bellow shook the air. Dark, corrupted tendrils of twisted red Mana pulsed through the holes in the walls. The Whalemaw was outside, only feet away, and it was bashing at them like a monkey with a coconut.

Flaring his Will, Felix climbed atop the tilted landscape. Pit did the same, though his wings were spread wide. The Maw hung strangely, completely unaffected by the impact as she studied the gate. The sound of leathery wings filled the air again, coming up the stairwell. Felix snarled at the Maw.

"It has to work! Figure it out! Or I swear I will throw myself into the Desolation rather than be eaten by that *thing* out there!"

The Maw's eyes widened until he could see the whites all around. Panic. And true fear. Felix might have enjoyed it, had he the time. The Voidbeasts had arrived.

"C'mon then!" he shouted, and activated his Skills.

Mantle of the Long Night!
Influence of the Wisp!
Reign of Vellus!

The area around them crackled with an icy chill as a maelstrom of freezing wind spun outward from Felix. Simultaneously, the first four Voidbeasts that crested the stairs were limned with ghostly blue fire and Enthralled. Felix didn't wait, instead launching himself at the creatures with a focused blast of Reign of Vellus, bringing his icy aura closer. He smashed through the first Tenebril with a punch, its body burning up and freezing at the same time. It exploded into gray ichor and streamers of rainbow vapor.

Corrosive Strike!

Blow after blow, he threw everything he had at the Voidbeasts, while Frost Spears and Wingblades ripped into either side of the crowd. Pit hovered near the ceiling, picking off whatever he could at range, though that didn't stop several Harrowings from coming after him. Felix couldn't do anything about that, though; he had enough to worry about.

His Mana was running low. Again.

Detonations went off outside the Temple, green fire reflecting through the holes in the structure's walls. More of them were hitting the Whalemaw's bulk than the Temple, proven when another resounding scream shook the air. He pulled his attention away, but it was hard. Like turning his back on a rabid lion.

His freezing aura slowed the monsters down considerably, but it was still a battle. The Harrowings' cloaking Skill was useless now that they were corrupted, but their talons were just as quick and sharp. Their slashing edges found Felix's flesh easily and often, sprinkling the growing rain of ichor with bright red blood. Felix roared in anger and pain, and he struck with everything he had. Skill after Skill flared and activated, each one a weapon or tool to maneuver or maim.

"Get off me!" Felix smashed through a Harrowing's angular face and tore off its razor-sharp beak, carelessly tearing open his palm. The rage, pain, and terror he'd been feeling rose to the surface, buried for so long, ever since he'd found he'd survived the Maw. Now, it exploded outward in a flurry of violence that only blood could quench.

SILENCE

The Temple rocked again. This time, the Corrupted Narhollow's bellow was far closer, and massive teeth pierced through one of the far walls. A staccato crunch and the stone came apart, ripping back and into the dripping jaws of the nightmare beast as it undulated backwards. Its body was utterly transformed and was now pocked with weeping sores and fleshy red tendrils that writhed along its entire form. More green fire bloomed along its back and head, and it reared up again in a fury.

"We have to hurry!" Felix turned to the Maw, who was floating upside down before the gate. He blasted out with Reign of Vellus and drove twenty more Voidbeasts back against the walls.

Of course! The Bloodmoon! I need your blood! The Maw stared at him, its blue-green eyes glinting as it held out a hand.

"What? No!" Felix lashed out with Corrosive Strike, burying his arm in another Tenebril. "Never again!"

You idiot! For the Gate! It's a Bloodgate! It was pointing to some sort of markings on the triangular gateway. They looked like a series of circles. *The inscription says the blood must be sacrificed to Vellus to operate the Gate! ARGH! But this requires a Master Tier at least to function!*

"A what?" Felix ducked another flurry of talons, then spun below and grabbed it by its wings. He yanked it apart in a shower of ichor.

A Master Tier, you imbecile! Someone far above your Apprentice Tier!

"Goddamn it!" Felix ducked and dodged a sweeping talon strike, only to run into a second Harrowing's attack. "All this way, and we can't even use it?!"

The Maw laughed, bitterly, insanely. *I was beyond Master Tier before you entered my life, Felix Nevarre. I was perfection! So mighty it would take a hundred Masters to merely stop my onslaught for a moment! Now I die, here, with you. So if you weep for anyone, weep for me! For the death of utter glory and magnificence!*

Wait. Felix's hands stopped dead, his grip strangling the wedge-shape head of a Harrowing. It clawed at him, drawing hot furrows down his burnt arm. He hissed in pain and throttled the Voidbeast. *Wait a damn minute.* He looked up at the Whalemaw still struggling to chew through the Temple.

"Pit! Cover me!"

A flurry of Frost Spears slammed into the ground around Felix, cutting him off from the Voidbeasts for a moment. Appreciation surged through his bond, and Felix leaped toward the Whalemaw. The Gate needed blood? He knew a perfect source!

Wrack and Ruin!

Shadow Whip!

The orb of acid rocketed from his grasp and splashed into the Whalemaw's furious, ever-shifting eyes. It punched through, bursting vile sclera and drove deeper into the thing's twisted insides. Behind it, Felix's desperate whip slashed out. Dexterity-propelled, it sank arm deep into the wound, and he spread its head so it gripped.

Felix yanked with everything he had, and a flood of putrid ichor *poured* out of the Whalemaw's eye. It splashed down, over him, and over everything in the room.

You mad, brilliant boy!

The Temple shook again, tumbling once again, end over end. The white, impossibly bright light outside filled the windows and cracks with a powerful, unstoppable radiance. The Whalemaw screamed again, a many-voiced cry of dissonance that sent everyone reeling.

Everyone but Felix.

Convergence!

Across the room, Pit disappeared in a flash, and Felix flung himself toward the Maw. Felix slammed his wounded palm against the frame of the Bloodgate.

Lightning burst from the once-inert gate, an azure energy that swept outward and upward in an instant.

They were gone.

CHAPTER FORTY-TWO

"Until such time that the Foglands are deemed safe, the Haargate shall henceforth be shut! If any seek to use the Haargate, they must first gain a Writ of Permission from an Initiate of the Order. All others are forbidden, on pain of death!" The Inquisitor who spoke was old, but possessed of a vibrancy that couldn't be denied. He jabbed a finger at the gates. "Worse than death stalks those forests! We have come to eradicate that threat, so worry no more!"

The early morning sun glinted off of white-enameled plate and golden sunbursts as the edict rang out. Harn leaned casually against a lamppost, his armor left behind for once, and scowled through the tumultuous crowd. Cheers chased boos, while the sharp eyes of the Acolytes fruitlessly sought out the latter. A crowd this big, no Apprentice Tier redcloak was spotting anything worthwhile. Still, that didn't stop their six-deep formation from glowering at everything from behind their sallet helms.

Behind them all, the massive red-gold edifice of the Wall stretched into the sky, bigger than every building in Haarwatch save the Eyrie itself. Doors slammed shut, made of the same orichalcum as the Wall, and brilliant streamers of Mana flared so potent that even the Mana-blind like Harn could see them. The doors were sealed.

"If you wish to obtain a Writ of Permission, line up to the left side of the thoroughfare to begin!"

"Damn redcloaks," Harn cursed. "First they lock us out, then they start comin' for folks. Mark my words."

"Not questioning it," Yan said. He tugged his hood up over his bald head, though it was unnecessary. The man was a head shorter than most in the crowd. "Just keep it down. Last thing we want is attention."

"Aye, aye. Let's begone from this place. Ain't completing any more jobs now." Harn started pushing his way through the crowd. After glimpsing his scarred face, most folk let him. They had come down to the Haargate to make good on the Hunting jobs they'd managed to find, but the Inquisition had blocked off the gates with their little soldiers.

"We aren't gonna try to get a Writ?" Yan ran a finger through his mustache, eyeing the gate.

"You wanna be on their little list, Yan? So they can harass us for the privilege of using the Foglands?" Harn asked. "Twin's teeth, I don't."

"Think we should leave? Make a run for Setoria?"

Harn grunted. "We'll leave that up to Cal. You and me, we're no thinkers. We're here to kill and to look good doin' it."

Yan laughed as they slipped out of the crowd. "Not arguin' with that!"

Cal did want to leave, but before they had even gathered up their belongings, word reached them that the Sunrise Gate—the lone access to the Verdant Pass and distant Setoria—was also closed. Restricted, it was said, though only Inquisitors could be seen moving back and forth.

The news did not sit well with the woman, but more than

conniving redcloaks had her attention. She'd learned—far, far too late—that Evie and Harn had slipped into the Eyrie and stolen Magda's body. Her rage and fear were tempered heavily by the enormity of what they'd done and what it meant. There'd been more than a little hectic hand-wringing in the week that followed, most of it her own. Cal had been convinced the Guild would have come down on them like a hammer. Yet only silence had met her anxiety. Either Magda's body hadn't meant much to them—which infuriated her in ways she couldn't fully speak to—or they hadn't noticed.

Or something worse.

Cal shook herself, pulling from her memories and anxious contemplation. Today, at least, was to be an end to all of that. The lot of them stood in the center of an abandoned lot in the Dust Quarter, ringed about a pyre that was wreathed in ribbons. She looked to her right, where Evie stood, dressed in mourning silver slashed with crimson. All of her team was: Harn, Yan, Bodie, every single one. Most had only managed a shawl or kerchief to mark themselves, but all wore it with a solemn pride. Evie glanced back at her, a sad smile on her face, and Cal squeezed her hand.

"You did good, Evie," Cal said. "Mags would've been proud."

The teen—*young woman*, she corrected herself—worked her jaw, but nothing came out. Her eyes were bright with unshed tears. "I hope so."

Mags' body had been laid down atop the pyre, her body fitted with plate armor and the scrapped remnant of her mithril shield. She looked waxy and gaunt, having lost something more than just her life in the intervening months. Stasis arrays had kept her body from rotting away, but there was a… diminishment that tore Cal's heart in half. It wasn't Mags that they watched over now, she knew that in her Spirit. But Evie needed this, Siva's grace, so did Harn. The stoic warrior was crying, a man she'd seen take a lance to the chest without blinking.

Evie stepped up and whispered something to her sister,

something no one else made any attempt to hear. Advanced Perception or no, there were things that should remain private. She returned in a few short minutes, her eyes red and shoulders shaking. It was Cal's turn next.

Cal lifted her hand, looking at her own triangular pendant, one that had been returned to her by Magda when they had reunited.

Name: Twin-Touched Locket
Type: Enchanted Accessory
Lore: Used by many to keep images of their loved ones close. Always paired.

"You should wear this, Mags," Cal managed to say before she couldn't say anything else. Silently, she took off the locket and placed it around Magda's throat. Her fingers trembled. "I almost can't bear to leave it here," she laughed, quietly. "I wish I knew where yours went... I wish so much had been different."

She breathed unsteadily. "I don't blame you. I always wanted to say that. I don't blame you for running or saying no or... I wish I could, being mad might've made this easier." She put two fingers to Magda's cheek. Tears splashed against her, but Cal left them. "I love you. I'll miss you, forever.

"Go into the Ethereal, Mags." She stepped back, wiping at her eyes. "Karp?"

"Aye, Cal." The bearded archer lifted his bow, arrow nocked, and whispered a soft word. The tip of the arrow ignited with a green-gold fire. He loosed it into the pyre, and the entire thing caught into a six foot tall column of green-gold flame.

Later that night, Cal briefly recalled someone singing a dirge, but couldn't remember who. It all passed in a numb blur until only Evie and Cal remained nearby, watching the pyre burn away. They hadn't talked in a half glass, but it was a comfortable sort of silence. Companionable. Sisterly, she hoped.

"I gave her my half of the locket," Cal admitted, before she realized what she was saying.

"What?"

"I just... I wanted her to have it. She lost her own." Cal swallowed. Her throat still hurt. "You know, it was the only portrait I had of her. I should have given it to you. Gods, I don't know why I did it. I thought, maybe—"

"Dunno that Maggie ever believed in the gods much, but she liked to tell me stories of it," Evie said, interrupting her. Cal let her own words die, her own guilt silencing her. "Of the place our parents might've went, the light and eternal rest of the Ethereal. It was nice, maybe a bit too nice, but for a sad kid, it was the right thing to say." She smiled. "Maggie wasn't always the best with words, but she got it right with that one."

Evie laughed again, and it was a bright thing in the dark. Cal couldn't help her answering smile. "She also told me about the other places. The divine realm where heroes go to fight and drink and eat forever. That it's hard to get into the Hall of Heroes. Hard as anything ever done. But if anyone made it there, Maggie did." Her voice turned fierce at the end, only spoiled by a faint crack. "Let her carry it with her a while. I've got my memory to keep her alive, yeah?"

Evie looked into the dwindling fire, watching a point that still blazed hotter than the rest and knowing it for the enchanted locket.

"Maybe now we can get there, too. Just follow the light."

They held each other until the pyre burnt out.

The false sun was hot overhead as the last of the subjects were moved into the grounds of the old keep. Elder Teine felt none of the heat, of course, but he knew it wouldn't do for his experiments to be blistered by the cruel orb above. The desert type of the Domain below Haarwatch meant it was always boiling hot during the day cycle and freezing cold during the night cycle, and he had instructed his assistants to take every precaution to keep their subjects safe.

He sighed as he walked the battlements, peering out over the rolling dunes of the landscape. He had been forced to move his entire operation, thanks to the arrival of the cursed Inquisition, as not even High Elder Fairbanks had spine enough to stand up to those puffed up popinjays.

Redcloaks. Pfah!

At least with his experiments in the Guild-controlled Domain, he could access them fairly easily. It would not impact his project too much, or so he hoped.

"Sir! Elder, sir!" Someone came running up to him, utilizing some sort of hopping movement Skill. It was ungainly, but useful, Teine supposed. Perhaps if it were applied to—he recalled that the messenger was speaking and began to listen.

"—survivor escaped and attacked us! One of the Bronze Ranks was bitten!"

"*Really?*" Teine's interest was piqued. "What will happen, do you think?"

The messenger looked at him with eyes wide with fear. "Uhm, uh, he will be healed?"

"In due time. In due time," Teine clapped the boy upon the back, neatly staggering him. "Restrain the subject and the Bronze Rank. Use elision collars if the inscribed chains aren't enough, but keep them docile."

"The Bronze Rank as well, sir? He's only injured—"

"Do as I said, child," Teine snapped. The boy shrank under his intense gaze, so fearful even without Teine utilizing his Spirit to press him. "Do not make me tell you again."

The boy scurried off, so afraid he didn't leap once. Teine nodded in satisfaction. Yes, he could accomplish much in the Domain, where he was free of oversight. Without the High Elder breathing down his back, looking for results, Teine would see miracles done.

Screams came from below, Human and distinctly otherwise.

Yes. Much to do. Much to discover.

"Get in there!"

The Envoy stumbled into the cell below the sands. It was dark there, but its eyes could easily pick out a single other Human sitting there. It chose to fall, to give the impression of weakness to the guards. It worked, and the Envoy could feel the guard sneering at its back.

"Didn't like that, did ya? You try and bite any others, and you'll see what *true* pain feels like, eh?" The guard rapped the bars of the cell with a flanged mace and stomped off. Another guard stepped up only seconds later, with two trays with some water and a mealy sort of slop. Their food, the Envoy hazarded.

The Envoy rolled over, still keenly aware of the other prisoner's eyes on its form. It reached a tentative hand to its neck, where a wide elision collar had been fitted, a device designed to shut off the flow of Mana to and from one's core and weaken one's Temper. It was largely ineffectual for one such as the Envoy, but these fools did not know that. It resembled a Human, after all.

"Hey, uh," said the other prisoner with a cough. It was an Elf, and he looked quite sick. "You okay, pal?"

"I am… I will be fine." The Envoy sat up with a feigned grunt and settled against the dusty stone wall. "Everything will be fine. My Father is coming, after all."

"Tch, you some nobleman's kid? I, uh, don't know how to tell you this, but nobles won't stand up to the Guild. Not in this town." The Elf spat out some blood and what looked like a tooth. "Teine's got em all wrapped around his finger."

The Envoy briefly considered educating the Elf on its Father, but there would be time for that later. For now, it stood and walked to the food. Bent over the bowls of mush, it accessed its core, the surging potency stored within its chest that its Father shaped from base metals into transcendent creation. There, among the inaccessible Mana it held, there was a reservoir of blood-red rot. It bubbled and hissed, kept separate from his core space by the ingenious script work of its Father and contained with a squarish device built into his side. The Envoy vented the rot out, directly into the mush.

"Here, you eat," the Envoy said to the man. "You need your strength, and I'm fine for now."

The Elf grunted a desultory thanks at the Envoy and took both portions, shoveling the lumpy gruel into his fleshy orifice. If he noticed the rot, he made no mention of it.

Only moments later, the Envoy could see it working, just as the infection had already spread among the others. The Envoy wasn't the source, not originally, but it certainly had helped it along. Its Father was quite interested in what the rot could do, and the Envoy could admit to itself a certain giddy curiosity.

Primordial Essence was hard to come by, after all.

They fell.

They rose.

Light and darkness, color and sound, all of it had ceased having any sort of meaning at all. Felix and Pit were stretched like taffy, pulled through something so infinitely powerful there had only been a single moment of terror before numb shock set in. Stars whirled by, planets maybe, lands of strange things and stranger entities, too many to count, too much. Too much.

Then, a pause.

The world froze, cracked, as something titanic considered him and his Companion. Sense-blind, Felix barely held onto himself, but could feel it still. A leviathan in a sea of blood. A mountain as big as a world. A figure, draped in chains and shadow, one that dwarfed it all. Eyes that burned like a living storm.

A screaming voice, Intent and thought more than anything else. *I survived, you colossal bitch! I survived and escaped!* The Maw railed into the nothing, into the eye of storms. Not in terror, but defiance.

That storm came at them like a comet, so fast and so hot it

threatened to burn everything that was Felix. To hollow him out as sure as a Manaship would have. Lightning and a relentless flood of crimson darkness crashed over them, choking the Maw's laughing visage and sending Felix spiraling outward.

A wild fall that made the luminescent Void around him crackle and shatter. A shimmering explosion consumed everything, pulling him core-first through the eye of a needle.

Out. Out into light.

"Pathless… anyone… if anyone can hear me," someone wept. "Please… save me."

Sunlight and the smell of leaves. Felix felt his feet hit solid ground, all of his aches and pains coming with him. There was a hissing noise nearby, and a terrified gasp, but he couldn't be concerned with either. Instead, he focused on the blue box notification that dominated his vision.

Congratulations!
You Have Returned To The Continent!

"Finally."

ABOUT NICOLI GONNELLA

Nicoli Gonnella spent his formative years atop a mountain, breathing deep of the world energy and expelling impurities from his soul. Also he went to school and stuff. He always wrote but now he's abandoned everything to do it full time. Readers give him strength, spirit bomb style, and there's no telling how strong he will become. This isn't even his final form.

He lives with his wife, two kids, and a corgi named Cornelius.

Connect with Nicoli Gonnella:
NicoliGonnella.com
Discord.gg/sqQvJQhY8F
Patreon.com/Necariin
RoyalRoad.com/fiction/30321/Unbound
Facebook.com/Nicoli-Gonnella-Author-347428719693359

ABOUT MOUNTAINDALE PRESS

Dakota and Danielle Krout, a husband and wife team, strive to create as well as publish excellent fantasy and science fiction novels. Self-publishing *The Divine Dungeon: Dungeon Born* in 2016 transformed their careers from Dakota's military and programming background and Danielle's Ph.D. in pharmacology to President and CEO, respectively, of a small press. Their goal is to share their success with other authors and provide captivating fiction to readers with the purpose of solidifying Mountaindale Press as the place 'Where Fantasy Transforms Reality.'

Connect with Mountaindale Press:
MountaindalePress.com
Facebook.com/MountaindalePress
Twitter.com/_Mountaindale
Instagram.com/MountaindalePress

MOUNTAINDALE PRESS TITLES
GameLit and LitRPG

The Completionist Chronicles,
The Divine Dungeon,
Full Murderhobo, and
Year of the Sword by Dakota Krout

Arcana Unlocked by Gregory Blackburn

A Touch of Power by Jay Boyce

Red Mage and
Farming Livia by Xander Boyce

Space Seasons by Dawn Chapman

Ether Collapse and
Ether Flows by Ryan DeBruyn

Dr. Druid by Maxwell Farmer

Bloodgames by Christian J. Gilliland

Unbound by Nicoli Gonnella

Threads of Fate by Michael Head

Lion's Lineage by Rohan Hublikar and Dakota Krout

Wolfman Warlock by James Hunter and Dakota Krout

Axe Druid,
Mephisto's Magic Online, and
High Table Hijinks by Christopher Johns

Skeleton in Space by Andries Louws

Dragon Core Chronicles by Lars Machmüller

Chronicles of Ethan by John L. Monk

Pixel Dust and
Necrotic Apocalypse by David Petrie

Viceroy's Pride by Cale Plamann

Henchman by Carl Stubblefield

Artorian's Archives by Dennis Vanderkerken and Dakota Krout

Vaudevillain by Alex Wolf

Made in the USA
Monee, IL
15 April 2025